THE EIGER CONTAGION

THE EIGER CONTAGION

by MATT HOWARTH

The Merry Blacksmith Press

2012

The Eiger Contagion
story and cover art © 2012 by Matt Howarth

For information, address:

The Merry Blacksmith Press
70 Lenox Ave.
West Warwick, RI 02893

merryblacksmith.com

Published in the USA by The Merry Blacksmith Press

ISBN— 978-0-61573-984-7
0-61573-984-9

1

Everybody on the Moon was crazy.

Only crazy people would leave Earth behind—friends and family and loved ones and air and food that didn't need rehydration—and trade it all for isolation and bottled air and drinking recycled urine. Some were driven by a lust for adventure, but most were drawn moonward by the lure of wealth. A fortune could be made prospecting, for the lunar landscape was ripe for exploitation.

Greed brought Riccardo Denk to the moon, not thrills. But after four months of commission slots on profitless runs, he found himself destitute. *I was crazy to come here,* he told himself. *This place is supposed to be a goldmine, but nobody has any respect for someone who deserves to strike it rich.* The last thing he wanted to do was call Daddy to bail him out. Then he heard about Moss.

Nobody would ship out with Moss. He was a crazy among crazies. He was reckless, knew it, and didn't care. He acted as if he had a death-wish. He regularly posted for a crew, but no one ever responded.

But Riccardo was desperate enough to ignore everybody's advice and answer Moss' posting. He had no choice. It was join Moss' crew or start selling body parts to pay the air tax.

Of course he got the job; he was the only applicant.

As Moss' entire crew, Riccardo was kept constantly busy. Moss' lunar tractor was woefully decrepit. His larder consisted of nothing but vacu-packed yogurt. And the man's personal hygiene would've gagged a maggot. Riccardo toiled endlessly to keep things clean and running. It was exhausting. And often precarious, for Riccardo's familiarity with machinery was at best deficient.

Being cooped up with Moss for weeks on end was maddening. The man was… crazy. Not just mutter-to-himself or forget-to-seal-the-inner-airlock-door crazy, although he was guilty of both on a regular basis. At times, though, Moss got wear-his-underwear-on-his-head loopy. These antics scared Riccardo. He regretted signing on with this lunatic.

By the middle of the third week, Moss had driven his tractor way out past Mare Humboldtianum, far beyond even the more remote hydrogen mining bases, into the wasteland. But Moss never conducted scans for mineral deposits, he took no core samples. All he did was cruise aimlessly across the lunar landscape.

After three weeks of this haphazardous methodology, Riccardo was compelled to challenge his employer. "This isn't prospecting, it's wanton blundering about."

"I'm searching," Moss declared.

"For what?"

They sat in the twin pilot seats at the nose of the module. Before them the domed windshield revealed a gray and airless terrain. The caldera of a crater loomed like a stadium on their left. To the left, the tableau was scattered with other distant craters. Their seats could swivel, giving them access to the module's cramped living quarters. The port wall could be folded down into bunks. A small table at the rear hosted the food dispenser. A hatch in the starboard wall led to the airlock, which opened upon a patio-like fender. Fundamentally, the vehicle was an oversized dump truck with giant inflatable treads instead of wheels. The living compartment was an egg-shaped tumor attached to the front of an oversized payload tank. So far, though, Moss had failed to gather anything of value in that storage bin.

"I won't find what I'm looking for in the dirt," Moss asserted. He hunched over the steering wheel. Once a burly individual, he'd let himself go flabby in the lunar gravity. His rotund face was drab; the only time Harold Moss showed emotion was when his behavior got loopy. His hygiene was deplorable, his hair and beard unsuitably shaggy.

"You're chasing vacuum," swore Riccardo. His snide tone matched his entitled attitude. His posture was habitually tense. He dispensed a percentage of his nervous energy by relentlessly tapping his right foot. In his mid-twenties, Riccardo Denk was swarthy and pudgy. His angular head featured a high forehead, long nose, and a prominent cleft chin. Despite the example set by Moss' lax attitude toward personal grooming, Riccardo used depilatory cream to keep his normally robust facial hair in check. His eyes were dark and routinely squinty. He constantly ran his fingers along the side of his head, toying with brown locks that should have been shaved away when he'd gotten moonside.

"I'm hunting for my wife…" Moss announced. "My wife and my family…"

This odd proclamation made Riccardo sit back, stunned wordless. "Yeah, uhh…" he muttered. "I heard about your family—your wife and kids perished in a shuttle crash a few years ago, right?"

"If I find the right spot," professed Moss, "I'll be reunited with them…"

"But they're dead…" And then the pieces fell into place in his head and Riccardo had a fearful inkling of what truly motivated the man these days. "You want to die!"

"Everybody dies," Moss assured him. His expression was placid, deceptively devoid of any madness.

Riccardo saw it now. Moss couldn't cope with the loss of his family. He longed to be reunited with them, but lacked the guts to kill himself outright. Everybody thought Moss was crazy—and in a way he was—but his lunacy also concealed a premeditated cunning. His rash and careless actions were intentional, affected in the hope that an accident would do what he couldn't. His recklessness was simply a cowardly way to achieve his speedy extinction.

"Hey, if you're going to kill yourself, I'd rather not be along for the ride."

"It's imminent," crooned Moss. "I can feel it out there…" He leaned forward until the steering wheel ground into his flabby chest. His suddenly euphoric face pressed against the inner surface of the windshield. He began licking the glass, leaving streaks of phlegmy saliva on the pane.

There's no point arguing with him now, fretted Riccardo. *He's gone loopy on me again.*

So far, Moss' lunacy had been disturbing but tolerable. Now, however, with his true psychosis revealed, his outlook became a viable threat to Riccardo Denk's well-being. Suicidal ambitions drove Moss' madness. At any moment he could decide to crash the tractor into a boulder or send it careening into a fissure.

If Riccardo didn't do something fast, Moss was liable to kill them both.

But what can I do?

All along, he had entertained the notion of ditching Moss if they found a profitable mineral deposit. That way, all the revenues would belong solely to Riccardo. It would be an easy move to lock Moss outside the tractor and leave him there to asphyxiate once his oxygen tanks were depleted. A nasty move, but nonetheless easy. A necessary move, too, if it guaranteed that Riccardo wouldn't languish in unpleasant poverty. He could hide the body and claim that Moss had simply wandered off and never come back. No one would question this story, for the man's craziness was widely renowned.

But now, in light of Moss' suicidal predilection, could Riccardo afford to wait for such an expedient opportunity to rid himself of the smelly prospector?

Violence was hardly a familiar trait for Riccardo Denk, so he was slow to accept it as his only recourse. The idea of physically attacking anyone made him uncomfortable. His personal morals had no problem with disposing of anyone who stood between him and what he wanted, he had employed this tactic time and again to reap rewards that were not rightfully his. On previous occasions he had always been able to hire lowlifes to handle such ugly chores; now, though, penniless and alone, this option was not available to Riccardo. He would have to do the dirtywork himself and that prospect annoyed him. He couldn't imagine resorting to brute force... but Moss' madness left him with no other choice. It was painfully clear that neither diplomacy nor reason—nor even guile—would have any effect on swaying the man from his suicidal dementia.

Having spent the majority of his life in pampered luxury, Riccardo had no faith in his naked fists. He looked around for something he could use to subdue the maniac at the wheel. There was nothing within reach. Getting up, he abandoned the piloting station and stumbled back through the claustrophobic domicile. Lost in his mania, Moss paid no attention to his departure. Riccardo searched, but the best weapon at hand was a plastic drinking cup. Everything was built-in or attached. In the tractor's tool kit he found a wrench.

Sneaking up on the man seemed pointless, Moss was completely immersed in his mania. His face remained pressed against the windshield as he released a low moan. Riccardo stepped close and raised his bludgeon.

At the last second, Moss pulled back from the windshield—and Riccardo's blow swept past him and landed on the control console. Constructed of brittle plastic, the panel came apart like the shell of a rotten egg. The wrench gouged down into the machinery beneath the switches and dials.

Sparks erupted from the cowling. A sooty cloud laced with electrical discharges billowed forth from the fracture.

"What the—" blurted Moss. Shock and outrage flickered across his glassy stare. "You're trying to stop me—"

Before Riccardo could lift his weapon for a second shot, the maniac set upon him. Moss hit him hard. The wrench flew from his grasp. Wailing like a banshee, Moss drove Riccardo back from the pilot seats. They tumbled into the living space. Riccardo was hard-pressed to defend himself against the man's fevered assault. He fought like—well, like a maniac. Kicking and punching and clawing, he even tried to bite Riccardo.

"Why?" wailed the madman. "Why would you want to keep me separated from my wife?"

"You're going to get us killed!" Riccardo snarled back. It felt odd to be fighting for survival instead of for wealth, but all the more imperative, since a dead Riccardo could no longer enjoy expensive amenities.

"That's the point!" Moss screamed in his face. "That's the damned point, you interfering idiot!"

Riccardo brought his knee up into Moss' gut. A grunt of pain interrupted the man's tirade and he rolled off Riccardo, allowing him to scrabble away. There wasn't much room inside the living quarters; no matter how far he crawled, the maniac could reach him in seconds. Too late Riccardo realized he should've pushed his advantage and attacked Moss while he'd been disoriented. Too late now. The madman lunged, and they were again locked in close combat.

Back and forth they rolled on the narrow floor, smashing again and again into the manifolds that housed grumbling machinery. Moss pummeled him. He got in a few good shots of his own, but they did little to daunt the madman's frenzy. Riccardo needed to fight harder. He must summon forth a more intense level of animosity if he wanted to save himself. He pounded Moss in the kidneys. He delivered a savage chop to his neck. He punched him in the side of the head. He kneed him in the groin. By the time the maniac fell back, Riccardo was too exhausted to follow up and subdue him. He lay gasping and aching for precious seconds.

He scrambled to his feet, half-climbing the wall to get himself standing. His head pounded. Clouds of smoke from the damaged controls blurred his vision. He slumped against the wall and found himself clutching a pressure suit hanging there. Responding to survival instincts, he grabbed the helmet. Instead of donning it, though, he swung around, wielded the headset like a bowling ball, and caught Moss in the face with it as the maniac rushed him. This blow put Moss on the floor, out cold.

Right now, all Riccardo wanted to do was sink to his knees and wallow in pain and exhaustion. But his gasps were uncomfortably tainted with smoke.

Choking on these fumes, Riccardo blindly crawled forward until he reached the nose of the module. Pulling a canister from beside the station, he sprayed flame-retardant foam on the sparking control console. Once he was certain the fire was out, Riccardo sank into one of the pilot seats and allowed himself to relax.

But that limp respite lasted only a moment. He couldn't rest yet. Before another moment could pass, he leaned forward to stop the tractor. He didn't want it running into anything. With the controls so extensively damaged, he was forced to delve deep into the machinery and unplug the tractor's engines before the vehicle ground to a halt. Then he activated cabin fans to draw off the contaminated gases and replace it with fresh air.

He took the time to gulp a few clean breaths before he scurried back to deal with Moss. A novice to violence, Riccardo had no idea how long the man would remain unconscious. Using a spool of wire from the tool kit, he trussed up the maniac while he was still disabled. Electrical tape was wound around his head, sealing his mouth. As an additional precaution, he dumped Moss in the shower stall and locked him in the lavatory.

Now he could relax.

It had always been his intention to take control of the tractor sooner or later... but only once the prospector had unearthed a rich mineral deposit. The man's suicidal mania had forced Riccardo's hand.

I had to do it, he grumbled to himself. *The fool went crazy. He was gonna get us both killed. I just didn't want to die.*

He was alive, but didn't know what to do now.

It turned out there wasn't much he *could* do.

The damage to the controls looked rather severe. A cursory examination confirmed his suspicion: even he could tell the entire board was dead. Everything, ignition, navigation, even the comm unit was useless. He doubted he could fix things with the sparse gear on-hand. Besides, he lacked the know-how to repair machinery like this.

I'm stranded out here... with no way to call for help. Closing his eyes, he lowered his head and cursed under his breath. *And it's my own damned fault.* His efforts to stop Moss had gone awry. His own attack had destroyed the tractor's controls. Riccardo Denk had become the fatal accident Moss had been hoping for.

How long could they survive out here? The tractor's atmo-recycler would keep the air fresh for a few months, but the food would run out long before that.

Where were they? No way of knowing. The astrogator equipment was intact, but his ability to access data from it—or any machinery—was dependent on the smashed console. This was the true irony: the motor was still functional, but he couldn't activate or control it.

If Riccardo took a pressure suit, could he walk to safety? No... Moss had been driving for weeks; the tractor was deep in the outlands. Even a sled piled with oxygen canisters wouldn't provide Riccardo with enough air to reach civilization. He would never survive the long trek.

Maybe somebody would spot them and come to their rescue... Again, the tractor had traveled far beyond conventional prospecting territory. The chances were dauntingly dim that anyone would be as reckless as Crazy Moss and come out this far.

Every way he looked at it, Riccardo was screwed.

A muffled *thump* told him that Moss was rousing in the lavatory.

I hope you're satisfied, you bastard. You're going to be reunited with your family. Well, set another place at the Moss family table in the afterlife, because you're dragging me to dinner along with you.

He had no intention of untying Moss. Right now, he didn't even want to acknowledge the man's existence. The bastard was to blame for Riccardo's present predicament. If the smelly fool hadn't leaned back, had just let Riccardo brain him with the wrench... but no, Moss *had* to dodge and let the wrench destroy the control console. As far as Riccardo was concerned, he was stranded out here all alone.

Lifting his head, he stared outside and gasped. The smoke had cleared enough in the cabin so that he could see again. The view beyond the windshield startled him—it was all wrong, drastically wrong. Instead of a stretch of gray moondust punctuated by various craters, another environment was spread before the tractor. It was green and quite pastoral. A carpet of verdant grass swept into a shallow valley filled with trees. The lush foliage obscured any trace of lunar craters. As he gawked, a pair of birds—brown sparrows, extinct on Earth for decades—soared across the tableau to disappear into the far trees. Although a gloom permeated the greater countryside, for it was the dark side of the Moon, pleasant sunlight basked the wooded area. A clearing ran down the center of the valley, leading to something sitting in the distance. Neither the ambient lighting nor the tractor's headlamps were strong enough to reveal what that something was.

Riccardo closed his eyes and shook his head, but when he looked again the impossible spectacle was still there. A green valley in the middle of the lunar landscape. That was the creepiest part: right beyond the edge of the valley the terrain switched back to lifeless moondust. The colorful vegetation confined itself to just the glen.

"This is impossible," he choked out, but his declaration was so weak it didn't even convince him. "It *has* to be impossible…"

A flurry of confusion swamped Riccardo's concentration. He reached out a fearful hand, then recoiled when his palm touched a damp smear on the pane. His eyes flickered to study his wet hand, but the idyllic tableau kept hauling his attention back outside. He couldn't ignore it any more than he could explain it.

"Maybe Moss drugged me…" But he felt no flush or wooziness which would betray a narcotic in his bloodstream. From his high society days, Riccardo had enough familiarity with a wide range of recreational drugs; he would recognize an altered mental state.

"Then it has to be fake," he decreed. But that answer was just as implausible. The pastoral scenario was remarkably realistic. It couldn't be—trees and grass and birds couldn't thrive in the lunar vacuum. The tableau had to be artificial—but who would construct such an extravagant diorama this far in the outlands? And why?

Nothing made any sense to Riccardo.

Enraged by his bound and gagged condition, Moss was making an uproar in the lavatory. Riccardo doubted the madman had gotten loose; he was just flailing about.

"Quiet down in there," he muttered, too low for Moss to hear him. He was too weirded out by the woodland valley to care about Moss' tantrum.

The whole thing was too impossible. He needed to verify that it was a mirage. To do that he would have to go outside. Only by touching—or failing to touch the trees could Riccardo prove the glen wasn't real.

Retreating from the nose of the module, Riccardo clambered into a pressure suit. He strapped on life-support gear and clipped the fishbowl helmet to the suit's wide collar. Squeezing through the hatch, he initiated the airlock sequence. He took his wrench with him, a precaution against… what? He had no idea, but felt better with the hard metal tool in his hand. Within a minute he stood on the tractor's high fender.

The glen was still there.

He carefully hopped down from the elevated manifold, his awkward landing kicking up loose dust. He was too new to the low gravity to have mastered traveling by expansive jumps, so with cautious steps he approached the mouth of the verdant valley. Now that his view wasn't constrained by the windshield frame, he saw how the valley was actually a ravine between two large craters. Their flanking calderas loomed behind the trees, visible evidence of the airless wasteland that surrounded him. If anything, this made the spectacle all the more surreal.

He paused before treading on the grassy carpet. Up close everything looked real. He could see hundreds—thousands of blades of grass. There was an astounding attention to detail in the trees' coarse bark, ridges and whorls and fledgling branches. The older branches rose like curvaceous fingers, disappearing into the thick foliage. An impossible breeze stirred the leaves. Everything was rooted in brown soil, not gray moondust.

He took a hesitant step into the valley. The ground definitely felt spongy beneath his boots. And he swore he weighed more now. When he was close enough, he reached out and touched one of the noble trees. Actually *touched* it! His gloved hand pressed against the trunk. It was a tree and it was real. Disbelief rose and clogged his throat.

The path led off into the distance. Something lay at the end of the trail, but he still couldn't make out what it was. The structure possessed a wobbly haziness, as if a region of super-heated air lay between it and Riccardo. This eerie aspect fascinated him. He headed off down the path, deeper into the impossible glen.

He definitely weighed more—or more precisely, a stronger field of gravity now exerted itself on his body. His stride grew cumbersome as the bulky life-support gear strapped to the suit dragged him down with their suddenly increased weight. Under normal lunar conditions, nobody was hampered by the ponderous mass of their pressure suit and its attachments—but here in this impossible valley, it felt as if his unsteady legs supported several anvils. Each step became an arduous ordeal. He'd been moonside too long, his muscles had acclimated to the lesser G forces.

"This is ridiculous," he muttered to himself.

His awkward progress frightened birds and small animals lurking in the woods. He caught flashes of these beasts as they took refuge among the lush canopy supported by the trees.

The path ahead drew narrow… or had the woods reached out to crowd his way?

The ground seemed more brittle, and when he glanced down he saw that the soil had become graveled. Larger stones lay among the pebbles.

When he stepped on these bigger stones, they crumpled with a glassy tinkle and released puffs of vile-colored fog. To his horror, this gas appeared to be corrosive. "It's eating through the fabric of my boots!"

Before Riccardo could come to grips with this absurd development, the rest of the environment turned hostile. He hadn't imagined it—branches *were* reaching out for him. Each bough bore clusters of leaves—and those leaves were suddenly curling into razor-edged cusps. These green talons clawed at him. As he watched, fresh wooden extensions burst forth to stab in his direction. The path had become a gauntlet of emerald knives.

He was in too deep. He couldn't turn back, he had to keep moving forward, ponderously and with much exertion. Only now an edge of panic was added to his frustration.

The assailing branches closed in on him. Putting on an endorphin-born burst of speed, he blundered through these tangled adversaries. The leaves sliced his pressure suit to shreds. He tensed, expecting abrupt decompression and exposure to the deadly vacuum to boil him alive... but no excruciating blast of agony occurred. For a brief instant he staggered in shock, unable to believe he was still alive. *The glen's real,* he told himself. That was the only answer. Here there was no vacuum, the woods existed in a pocket of atmosphere. Impossible—but apparently the case.

Then he resumed his forward struggle, crashing through the extended branches. The sharp leaves continued to rip his pressure suit until only isolated tatters hung on him. His clothes and flesh were suffering cuts now. The emerald blades sliced right through the reinforced crystal of his helmet, exposing his frantic head to their curved rapiers.

Tears and stress blurred his vision—but the structure at the end of the path was near enough to identify it. *Weirder and weirder...* It was a quaint cottage with a small porch. A trail of smoke lifted from the antique chimney. A pair of windows were lit; someone moved about inside.

He forged ahead, more to escape the punishing branches than to reach the sweet cottage. It was all too weird for Riccardo to fathom. His reactions were motivated by base sensory stimuli. The trees were hurting him—get away from them. The cottage offered potential shelter from the savage foliage—head for it.

As he drew near the cottage, the plants fell behind... or backed off... or maybe they'd reached out as far as they could. Whatever the reason, Riccardo was breathlessly grateful. He staggered up to the porch and almost collapsed onto it in his desperate enthusiasm.

Things took another strange twist. The cottage's door was a pressurized metal hatch. He fumbled at its controls, punching random sequences of numbers into the exposed keypad—but all to no avail. The hatch remained hermetically sealed. He clawed at the controls and mewled like a child.

Behind him, he could sense the trees brazenly edging closer. They wanted to snatch him away from the doorway. They would drag him in and dissect him in minutes. He had to get away—had to get inside the cottage.

"—let me in," whimpered Riccardo. "Oh please, open up and please save me—"

Pressed against the hatch as he was, he felt a slight tremor vibrate its cold hard surface. He flinched back, equally scared shitless and desperately hopeful.

The hatch opened—and a crimson wave engulfed him.

As his consciousness succumbed to this scarlet tide, he thought he saw a faint figure deep in the red glare. The cottage's occupant? If so, they were awfully small… and appeared to have four legs and a tail…

2

Sliding out of bed, Sergio Denk left behind a sated lady.

He moved deftly through the gloom, slipping away like a naked ghost. Out in the living room, he left the lights off, for their brilliance would ruin his post-coital euphoria. The domicile was small enough that he didn't have to move far to touch a wall with an extended arm. He folded a chair from its hiding place and settled into it. He felt around until his fingers located the fridge. Popping it open, he rooted through the sparse contents, finally selecting a small bulb of synth-fruit juice.

"You're such a cad," he chuckled to himself as he drained the plastic-tasting liquid. "You tap his wife, then you drink his last juice bulb. You're a bad boy."

Aw, but Major Dummheit had earned his share of humiliation. No one on Station 51, fellow officers or any of the innumerable jarheads, liked the man. He treated the troops under his jurisdiction like morons instead of the highly trained professionals they were (perhaps out of jealousy, for they matched his incompetence with their own seasoned expertise). He was the worst Marine officer Sergio had even encountered. He jumbled crews until everybody was badly partnered. He sent them off on demeaning missions, often scutwork that should've been handled by janitorial technicians. On more than one occasion, Sergio had been assigned to squads which the blustery Major had sent out to scrub the hull.

Sergio loathed being outside. It was one thing to ride through outer space in rocketships or to live in barracks that were contained in a metal shell hanging in the interplanetary void—it was quite another thing to go for a spacewalk. All that vast open area intimidated Sergio, and Sergio didn't like anything that threatened his macho self-image.

The general consensus held that Dummheit was just an asshole. Nobody wasted any effort in exploring the psychological roots of the man's unpleasant persona, it was easier to just follow his inappropriate orders and avoid his often-flamboyant wrath.

Dummheit vented so much fury on his soldiers, the man had no passion left for his wife. Consequently, the bed of his lonely, quite buxom and very attractive wife was open to all comers. Sergio was well aware that he was only a one-night stand for the lady, a blip in an endless series of lovers as the woman sought to satisfy her neglected needs. But it had been a thoroughly enjoyable one-night stand. She'd been a hellion in the sack, remarkably adept at zero-G antics. She ranked among the top ten percent of the women he had bedded, and that roster was quite an extensive one.

Without a trace of hauteur, Sergio knew how handsome he was. His physique was lean and tawny, his flesh bronzed by interplanetary radiation. A series of military tattoos decorated his arms and portions of his torso, ranks and medals intermixed with tapered designs that enhanced the articulation of his buff sinews. His angular head possessed a high forehead, a long nose, and a cleft chin that most women found irresistible. His face was clean-shaven and his scalp featured a buzzcut of brown bristle. He also knew how good he was in the sack. Frequent practice had honed those skills, not to mention a personal preference for sexual activity over basic bodybuilding gymnastics. His exploits had gained him notoriety as a talented lothario around the barracks.

This time, though, there was an extra perk to his latest conquest. He'd slept with the *Major's wife*. And he'd satisfied her in ways the pathetic idiot couldn't. Sergio had proven—if only to himself and the remarkably agile Tara Dummheit—who was the real man. Dummheit could prance about and bluster and think he was such hot shit, while Sergio would have the satisfaction of knowing who was the better soldier *and* the better lover.

Intoxicated by glee, he was entertaining the notion of going back for seconds… when a small noise stopped his bawdy ruminations, froze the breath in his throat, made his heart skip a beat in his muscular chest.

The door—someone was at the domicile's door. At this late hour, it couldn't be a social visitor. Anyway, a guest would've rung the buzzer. Whoever it was had a keycard, although from the fumbling scritching it sounded as if they were experiencing difficulty sliding the magnetic card through the slot.

A vortex of anxiety whirled through Sergio's thoughts.

—oh shit—it has to be Dummheit—this is bad—the short-tempered husband coming home early—to find me sitting naked in his living room—

His body leapt into motion seconds before his mind generated a flight response. Taking advantage of his weightless condition, he flew across the room and pressed himself into the wedge of wall above the doorway. He held his breath and clung there as the person finally managed to unlock the hatch. The portal hissed open and Major Dummheit floundered through the entrance.

An alcoholic stench accompanied him. He was grumbling to himself, cursing everyone and everything with inarticulate vehemence. Dummheit was known to hang around past his shift to prove how gung-ho he was, although he usually achieved nothing more than making a nuisance of himself among the late hour personnel. Afterward he invariably stopped off at a tavern on his way home to drown his exhaustion in booze. His shoulder hit the jamb as he came through the doorway, boosting his complaints from mutterings to a brief and vicious outburst, before he recoiled and slammed his other shoulder into the far side of the door frame, inciting a more vehement reprise of swearing.

A raucous guffaw threatened to erupt from Sergio; he bit his lip to prevent its escape. *The fool's been stationed on 51 for seven months, but he still stumbles around like it's his first hour in zero-G.*

Physically Dummheit was a particularly nondescript man. His height, his build, his pigmentation: all were average. While he wasn't flabby, his physique was hardly as tight as one would expect of a Marine Major. His face was quite unmemorable, his features bland and unsympathetic. Contrary to orbital duty guidelines, he maintained his blonde hair in long stylish waves which refused to stay in place. He habitually wore his uniform 24/7, a sartorial affectation even his wife disdained. Long before he opened his mouth, his smug posture marked him as an asshole to anyone who met him.

If he caught Sergio here, there'd be unpleasant consequences. The bastard would beat him to a pulp—or try to—and then court-martial him. Sergio had to escape without revealing himself. Outrageous as it may have seemed, *now* was his best chance. While the door was still open. While the man was fuddled by his intoxication and annoyed with his own clumsiness. Even if he spotted the fleeing lothario, the best Dummheit could muster in his current condition would be to thrash about and yell; he'd be incapable of giving chase.

Now! Sergio told himself. *Move now—or get trapped in here with the fool.*

Curling his fingers around the upper door frame, he swung himself down, through, and out. He let go and tumbled into the corridor. Before he reached the opposite wall, Sergio twisted in the air and brought his knees up against his hairless chest. As he hit, he kicked off, transforming his rebound into a flying leap that send him rocketing down the passageway. Expertly catching a strategically positioned rung, he swung around the first corner that presented itself. He disappeared down this side corridor before Dummheit came storming out of his apartment to demand an explanation of an empty hallway.

I made it.

He laughed his way back to the barracks, his fleet naked body drawing some amused stares from personnel who wandered the corridors at this late hour. A few of them could even guess where he'd been and why he fled now with such speed. No one would be gauche enough to report having seen him.

Slithering between the bunks, Sergio reached his berth and rolled into its netting. As he settled in, the berth next to his bulged and a face peered out of the sleep webbing and grinned at him.

"Out servicing the Major's wife, eh?"

Sergio confined his response to a noncommittal grunt.

"She's a tigress, ain't she?" cackled the other soldier.

In truth, Sergio barely knew this man. His name was Dennis or something. He was a big brute, with beefy arms decorated by pornographic tats. His blunt face reminded Sergio of a beaten pillow. Dennis was another example of the Major's foolishness, scrambling up teams so nobody knew each other, abolishing any camaraderie the soldiers established among their ranks. The best the men could do was try to befriend their new comrades before the Major shuffled up the ranks again.

"She's got all the right moves," he confided in an effort to establish a rapport with Dennis.

"Thinking about her makes me hard," whispered Dennis. "Have to wait until the weekend, though. That's when it's *my* turn at her."

With the exception of her negligent husband, all were welcome in Tara Dummheit's bed.

"Be careful," Sergio warned him. He advised his new friend how the Major had come home early and nearly caught him.

"Don't worry," Dennis assured him. "You've been here all night—*I* can testify to that."

"Thanks."

No matter how hard Major Dummheit labored to undermine the squad's esprit de corps, the men thwarted him by striking up new friendships. Every jarhead aboard 51 hated Dummheit. From that common sentiment they could build the stronger bonds necessary among soldiers.

Come morning, Sergio and Dennis (who was actually named Danford) would be tight buddies.

A buzz inside his head woke Sergio.

Responding by reflex, he activated his earbud and answered the call that had roused him.

"Corporal Denk, C12-638, reporting," he whispered inside his sleep webbing. Having no idea what time it was, he didn't want to disturb anybody sleeping nearby.

He listened to the codes that spilled over the comm-link. They triggered conditioned responses in him. Dragging clothing from the satchel that formed one end of his hammock, he dressed hurriedly. Within minutes he was squirming free of his tubular bunk.

He was not alone. Six soldiers were wriggling out of their berths and swimming toward the lift pole. Danford was among them, and Sergio recognized two of the others. Propelling himself from his hammock, Sergio joined the small swarm as they converged on the travel rod. Positioned parallel to the array of webbing bunks, this metal shaft sported lateral bars; troops were supposed to use it as a ladder, but most jarheads informally relied on personal agility to reach the barracks' exits. This morning was different, their response performance was probably being monitored. Snagging a bar, Sergio climbed to the dispatch hangar where the group would be geared up and shipped out.

If they were *really* shipping out.

The chance existed that this was just another one of the Major's pointless drills. Exhibiting no faith in the capabilities of the soldiers under his command, Dummheit was constantly subjecting them to false alerts which only inspired their resentment.

If they did ship out, though, that didn't mean they were going on a military mission. The Major had his troops running errands for everyone from repair staff to hull scrubbers. More often than not, a launch code would send a squad of wired trigger-hungry soldiers to do menial tasks. Sometimes they got to provide an armed escort for some VIC (Very Important Cargo), which invariably turned out to be elite cuisine for the Big Brass.

Although there were at least four wars going on Earthside to which they could've been allocated, not to mention innumerable terrorist strikes and cases of civil insurrection, actual missions that warranted their combat skills were extremely rare. Sometimes it seemed as if the Major was reluctant to send his troops into battle. After all of the Major's menial assignments, Sergio wasn't the only jarhead who pined for combat situations. It was demeaning to carry around all this training and expertise and have to spend his hours scrubbing hulls.

Sergio could tell right away this wasn't a drill.

A ship was definitely docked and waiting for them. From the glimpse Sergio caught, it looked like a shuttle that handled short-range transport, so their destination was not liable to be Earthside. Major Dummheit bullied them aboard and—to everyone's surprise—joined them in the carrier. Combat gear was distributed among the squad. Even the Major suited up.

If the Major's coming along, Sergio mused, *this isn't going to be a scrub job. This is something important enough that the pompous fool wants to be directly associated with it. He'll send his troops in to do the hard work, then he'll reap the rewards for our success. Scumbag.*

Once geared up, each soldier settled on fold-down benches that lined the transport compartment. The team numbered seven members, counting Sergio—but not counting the Major. He was not one of *them.*

At Sergio's side was seated Private Emil Danford, his beefy figure made all the more bulky by the armor he wore. In better light, his face wasn't as shapeless as it'd seemed the night before. His features conveyed a certain innocence, except for the many-times-broken nose.

Across from Sergio was Corporal Jack Hibbs, a rugged bear-like man like Danny-Boy. Hibbs carried himself with the suave aplomb of an automaton, always alert despite the half-dozing cast of his eyes. Sergio knew him well; they had served together on several groundside missions and had remained close buddies despite the Major's rotations of troops among 51's various barracks. Hibbs was a good fighter and a worthy adversary at cards.

Next to Hibbs sat Corporal Anne Marshall, another jarhead who was more than familiar to Sergio. Raven-haired and sharp-featured, Marsh was wiry babe with a predilection for practical jokes in the sack, an annoying quirk that had annoyed Sergio on more than one recreational occasion. She was a hotshot computer specialist.

The remaining three were relatively unknown to Sergio, but from reading their suit displays, he found that two of them were: Corporal Green, a lanky fellow with a skeletal face; and Private Scarpetti, a pert little blonde whose body armor couldn't disguise her bombshell body. He'd heard of Green, a longtime veteran with numerous battle commendations.

The last member of the squad was a school-marmish woman, mid thirties, with good bone structure and decent padding, but a facial expression that remained prissy. She never once looked at any of the others seated around her, as if she felt superior to them. Her body armor hung cockeyed on her narrow shoulders; she'd probably cinched the straps too tight, a mistake no soldier would make. She had to be a civilian.

And there was Major Dummheit, standing over them like a demonstrative general.

"So," Danny-Boy broke the silence, "what's up, Boss?"

The Major gave him a withering look, then puffed up to broadcast importance. "A rescue mission."

"Earthside?" Hibbs grunted hopefully.

"Moonside."

Several shoulders slumped at word of their destination. They all yearned for planetary battlefields. Grubbing about in lunar dust was less than thrilling.

"I want to see enthusiasm!" the Major commanded them.

Why? Sergio moaned to himself. *Because you think this sort of shit actually gets us hot?*

"This mission has high security implications," the Major informed them. "You'll see."

Another of the scumbag's annoying habits was to wait until the last minute before dispensing briefing packets. For some twisted psychobabble reason, Dummheit believed it best to surprise his troops at the eleventh hour with information regarding their assignment. Something about keeping soldiers quick-witted. *More like keeping us unprepared.*

Well, at least now he knew why the Major was along for the ride. A high security matter was bound to come to the attention of the Big Brass. *Great,* he lamented, *now we'll have to put up with him prancing about and acting all commander-like.*

Meeting Hibbs' eyes, Sergio saw the same prospect had dawned on his buddy. Both of them had been witness to the Major's ridiculous attempts to impress his superiors on prior occasions. They remembered how terribly wrong things had gone those times, invariably because of Dummheit's inept guidance.

This better be a cake-walk... or he's liable to get us killed...

It took several hours to reach the Moon. During that time, the squad sat in stone-faced silence, for idle chatter was another pastime of which the Major sternly disapproved. Marshall busied herself reviewing a technical journal on her wrist pad. Hibbs and Green appeared to doze, catching a bit of rest before the mission began. Danny-Boy and Bombshell Scarpetti fidgeted but were smart enough to restrain their nervous energy from going verbal. The civilian sat with her head lowered as she studied some report on her suit's wrist pad.

Sergio tried to mirror Hibbs' tactic, but a nagging bad feeling refused to let his thoughts relax. Something was wrong, but he couldn't figure out what it could be. Knowing nothing about their assignment didn't help. He felt as if he were perched at the brink of a cliff with no idea how deep the chasm was. His apprehension gnawed at his professional cool. Like any decent soldier, he hated going in not knowing what was in store for them.

Was it something about the mission that made him uneasy? Or was Major Dummheit the cause of his anxiety? While he seriously doubted the man suspected Sergio Denk had been the mysterious intruder in his apartment the night before, Sergio covertly watched the Major, and at one point caught the C.O. staring intently at him, but after a few minutes the Major shifted his stare to another one of the troops. One by one he was studying his crew, undoubtedly calculating their faults and weaknesses for later cataloging. Dummheit's assessments would be entirely erroneous, but that never stopped the fool from openly distributing his scorn.

The Major finally announced it was time to activate their briefing memos. He typed a control command on his wrist pad and each soldier's earbud caught the transmission burst.

The instructions were pretty simple: the squad was to find out why Eiger base had gone dark. It was a research facility manned by seventeen people, all civilian scientists. No mention was made concerning the facility's purpose, which clearly marked the research as classified. A flash file of the underground installation's schematics was logged in his implant HD; if and when needed he could call them up on his ocular scan and consult them. There was a surface bunker that housed a high security airlock entrance, then a deep shaft descended into the lunar mantle to an aggregation of unlabelled levels. Whatever these scientists were studying, they'd had to dig down to reach it... or to hide it.

Being callow, Danford inquired, "What's this place all about, Boss?"

Sergio caught the civilian throwing a tense scowl in the Major's direction.

"That information isn't included in your briefing, so you don't need to know it," came the Major's terse retort.

"It might be relevant, though," Danny-Boy persisted. "Like if they do weapons R&D, we can expect them to be armed?"

"If it isn't in the briefing, Private, then men a thousand times smarter than you decided you didn't need to know it."

"This is supposed to be a rescue mission, right?" interjected Hibbs.

"It remains to be seen whether or not anybody needs rescuing," spoke the civilian. Her voice was husky yet silken.

"Dr. Holmes is correct," the Major jumped in, reasserting his command of the discussion. "We're going in to determine the status of the facility. Obviously, though, if there are any survivors, we will rescue them."

"Why would there be 'survivors'?" asked Hibbs.

"Clearly something has gone wrong," Dr. Holmes shook her head abstractly, momentarily lost in her own ruminations. "Otherwise they wouldn't have cut off their comm-lines."

"So you anticipate hostile circumstances…"

"We don't 'anticipate' anything, Corporal," snapped the Major. "We wait and assess the facts as we encounter them."

Hibbs nursed a frown for a minute, then protested, "I gotta side with the newbie, Boss. If we're going into a potentially hostile situation, it'd be mighty helpful to know what kind of research the base was conducting."

"That information is classified, Corporal. Drop it."

Sergio saw Marshall settle back and covertly pitter away at her wrist pad. If there was anything on the internet about the place, she would find it.

All this talk about potentially hostile circumstances was getting Sergio excited. He wasn't the only one, either. Hibbs and Green, both veterans, hoped for the prospect of combat. The others just looked confused. This was probably their first exposure to the Major's idiosyncratic style of bad command skills.

Get used to it, guys, he privately warned them. *You gotta rely on your own wits out there, because the Major sure don't have any.*

The shuttle landed; they felt the shudder as it touched down. Everyone sealed their helmets. A moment later a wall lowered to become a ramp leading down to the lunar surface. With dramatic flourish, the Major ordered them into motion. The squad bustled out onto the gray terrain and took up positions around the shuttle. The Major brought up the rear, escorting Dr. Holmes down the ramp.

As soon as all eight of them had disembarked, the ramp retracted and sealed itself. A moment later the shuttle's exhaust jets fired, generating a cloud of moondust as the vessel lifted from the surface. The carrier continued to rise until the murky gloom swallowed it, leaving the squad alone on the ground.

Their suit lamps revealed a typical drab lunar landscape. Gray dust everywhere. A pair of large craters loomed nearby, so close to each other their calderas almost merged at one point. No Earth hung in the sky, so this secret base must have been hidden on the dark side of the Moon. Initially Sergio saw no sign of any artificial structure, though.

What he did see—right away—was an industrial dump truck parked at the mouth of the ravine created by the conjoined craters. The vehicle's headlights threw additional illumination across the scene, revealing a concrete structure butted against an escarpment of rock. This would be the facility's entrance. But—what the hell was a commercial mining vehicle doing here? Had the installation been compromised by outsiders?

"What the hell is *that* doing here?" the Major's incredulous exclamation sounded in each of their earbuds. Everyone presumed he was referring to the truck.

"It's a commercial mining truck," remarked Danny-Boy.

"I can see that, you moron!" thundered the Major. "Go check it out."

When the soldiers fanned out, Bombshell Scarpetti found a trail of footprints that led away from the truck through the dust. The tracks stretched off in the direction of the base's entry bunker. Marshall and Green climbed up to the vehicle's domicile module; they carefully entered its airlock. Sergio moved around back and checked the storage bin; it was empty. They all reported their findings to their useless C.O.. A moment later, Marshall advised that the truck contained a single occupant: a man who was bound and gagged and stashed in the module's lavatory.

This development sent the Major scurrying aboard the truck.

The others milled about outside, warily scanning the area for anything suspicious. Rather than risk being overheard using their comm-links, the soldiers swapped comments on their wrist pads.

Hibbs: 50 to 1 odds against the Major cracking the guy.

Danny-Boy: You think he's a pirate?

Hibbs: As far as the Major's concerned, *everybody's* a terrorist.

Bombshell Scarpetti: Why would terrorists raid the base?

Sergio: And why's the guy tied up?

Hibbs: Whoever did it is probably still around here.

They nervously lifted their weapons, waving the nozzles around with sudden caution.

Dr. Holmes stood a few meters off. The woman stared at the installation's entry bunker. She was clearly itchy to get down into the base, but apprehensive about being the first one. Sergio didn't like the implications of her reluctance.

She knows what we're going to find down there, he intuited. *And it scares her.*

He wanted to share his suspicions with someone, but of the squad members he actually knew, Marshall was in the truck. While Danny-Boy was a new comrade, the bruiser was too new to the corps to harbor any helpful opinions. And Hibbs... well, Hibbs was a rugged veteran, he wouldn't be put off by the prospect of unexpected bloodshed.

In all truth, neither was Sergio—but he'd like to be a little better prepared for whatever fiasco lay ahead. The soldiers could expect no clues from Major Dummheit, the fool was playing his no-preconceived-expectations game. That left Dr. Holmes as the sole source for pertinent information.

Sergio sauntered over next to the woman. He tried to act casual, but lumbering about in battle armor in the Moon's decreased gravity was not done gracefully, not even by a spacehound like Sergio Denk. Nudging her, he indicated she should look at her wrist pad. Dr. Holmes was unfamiliar with her pressure suit's capabilities; it took him a moment to get her to understand he wished to converse with her via texting.

Sergio: So what can you tell us?

Dr. Holmes gave him a bewildered frown, then typed back: About what? I know nothing about this commercial vehicle—other than it definitely should not be here.

Sergio: I meant about the base.

Dr. Holmes: The research conducted here at Eiger base is classified.

Sergio: But you know what it is, right?

Dr. Holmes: I'm not allowed to tell you—or anyone.

Now—there was a tantalizing hint. If "no one" was allowed to know the nature of this facility's research, did that mean the Major was in the dark too?

Sergio: You realize that ignorance could get us killed... and you as well.

She gave him a haunted look.

There it is, he told himself. Her weakness. Whatever secret knowledge she had, it made her worry about her own safety.

Sergio: Help us keep you alive down there.

Before she could respond, the Major and Corporal Green came hopping down from the truck's ledge-like fender. Not surprisingly Major Dummheit hit the ground and stumbled, almost falling on his armored ass. Once the fool regained his balance, he started issuing orders.

"Private Danford, stay here and guard this vehicle. Do not go inside. Corporal Marshall has the prisoner in custody." He strode toward the other members of the loosely clustered squad, his unsteady gait undermining his magisterial stature. "The rest of you—we're heading down into the base."

Dr. Holmes reached out to touch the Major as he clumsily strutted past her. "Who is this intruder?" she addressed him over the open comm-link. "Did you find out what he's doing here?"

"He refused to cooperate," Major Dummheit snarled with surly emphasis. (Was Sergio mistaken or did the Major glance at him and curl his lip?) Dummheit wasn't happy that he hadn't been able to crack the intruder. If anyone had taken Hibbs' odds, they'd've been a rich man now.

Ignoring the Major's vacuum of useful information, Hibbs texted to Green: What happened?

The others read Green's reply: The guy's name is Moss. He's a freelance prospector. According to his papers, the truck belongs to him.

Hibbs: Is he a terrorist?

Green: He's a complete wacko. He claims Denk tied him up and stuffed him in the bathroom. Called him by name, too.

Me?

Everyone (Hibbs, Bombshell Scarpetti, even Green) threw Sergio a puzzled look.

Nodding in Sergio's direction, Green continued: Oh yeah—and you're supposed to have murdered his wife and kids too. The guy's a raving lunatic.

The others kept skeptical stares fixed on Sergio.

He was forced to defend himself: Never heard of him. And I've never killed any children.

Bombshell Scarpetti: To the best of your knowledge...

Sergio fixed her with a bold scowl and texted: Never.

"Let's go!" cajoled the Major. He stood aside and urged his troops on.

Hibbs and Green led the way, brandishing their weapons. The Bombshell and Sergio followed, their weapons drawn and ready. The Major and Dr. Holmes brought up the rear.

Sergio glanced back and gave Danny-Boy a parting wave. The newbie was not happy about staying topside while the rest of the squad ventured down into whatever miasma had silenced the installation.

"Corporal Denk." The Major's voice rang in Sergio's earbud. He could tell from the tinny quality that the C.O. was speaking to him on a private comm-link.

"Yes sir," he responded.

"Are you acquainted with a Harold Moss?"

"Never heard of him."

"You're certain."

Turning to peer at the Major over his shoulder, Sergio assured his C.O. that he was certain. Then he inquired, "Is he the guy in the truck?" It was best not to reveal that Green had apprised him of the madman's accusation.

"He claims to know you."

"Never heard of him, sir."

"He claims you attacked him and tied him up," the Major uncharacteristically explained.

Sergio laughed. "When was I supposed to do that, sir? While I was in the shuttle with you and the rest of the squad? Or back when I was still on Station 51, asleep in the barracks?" *Or maybe while I was sticking it to your wife?*

"Yes, I suppose you have an alibi…"

An "alibi"? What the hell—you were with me on the transport, you know I didn't sneak off to the Moon ahead of the shuttle. You bastard, you actually want to believe that I might be guilty of this. You just can't figure out how I did it…

"He insists you attacked him roughly two hours ago."

"I was on the shuttle with you, sir."

"This Moss fellow is clearly delusional."

Don't sound so disappointed, you bastard.

Things started to get weird once they got within twenty meters of the bunker. Sergio could only attest to his own difficulties, but from the sound of things similar quandaries plagued the others.

The first thing Sergio noticed was his battle armor getting heavier. Even his plasma rifle seemed to weigh more with each progressive step.

And speaking of those steps—they were dragging, as if he suddenly plowed through mud instead of vacuum.

"Anybody else feeling that?" came Hibbs' voice over Sergio's earbud.

"Everything feels heavy," the Bombshell's husky voice was tinged with distress.

"Deal with it and shut up!" snapped Major Dummheit. "Maintain radio silence!"

"What the hell—" yelled a voice Sergio didn't recognize. It was probably Green.

A second later, Sergio and the others echoed that startled exclamation. Even the Major violated his decreed radio silence.

An orange mist was rising from the ground. Instead of dissipating in the vacuum, though, the fog maintained a particular density. It separated, clustered around each squad member. Even creepier: these attendant fogs moved along with the soldiers, keeping the men and women centered in their gaseous dominion.

As Sergio watched, things manifested in the mist—impossible things. Hovering right before him, a globular mass writhed until it resembled a lithe torso. The figure's limbs and body undulated as if it were boneless. Its mouth stretched into an exaggerated maw. Its hands elongated into malicious claws. Other regions of the fog were coalescing into additional vaporous figures, surrounding him with antagonists.

Sergio had no idea what to do about this development; it was simply too outrageous. He risked a quick glance at the others and saw that most of them either sagged under a ghostly weight or flailed at foes hidden within each of their attendant mists. So this attack was unilateral, not just aimed at him. Somehow, that didn't make him feel any better. Not even seeing the Major capering about like a madman, swatting at phantoms, alleviated Sergio's stress.

Somebody set some weird kind of ambush for us.

Not just weird, but elaborate. The mist could be staged with gas canisters buried in the moondust. A gravity generator could be focused on the squad, that would explain the increase in the weight of their armor and weaponry. These were expensive measures, though, to use against a rescue squad.

But the wraiths swimming out of the fog—*they* were harder to rationalize away. Granted, a holo projector could be producing the images, but if that was the case how could Sergio's tormentors look like bullies who had tormented him back in grade school?

And there was an itch at the back of his neck that he knew he'd never be able to scratch, even if he unclipped his helmet, for the irritant tingle lay deep inside his head.

Clearly the ambush involved some psychotropic element that was inducing hallucinations in the squad.

And then one of the wraiths slammed into Sergio and knocked him on his butt.

Okay—that *wasn't a hallucination. That thing was real*—

As ludicrous as it seemed, Sergio found himself fighting off a swarm of these juvenile specters. Possessed of physicality, they attacked him, and in turn their substance enabled him to fight back. At first he batted them aside with the barrel of his rifle. When a cluster clawed at him, he fired a blast into their midst. Unbothered by the plasma blast, they pounced on him and pummeled him with their gnarled fists. Their bratty mouths twisted with denunciations which Sergio couldn't hear.

Okay—*energy blasts have no effect on them, but they feel my gun when I wield it like a truncheon. That's something. Not much, but something I can use.*

Shifting his grip on the plasma rifle, Sergio swung it like a club. A rank of snarling wraiths went down under his initial swing. His backswing caught another gaggle and sent them tumbling.

The fog had thickened. By this point it obscured the lunar landscape. He could no longer see the concrete bunker that housed the installation's entrance hatch. From his memory, the terrain wasn't intrinsically hazardous; no fissures or large boulders, just a sloping ravine with the building located at the end of the escarpment. He should be able to maneuver without fear of stumbling over anything or pitching into some abyss.

As he laid into the remainder of the swarm with his bludgeon, a strange feeling crept up his legs… a wetness… as if the legs of his pressure suit were filling with liquid. Which was utterly impossible. Yet the sensation persisted, mounting as the ghostly fluid rapidly seeped across his chest. Where was it coming from? As the baffling tide rode to his chin, Sergio got a whiff of the fluid. It was too glutinous to be water, too malodorous. The stench was incredibly vile; it made him wish he could shove rotten eggs up his nose to drown out the fluid's stink. He trembled as the gummy mass oozed over his face. He choked and thrashed his head in the hope of dislodging the jelly-like substance. But it clung to his skin, and soon he felt it close over the top of his buzz-cut head. The goo had flooded his entire suit.

Blinded by this translucent gelatin, Sergio dropped his rifle/club and clawed at himself. He was suffocating in his pressure suit—but ripping it open would only expose him to freezing vacuum. In or out of the suit, he was damned.

He stumbled against something. His face pressed close enough to the shell of his helmet and he caught a glimpse of a control panel with a small keypad.

The bunker—he'd stumbled upon the bunker and had fallen against the entry hatch.

There's air in there, he realized. *In the base.* If Sergio could open the hatch and gain access to the airlock, he might stand a chance of survival. Once he was safely inside, he could twist off his helmet and tear away the goo that prevented him from gulping air into his mouth.

He fumbled with the controls, but had no idea what code would open the portal. He had to pause and marshal his inner resolve to calm his panic. He needed to concentrate to call up the installation's schematics. Then he struggled to maintain that focus as he rooted through the map for subfiles related to the map. There it was—the entry airlock. A notation gave the proper code that would open the hatch. As he punched it in, a pounding inside his head grew deafening and extinguished his desperation like an ocean dumped on a lone cinder.

The hatch slid aside, and his unconscious body fell into the murky depths of the airlock.

3

ergio Denk woke to find himself no longer encased in suffocating goo. His pressure suit was dry, and it weighed what it should have. He was propped against a wall.

"Surge is with us again," he heard someone proclaim. Sergio was too groggy to identify the speaker, but it was probably Hibbs or Green, for only the veterans would call him by that moniker.

"About time, the slacker," muttered the Major. *His* voice, with that ever-present trace of disdain, was instantly recognizable.

"Hey," objected someone—a girl. Was it Marshall? No, she was back in the prospector's truck. So, that meant it was the Bombshell. "He's the one who made it to the hatch and got it open."

"Big accomplishment," sneered Major Dummheit. "He opened a door."

"While the rest of us were fighting off monsters."

"Keep a civil tongue, Private."

"Sir," Bombshell Scarpetti grunted sternly.

"What happened?" Sergio finally managed to croak. His throat felt as if he'd swallowed an acre of moondust.

Someone crouched down beside him—Hibbs—and plugged a squeeze bottle of water into a nozzle on the collar of Sergio's pressure suit. "Here, you sound terrible."

Taking the extended tube into his mouth, Sergio sucked a welcome gush of liquid into his parched mouth.

"You got the hatch open just in time, Surge. Another few minutes and those creatures would've killed us all."

"There were no creatures," snarled the Major. "It was all smoke and mirrors."

"Begging the Major's pardon," the Bombshell remarked, "but it takes more than smoke and mirrors to kill a man."

For a moment, it actually looked as if the Major was going to strike Bombshell Scarpetti. But he didn't. Perhaps he suspected the girl would hit him back. Whatever the reason, the Major suppressed his rage and stormed off.

"What the hell happened?" Sergio asked again.

"Green didn't make it," sighed Hibbs.

"Huh?"

"The creatures—whatever they were—they got him."

"What?"

"He's still scrambled," Bombshell Scarpetti muttered and turned away.

As the woman, still wearing her armor, moved off to another region of the murky chamber, Hibbs shook his head and grumbled, more to himself than to Sergio, "We're all scrambled after that shit…"

"What the hell are you guys talking about?" demanded Sergio. Past Hibbs, he could see they were in a passage whose walls were hewn rock. Faint light came from the direction that had swallowed the Major and the Bombshell.

Hibbs explained: the squad had encountered mystifying defenses outside the base's entrance. Monsters—creatures—things—had attacked the soldiers. Apparently each person had seen and fought off different adversaries. For Hibbs, it'd been giant spiders. The Major blamed a narcotic gas for the whole incident, but could offer no explanation for how this gas had been able to penetrate everyone's pressure suits. Hibbs didn't care what had generated the creatures, he was simply grateful they were gone. The squad had Surge to thank for their survival. While everyone had been preoccupied fighting their personal demons, Surge had lived up to his nickname and managed to reach the bunker and open the hatch. The rest of the squad had followed him inside, escaping their monstrous tormentors, for the creatures had not pursued them into the airlock. Only then had they discovered that Corporal Green was no longer with them. He hadn't gotten through the hatch. Accessing an external camera, they'd spotted his dead body outside. "Dead… and torn to pieces," muttered Hibbs.

"Green is dead?" whispered Sergio. That didn't seem possible. Although Sergio hadn't really known him, Green's reputation made him to be an iron-willed jarhead. He'd suffered enemy fire on more than occasion and popped back healthy as ever. Sergio just couldn't imagine the veteran being taken out by an hallucination.

"Oh, those things were more than hallucinations," interjected Bombshell Scarpetti. She hadn't gone far and had wandered back during Hibbs' grim recap. "Hallucinations are figments of the mind. Whatever assaulted us had physical form. Their hits hurt." She winced and massaged her side—something had broken a chunk from her armor.

Remembering the tide of goo that had filled his pressure suit, Sergio empathized with her unpleasant memories. Their attackers had certainly exhibited all the traits that go along with physicality.

"The Major thinks we were drugged," she spat.

Hibbs texted them: The Major's an idiot.

Climbing to his feet, Sergio mumbled, "So—we're inside the base now?"

"Not yet. This tunnel leads from the airlock to an elevator that goes down to the underground installation."

With a contemptuous snort, the Bombshell added, "The Egghead can't crack the elevator's access code."

The Egghead? Oh, right—she means Dr. Holmes. Sergio had almost forgotten about the woman. It seemed unjust that the hallucinatory creatures had killed Corporal Green but had left the civilian unharmed. Then his mind took a good look at that last thought and realized how deeply wrong it was.

"Wait a second," Sergio vocalized his confusion. "How did a defenseless woman survive an attack by imaginary monsters that took out a trained soldier?"

"Huh—" grunted the Bombshell.

"You've got a point there, Surge," Hibbs nodded slowly. He threw a glance down the lit portion of the corridor. "If anybody should be dead, it should be her, not Green."

"I don't trust her," the Bombshell confided to them.

Sergio shrugged. To Sergio, the problem seemed more one of getting the woman to trust them. It was clear that Dr. Holmes knew something important, something that might help the soldiers cope with whatever had befallen the hidden research base, but protocol forbid her from revealing anything. During his brief conversation with the Egghead, Sergio had sensed the woman's frustration concerning her forced silence. He believed she was inherently sympathetic to his requests.

Already one soldier was dead, and they'd only gotten as far as the outer entrance. How bad did things have to get before Dr. Holmes chose common sense over security concerns and shared her knowledge with the squad?

When the time came, their lives might depend on trusting the woman.

As the three soldiers rejoined the others, Major Dummheit chastised them, "Where've you been, dammit? Get over here."

"Sir." they grunted in automatic response.

"This damned door won't acknowledge Dr. Holmes' codes," the Major announced. "I want you to blow it open."

"Is that wise?" Hibbs asked.

"It's an order!" the Major snapped back. "You'll do as you're—"

Hibbs posed further questions to the Egghead, not his C.O. "How structurally sound is this corridor? Could a blast collapse the passageway? Or damage the elevator cubicle? Is the shaft reinforced? Is there a chance of an explosion caving in the shaft?"

She turned a frustrated gaze on him. "I'm familiar with the base's staff and research, not the details of the installation's construction."

"She can't unlock the door," the Major proclaimed. "So we have to blow it open."

"Hang on," Sergio told everyone. "I think I've got some answers… just give me a second… accessing the base's schematics."

"You shouldn't have those!" squealed the Egghead. "Where did you get them?"

"They were contained in our briefing," Sergio muttered. He shuffled through the blueprints, keying past the images thrown up on the microscopic display included in his ocular implant. Moving methodically through the data arrays, he searched for the files pertaining to the entrance. There they were…

Dr. Holmes was throwing a tantrum on the Major. "Why does he have schematics? That's classified data! What else do you know that you're not supposed to?"

Flinching back from her tirade, the Major sputtered, "Don't blame me for that. Somebody else compiled our briefing, somebody higher up the chain of command."

According to the schematics, the access corridor wasn't reinforced, it was simply a tunnel burrowed into the porous lunar rock. *Would an explosion disturb things? Hell, a loud shout could bring down the ceiling.*

The elevator shaft would fare better, but not by much. Although struts ran the length of the deep shaft, their strength wouldn't hold up to a C4 blast. The damage might not be enough to cave in the entire shaft, for it was deep. The squad could easily climb down the shaft if necessary. If the elevator cubicle was at this level, the blast would crumple the cage and render it incapable of safely transporting anyone.

He apprised everyone of his findings. Use of explosives was ill-advised under the prevalent circumstances. Furthermore, he could find no sub-file that contained the password necessary to unlock this door.

This news infuriated the Major. Unwilling to give Corporal Denk's assessment any credence, the C.O. demanded that they "open the damned door!"

"Let me try," the Bombshell stepped forth. Her brazen advance made both the Major and the Egghead edge back, giving her clear access to the closed threshold. As she examined the control panel set next to the doorway, she unzipped her right glove and pulled it off. She pried open a small panel and peered at the tight machinery contained within the exposed compartment. For a few moments she poked at the circuitboards and wiring. Then her naked fingers tickled the keypad buttons. Nothing happened. Again she probed inside the tiny compartment, again she tried a fresh code. Again nothing happened.

"Stop this foolery," commanded the Major, "and blow the thing open!"

"Give her a chance," Hibbs muttered to his C.O..

"She's had her—" the Major started.

A third fiddling and numeric sequence had been engaged while the Major blustered, and this time the door slid open with a tart hiss.

The Major's rant devolved into a breathy "—what the—"

"She did it," gasped Dr. Holmes. "But this facility's security should be uncrackable…"

"Hey," Bombshell Scarpetti chuckled as she stepped back, "I grew up in the Chicago projects, I've been cracking security locks since before I had tits."

Hibbs slapped her on the shoulder. "Good going, girl."

"Quickly," the Egghead insisted. "Into the elevator—before it closes on us."

The cubicle was large enough to accommodate at least ten people, but with the added bulk of their battle armor, the squad barely fit. Instinctively edging the civilian to the rear of the cage, the soldiers faced the doorway, their guns in hand and ready to immediately snap down into firing position if the need arose. The Major deftly sidled his way to the back of the cubicle, hiding behind his troops.

Hibbs pressed the only button on the panel inside the elevator. The door closed and the cubicle descended with a subtle lurch.

Catching the Egghead's eye, Sergio muttered softly to her via the comm-line, "Last chance, Doc, to warn us what to expect before we have to face it."

For an instant, he thought she was going to spill, but then her adherence to security won out. Her disoriented expression hardened into a haughty mask. Her lips pursed with defiance and gave a head a single severe sideways jerk.

It was worth a shot.

The Major glared at him with revitalized rancor. Apparently his ears had caught Sergio's remark. The C.O. had prohibited the subject from discussion, and here one of his men was flagrantly violating his decree. Sergio could expect a strong tongue-lashing down the road for this transgression.

Sergio shrugged. *Let him hold a grudge—who cares. Major Dummy and his pompous stupidity.* Anything that increased their readiness was worth grabbing for. Considering the weirdness they'd faced getting to the entry hatch topside, who knew what monstrosities the squad had to look forward to down in the bowels of the secret installation.

The ride was smooth and surprisingly brief. Within minutes the cage reached its destination and halted. Everyone held their breath as the door slid open.

The elevator door opened on a murky gloom. When the soldiers played their lamps into the corridor, the beams of light revealed the air was heavy with a gray pall.

"More narcotic gas!" exclaimed the Major.

But Hibbs conducted a scan and announced, "Just carbon traces."

"Smoke," grunted Bombshell Scarpetti.

"Surge and I will take point," Hibbs decided. They stepped from the elevator and advanced slowly down the murky corridor. Their weapons tracked back and forth.

Dr. Holmes wanted to go with them, but the Major forced the woman to remain with him inside the cubicle.

The Bombshell took up a defensive position in the elevator threshold, blocking the door from closing.

This passageway sported plastiform walls, a poured concrete floor, and a ceiling of sponge-board tiles interspersed with tepid glow strips. No furnishings were evident. As Sergio and Hibbs progressed along the corridor, they detected doorways lining the passage. These doors were all closed.

"I'm picking up no heat signatures," Sergio remarked.

"Nothing on the motion sensors, either," added Hibbs.

Listening in on the comm-link, Major Dummheit deduced, "This level's empty."

"Let's just check to make sure," cautioned Hibbs.

Sergio agreed with his comrade. He took the left side of the hallway.

The first door was locked. So flimsy was its construction, though, Sergio easily bashed the lock to pieces with the stock of his plasma rifle. Nudging the door open, he panned his headlamp across the room. "A storage room," he reported. "Just boxes, no bodies."

Behind him, Hibbs had battered his way into his first room, which he announced was an empty office of some sort.

The two of them moved their way along the corridor, finding more of the same—until Sergio discovered a locker room where visitors could shed their bulky pressure suits and adopt more comfortable attire. A scorched mound of something was piled in the center of the chamber. It took him a minute to realize what it was.

Hibbs joined him in the locker room. They shared "what the hell" looks.

"Well?" came the Major's impatient call.

"All clear," Hibbs assured him.

A moment later the others gathered in the locker room doorway.

"What's that stuff?" demanded the Major.

"It used to be pressure suits," Sergio guessed. A considerable amount of heat had been employed to torch them. The suits had melted together in a grotesque semblance of a pile of bodies. To one side lay the shards of smashed helmets.

"Why would the personnel destroy their pressure suits?" muttered the C.O. "They couldn't leave the base without them."

"Somebody didn't want anybody to leave," Hibbs asserted.

"This must be the work of the invaders," proclaimed Major Dummheit. "So Moss did have accomplices, and they broke in here."

Pressure suits are expensive gear, Sergio mulled. *Why burn them when you could steal them?* Something about this act of destruction was not what it appeared to be.

Was it possible they were still experiencing hallucinations? Was there really a pile of burned pressure suits on the locker room floor? Or was this a mirage induced by whatever narcotic they'd been exposed to? Could they trust any of their perceptions?

I think, therefore I am. I question, therefore I might not be.

With the toe of his boot, he nudged the fused mound on the floor. It certainly seemed real to him. But then, the delusions he had suffered topside had seemed real, too.

"We need to find the staff," insisted Dr. Holmes. She pulled back out into the corridor. The pointmen had gone through all the other rooms, the group was at the end of the level now. Nearby lay an open staircase, she stared at it with trembling excitement. She wanted to rush down its steps but didn't want to face what she might find.

The Major reached out and grabbed her arm, restraining the woman. "No," he growled. "My men go first."

Right, Sergio sighed to himself. *We're expendable.*

Again, Sergio and Hibbs went first. Of the three soldiers left, they were the more seasoned warriors. If any of the hypothetical invaders waited down below, they'd face two highly trained and currently wired adversaries. The soldiers encountered no one during the descent.

One second Sergio was edging carefully down, for his boots were slightly wider than the steps, making footing precarious.

The next he was sinking into the stairs. A nasty tingle numbed his feet. He flailed, reaching out to steady himself—and his arm passed through the wall as if it were just a projection. "What the hell—" he shouted. As the steps swallowed Sergio, he saw that Hibbs continued on, unbothered by this latest delusion. Twisting around, he found that the Bombshell was also unaffected by sudden immateriality. As he sank away, he saw her face expand with incredulous surprise as she watched him disappear.

Darkness engulfed Sergio, forcing him to curl into a fetal ball.

But the darkness lasted only a few seconds.

And he fell from the ceiling of the installation's next lower level. At least, that's where he expected to come out. But when he pushed himself erect, Sergio found himself at the bottom of a grotto. Steep walls of rock rose all about him. A feeble waterfall, actually no more than a trickle of silvery water, flowed down one side into the pool that was gradually filling the pit.

None of the rock looked like lunar material. The colors were all wrong. Everything on the moon was drab gray, but this grotto featured a spread of earth tones. The really jarring part was the sky. Although only a small bit of it was visible past the mouth of the hollow, these heavens were as blue as an ingenue's eyes. There shouldn't be a sky—much less a blue one—down underground.

As he gawked, an animal crept into view atop the grotto. The creature perched above him and released a fearsome growl. It looked like an oversized cat, tawny legs and a sleep body covered with short black fur. It was, he realized, a panther.

No panthers on the moon, Sergio reminded himself. All of this was another hallucination. *At least, it'd* better *be an hallucination.* He nervously eyed the jet black predator as it pawed the ground with menacing intent. Its activity dislodged a spray of stones that came cascading down upon the soldier. Each pebble clattered against his armor before disappearing into the rising water.

"To hell with this shit," he declared. Swinging up his rifle, he fired a plasma blast at the threatening panther. The beast moved with incredible speed, deftly avoiding his shot. Hitting unoccupied rock, the blast fragmented a portion of the grotto's mouth and another avalanche tumbled down upon Sergio.

This time some of the falling chunks were big enough to give him cause for concern; if a large one struck his helmet it might crack the crystal and render the pressure suit useless as protection against the vacuum. While military helmets were generally designed to withstand high impacts, even the best impact-resistant materials couldn't survive getting smacked with a hunk of stone as big as a man's torso. Much less, his ponderous weight told Sergio he was again in the thrall of higher than lunar gravity; this debris was coming down fast and heavy.

The grotto's escarpment crowded in on him. There wasn't enough room for him to dodge all of the falling rubble. Another means of escape was necessary.

Squeezing the trigger of his still-raised rifle, he swung the barrel back and forth. The plasma beam vaporized the smaller pieces of falling debris; the larger masses came apart into tinier molten pieces that summarily disappeared in dusty puffs. A rain of minute pebbles peppered the pool of water around him.

That pool was another problem-in-the-making. Already the water level had risen above his waist. If the waterfall maintained its flow, he'd be completely submerged within minutes. Encased in body armor as he was, Sergio would remain stranded at the bottom of the flooded pit. He wouldn't suffocate, for his suit would provide him with breathable air... but for how long? Would someone come along and rescue him before his bottled oxygen ran out? He didn't even know where he was—other than possibly trapped in a drug-induced delusion. How did one get rescued from a mirage?

Logically, he should still be in the stairwell, probably slumped over in a coma. Hibbs and the Bombshell would take care of his real body. All Sergio had to worry about was his sanity.

"None of this is real," he told himself. "Shake it off. You're stronger than some narcotic gas."

The problem was: Sergio was skilled in physical combat, but when it came to cerebral matters he was an average joe. He had no idea how to fight off a psychological glitch. The hallucination won out by virtue of its unfamiliarity, not to mention its implausibility.

The best he could do was wait it out… and pray that this latest fugue wasn't permanent.

Maybe I can climb out…

A throaty growl above him reminded Sergio that the panther still lurked up there. Peering up, he saw it prowling the circumference of the grotto's mouth. Around and around it went, its tail lifted against the azure sky, the tip twitching with rancorous fervor. The beast's head was lowered as it gazed down upon him. Its pink tongue darted out between rows of yellowed fangs and licked its ebony snout. Its eyes glowed an unnatural red.

It's going to pounce… He didn't need an intimate knowledge of feline behavior to tell that much. *Look at the claws on that thing—it's going to tear my armor and suit apart—then I* will *drown down here.* The panther's leg muscles bunched in preparation of the leap.

Hefting his weapon to bear, he fired a burst of plasma at the cat as it jumped. He was half-a-second too slow. And when he swung the energy beam to slice-and-dice the beast in-flight, the target gracefully contorted to avoid the incandescent needle. Sergio couldn't catch the panther's trajectory. The creature hadn't leaped straight down at him, but instead was descending on an angled path, bouncing off the steep walls of the grotto.

It hit him like an elephant, knocking Sergio from his feet. For a moment he floundered in the deep water, stunned and gasping for breath. His suit was still airtight. The beast's impact had literally knocked the wind from him. By the time he struggled erect, there was no sign of the panther.

No—there it was—atop the rocks, snarling and growling at him, pawing angrily at the ground and dislodging more debris to shower down upon him. *It's toying with me.* Instead of mauling Sergio in the pit, the beast had jumped back aloft to taunt him. At any moment it could pounce again and knock him on his ass. The creature had him trapped, it could keep up this game all day. If the cat was even really there…

Sergio had a strong suspicion, though, that he was going to come away from this hallucination with a mighty bruise across his shoulder where the imaginary panther had hit him.

This is ridiculous. I can't climb out with that thing waiting up there, and if I stay here the waterfall will fill the grotto and strand me underwater.

Eventually the steadily rising water engulfed Sergio. Annoyed by his predicament, he sat down and tried to think of a way out of the mirage. He closed his eyes and envisioned himself back in the installation stairwell. *That's where I really am… not here in a flooded pit guarded by a bad-tempered panther. If I can just make a connection with the real world…*

Something was happening—the pit trembled under him. Vibrations traveled through his armor, through his suit, tingled his skin and penetrated into his muscles and his internal organs. They started low, little more than quivers, swelling in force until it felt as if he were riding a rocket on takeoff. *An earthquake!* Immersed as he was, he moved in slow motion, scrambling to his feet. Fierce tremors shook the grotto. The sensors in his gear revealed to him the surroundings he could not clearly see through the churning water. The geological upheaval ripped the grotto to pieces. The walls caved in on Sergio. Large chunks of debris fell upon him, pressed him down. He was swiftly buried under tons of rock.

Incredible weight crushed him. His armor fractured under the pressure. A wave of pain flooded his mind as the compression reached his body. The ache of his muscles soon gave way to excruciating agony as his bones fractured and shattered. The increasing pressure squeezed his chest, his guts, his head. Darkness forced itself upon him.

4

Grumbling to herself, Corporal Anne Marshall settled into one of the tractor's pilot seats and gazed out at the lunar landscape. She really resented being stuck guarding the commercial vehicle and its solitary passenger. She was a soldier, not a baby-sitter. Her computer skills alone should've guaranteed a place on the team that went down into the installation. But no, in his infinite stupidity, the Major had ordered her "to guard the terrorist and his tank."

Moss wasn't a terrorist, he was a pathetic lunatic.

And by no stretch of anyone's imagination was this vehicle a tank. Even a child could see it was just a commercial mining tractor. But the Major had decreed it was a *tank* and it belonged to *terrorists*—and there was no arguing with Major Dummy's proclamation. The fool believed terrorists lurked around every corner.

So here she was: stranded out here while the rest of the squad got to do their job. Her talents and time were being flagrantly wasted. It was no consolation that Private Danford had been posted outside, so he'd be missing all the action too.

She barely knew Danford—and quickly found she didn't like his pushy nature. Initially he had attempted to engage her in idle conversation, but his topics invariably turned risqué. His innuendoes were crude, so much so that they couldn't be considered tantalizing insinuations. He openly bragged about his sexual prowess, bluntly advising her that she would be a fool if she didn't try him out. He had no couth. He made a lousy comrade in exile. Eventually Anne muted her earbud to spare herself his ribald crowing.

There was nothing to do.

Her search of the cramped living quarters had unearthed no secret hidden caches, the place was clean of any weapons or seditious material.

Tapping the tractor's database, she'd found nothing incriminating there, either. Moss was exactly what he claimed to be (in-between the crazy babble): a lunar prospector. Accounts showed he was a terribly unprofitable one, too.

Moss did a lot of babbling, but his subject material was severely limited. If he wasn't moaning about his dead wife and kids, he was ranting about how Denk had attacked him, how Dent had killed his family, how Denk had wanted to hijack his valuable tractor, how Denk was a scoundrel and a murderer and a nuisance, how he'd tied him up and dumped him in the bathroom and on and on and endlessly on. After a while, Anne donned her helmet and killed her external audio input.

She wondered if Moss even had a dead wife. In light of the rest of his outrageous story, how could there be credence to any of his claims? Moss was adamant that Denk had assaulted him—and that couldn't be. Sergio Denk had been aboard the shuttle, en route here from Station 51 in Earth orbit. In her opinion, Sergio was an amazing individual in many ways (a lewd smirk curled her pouty lips as she recalled their trysts), but being in two different places at the same time was beyond even his skills. Moss' accusations were blatant nonsense.

Outside, the squad approached the base's entrance structure. They were the lucky ones. They got to do something, while she was forced to sit and watch. And soon they'd go inside and there'd be nothing for her to watch.

It seemed to her that the figures were moving strangely. They'd almost reached the bunker, but some of them plodded as if mired in mud, while others waved their arms about in dismay.

She reactivated her comm-link. "What's going on out there, Danford?"

"What—" Danford stepped into sight. Once she had spurned the man's obscene propositions, he'd wandered off beyond her view through the tractor's windshield. "I can't see from here."

Switching to the communal frequency, Anne called, "Major, is anything wrong out there?"

After a silent minute it became obvious that the Major wasn't going to respond—or couldn't.

"Why isn't he answering?" muttered Danford. He took a few hesitant steps in the direction of the squad.

"They're in trouble," Anne told him. "Go—help them!"

"But the Major ordered me to stay here..."

"There's something wrong with the squad," she yelled. "You moron—"

The moron was too green. Danford knew his C.O. was an idiot, but he lacked the gumption to disobey the idiot's commands and do the right thing. There were occasions during battle when one had to violate directives and adapt to the ongoing crisis. Okay, this wasn't per se a battle, but something was definitely amiss with the squad out there. They were clearly in distress. The circumstances called for action, not blind adherence to an idiot's orders. Alas, Private Danford wasn't about to use his head. Going proactive was going to fall to Marshall.

Evacuating the tractor and running to the aid of the squad would be a wasteful response, especially if every second counted. It was easier, faster—and smarter—to drive there. She had the feeling her jarhead comrades would really appreciate it if she showed up right now with a rescue vehicle.

Her hands flew to the tractor's controls—and at the last instant she recalled that the console was damaged. The tractor was dead—another crime Moss had blamed on Denk. Without extensive repairs the tractor was going nowhere.

Dammit—

Scrambling from her seat, Anne assailed the tractor's airlock. Her gloved fingers fumbled on the keypad, and the airlock took a vexatious long time to go through its cycle, withdrawing air from the interim compartment for storage instead of wastefully venting it into the vacuum. She hopped from the outer hatch to the fender and down to the ground. She landed running.

And passed Danford as she raced for the base's entrance. The man fidgeted where he stood. His protests, chattering in her earbud, sounded feeble, as if even he realized what a moron he was being. Finally he gave in and dashed after her.

By the time Marshall arrived at the bunker, the squad was gone. The terrain was marked by tracks and scuffmarks, showing they had all gone through the hatch.

Somebody hadn't made it. A body lay on the ground. Something had ripped open the man's pressure suit and had then eviscerated him. Freeze-dried remains of his organs were strewn about in the moondust.

Coming up beside her, Private Danford gawked at the mutilated corpse. His raspy voice sounded over the comm-link: "Oh my God—can you tell who it was?"

"It's Corporal Green," Anne replied.

She was stunned. She'd known Green. The man was a decorated veteran of several Earthside battles. He was a soldier's soldier, a real hardass. And now he was dead—torn to pieces. What could have done this to him?

"What the hell happened...?"

"Damifino," she whispered.

"It looks like an animal mauled him."

"There aren't any animals on the Moon."

"Get real, Marshall," he chastised her. "No human being did that... unless somebody mounted bear-claws on a chainsaw."

She threw a nervous glance at their surroundings. What the hell had attacked the squad? She'd only seen them responding to some interference. She'd spotted no adversaries, nor did she now. In fact, whatever had gutted Green had left no tracks in the moondust.

That observation stopped Anne's rumination. She peered around at the rest of the area. There were only six sets of scuffmarks disturbing the moondust. Whoever—whatever—had attacked the squad had left no footprints in the granular groundcover. *That* was impossible.

Just as impossible as Green being eviscerated by an animal out on the lunar surface.

Anne suddenly wanted to retreat to a safe position—fast—now.

She took a backwards step.

"Where you going?"

"It isn't safe here," she muttered.

Danford laughed, "What—scared of ghosts?"

She continued moving away from the corpse and the mystifying scenario. Her mind rebelled at the inexplicable evidence, or lack thereof. There had to be a rational explanation for this horrible event... but for the life of her she couldn't think of one. Faced with this quandary, she didn't know what to do. The squad was gone, they'd escaped into the base. Not knowing the access codes, she couldn't follow them. Retreat seemed her only option.

"We can't leave him like this," Danford called after her.

He had a point. Green deserved some respectful treatment. But she found herself unable to help. Although not squeamish by nature, this time she was repulsed by the notion of touching his grotesque remains.

"Where are we going to store him?" she asked. She'd paused in her retreat. "The tractor's cramped it is."

Danford bent down and hooked his hands in the corpse's armpits. He dragged the body around and back-stepped his way toward where Anne stood waiting.

She winced to see how parts of Green, some of them rather large, remained behind, torn free from the cadaver by some beast that left no footprints. Decency dictated that somebody collect the rest of him—but it wasn't going to be her.

Danford and his grisly burden were less than two meters from her when the Private seemed to stumble. He fell backwards, toward her. She capered back to avoid him colliding with her—and saw that Green's corpse was falling with him. No, if Danford had tripped over something, he wouldn't have pulled Green's corpse into the air like it was right now. The body should've stayed on the ground—but instead it appeared to be tackling Danford.

A wail swelled from her throat as she saw Green's corpse move. These weren't random movements, either. They were purposeful and murderous. Green's arms lunged down to pummel a very startled Danford. Now the Private's startled shout rang in her earbud. With an attack that was entirely bestial, Green battered at his victim with dead fists. Danford was too shocked to effectively fight back.

Marshall plucked her hand gun from its hip-mounted holster. Before she could lift and aim the weapon, the zombie had managed to unscrew Danford's helmet. A burst of flash-frozen air billowed forth from the Private's collar, momentarily concealing the ghastly transformation his head underwent upon sudden exposure to the vacuum. Too late she pumped four bullets into Green's forehead. The shots sent him tumbling away.

A dead Danford sank to the ground, his head a swollen abomination.

Realizing she was hyperventilating, Anne struggled to compose her breathing. What the hell had just happened? Green's mutilated corpse had come back to life and murdered Danford. There was absolutely no chance that Green hadn't been dead; between his extensive injuries, air loss, and the vacuum—the man had suffered overkill. His body couldn't move of its own volition—yet she'd witnessed it do exactly that.

In fact—the shocks just kept on coming—Green's corpse was still kicking. Despite the slugs she'd put into his brain, he was clumsily scrambling to his feet. As he pushed himself erect, brittle pieces of his exposed guts broke off and drifted to the ground. His dead face leered at her inside the helmet. Her shots hadn't stopped him. But—why should they have?

He was already dead, a few head shots weren't going to make him any *more* dead. He was a zombie.

Zombies don't exist, they're figments of horror movies.

Yet Green's reanimated corpse didn't care about such distinctions. It was up and moving, and it was coming to get Anne.

Throwing logic to the wind, she let her warrior instincts kick in.

She dropped her revolver; it hadn't been enough firepower to stop her attacker.

This time she dragged her plasma rifle from her shoulder. Thumbing the gun to wide spray, she fired. The pointblank blast caught the zombie in the stomach as it lurched upon her. She held the trigger, and the rifle basked the monster with a steady burst of hellfire. Gloppy pieces flowed into the moondust as the corpse came apart. She kept her weapon trained on the cadaver until the blast had scorched the molten remains to cinders. Human ash mixed with the lunar powder.

The plasma charge ran dry before Anne consciously stopped firing the weapon. Suddenly incredibly heavy, the rifle slipped from her grasp and fell at her feet. To her surprise she found she was panting. She sagged with stress-induced exhaustion; only her body armor kept her standing.

She threw a trepid glance at Private Danford's body. There was nothing she could do for him. He was unquestionably dead.

A numbness filled her head, preventing her from assembling any thoughts.

Somehow Anne got moving. She staggered unsteadily away from the gore-splattered region. When she reached the dead tractor, she had no recollection of climbing up to the elevated fender nor any memory gaining access to the vehicle's airlock.

The next thing she knew, Marshall sat slumped in one of the tractor's pilot seats. Her back to the windshield, she stared into the habitat module's living area. Moss lay there, unconscious or dead—she really didn't much care which.

Gradually she fought her way free of the traumatic quagmire churning between her ears. Her cognitive ability returned, and with it came a sense of vivid disbelief. The things she remembered couldn't possibly have happened.

Swiveling the chair, Anne peered through the windshield. The charred husk that had one been Green's reanimated corpse lay about ten meters from the tractor.

What the hell's going on here? she fretted. *Dead bodies don't start moving or attacking people—maybe in horror films, but not in real life. Yet—I saw it happen!*

Ah, but she didn't have to trust her perceptions. Her suit-cam would've caught the entire impossible affair. All she had to do was play it back to reveal the truth.

As she reached for her suit controls, though, Anne paused. Did she really want this frightening delusion verified? And what if the record showed no zombie attack? Either way, her sanity would be in question. She wanted to know the truth, but wasn't sure she could handle it.

Ultimately, she needed to know. If she'd cracked under the pressure, she needed to know. If she was suddenly living a horror film, she needed to know.

Flipping open the panel on her forearm, her fingers manipulated the controls. She accessed the digital recording and ran it through her ocular implant.

She watched the last half-hour replay itself… her dash out to the bunker, her discovery of Green's gruesome remains, her initial retreat from the scene, Danford's valiant effort to retrieve the Corporal's body, and the lethal reward he received for his respectful actions. She watched the cadaver attack him. She watched it kill him. She watched her plasma blast fry the murderous corpse.

Stopping the video feed, Anne sat and suffered a surge of self-doubt. She couldn't argue with digital documentation. Green's corpse *had* come back to life. She had the proof, but still lacked the ability to believe it.

A noise shattered her fearful reverie, dragging her attention back to the real world. She was surprised to discover that at some point she'd unscrewed her helmet. She swiveled her seat and surveyed the cramped habitat. Moss still lay inert. The sound she'd heard hadn't come from him. Her eyes scanned the rest of the chamber. Nothing looked out of place.

And then the noise came again, and she recognized it. The airlock. Someone was opening the outer hatch.

Who could it be? Corporal Green and Private Danford were both dead. And the rest of the squad was down in Eiger base. Had someone returned to the surface?

Transmitting on the squad's open frequency, Marshall demanded, 'Who's there? Identify yourself!"

No reply.

It was possible that one of her comrades' comm unit was malfunctioning... but she had a dreadful premonition that the truth was a lot uglier—and less believable.

A quick glance out the windshield revealed that Danford's body no longer lay on the ground next to the incinerated residue of Green's zombie.

Leaping to the inner hatch, Anne got it open. She wedged a toolbox in place to prevent the door from closing. As long as the inner hatch was open, automatic safety protocols would keep the outer door sealed. Whoever was out there wasn't coming in here.

She staggered back and sagged against the habitat's side wall.

I have to find out who's out there.

She had no idea if the tractor was equipped with external cameras. Even if so, there was no way she could activate them, not with the control console smashed.

The only way she was going to identify this intruder was to meet him face-to-face.

5

Sergio Denk was adrift in a comfortable darkness, and to his embarrassment he liked it. There were no worries here, nothing existed, so nothing mattered. Not even himself. He was just a tiny portion of a greater void, where everything was equal in its insignificance.

No more bad days. No more dodging artillery in grungy skirmishes. No more getting conscripted to scrub 51's hull. No more shit from Major Dummy.

But there'd also be no more chasing girls. He would miss that delightful pastime.

Pastimes had no place in oblivion. Here, there was only—

Ow!

A sharp pain in his side. The sensation dragged Sergio's consciousness from the cherished embrace of the dark void. Other sensations bullied their way to his attention. A hard surface pressed against his back—a floor. The air tasted terrible, as if he'd vomited in his suit. His vision was still too murky for him to make out anything. A murmur rose to congeal into words.

"At attention, soldier!"

Sergio spontaneously responded to the command. He jolted himself awake enough to clamber to his feet. When his vision finally caught up with the rest of his returning senses, he saw Major Dummheit scowling in his face.

"What the blazes are you doing down here?" the Major hollered at him. "Did I tell you to wander off? Looking for some booty to pocket, weren't you?"

Sergio had no memory of "wandering off"...

"We told you, sir," interjected Bombshell Scarpetti. She moved forward into Sergio's range of bleary vision. "He didn't wander off."

Hibbs loitered at the edge of Sergio's returning clarity. He added, "Surge fell down a hole in the stairwell."

Turning on them, the C.O. snapped, "I didn't see this hole, so there was no hole. You're just covering for him going looting. Expect to get a cut of whatever he found, eh?"

"Permission to speak freely, sir?"

The Major waved a glove at Hibbs.

"I'm a Marine, sir. An honorable soldier. Honorable soldiers do not engage in looting." Hibbs spoke with a terse tone. His stare was ferocious, locked with the Major's weak eyes. "With all due respect, sir, if you ever impugn my honor again without evidence, I will rip off your head and shit down your throat. Sir."

Sergio stifled a guffaw, but a grin leaked out across his face.

"I'll have you court-martialed—" blurted the Major.

"All this bickering is counterproductive!" Dr. Holmes yelled. She pushed her way past the soldiers to confront them. "We're here to determine why this base went dark."

"This is a disciplinary matter, Miss," the Major chastised her. "I do not tolerate insolence among my troops."

"Your primary concern should be investigating this facility, not reprobating your soldiers."

"I am the Commanding Officer here, Dr. Holmes. You are just a civilian consultant. *I* decide priorities and procedures, not you."

"From what I've seen, Major, you make a terrible Commanding Officer. You're lucky your soldiers know what to do when you misguide them."

The Major bridled with indignity. "You know nothing—"

"Like now," Dr. Holmes accused him. "You're wasting time threatening this man—instead of finding out what happened to him." Turning to Sergio, she asked, "What happened, soldier?"

"I… I don't know," mumbled Sergio. He couldn't remember… wandering off or falling into a hole. Scavenging through his memories all he could find were fragments of being attacked by a panther—and they clearly belonged to a dream he'd had while unconscious. There were no wild panthers on the Moon. He could locate no synapses that offered a plausible explanation for his obviously errant actions. "The last thing I remember is descending the stairs."

"You fell through a hole," insisted Hibbs. "The fall must've knocked you out. You probably landed on your head." The Corporal voiced a forced chuckle.

The Bombshell gave him a strange look.

"There will be no more falling down holes, soldier!" ranted the Major. "Do you hear me?"

"Sir yes sir." Sergio was too scrambled to bother objecting to the Major's pompous tirade. Sergio's memory lapse was more troubling. He'd never before suffered amnesia. As new experiences went, it was a thoroughly unpleasant condition. There was a gap in his mind, an inexplicable void. A section of his life was lost. He felt violated, and annoyed that he didn't know who to blame.

Again he wondered if narcotic gases had been released in the installation. That might explain his amnesia.

It also seemed to Sergio that the Major was being awfully stupid about things—but that was par for Major Dummy. He paid more attention to his snap judgments than to the reality of any given situation. And once the Major had decided what was going on, no amount of empirical evidence could dissuade him from his erroneous opinion.

Like now: it was obvious that something hinky was going on at Eiger base. The personally-tailored hallucinations that had beset the squad as they'd approached the entry hatch topside. Those weird delusions had managed to kill a seasoned combat veteran. The squad had encountered no one since entering the installation.

"Go reconnoiter this level," the Major ordered his troops.

They set off, Hibbs checking the rooms on the right, Sergio taking the rooms on the left, while the Bombshell stayed in the corridor as backup. As they progressed down the hallway, the Major and Dr. Holmes launched into what appeared to be a vitreous quarrel. The pair conducted their argument on a private frequency. Using an auxiliary channel, the jarheads conferred with each other.

"So, Surge, you really don't remember falling down a hole?" inquired Hibbs.

"Sorry," Sergio replied. "Between the stairwell and the Major kicking me awake, it's a complete blank."

The Bombshell shared a derisive snort with them, then challenged Hibbs, "Why are you asking him about a hole? There was no hole, dammit. You saw what happened as well as I did, Hibbs."

"What's she talking about?" muttered a suddenly suspicious Sergio. He knew Hibbs, they were longtime comrades. Why would he make up a fictitious hole?

"I know what we saw, Scarpetti," snarled Hibbs over their three-way comm-link. "I just don't believe it—and neither should you. People don't sink through the floor like ghosts."

"I sank through the floor?" Sergio definitely didn't like the sound of that. Hibbs was right: shit like that didn't happen.

"Listen," confided the Bombshell, "I'll tell you what I saw—for what it's worth. You make up your own mind."

"Fair enough."

"We were descending the stairs," she began, "and you—well, I thought you stumbled… but then I saw your feet had disappeared into the steps. Whatever was happening to you, you knew about it—you were struggling, grabbing the walls for support… but your hands went right through the concrete."

"She warned me," added Hibbs, "and I turned around in time to see you sink into the floor."

"It was like you suddenly became a ghost," the Bombshell remarked. "Devoid of any substance."

"You really don't remember any of this," Hibbs probed.

"Nothing," admitted Sergio. He was growing weary of professing his ignorance.

"Naturally, the Major refuses to believe it happened."

Bombshell Scarpetti sneered, "Even after viewing the video footage shot by both of our suit-cams."

"Can I see that?" If his comrades had footage of a portion of his blackout, Sergio was desperate to view it. Perhaps witnessing the sequence might trigger a memory renewal in him.

They fed patchcords into the input on his gauntlet, the Bombshell first, then Hibbs. The videos flashed on his ocular display; each one lasted only a moment. He beheld himself stumble and sink into the concrete steps. He observed himself flail about, clutching for a handhold that would prevent his descent. The Bombshell's view was from behind, but for a few seconds in Hibbs' video record he saw his face contorted with a look of utter panic. The footage answered nothing, sparked no lost memories. If anything, it made Sergio uneasy to see himself undergoing a patently impossible plummet through solid concrete. He didn't remember it happening, yet here was incontrovertible proof that it had.

"The Major claims you slipped off into a secret passage," muttered the Bombshell.

"How am I supposed to have known about a secret trapdoor?" Sergio laughed. "I've never been here before."

Hibbs growled, "You know better than to try to apply logic to one of the Major's inarguable judgments."

Yes, he did.

"It's so typical of Major Dummy to overlook the circumstances and argue in favor of an explanation that ignores most of the facts," grumbled Sergio.

"Terrorists!" Hibbs scoffed. "What kind of terrorists are capable of conjuring imaginary monsters that can kill? Anyway—if there are terrorists, where are they?"

"Maybe they're as invisible as the creatures that do their dirtywork," chuckled the Bombshell.

During the course of their conversation, the three had moved along the corridor and carefully checked each room. This level was devoted to recreational facilities: a small auditorium with a wall screen for showing movies, a gaming room, a gym, and an indoor swimming pool. The water had been drained from the latter, then the tiled pit had been filled with broken furniture and clothing and what looked like pieces of semi-dismantled scientific equipment. There were no signs of the installation's personnel.

"The Major's not going to like this," the Bombshell remarked as they headed back to where their C.O. awaited their report.

Hibbs groused, "Major Dummy won't be happy unless we uncover a nest of seditious terrorists."

Drawing near, they saw that their C.O. was still engaged in a vehement disagreement with the civilian consultant. It appeared that Dr. Holmes was holding her own against the pompous Major.

Having witnessed his inept command skills, not to mention his questionable judgment, she contested his ability to lead this mission.

In turn, he defended his superiority, reminding her over and over, like a skipping music track, that *he* was in command here.

Unimpressed by his rank, the woman insisted that the classified nature of this mission put her in charge. Her familiarity with the Eiger installation made her the obvious leader. She knew what they were looking for and what to do when they found it.

Sergio was intrigued by the vague clues hidden in her argument. Officially the squad had been dispatched to rescue the Eiger staff, but apparently she was looking for something more than survivors.

When the soldiers rejoined them, the Major curtailed their argument. He demanded a detailed report, and although Hibbs jazzed up his account with strings of descriptive adjectives, the gist remained the same: nothing of significance had been found. No base staff. No terrorists. The trash piled in the drained swimming pool served as a high point in Hibbs' account.

"These are especially cunning terrorists," snarled the Major. "They're hiding in one of the lower levels."

"Well then, by all means, let's go find them," Hibbs chirped. Spinning on his bulky heel, he marched off toward the stairwell. Sergio caught the sardonic smirk on the Corporal's face as he passed. He was mocking the C.O.

The Bombshell fell into step behind Hibbs; Sergio joined them, leaving the Major and the Doc to scurry after them.

Dr. Holmes was clearly distressed that her argument with the Major had been interrupted before she could convince him of her superior status as far as the mission was concerned. In her own way, she was as obstinate as the Major. Both of them vied for the command position; she out of concern for the facility's research, he to keep his ego inflated. His refusal to use common sense was every bit as strong as the woman's resolve to reveal nothing about the installation.

What a motley crew we are, mused Sergio. *Three jarheads being goaded on by a pair of dueling commanders.* In all honesty, he wasn't sure which one of them he'd rather follow—the idiot Major with his smash-his-troops'-heads-against-the-wall strategies, or the woman who refused to warn them what to expect. *While the rest of us are just flat-out confused.*

They ventured deeper into the underground installation.

The next floor provided accommodations for the Eiger personnel. Here, four hallways converged on the centrally located stairwell; twenty apartments were arranged along these dreary plastic passages.

The soldiers wanted to fan out to check the rooms, but the Major insisted they all stay together. It was, he claimed, for their own safety, but Sergio suspected the man didn't want to get stuck alone with Dr. Holmes again, fearing she would continue to argue with him. She was a strong-willed individual, perhaps not equal to the Major's obstinate resolve, but persistent enough to tax his patience. Major Dummheit was used to people doing what he told them to do. This time, however, his adversary was not a soldier under his command—worse, in all likelihood Dr. Holmes probably had the authority to overrule his decisions. As long as the squad was in the field, though, the C.O. had the upper hand, for he could make life unbearable for any enlisted grunt who refused to follow his orders.

Doc Holmes would have to wait until the squad returned to Station 51 to lodge her complaints.

The rooms were narrow and sparsely furnished. The beds comprised little more than elevated slabs of foam. The dressers were plastiform cabinets with recessed handles. Work desks had computers built into them and featured chairs designed to provide the antithesis of comfort. While most of these quarters were undecorated, a few of the occupants had taped posters on the walls. No, "posters" was an inaccurate description. When Sergio examined them, he saw the printout sheets didn't feature pictures, just graphs annotated with illegible remarks. The closets were full of dreary clothing. The desks contained innocuous personal effects that offered no hints as to the personalities of their owners. Each medicine cabinet was stocked with toiletries and all-purpose pharmaceuticals. None of the beds looked as if they'd been slept in for days.

Concluding his examination of the third homogenous domicile, Corporal Hibbs returned to the hallway to report in a drab monotone, "Nothing again, sir."

As the soldiers started off down the corridor to check out the next apartment, the Major summoned the Bombshell. "Check the computer for a diary or anything that might shed light on the staff's disappearance."

Dr. Holmes promptly forbid any such action. "The contents of these harddrives are highly classified," she protested. "None of you have the security clearance necessary to touch these computers."

Treating the woman to a dismissive sneer, Major Dummheit urged Scarpetti to follow his orders.

For once, Sergio had to agree with the Major's belligerent attitude. For Major Dummy, it was purely a matter of triumph over the uppity civilian. As far as the troops were concerned, however, they needed some information regarding the base, its personnel and operations. If Dr. Holmes wasn't going to provide any, the squad had to find it somewhere else. The personal computers of the missing staff were as good a place as any to begin.

Ignoring the civilian's protests, the Bombshell approached the desk and set to work on the computer. After a while, she stepped back to announce her failure.

"What do you mean?" the Major berated her

"I can't access any of the files," she explained the obvious with a weary sigh.

"Try again," insisted the C.O..

"I tried several times, sir. Everything's password protected."

"Crack them."

"I'm no hacker," she complained.

"That's Marsh's thing, sir," Hibbs reminded the Major.

"What about you—" The Major turned on Sergio. "The schematics you found in the briefing—they had passwords in them. You found one to open the topside airlock."

"That was different, sir. That was a general access code." He quickly scanned the files to verify his snap judgment. Besides the access code to the topside hatch, there were no other passwords included in the data. "These are personal units, each individual user will have set up their own private passwords."

Twirling on his heel (not a particularly easy maneuver when wearing a pressure suit mounted with body armor), the Major stormed off. He brusquely pushed Dr. Holmes from the apartment's doorway.

Sergio, Hibbs and the Bombshell shared "what an asshole" looks before dutifully following their C.O. Dr. Holmes stepped aside to let them through the doorway.

Stomping away down the corridor, the Major reached the next door. As he yanked it open, a shape spilled from the room and pounced on the man. He staggered back, flailing his arms and filling everybody's comm-lines with a high-pitched screech.

By the time the soldiers dashed forward, the Major's assailant had scurried off and vanished into another apartment down the hall.

Scarpetti crouched by the fallen C.O. and asked if he was okay. Keen to hide any weakness, he brushed her aside.

Sergio and Hibbs paid little attention to the Major's well-being, they chased after his assailant. Although Sergio had gotten only a fleeting glimpse of the figure, it had looked human, not monstrous at all. Maybe this time they were facing a non-hallucinatory opponent.

They entered the room, Surge going first. He dove into the apartment; his weapon was at the ready, but he was fundamentally reticent to shoot the attacker until they determined whether or not they were dangerous. A blow from the rifle stock would suffice to disable the person for later questioning.

This apartment offered no drastic variations from the ones they'd previously searched. The bedcovers were unrumpled. Another assortment of enigmatic printouts were taped to the walls. The desk was uncluttered by any personal items. The only difference here was the noise coming from whoever hid in the closet.

Sergio and Hibbs flanked this closet. On the count of three, Sergio pulled open the door and Hibbs reached in to drag out the occupant. He flung the person into a far corner.

It was a man, naked, fortyish, balding with a pot-belly and skinny legs. His features were contorted by a furious insanity. His mouth twisted and spat bestial sounds. His eyes rolled up with porcine panic. His forehead wrinkled with heartfelt anxiety. He cowered into the corner, clawing at the wall as if seeking a secret escape panel.

"That's Professor Hoek," exclaimed Dr. Holmes. She stood in the apartment doorway, gawking at the naked savage. "Don't hurt him! He's one of the base's heads of staff."

She took a step into the room, her hand lifted in a reassuring position. "Professor Hoek, we're here to help you. There's nothing to be afraid of."

Flinching away from her approach, the unshaven wretch gibbered, "Better off dead!"

"That's not so, Professor," Dr. Holmes assured the pathetic man.

"But," he wailed, "she doesn't want to kill you!"

"Nobody wants to kill you, Professor."

The madman gave her an urgent look and hissed, "She has more fun with living playtoys!"

When she kept coming, Professor Hoek's hysteria climaxed, sending him into a violent frenzy. He scrambled to crawl past her and escape, but the two soldiers moved to block his exodus. Trapped, he retreated to the bed where he pressed his back against the wall. His head rolled back and he avowed through clenched teeth, "Better off dead! Better off dead! Better off dead!" Reaching up, the man ripped out his own throat.

With a unified outcry, Sergio and Hibbs leaped to stop him, but Hoek knew his anatomy. Despite the dementia characterized by his behavior, his self-mutilation was carefully targeted. His fingers dug through his flesh to snag his carotid artery. With a pitiful moan, he tore the pliant tube from his neck. His blood sprayed forth, dousing Sergio and Hibbs as they arrived too late.

"What did you do to him?" screamed Dr. Holmes. She pushed past the soldiers and bent to try to revive Hoek. Her pressure suit gloves made her efforts clumsy.

Within seconds, the madman was dead.

"We didn't do anything," Sergio protested.

"He ripped out his own throat," gasped Hibbs. There was a distinctly queasy edge to the veteran's voice; even the battle-seasoned Corporal was disturbed by Hoek's gruesome suicide.

"He was a sane man—a scientist!" she shouted at them. "You frightened him into doing this!"

"Lady, it wasn't *us* that scared him."

The Major arrived, full of bluster and the desire for vengeance. He showed no regret that his attacker was dead, only annoyance that he had missed his enemy's demise. Stonefaced, he listened to accounts of what had happened, from his soldiers and from the outraged civilian. He preferred to believe Dr. Holmes' version, that Sergio and Hibbs had attacked Hoek. How could anyone rip out their own throat? He commended his men for their efficient efforts in "putting down that terrorist animal."

"Professor Hoek was a man—a scientist—not an animal!" argued Dr. Holmes. "He wasn't a terrorist—he was a head of staff here at Eiger base! He's one of the people we came here to rescue!"

"He attacked me," was the Major's snide retort. "The terrorists must have turned him."

"The guy was scared shitless," remarked Hibbs.

Reluctantly leaving the dead man's body sprawled on the bed, Dr. Holmes turned her full wrath on the Major. "You stupid moron! This man was worth a hundred of you! He—"

Casting off his smug satisfaction, the Major gave her a mighty shove that propelled the woman across the room. Her armor crashed into the wall, cracking the plastic sheeting. Dummheit followed to loom over her. Drawing a handgun, he pointed it down at her and snarled, "I've had enough of you and your damned interference, bitch. Nobody is worth a hundred mes—not that slob, not you. It's time you learned your place. This isn't some government office—this is a battlefield—and out here, *I'm* in command. My orders are the only ones that matter. Cross me again, and it'll be the last thing you ever do!" He waggled the gun in her wincing face. "Do you hear me?"

Stunned into immobility, Sergio and Hibbs stared at their C.O. as he openly threatened the woman. The Bombshell stood in the apartment's doorway and gawked.

Whirling on his soldiers, Major Dummheit declared, "I want this woman locked up! She's clearly working with the terrorists."

"No!" she whimpered. "There are no terrorists—"

He silenced her with a kick.

"Out of that suit," he ordered. "C'mon—strip—now!"

"Sir," mumbled Sergio. "Is that necessary?"

"I can't risk her eavesdropping on my strategies."

Too terrified to respond, Dr. Holmes cowered on the floor. The Major leaned over and pressed the nozzle of his gun against the crystal shell of her helmet. "Off with it—now—or I put a bullet in your head."

Moving jerkily, the woman struggled to comply. Her unfamiliarity with the suit left her frustrated and panicky. The Bombshell stepped forward to help her.

On the pretext of "Further orders, sir?" Sergio and Hibbs got the Major to retreat to the hallway. They wanted to separate him from Holmes before his rage turned the situation any uglier than it had already gotten.

"I need to know how widespread this terrorist infestation is," asserted the Major. "You two go check out the next level. Report back to me here."

"We haven't finished examining the rest of the rooms here, sir," Sergio pointed out.

"Private Scarpetti will handle that. You two take the lower level."

"What about you?" asked Hibbs.

"I'll stay here to guard the prisoner."

"Prisoner…?" mumbled Sergio.

"The spy—that bitch." The Major tossed a significant scowl in the direction of the room where Scarpetti was helping Doc Holmes divest herself of her pressure suit. His glare lingered, as if he expected one of the women to offer some criticism. "I'll be here… to make sure… the bitch doesn't turn the Private… against us…"

The two soldiers waited. With the Major's disjointed speech pattern, they couldn't tell if he had finished his statement or not. After a moment they decided there were no more forthcoming instructions.

"So," remarked Hibbs, "we'll go reconn the next level…"

They moved off in the direction of the central stairwell.

"Don't screw up," the Major called after them. "I'll hunt you down and punish you if you screw up."

If we screw up, it's liable to get us killed, reflected Sergio. *If you want to follow us into the afterlife, be my guest, you asshole.*

"He's lost it," grumbled Hibbs.

"No shit."

They were making their way down the murky steps. The only light came from the halogen lamps attached to their suits; the illumination was so bright it made everything look like a backdrop from a high-contrast cartoon.

"How wise is it to leave Holmes back there with Major Crazy?"

"She'll be okay," Sergio replied. "The Bombshell won't let him hurt her. She's a good kid."

"The 'Bombshell'?"

"Private Scarpetti."

"Oh." A ribald chuckle escaped Hibbs' lips. It sounded artificial coming through Sergio's earbud. "Good one, Surge. Yeah, she's a hot little piece."

Sergio gave an agreeing grunt.

"I guess you're right," commented Hibbs. "She seems level-headed enough to stop the Major from doing something stupid."

"Everything the Major does is stupid," Sergio muttered to himself.

"Yeah..."

They'd reached the doorway that gave off to the next lower floor. As usual, Sergio went through the doorway first. After peering about to ascertain the level's overall safety, he sent Hibbs two clicks—the signal that all was okay. (One click meant danger, two implied safety. The theory was that a warning needed to be swift, while speed was an unnecessary factor in an all-clear signal.) The Corporal followed Sergio through the access door.

More corridors, this time numerous ones, all converging like the spokes of a wheel on the stairwell hub. Although it seemed hard to believe, these passages looked even more drab than the pale gray hallways they'd encountered above.

When Sergio moved to begin searching the rooms that lined one corridor, Hibbs accompanied him instead of taking another hall. "Safer this way," he told Sergio.

Sergio wasn't about to complain. After the weirdness they'd seen, he felt better with a trustworthy comrade at his side.

The first room proved to be an office. Metal cabinets lined the walls, their drawers were intended to contain arrays of data chips, but the drawers were mostly empty. The few remaining chips were each labeled with a tiny piece of masking tape bearing a sequence of numerals. A computer sat on a desk, but its screen was smashed. A closer examination revealed traces of a brownish sap crusted on the edges of the broken crystal shards.

"I think that's blood," remarked Hibbs. "Somebody put their fist through the monitor screen."

They both looked at the objects laying atop the desk—a slim remote control unit, a stapler, a lucite cube holding down a stack of papers, a stack of empty data chip cases.

"Why would someone would use their bare fist instead of one of these heavier objects to smash the computer screen?" Sergio wondered aloud.

Hibbs examined the papers, but they were covered with calculations that meant nothing to him (nor to Sergio when he consulted them). The Corporal rifled through the desk's drawers but found nothing helpful, just more algebraic printouts and a box of hard candy.

Any one of the surviving data chips might have offered information concerning the base's doings and downfall, but without a working monitor screen there was no way to read the files. *Besides,* mused Sergio, *they're probably password protected like everything else in this place. And what else would you expect in a secret research facility?*

They continued on to the next room, which turned out to be another clerical office. More cabinets filled with a poignant absence of data chips. Here too the desktop computer had been assaulted, this time a paperweight had been used to shatter the monitor.

Several more rooms were the same. In a few they found semi-melted mounds on the floor where somebody had incinerated piles of data chips.

"Something very bad went wrong here," remarked Hibbs. "They wanted to destroy any evidence of the research before they got away."

"But—they didn't get away," Sergio reminded him. "They burned their pressure suits, stranding themselves here."

"So where are they?"

"We just haven't found them yet."

"Why would they hide from a rescue team?"

Sergio shrugged. "Maybe they're all dead."

"Then where are their bodies?"

Alas, Sergio had no inkling of an explanation, just a bad feeling in his gut. Everything about Eiger base creeped him out.

Returning to the hub, they paused at the doorway to the stairwell.

"The Major isn't going to be happy that we found nothing."

"I'm inclined to forage deeper into the installation," suggested Hibbs. "Not much point in going back until we have something useful to report."

"Okay."

According to the schematic he carried in his head, there was only one more level beneath where they stood. If the scientists weren't hiding down there… where the hell were they?

They headed down the steps.

At the next landing they found a massive hatch instead of a conventional doorway. The hatch was heavily armored. They doubted even a plasma blast would penetrate the barrier. Its security lock confounded their efforts to open it.

Hibbs' exasperated sigh resounded in Sergio's earbud.

"Yeah," he agreed with the Corporal. "I guess we're stuck going back to the Major with nothing but bad news."

6

A jolt roused her. Corporal Marshall didn't recall drifting off. The stress of her predicament had clearly overtaxed her normally indefatigable stamina.

Maybe that predicament itself wasn't real, perhaps it'd just been a dream from which she was now awaking. That would be a wonderful relief. So much of the circumstances had been nightmarish, but now that she was awake all those horrific aspects would evaporate, stranded in the realm of dreams.

Another jolt occurred, and Anne realized she couldn't move. Dressed in her armored pressure suit, she was seated in a chair—a pilot's seat—in the dead mining tractor. With the crazy prospector. She struggled, but someone had tied her in place. Peering down at herself, she saw that a sturdy electrical wire was wound around her, securing her to the chair. Although it was awkward, Anne could manage to swivel the seat around so she could see into the module's living space. Moss the madman no long lay on the floor, unconscious and trussed.

He was up and active—and donning the decrepit pressure suit that hung next to the airlock.

"What are you doing?" she barked at him. But he showed no sign of hearing her. Her external speaker was off; she'd deactivated it to cut herself off from the intruder's angry ruckus.

And in an unwanted flash, the really unpleasant part of her not-a-nightmare came flooding back into her mind. The intruder—the one she'd prayed was a member of her squad returning topside from the secret research base... all the while dreading that it was something unholy and malicious. The intruder had banged on the tractor's outer hull for a long time, forcing her to deactivate her exterior microphone to preserve her sanity. She'd cowered near the rear of the tractor's cabin, afraid of monsters that couldn't exist. And then she'd caught a glimpse of the intruder through the front windshield. Morbid fascination had dragged her forward to gawk at the figure outside. It had been one of her squad-mates, but not one that should've been up and walking around. It'd been Private Danford. Still minus his helmet—shudder, she recalled how Corporal Green's reanimated corpse had unscrewed that, exposing Danford to the lethal vacuum—the Private's corpse had stood outside and stared at her with its empty eye sockets. Depressurization had blown the eyeballs out of his head, while abrupt vacu-freezing had drawn the skin taut across his wide face, changing the man's otherwise jocular grin into a gruesome rictus. She'd screamed when he'd lifted his dead arms to wriggle his gloved fingers in her direction.

The dead are up and walking—well, technically shambling, she'd privately lamented. *He's terribly unsteady in the lunar gravity.* Hysteria had welled in her. Here she was facing impossible circumstances—and she couldn't stop being analytical about it, nit-picking over terminology in her attempts to cope with this supernatural state of affairs. There was nothing rational about the dead walking around; it was an act of stupid futility on her part to try and fathom the mechanics of such a fantastic turn of events. But she couldn't stop doing so, as if swaddling herself in logic might protect her from the chimerical phenomenon.

But that hadn't worked. The undead figure had still stood out there, reaching for her with writhing fingers that wanted something.

The zombie's desire wasn't that hard to guess—it wanted to kill her. Green's reanimated corpse had murdered Danford, and now it was his turn to kill somebody.

To escape all this ludicrous necromancy, Marshall had retreated into a semi-conscious state. She remembered that now. But during her fugue, unexpected developments had complicated matters. Crazy Moss had awakened and gotten free, then he'd tied her up with the very wire she'd used to bind him. Now he was putting on his tattered pressure suit.

Activating her external voice system, Anne repeated her protest, "What are you doing?"

Moss swung around to squint at her. Full-blown madness contorted his angular face into a mask of antagonism. He barred his teeth and hissed at her before he growled, "You're in league with Denk—don't bother denying it." He continued to climb into his pressure suit.

"Where do you think you're going?"

"After him, of course." Fevered hate gleamed in his manic eyes. "The bastard has to die."

"You don't want to go out there…"

"Why not?" Moss sneered.

And Anne realized how insane her reasons would sound. *If you go outside, an undead zombie is waiting kill you.* Was Moss crazy enough to play along with this lunacy?

The man dismissively waved a gloved hand at her. "Don't bother—I won't believe anything you tell me. You'll say anything to protect Denk."

Adrenaline flowed rich in her bloodstream right now. Her heart pounded with the frantic need to stop the maniac from opening the air-lock. She needed some wild trump card that would dissuade Moss from venturing forth on his misguided quest for vengeance. Fragments of data fell into a weird alignment in her head, spawning an outrageous bluff.

"Your family isn't dead!" she yelled. "Denk didn't kill them—he's gone to rescue them."

Moss paused zipping up his suit and threw a suspicious glower in her direction. "Lies," he snarled.

"No—it's the truth. The accident—" She searched her memory for what kind of accident it'd been; the man had babbled enough about it. "The shuttle accident—it happened to you, not your wife and kids."

"You're saying *I'm* dead?"

"No—you suffered a head injury—it's scrambled your memories, made you think Denk is a villain—where he's actually your… your pros-pecting partner." It was a stretch, but to convince Moss she needed to tie together all the parts of his delusion, and Denk was apparently a vivid element in his fantasy. She had to work Sergio in somehow. "He's trying to help you reunite with your family."

"If they're not dead, why does Denk have to rescue them?"

Loose hole—plug it quick. "You found a super-rich deposit—iron—and these scoundrels are trying to steal your claim. They kidnapped your family to force you to sign over the site's rights to them. And Denk has gone off to rescue them."

"Why didn't I go along? If anyone's going to rescue my family, it's go-ing to be me!"

"The kidnappers have sensors cued to your brain pattern." Her story was growing wilder and wilder, but she suspected Moss was so far gone that even the wildest explanation might sound logical to him. "They'll kill your family if you come after them. So Denk went alone."

For a moment, needy faith burned in Moss' eyes—he so wanted to believe his family was still alive—but then suspicion furrowed his brow.

"And who are *you* supposed to be?"

"You keep forgetting who I am, Moss. I'm Marshall, a freelance mercenary. Denk hired me to assist on this rescue mission. You need to untie me."

"Why do I keep forgetting you?" Moss lowered his head until his chin rested on the pressure suit's raised circular collar. Tears leaked from his scrunched-shut eyes. "Maybe because you're not who you claim to be." He raised his head to glare at her. "You're in league with Denk—you probably helped him kill my family."

Wo—things going awry. He really has a deeply-ingrained hate for Sergio. Lord only knows where he got that?

"Listen," she urged him, "we're in danger right now. The tractor's disabled—and there are hostiles outside, agents of the kidnappers. You mustn't go out there."

"I don't believe you," Moss declared. He hoisted his helmet over his head and gave it a twist, securing it to the rigid collar.

"No—wait—" But it was too late. He'd shut himself off from her voice.

Turning to the airlock, Moss discovered the toolbox she had used to prop open the inner hatch. With an annoyed kick, he knocked the crate out of place and stepped into the airlock.

Anne struggled with renewed vigor. She strained and rocked and flexed her arms and pushed with her legs. Gradually she felt her bindings loosen; Moss had been slipshod with his shackles. Freedom was imminent—but still too far off.

Moss pulled shut the inner airlock door. Through the portal set into the hatch, she could see him initiating the outer door's release.

The wire loops finally slackened enough for Anne to slip from the chair. She stumbled across the narrow cabin, almost falling upon the airlock in her urgency. Her fingers clawed at the small control panel set next to the hatch, but the machinery ignored her input. Once the outer door started its opening procedure, the inner door was firmly sealed.

Too late, she moaned to herself. The moron was gone—outside into the monster's waiting embrace. Moss was unarmed and had no idea that any threat existed out there. Anne, though, had weaponry perfectly suitable for blowing away the murderous corpse. Against her better judgment, she knew she had to go after the crazy prospector.

For all his urgency to chase after Denk, Moss unhurriedly exited through the outer hatch and before freeing up the airlock for another cycle, leaving Marshall twitchy with frantic impatience. The damned tractor was so old and decrepit, its machinery operated so slowly. *By the time I get outside,* Anne fretted, *Danford's corpse will have gotten to Moss and murdered him.*

Was Moss spry enough to avoid the corpse's shambling assault? And what if the maniac eluded Danford? Well, that much was obvious: Moss would seek out Sergio and murder him, a development Anne resolutely sought to prevent.

But first she had to see to her own survival, and the survival of the madman too. Just because Moss was crazy was no reason to let him blunder into a fatal encounter with Danford's reanimated cadaver.

The airlock's lethargic cycle afforded Anne the opportunity to check her weaponry, to make sure she had ample ammunition for her rifle and handgun. She'd lost her plasma rifle outside after using it to incinerate Green's corpse. She ran diagnostics, confirming that her suit and armor were still operating at maximum efficiency. She topped off her oxygen reserves from the tractor's tanks. Now that she had rallied her psychological resolve, she was keen on making sure her gear would not let her down.

Her earlier fear and shock had faded, replaced by determination and fortitude. No rationalization existed for the zombies, but she had moved past any need for explanations, taking refuge in a soldier's doctrine to face any foe with resolve and courage. It didn't matter whether Danford's undead corpse was possible or impossible, credible or incredible, it was an adversary that must be met and defeated. The absurdity of killing something that was already dead was moot.

When the airlock finally released its inner hatch, Marshall hastily plunged through it and eagerly assailed its controls. And discovered why Moss had lingered so long here before escaping to the outside. He'd set the controls to respond to a password. Without the proper coded sequence, the outer hatch would never open. He'd effectively trapped her within the tractor—or so he'd thought.

Marshall was quite adept with computer systems. Given the time, she could break any security code. Here and now, however, she really didn't have the time to spend hacking a go-around to gain control of the airlock. The few minutes it would take her could be enough of an interval for Danford's zombie to catch and slaughter Moss.

Immediate action was requisite.

From a compartment at her waist she drew a brick of C-4. She didn't need the entire slab, a pinch would suffice. Her glove's padded fingers were too bulky to effectively detach a small chunk of the plastique explosive, so she unzipped her gauntlet and pulled it off. Crimping a bit of the soft putty, she stuck it to the outer hatch's secured locking mechanism, then plugged a charge-prong into the volatile glob. She programmed the detonator for ten seconds. She retreated to the relative safety of the tractor's living module—barely in time.

Despite the small amount of C-4 she used, the blast rocked the tractor. The concussion wave flung her against the far wall of the domicile, momentarily stunning her. She was dimly aware of a high-pitched whistle as the air evacuated the tractor. Before she could regain her wits, a powerful suction pulled Anne across the module and flung her through the blown-open hatch.

She tumbled outside across the lip of the tractor's extended fender and landed on her back on the granular ground. Her impact generated a cloud of moondust that briefly engulfed her, blinding Anne to her immediate surroundings. Fighting off her disorientation, she extracted her handgun from its holster. For all she knew, Danford's zombie was skulking by the tractor, waiting to pounce on her. At least now she was armed.

Too impatient to wait for the dust to settle, Anne rolled aside to avoid any ambush. By the time she scrambled to her feet, she could tell that no one—dead or alive—lurked in her immediate proximity.

So—where are they?

She activated her suit's sensors, and within seconds a scan of the region told her everybody's location.

Moss was traveling briskly across the terrain, headed for Eiger base's entrance bunker. His loping gait showed an expert familiarity with lunar conditions.

The zombie was not giving chase. The undead figure stood a few meters ahead of the tractor; its shriveled head uptilted and focused on the vehicle's windshield. Its arms hung at its side, passive and unthreatening.

This turn of events changed Anne's priorities. Moss had eluded the zombie, he no longer needed saving. But she had to catch Moss before he could get into the base and hunt down Sergio. (Would Moss even recognize him? The prospector was driven by a savage hate for Denk, but—as far as Anne knew—Moss had never met Sergio. What face did Moss' delusional Denk wear?) The role of adversary had shifted from Danford's corpse to the lunatic prospector.

Ignoring the zombie, Anne pursued the fleeing madman. Trained to cope with diverse environments, her skill at moving in low gravity rivaled Moss' homeland advantage. She would've caught up with him too—if not for the slab of basalt that got impossibly in her way.

The ground just ahead of her erupted and a stone buttress rose from the underground depths to loom twenty meters above her. Since each of her steps propelled her four meters off the ground to land ten meters ahead, she had no opportunity to halt or deviate from her course. She hit the barricade full-on. The impact knocked the wind from her. Luckily she had reflexively thrown up her arms to protect her head so that her helmet didn't crash into the rockface. Dazed and bruised, she slid down the coarse barrier to crumple at the base of the new mountain.

The geological phenomenon stymied Anne. That it had happened at all was quite incredible, but that the lunar surface had intervened to help Moss escape her—*that* was absurd. Yet—it had happened, there was no denying that. Her aches and dizziness attested to the rock slab's tangible existence. It completely blocked her from Moss, she couldn't see him at all. In order to chase him she would have to race around this stony protrusion.

Apparently the terrain wasn't going to allow her to do that. As soon as she started running along the base of the new cliff, another boulder burst from the ground to block her path. Each time she tried to dodge around one obstacle, another obstruction would pop up. While these new boulders weren't as massive as the first, their dimensions were enough to hinder her progress.

She ran a winding course through these obstacles, undaunted by their impossible advent. At one point she tried to leap over one, only to be thwarted by a fresh crag that rose fast and high to prevent her escape. More than just impeding Anne, these boulders were erecting walls to cage her in.

Her wide scans alerted her that Danford's corpse was lumbering after her. Only the zombie's clumsy lethargy kept it from catching up to her. But if these emerging barriers continued to block her way, the corpse would soon reach her and add to her troubles. She needed to get past this forest of rock, then the boulders would hamper the zombie's progress.

Extreme measures were called for.

The jets embedded in her boots would gain her a speedy release, but at considerable cost of her resources. Firing those jets would drastically deplete her energy reserves. She was loath to waste so much power, but she couldn't think of another solution. If she didn't find a way around the boulders soon, Moss would escape and Danford's zombie would catch her.

Thanks to the Moon's meager gravity and airless atmosphere, only short bursts were necessary to send her flying into the sky. Leaving the stone maze far below, she angled her short flight to carry her in the direction of the Eiger bunker.

With a startling degree of violence, the ground spat a large boulder into the air. The rock lifted to block her aerial path. Unless she changed her trajectory, it looked as if she was going to fly right into the thing. She cursed at the necessity of expending another burst of her jets—but then saw that secondary blasts might not be requisite.

The huge projectile's upward momentum was moderate, and its ponderous weight prevented it from soaring to an exceptional height. Although it initially rose high enough to obstruct her, by the time she reached the boulder it had achieved the zenith of its ascent and was already falling back to the lunar surface. She still hit the boulder, but was able to transform that impact into a leap which added more elevation to her flight.

The ground spewed forth a few more rocks at her, but none of these projectiles reached her new altitude. She soared above the lunar valley, at a height almost equal to the lips of the nearby craters. The view was spectacular, but her attention was directed elsewhere.

Eagerly scanning the area around the Eiger bunker, she spotted Moss. The madman was within four meters of the entrance hatch. She'd never reach him in time. But then he would spend valuable time fumbling with the entry controls. This place was a secret base, a raggedy prospector couldn't possibly know the codes that would open its front door. Anne would definitely be upon him before he—

What the hell—

She gawked as the bunker's hatch slid open long before Moss reached it. The madman raced through the portal. As soon as he was inside, the hatch closed.

What the frigging hell—

Someone in the base had opened the doorway for Moss. It was highly doubtful that any member of Marshall's squad would've let him in. Did the lunatic have an accomplice?

"Accomplice"—damn, I'm starting to sound like Major Dummy. Moss is no terrorist. He's just a crazy lunar prospector. So—who had opened the hatch for the man?

Her flight brought her down a few meters from the bunker. As she landed, she vented a microscopic burst of air from a vent located along her upper back, counteracting her momentum and preventing her from bouncing back into the air. She half expected more rocks to surge forth from the ground to impede her, but none did. Maybe the ground here was too hard to easily eject buried boulders. Grateful but unconcerned with explanations right now, Anne dashed to the hatch. She examined the controls.

A simple keypad affair. She calculated that hacking past its safeguard protocols would be child's-play for her superior skills. Popping the unit's panel, she drew a selection of fiber-optic lines from her wrist and attached them to strategic points among the exposed machinery. Using a keyboard mounted on the forearm of her glove, she proceeded to infiltrate the hatch's operating system. The security firewall was pathetic; she was through it in seconds. And seconds later she had located the triggers to open and close the hatch.

To her utter surprise, the entrance controls refused to succumb her to reprogramming. She flexed her digital imperatives, but still the system resisted her efforts to activate the doorway. She doubled her commanded—to no avail.

The hatch was locked shut.

Whoever had let Moss inside was determined to keep Marshall outside.

7

As soon as the insolent Corporals were gone, Major Dummheit summoned his remaining soldier.

"I need you to search the rest of this floor," he informed Private Scarpetti. "Make sure there are no more hostiles hiding to ambush us."

"What about Dr. Holmes, sir?" chirped the buxom soldier.

"I'll watch the traitor."

"You think she led us into a trap?"

"From this point on," he advised her, "we must assume that everyone is in league with the enemy. The staff are to be considered hostiles and treated as such."

"What does that mean, sir?" The girl gave him a puzzled look. "Specifically..."

"I'm authorizing lethal terms of engagement, Private."

"Kill them...? But sir... aren't we here to rescue them?"

"You don't realize the volatile nature of this situation, Private," Major Dummheit snapped back. "This entire facility has been infested by terrorists!"

"But shouldn't we try to rescue the staff from the terrorists, sir?"

"We're too late. They've all been turned."

It vexed him that the stupid girl didn't understand. Not that "understanding" was necessary—she should follow his orders without question. Clearly the riffraff had tainted Scarpetti with their insolent conduct. *Another one lost,* he mulled. He'd harbored hopes for this new recruit, but she'd gone the way of the rest of them.

Major Dummheit often lamented the uselessness of his troops. They were rowdy and lazy. Disrespect was rife among the ranks aboard Station 51. Major Dummheit couldn't believe the sloppy discipline exhibited by the troops under his command. They had no respect for his authority.

Nothing he did managed to bring them into line. Their impertinence was insufferable. He couldn't imagine how such a multitude of contemptuous lowlifes had gotten accepted into the Marine Corps in the first place.

It galled him to be stuck commanding a regiment of losers. He deserved more, certainly a better chance to prove his worth. He had high aspirations for himself, perhaps a position in the Global Senate. It wasn't fair that so far his military career had failed to show his true promise. Those damned lowlife servicemen were to blame, always making him look bad. Some of them had even had the audacity to accuse *him* of faulty command decisions. Not that the Big Brass had put much credence in those callous lies. Even so, the allegations became a black mark on his record, threatening to abolish his political career before it'd even begun.

To be perfectly frank, he hated the wretches under his command. They were scum and deserved far worse than the demeaning assignments he arranged for them. Scrubbing hulls should've built their character—or at least humbled them. But no, they continued to flaunt their mutinous demeanor. And he loathed them all the more for their tenacious scorn.

He felt no remorse over Corporal Green's demise. The soldier had repeatedly used his status as a veteran to undermine the Major's authority, scoffing at regulations and challenging every directive. The squad would function better without the troublemaker.

Alas, they were all troublemakers.

Corporal Hibbs had a charismatic mouth on him, and he used it to voice all kinds of subversive criticism. Early on Dummheit had recognized Hibbs' rabble-rousing tendencies. He was the one to watch. He was ballsy enough to act on his seditious opinions.

The buxom Private was already showing signs of rebellion.

And Denk—Major Dummheit resented Corporal Denk's suave calm. The man never sweated, never showed a trace of uncertainty. His brimming self-confidence and good looks rankled Dummheit. In all truth, Denk was a superb soldier—and Dummheit hated him for it. He sought ways to debase Denk, to waste his talents, to diminish his popularity among the ranks. But nothing ever broke the bastard's spirit. Sometimes Dummheit wished he could find a reason to put a bullet in Denk's brain.

Hackhead Marshall and Newby Danford were topside. They posed no threat to Major Dummheit's authority down here.

But Dr. Holmes—that bitch had brazenly tried to usurp his command again and again. He'd not been surprised to discover she was in league with the terrorists. She'd been leading the Major and his squad into a trap.

It was all well and good to send Scarpetti to search the other rooms on this floor… but Major Dummheit knew that questioning Dr. Holmes would prove more fruitful when it came to ferreting out information about the enemy.

During his ruminations, the Major had strolled over to the room where the woman was incarcerated. He stood in the door and studied her. Without her pressure suit she looked small, petty, scared. She cowered under his stern regard, showing her inherent weakness. She would talk, she would spill everything, eagerly confessing every transgression she'd ever made going all the way back to her childhood. For all her bluster, Dummheit could tell she had no resolve. She would crack all too soon, cutting short any fun for him. For once he'd have to forego amusement in the name of self-preservation.

"Where are they hiding?" he barked. Through activated speakers in his suit, his voice boomed in the narrow room.

The woman flinched. She edged back on the bed where she sat. But then her eyes flashed with defiance. She yelled at him, "You can't do this to me! My security clearance is—"

"Any status you had was forfeit when you colluded with the enemy, woman," Major Dummheit spat back. "Traitors deserve no special treatment."

"You're insane!" wailed Dr. Holmes. "How can you call me a traitor? *You* had Professor Hoek killed! You were sent here to rescue the researchers—not to kill them!"

"He attacked me. He got what he deserved." Moving closer, Major Dummheit loomed over the woman. "If you know what's good for you, you'll advise me on the whereabouts of your terrorist associates."

"What terrorists? There are no terrorists!"

"If that's the way you want to play it, bitch…" He reached out and cupped her face with his gauntlet. "I'm perfectly willing to force the truth out of you." With each word he tightened his grip until her cheeks whitened under his bulky fingers.

Her defiance sputtered out, leaving only mortal panic smoldering in her eyes. He squeezed her mouth shut lest she spoil his fun with any premature confessions. She squirmed and he forced her back against the wall. A bloodthirsty glee boiled up in him. This was going to be—

"Sir," came an interfering declaration.

Major Dummheit twisted around to glare at the figures standing the apartment's doorway. The Corporals had picked a most inconvenient moment to return.

"What?" he snarled at them.

"The next lower level is abandoned," reported Corporal Hibbs.

"Then go assist Private Scarpetti," the Major replied. "She's searching this floor for any more hiding terrorists. I'm busy forcing a confession out of this traitor."

For a moment neither of the Corporals moved. They lingered in the doorway, regarding him with their idiosyncratic insolence. Were these lowlifes actually about to challenge his command?

"Go help Private Scarpetti," growled Major Dummheit. "I want this floor secured against terrorist infiltration."

Before the Corporals got the chance to mutiny or comply, an uproar erupted out in the hallway. The soldiers promptly rushed off to investigate it. Releasing his intended victim, Major Dummheit crept over to peer around the door jamb.

He saw nothing more than the Corporals disappearing around a corner down the corridor as they sought the source of the bedlam. (The scene stirred unpleasant memories for him from the night before when he had watched some brazen intruder flee his apartment.) Besides the noise of breaking furniture, more than one voice was screaming—and not all of them sounded human.

Although he was curious about what was going on, Major Dummheit was also cautious enough to stay where he was until he found out. As Commanding Officer it was not his place to be in the thick of battle, he needed to remain safe so he could continue to command.

He heard gunshots. The shots didn't stop. They kept on resounding down the hallways, as if the slugs weren't bringing down their target.

He cringed back, suddenly worried that his remaining soldiers were being overwhelmed by a terrorist horde. Worthless though his troops were, these three grunts were all the Major had right now. Any further losses would weaken his defensive position, especially if he was suddenly faced with an army of terrorists.

Reacting to this train of thought, the Major ducked back into the room and closed the door. He secured it as best he could.

At least now he was safe from whatever the hell was going on out there.

8

When Corporals Denk and Hibbs returned to report to their C.O., they found Major Dummheit alone with Dr. Holmes. They saw no sign of Private Scarpetti.

Sergio was impressed by Dr. Holmes in her underwear. Shorn of her bulky pressure suit, she looked less like a scientist and more like a babe. Her body was remarkably toned for a desk-jockey. Her demure underwear hid none of her curves. With a different, less pretentious personality she might have made a tempting conquest.

Watching the confrontation for a moment, the two conferred via their wrist-pads. Sergio had a bad feeling about what they saw.

Sergio: What's he doing?

Hibbs: I suspect he thinks he's interrogating her.

Sergio: Looks more like intimidation to me.

Hibbs: A classic style… always popular despite its unethical nature.

Sergio: He's going to hurt her.

"Sir," Hibbs brusquely announced their presence.

The Major twisted around to gawk at them. His surprise was tinged with obvious annoyance that they had interrupted his inquisition. "What?" he snarled at them.

"The next lower level is abandoned," reported Corporal Hibbs.

"Then go assist Private Scarpetti," the Major replied. "She's searching this floor for any more hiding terrorists. I'm busy forcing a confession out of this traitor."

For a moment neither Sergio nor Hibbs moved. They lingered in the doorway, uncertain how to handle the situation. Sergio had no intention of leaving the Doc to Major Dummy's sadistic persecution. The asswipe's idea of an interrogation would turn ugly when his prisoner failed to spill the info he wanted. How could she confess anything to him? There were no terrorists; they existed only in Dummheit's warped mind. Once again, Major Dummy had concocted a tangled web of irrationalities to support his obsession, only this time his reckless mania was endangering more than just a squad of his own troops—this time his lunacy was putting a civilian in harm's way.

Exchanging a concerned glance with Hibbs, Sergio could see that the Corporal was as troubled as he was by this turn of events. In good conscience, neither of them could allow Dummheit to torture his captive.

"Go help Private Scarpetti," growled the Major. "I want this floor secured against terrorist infiltration."

Before the Corporals got the chance to concoct some additional delay, an uproar erupted down the hallway.

What the hell— Sergio recoiled from the awful noise. At his side, Corporal Hibbs reacted likewise.

Together, they launched into action. They raced down the corridor, drawing weapons as they ran. Their response was automatic and fearless. Someone was in trouble—honorable soldiers had to help.

"This is Hibbs, Scarpetti," Sergio heard the Corporal yell over the squad's comm-lines. "Where are you? What's happening? Report, girl!"

Chasing the screams to their source, they rounded a corner and dashed down another hallway. Dim light strips ran along the ceiling, but more vivid lighting flashed in a room at the far end of the passageway.

She's a newbie, fretted Sergio. *She's too busy defending herself to respond.*

When they reached the room, the men beheld a ghastly tableau. It was a cafeteria with utilitarian dining tables and uncomfortable plastic chairs. The walls were decorated with floor-to-ceiling jungleland murals. One side of the room served as a kitchen where the staff could cook meals instead of relying on freeze-dried cuisine. Human corpses hung from large meat hooks, their withered limbs entwined with each other as if these people had died as lovers.

The noise came from Private Scarpetti. Crouched down behind a cafeteria table, the Bombshell was firing sporadic rifle bursts across the room. If she was aiming at a target, though, it was invisible. Her shots chewed up a jungle mural. All the while, she screamed with hysterical fervor.

"Big—big cat—big black cat—"

She's lost it.

But then Sergio saw something move inside the two-dimensional mural—and he realized that the Bombshell hadn't lost it. The figure of a large panther skulked among the lush foliage. She was firing at this ene-my. Her bullets failed to reach the phantasm, though, lodging themselves in the wall's cement surface. The beast swung its dark sleek head to peer at the newcomers. Baring its impressive fangs, the panther issued a throaty growl.

Sight of the beast brought a flood of memories blooming in his head, filling his amnesiac gap with experiences that were thoroughly preposter-ous. He remembered sinking like a ghost through the solid concrete… only to find himself trapped in a grotto. He remembered the panther, the wa-terfall, the creature's taunting harassment, the pit's collapse. Despite their outright implausibility, these events had happened to him. They were not a nightmare he had suppressed, he had actually suffered through these ab-surd circumstances. The panther had been real—and here it was again.

"What the hell—" exclaimed Hibbs. Apparently he too saw—and heard—the imaginary cat.

Then things got weirder.

The bodies hanging along the length of the kitchen began to twitch and moan. Their arms clutched at each other, all implied affection fled now as the corpses clawed wildly among themselves. One tore out the eyes of another, while a twentysomething clerk-type disemboweled his meat hook neighbor. Stagnant blood and viscera spilled down upon the Bombshell in her hiding spot.

This time Corporal Hibbs' exclamation was more guttural. "Oh my God—"

Sergio was speechless. His gaze returned to watch the panther slip easily through the shrubbery. Their eyes locked and Sergio felt the feral hostility churning behind the cat's deadly stare.

Shaking off shock and disgust, Hibbs scurried over to Scarpetti's side. He dragged her from under the table and shoved her for the doorway.

"Stop shooting!" Hibbs loudly advised the Bombshell, but if she heard him she didn't heed him. "You're only wasting ammo!" Before he followed her, the Corporal threw a haggard glance at the writhing kitchen corpses, as if hoping that up close he might spot the stage trickery involved in this gruesome show.

As Sergio herded the Bombshell from the cafeteria, he saw the pan-ther bound from the jungle. He had a bad feeling the beast was about to do something utterly impossible—and the brute didn't disappoint him. A three-dimensional panther emerged from the flat mural. Crossing the room in a dark flash, the cat pounced on Hibbs.

The Corporal went down under the beast's mighty attack. Straddling him, the cat's mass pinned Hibbs to the floor. Its teeth closed on his helmet, but the reinforced glass proved to be stronger than the creature's jaws. Enraged by its inability to bite off Hibbs' head, the panther's hind legs clawed him with bestial frenzy and shredded his pressure suit.

Leveling his gun at the beast, Sergio fired off several shots. More than half of them hit the creature, but it didn't go down. Undaunted by these injuries, the panther kept on mauling its prey.

A blinding blast erupted in the cafeteria, and when Sergio's eyesight cleared, he saw the panther had been thrown back and Hibbs was scrambling for the doorway. A wisp of smoke coming from the nozzle of his plasma rifle explained the flash, as did the crater raggedly gouged into the ceiling.

Hibbs had shot the panther with a plasma blast—but the beast was still kicking. Hell, the thing wasn't even scorched. No natural animal could withstand such forces—it had to be a *thing*.

Just like the thrashing corpses were *things*. Maybe once they'd been people, but someone had mutilated and killed them. None of them could've survived their grisly wounds—yet they were moving and moaning. And now they were climbing down from the meat hooks. They were coming after the soldiers.

Sergio fired at the group—and was surprised to see several of the shambling zombies twitch from those shots. They didn't fall dead—they were *already* dead—but the bullets had a discernible effect on the corpses.

The unkillable panther had regained its wits. It started after Hibbs, snarling with emphatic animosity. Twisting around in the doorway, Hibbs hit the beast with another plasma blast. As the energy burst momentarily hampered the creature's advance, Sergio yanked him out into the hall and slammed shut the door. He locked it down.

"What the hell was all that?" gasped Sergio. "More hallucinations like topside?"

"Look at your suit," Hibbs grunted. "Hallucinations don't usually leave marks."

Long tears in the Corporal's suit hung open, revealing bloody scratches. Even his armor plates showed signs of laceration.

"It came out of the wall!" moaned the Bombshell. She stood a few meters down the corridor, still twitching with hysteria. "It couldn't've been real!"

Before Sergio could point out that he'd encountered the panther in a prior delusion, the beast pulled another impossible trick.

It came right through the closed door as if the metal barrier was no more than a hologram. Everybody suddenly filled the comm-line with panicky screams. The beast added to the din with its ferocious growl.

The soldiers retreated post haste. Hibbs brought up the rear, firing tentative plasma bolts to hold the creature off. They scurried along the hallway.

When they reached the apartment Major Dummheit had designated as his prisoner's holding cell, they found that door was closed.

"Major—it's Private Scarpetti. Corporals Hibbs and Denk are with me," the Bombshell signaled their C.O. "Let us in, sir! We're under attack out here!"

Sergio ceased struggling with the door's immobilized latch. He snarled, "Bastard's locked himself in."

Pushing him aside, Scarpetti cursed, "Let me at the damned thing. I'll open the door."

He backed off. The woman had shown expertise with locks. Hopefully her magic fingers would prove superior to his own brute force efforts to open the door.

From inside the room, they heard somebody bang a fist against the door. Over their comm-line they heard the Major's voice: "Go away! I won't let you in! The terrorists have contaminated you!"

The Major and his goddamn terrorists, Sergio grumbled to himself. There was no point vocalizing his complaint, the others were indubitably thinking the same thing.

"If we're stuck out here, we need to figure a way to incapacitate that monster," announced Hibbs. "These plasma blasts are barely holding it back. I know it sounds crazy, but it's almost as if the thing's adapting to them… or absorbing them…"

"Compared to all this, nothing seems crazy," Sergio advised the man.

Having paused at the corner the soldiers had turned, the panther cagily hesitated to follow them. It peered at them from there, its huge eyes luminous with rancor—and a touch of cunning. Right now the beast was relatively safe from the blasts of Hibbs' plasma rifle, but it sorely wanted to chase after the soldiers, to catch them and rip them to pieces. Sergio got the distinct impression that the panther's animosity went far beyond any basic bestial predatory nature—this creature's hate was almost human in its ravenous intensity… as if the soldiers had egregiously offended the beast or slaughtered its mate.

"What's holding it back?" muttered Sergio. The beast could pass right through solid walls, much less it had developed an immunity to Hibbs' blasts. As far as Sergio could tell, the creature had nothing to fear from them. So—what was stopping it from continuing its attack?

As they watched and waited, weapons ready despite the uselessness of their ammunition, the panther gave a fierce growl and withdrew.

Had something—or someone—reined it in?

A career soldier like Hibbs wasted no time taking advantage of an enemy's retreat. He boldly raced after the departing panther.

"Watch out," Sergio called out to him. "The thing might just be faking retreat."

Sergio cast a nervous glance around the corridor. For all they knew the beast was sneaking upon them by slipping through the unoccupied rooms. They needed to stay wary—although he wasn't sure that any degree of caution would help if the creature came pouncing from a solid wall to tear them to pieces with its deadly claws.

Behind him, Sergio heard the Bombshell exclaim, "Got it!" He turned as she flung open the door—just in time to see a hail of bullets spew forth. Ricocheting off Scarpetti's armor, the slugs inflicted no real damage, but the shock of the attack made her stagger back.

This outrageous development stunned Sergio. The Major was actually firing on his own troops.

Flattening against the corridor wall, Sergio removed himself from the Major's line of sight. The Bombshell followed suit and took a position to the right of the apartment door.

"What the hell are you doing, sir?" demanded Scarpetti. Her usually husky voice trembled with barely restrained anger. "We're supposed to be on the same side!"

Dummheit's caustic denunciation sounded in Sergio's earbud, "You can't fool me. The terrorists got to you. They brainwashed you and sent you to kill me."

"There aren't any terrorists," the Bombshell advised him.

"No," came the Major's snide retort, "they never think of themselves as 'terrorists,' do they? They're always freedom fighters."

He's crazy, she texted Sergio.

He sent back: "Just picking up on that, are you?"

"There aren't any terrorists, sir," she called to the Major. "Just a spooky big cat."

Oh good, Sergio flinched. *Start telling the crazyman about things crazier than just terrorists.*

"You can't fool me—" the Major's voice started to decree, but suddenly cut into a hoarse "—ooof—"

Followed by Dr. Holmes' screeched plea for help, "I have him—come quick—I—ooof—"

Despite the implausible scenario that Doc Holmes could've overpowered Major Psycho, Sergio's reflexes carried him through the doorway. He gambled and he won. Against outstanding odds, the civilian had indeed disabled the Major, albeit only momentarily. Jumping him from behind, she'd knocked him to the floor, trapping the gun he held underneath his torso. Her semi-naked figure spread atop him, her limbs splayed in a futile effort to keep the man pinned down.

As the Major threw off his feeble assailant and lurched erect, Sergio stepped in and snatched the gun from his clutches.

Space Marine armor was the best there was, it had to be. But any competent jarhead who'd worn space armor under serious combat conditions knew the gear had weak points. Sergio knew several ways to incapacitate the Major. His strike disabled the motors that augmented the wearer's ability to move the suit's ponderous joints. Major Psycho was effectively immobilized in his suit until somebody reset his servos' motors.

The Bombshell rushed to check on Dr. Holmes. The Doc wasn't badly hurt from her abrupt ejection, although that pale skin of hers would undoubtedly soon be sporting several vividly colored bruises.

A moment later, Hibbs rejoined them. "Damned thing got away. It melted right through the cafeteria door. I chased it inside and watched it go back into the jungle mural. It disappeared into the mural's shrubbery. Damnedest thing I ever saw."

"It's a day for damnedest things," muttered Sergio.

9

With the Major indisposed with psychological problems, Corporal Hibbs assumed command of the squad. He promptly advised Dr. Holmes to put her pressure suit back on. He could tell Denk was distracted by her exposed flesh. At any other time he'd've cheered on Surge's randy nature, but Hibbs wanted him sharp and focused in case that damned ghost panther returned. *Besides,* he mused, *getting the Doc back in her suit will boost her confidence, and that's just as important at this stage. After all, she's the only one who knows anything about what the hell's going on in this damned place.* By this point Hibbs was convinced that whatever disaster had befallen the Eiger base went far beyond any conventional threat assessment. Dr. Holmes' knowledge could prove to be the deciding factor between the squad's life and death. Ruefully, he had scarce hope of finding any members of the facility's staff alive, not after the abattoir he'd seen in the cafeteria.

Once Holmes was ensconced inside her pressure suit, Hibbs told her what he and Surge had found below: the empty office level with its smashed computers and piles of melted data chips. "We tried going lower, but the door to the level beneath that is like bank vault."

"The labs," she muttered.

"We couldn't open the thing," added Surge.

"No, you wouldn't be able to," remarked Dr. Holmes. Despite her earlier pompous scorn toward military intelligence, this time her statement sounded more declarative than denunciating. "You don't have the access code."

"But you do," Hibbs countered politely.

She flashed him a suspicious look, but then shrugged. "Yes." The woman finally realized the foolishness of security in their present predicament. "I know the base's access codes. Not all of them, just the important ones."

From the side where she guarded the doorway, Private Scarpetti snorted, "If you ask me, codes to open the front door and activate the elevator are kinda important, too."

Propped in a corner and still immobilized, Major Dummy ranted and flashed rancorous glares at the rest of them. Hibbs had confiscated the Major's earbud and deactivated his suit's comm unit. Nobody wanted to hear his infuriated tirade, and Hibbs didn't want him listening in on their discussions.

"If there's anyone left alive," mumbled Dr. Holmes, "they'll be down there. The labs are the facility's most secure chambers. It makes sense that the staff would lock themselves in the labs for their own safety."

Remembering the panther's ability to pass through locked doors, Hibbs didn't think anywhere was actually "safe."

"Well, we're here to rescue them," Hibbs declared. "So let's get moving."

"Begging the Corporal's pardon," remarked the Bombshell, "but I really feel we need to reevaluate that mission objective…"

"What?" Dr. Holmes gave a horrified gasp. "We have to—"

"Am I the only one who's picking up on all the nasty clues?" queried Scarpetti.

"What clues?" grunted Hibbs.

"We know there aren't any terrorists, so the Eiger staff had to be the ones who burned their pressure suits and locked themselves in here. Why would they do that? I think this place was a germ factory and some nasty plague got loose. So the scientists tried to quarantine the base."

Hibbs nodded. The Bombshell's deductions made sense. Why would the staff sequester themselves in such a drastic manner? Maybe "sequester" wasn't the right term, maybe "quarantine" was more accurate. Whatever they were cooking up got out of control. Was this why the squad had found nobody in the base? Had the plague wiped them all out? That would account for the base going dark.

"The staff don't want to be rescued," insisted Scarpetti. "They've done everything they can to contain the plague."

"No," Holmes protested. "That couldn't happen. The Eiger research isn't biological in nature."

"What is it, then?" chirped Surge.

"I can't tell you." Her face darkened. "But I assure you—no part of it could have accidentally produced a rogue disease."

"I dunno, Doc," reflected Hibbs. "The empirical evidence says otherwise. I think Scarpetti's right. Every sign points to the staff quarantining themselves." He paused to frown. "If that's the case, do we want to risk unleashing this plague?"

"There is no plague," Holmes argued. "Just a research staff who need to be rescued."

"Unfortunately," sighed Hibbs, "the only way to determine what's going on is to open the labs and see for ourselves."

"That's right," Holmes asserted.

"But we're going to be careful about this…"

"What's that supposed to mean?"

"It means the Doc and I will go down and unlock the labs. You two stay up here, hopefully beyond the reach of anything we might let out by opening the lab's entry hatch. We'll be real quick about it—open the hatch, go in, and immediately seal it back up. We'll use our comm-line to report what we find."

"What if you don't report back?" ventured Scarpetti.

"That's a defeatist attitude," Dr. Holmes complained.

"No," Hibbs corrected her. "She has a valid point. There's a fifty-fifty chance we're going to find something extremely unpleasant inside the labs. If the Doc's right, then we can proceed with rescue protocol. But—if the situation is dangerous, we might not survive to report anything." He turned to face Surge and Scarpetti. "If that happens, you two have to decide whether you stay or get the hell outta here. It's your call."

They nodded grimly.

"What about him?" Surge nodded toward their deactivated C.O.

"Haul him out with you," Hibbs recommended. "Your video logs will justify our removing him from command."

"If there's a risk of contamination—" Scarpetti started.

Holmes interjected, "There isn't!"

"But—" continued the Bombshell, "if there *is*—you can't go down there, Corporal Hibbs."

"Why not?" he laughed.

"Your suit's all torn up."

Dammit—she's right. I forgot about that. The damned panther ripped my suit back in our cafeteria scuffle. While he wasn't entirely convinced any contagious risk existed, Hibbs had to admit he'd rather err on the safe side. Going down into the labs dressed like this would be reckless.

"Take the Major's," suggested the Bombshell.

Hibbs gave a nervous laugh. "Poetic justice aside, I'd rather not. Besides, I don't think it'd fit me." He was a big man, while Dummheit was average-sized, albeit dumpy.

"You can borrow my suit," offered Surge.

"No, then you won't be able to leave the base."

"Nobody gets left behind."

Hibbs nodded. He knew Surge. The man was a true Marine, he'd never abandon a comrade. And ever since he'd gotten his nickname he'd become all the more courageous. "Unless we find an intact pressure suit down in the labs, *somebody's* going to have to stay in the base until another suit can be brought from outside. As your current C.O., I'm drawing that short straw. No arguments. If the Doc and I don't come back, you get the hell outta here. You don't be stupid, you don't come after us. You go get help."

"Scarpetti can go get help," insisted Surge. "There's probably an extra pressure suit in the prospector's tractor; she can go get that. But *I'm* not leaving here without you, Hibbs."

"This is all so melodramatic and moot," grumbled Dr. Holmes. "There's no plague to worry about. The torn condition of Corporal Hibbs' suit does prevent him from leaving the base unless a replacement is found. But as Corporal Denk just pointed out, the tractor topside is certain to have extra suits. So in the end there is no problem."

"Should I go fetch it now?" Scarpetti asked with evident uncertainty.

"Leave it for later," advised Hibbs. "Bad enough we're splitting the squad into two groups. You two stick together." He jerked his head at the incapacitated Major. "And don't leave him out as panther bait, tempting though it may seem."

The two gave token chuckles.

"So," grunted Surge. "You want to borrow my suit or the Major's?"

"No contest."

Denk proceeded to peel away his armor and squirm out of his pressure suit.

As Hibbs descended the stairwell with Dr. Holmes, he thought about Surge. *He's a devout Marine, a true warrior, but ever since Madrid he's become a thrill junkie. His first taste of being the front line. And now he's always got to be the first into battle. Madrid's when he suddenly developed an overactive libido, too. Madrid changed him.*

Madrid changed a lot of things, personal and cultural. Private Denk and Corporal Hibbs hadn't been the only ones scarred by that day.

They'd known right away that it was a combat mission. Several squads had been deployed over the past week as civil unrest had blossomed into bloodstained anarchy across Europe. The economic collapse of the Euro had triggered widespread riots, and terrorist groups had seized the moment to instigate innumerable crash-n-burn runs, adding to the overall pandemonium. Global troops had been summoned to reestablish order.

Corporal Jack Hibbs and Sergio Denk (then just a Private) were in the 23rd squad sent groundside. After weeks of warming their bunks with their butts, both of them were juiced for some excitement. Neither of them had any idea what they were about to face.

Their briefings told them the shuttle was depositing them in Madrid, otherwise they'd never have known. Destruction was rampant enough to render the city into unrecognizable ruins. Buildings slumped in upon themselves, collapsed mounds of rubble. The streets were clogged with abandoned cars, many of them torched and still burning. The sky was murky with the city's incinerated remains.

The people were the worst of it. Everyone wild-eyed and frantic, scrabbling with a mania that blurred the distinctions between survival and hostility. Dressed in tatters, many had looted sporting goods shops and armed themselves. Most of them were prone to shoot first and questions be damned. It was impossible to tell the difference between civilians and terrorists. Social decay had so eradicated propriety that there really was no difference anymore. The soldiers were forced to defend themselves against the very people they'd been sent to safeguard.

This blurring of any distinction between hostiles and civilians created an insurmountable obstacle to the restoration of order in Europe. From this day on, all battles would be fought unilaterally against everyone. Realistically, Global couldn't condone slaughtering innocent civilians, and so the majority of forces were withdrawn from the European continent. The theory was that sooner or later the Europeans would come to their senses, and once sanity prevailed, then troops could return to help the survivors. Alas, the lunacy remained quite prevalent among the Europeans. For five years, Global Forces adopted a posture of noninvolvement, although particularly bad catastrophes would prompt deploying emergency troops to quell pandemonium. The region became a 24/7 battleground.

Late that afternoon, the squad encountered a gang that had commandeered a section of what-had-once-been-a-city, roughly six square blocks of inhabitable wreckage. The gang used a mostly-still-standing church as their lair.

The C.O. (who fortunately had not been Major Dummheit, this mission had happened before his arrival at Station 51) proposed a surround-

and-contain tactic, but the territory was too big for the fourteen-man squad to establish and police a secure perimeter. The Lieutenant was still stymied by the quandary when the squad stumbled on a roving group of gang members who sounded an alarm. Before a bloodthirsty horde could be summoned, Sergio Denk had vanguarded a direct charge on the church. His brazen strike caught the rest of the gang unawares and enabled the squad to dispatch the thugs with minimal casualties. It turned out the gang (a group of Shiva extremists) were holding several Spanish commissioners prisoner; the squad rescued the politicos and saw them safely delivered to the ruins of an old cinema house where the Global Forces had set up a temporary command post.

His bravery earned Denk a promotion and a nickname.

And ever since that day in Madrid, Surge had adopted an outlook of living to the fullest, in battle and in all walks of life—especially in bed. Not that Sergio had been a virgin before Madrid, but the day unleashed a womanizer that would screw everything in reach. Surge's conquests were legendary around the Station.

According to the latest gossip, the sly stud had bedded the Major's wife the night before they'd been sent on this rescue mission. Hibbs envied him his audacity.

"Corporal—" Dr. Holmes' voice interrupted Hibbs' reverie. "You told me the hatch was sealed."

"What?"

They'd arrived at the bottom of the stairs. And the vault-like security door stood wide open.

"That thing was locked tight when Surge and I left it," he declared.

Through the open portal lay a murky passageway with metal walls. It led to another suspiciously open hatch. From here, Hibbs couldn't tell anything about the chamber beyond that secondary hatch.

"Someone opened it," Dr. Holmes immediately assumed. "The staff must've noticed you out here, but by the time they got the doors open, you'd left."

"Why didn't they come after us?"

Dr. Holmes flapped her arms with frustration. "How should I know? The important part is this proves there was no disease outbreak. The staff want to be rescued."

If that's the case, then why do I feel like a fly entering a spider's web?

If there was any veracity to the Bombshell's hypothetical Eiger plague, it was too late to worry about containing the disease now. Whoever had opened the lab's hatch had unleashed the potential infection. Hibbs promptly commed this news to Surge and Scarpetti back on the residential level. It was only fair they understood the current risks of staying in the base.

Both of them insisted on staying. This was no surprise as far as Surge's behavior was concerned, he was more bravado than caution. While Hibbs suspected Scarpetti was just matching Surge's valor out of personal honor. He wished she'd show some common sense and get out of here. The quicker she went topside and fetched another pressure suit, the safer everybody would be. But no—the Bombshell needed to prove herself.

Hibbs decided to pull rank on Private Scarpetti. "Go topside, Private. Rendezvous with Danford and Marshall. Get one of the tractor's extra pressure suits and bring it back for Corporal Denk."

"But—" she tried to protest.

"Get going, girl. That's a direct order!"

She grumbled, but accepted his directive.

Hibbs advised Surge to make sure she went. He instructed the man to stay where he was until she returned with a suit for him.

"Are we going in now?" pouted Dr. Holmes. She was eager to locate the missing staff, but still reticent to go in alone.

"In a minute," Hibbs muttered.

He had little hope that Surge would follow the latter instruction. Surge's nature wouldn't let him sit on the sidelines when there was action in the offing. Hibbs' suspicions were valid, but Surge still had some surprises for him.

When he showed up moments later, Surge wore battle armor and a pressure suit. The impulsive hero had borrowed the Major's gear. In the sack or in the field, Surge's temerity never failed to amaze.

"I'll take point," Surge declared and did so.

Hibbs and Dr. Holmes followed him into the lab's inner depths.

10

The hatch had opened as he'd approached it. Things that might've seemed improbable to most men were easily assimilated into Moss' madness.

He was chasing Denk into the villain's underground lair where his family was held captive. Someone—a secret ally inside—had activated the surface hatch and granted him entrance. This reinforced his conviction that Denk had kidnapped his wife and children. Others saw and understood the injustices being inflicted on Harold Moss. Their sympathies were with him, they would help him catch and punish Denk for his heinous crimes.

Moss expected to meet this ally now that he was inside the lair, but all he found was an empty airlock and a tunnel that led him to a waiting elevator. He entered the car and rode it down.

The elevator door slid open and Moss gave a grunt of puzzled surprise. A cat sat there. It was jet black, small, and stared at him with flashing red eyes, a regard that sent shivers down Moss' spine. After a moment, it walked away. Pausing a few meters down the corridor, the cat turned to peer back at him. The cat was here to guide him.

Again, Moss' dementia took this strange development and plugged it right into his delusion. His secret ally couldn't afford to reveal themselves, so they'd sent him an escort. He liked cats. His wife had had a cat during their courtship, so he associated cats with her. It made perfect sense that a cat should lead him to her.

He followed his feline guide to a stairwell. The cat took him down a flight of steps to an access door he was reluctant to open lest he reveal his presence to Denk's henchmen. But the animal pawed at the door with more than a trace of impatience. Moss opened the door and the cat slipped through the portal, leaving him no choice but to accompany it.

The interior darkness seemed to be uninhabited. Glow-strips mounted along the ceiling cast feeble illumination, revealing an empty corridor lined with open doorways. When Moss ventured to examine the hallway, the cat did not come with him. The nearest door hung broken in its frame. The room appeared to be a storage area. He had no interest in whatever filled the crates kept there.

The cat had remained by the access door. Moss rejoined it—just in time to hear someone climbing the stairs beyond the closed portal.

Carefully opening the door a crack, he spied an armored figure tromp past heading topside. Obvious curves told him the person was female. He immediately presumed it was the woman who had held him captive in his tractor. His tormentor had pursued him, and now she was searching the underground lair for her escaped prisoner. He vowed that she would not recapture him. He was here to rescue his family, not join them in captivity.

Once the villainess had passed, the cat returned to the stairwell and resumed its descent. Moss dutifully followed his guide.

Two floors down, the cat stopped, and Moss knew to open that access door. Together they entered the residential quarters. The cat led him to a room where the door was locked.

"Here?" gasped Moss. "My family is locked up here?"

His guide sat on its butt and stared intently at the locked door.

"They're in there, aren't they!" he wailed inside his pressure suit. In his fervor, he'd neglected to activate an external speaker. The cat heard none of his words.

As far as Moss was concerned, though, the cat's silence was a stoic affirmation of his belief. His family was locked behind this door. He needed to open it and free them.

Giving in to a manic explosion of rage, Moss attacked the door. He kicked it and pounded it with his gloved fists. It took a long time and the task exhausted him, but after ten minutes of constant battering, the plastiform door came apart and fell open.

To his surprise and acute disappointment, the room wasn't occupied by his lost family. Instead there was a man—a man in his underwear. He knew this person—it was one of the men who had posed as soldiers back at his tractor. They had to be in league with Denk. They were Moss' enemy. He was not happy to find this wretch. The cat had promised his family was behind the locked door. The cat had lied to him.

As Moss turned to chastise the cat, the pretend-soldier assaulted him. Pudgy little Moss went down like a cardboard cutout under the soldier's fury. The man acted with a persecuted desperation, screaming something about that Denk bastard and fixing his mutinous ass. As Moss crumpled under the soldier's attack, it dawned on him that maybe this man wasn't in league with Denk. Was this Moss' secret ally? But—why was his ally attacking him? Had Moss stumbled into some rift among Denk's villainous cohorts?

He took these questions with him into the darkness that finally engulfed him.

With wicked glee, the cat watched Major Dummheit beat the crap out of Harold Moss.

11

Despite the inarguable logic of Corporal Hibbs' orders, Private Gina Scarpetti resented being stuck with gofer duty. It was demeaning and, she privately suspected, somewhat chauvinistic. Nobody ever gave Gina the chance to prove she was the equal of any macho jarhead. All they saw was her sexy bod.

That voluptuous anatomy had been Gina's bane ever since it had bloomed in her early teens. As a Chi-town gutter-brat, it had attracted unsavory interest, forcing her to learn to defend herself against adversaries twice her size. Later, during her attempt to pass among respectable society, her buxom beauty had marked Gina as an ingenue who couldn't possibly have a brain—eyecandy this hot was *never* intelligent. Suitors had treated her like a trophy. And when she'd joined the Forces, still nobody took her seriously. She was doomed to be Hotty Scarpetti.

Admittedly, there hadn't been anyone else to carry out Corporal Hibbs' orders. Denk had no protection against the raw lunar environs, and Major Dummheit couldn't be trusted to go fetch a pressure suit for him. Gina was the only one who could go. Still, it rankled her that fate had conspired to stick her with this menial duty.

To be fair, Corporal Hibbs really didn't treat her like a bimbo. He alone among the troops afforded her a modicum of respect. Most everyone else, though, only saw her tits and ass—like Denk. That boy's overactive libido was legendary among the barracks. He was, she conceded, cute and he had a decent physique. If only he would acknowledge her personality, she might try him out.

But first she had to fetch him a pressure suit. Without that, Denk wasn't going anywhere.

This entire mission had been plagued by misfortune and absurd threats. Brutish phantoms topside and a ghostly panther down in the installation. As if they hadn't been enough, the squad had to be stuck with Major Dummheit as their C.O. The Major's stubborn proclivity for ignoring the facts was just as dangerous as the things that had attacked the squad so far. So far... She shuddered, dreading whatever new madness the contaminated base had in store for them.

Gina was convinced that the Eiger staff had succumbed to an outbreak of some plague of their own design. All the evidence indicated as much. The infected personnel had quarantined themselves, then they'd tried to destroy the records of their research to prevent anyone discovering their new germ. The monster they had created had been *that* awful.

And here we come, she mulled, *a rescue party marching right into the contaminated zone.*

Now that she thought of it, she didn't think she would sleep with Denk even if he suddenly transformed into a decent person. He'd been exposed to the Eiger infection.

But then... the evidence implied they'd all been infected. Somehow the insidious germ had penetrated their pressure suits and generated perilous delusions in their minds.

Dammit, what does Denk need with a pressure suit? None of us are getting out of this alive.

She reached the surface hatch, and when she opened it, someone bullied their way in and then hurriedly resealed the portal.

"Corporal Marshall?"

The intruder grabbed Gina's shoulders and shook her with enthusiastic glee. "You saved me!"

"What's going on?" grunted Gina. "You're supposed to be guarding the prospector in his tractor."

"Things have gotten weird—ugly weird."

Tell me about it, Scarpetti sighed to herself. *You haven't seen weird until you've been chased by a panther that can leap through solid walls.*

A loud thump startled both of them.

As Gina reached to open the hatch, Marshall pushed her away from the controls. "No!"

"What's the matter?" protested Gina. "That's Danford, isn't it?"

"It... used to be Danford."

"What the hell is that supposed to mean?"

"You wouldn't believe me if I told you." The Corporal pointed to the screen mounted beside the doorway. "See for yourself."

Activating the exterior camera, Gina saw a figure standing outside the airlock. It was indeed Private Danford. And then she saw what Marshall had meant. Danford's helmet was missing. Depressurization had warped his head. There was no way he could have survived that. Yet he was still moving, angrily battering the outer hatch.

"What the—" choked Gina.

"Zombie," Marshall gasped. "It happened to Green, too. Danford went to retrieve Green's corpse and it attacked him, killed him. When Green's zombie came after me, I managed to vaporize it with a plasma blast. Then Danford's corpse came after me."

Gina looked at her with wide-eyed disbelief.

"I know how ridiculous it sounds, but that's what happened," Marshall insisted. "I can't explain it. Hell, I barely survived it."

Was the Corporal's story any less ridiculous that a ghost panther?

Before Gina could assure Marshall that she understood, the hatch next to them started to slide open. Neither of them had touched the controls. Neither had Danford's flailing corpse. The airlock was opening of its own accord.

She lunged to the controls and tried to input an override sequence, but it was too late. Half-open was enough to let Danford's zombie crawl through. It immediately lumbered toward Marshall.

The woman swung her rifle to bear and fired a short burst. The shots pulverized her attacker's head. The rest of the zombie's body remained, still staggering in her direction. Her next blast of bullets sent the headless thing reeling back through the hatch. It fell on the ground and lay there, finally dormant on the lunar dust.

"What the hell—?" growled Marshall.

"Don't look at me, I didn't open it."

"Well, close it before you let anything more in."

"But—I need to go out—to the tractor," Gina professed.

"What for?"

"Denk needs a pressure suit."

"Surge lost his pressure suit?" Marshall gasped with incredulous shock.

"No, he loaned it to Corporal Hibbs. The panther ripped Hibbs' suit."

"The panther...?"

"You've been harassed by zombies, we've been stalked by a panther that can walk through walls."

For a protracted moment the two woman stared at each other, their faces jumbled by a conglomeration of disbelief and stress.

"What the hell is with this place?" hissed Marshall.

Gina filled her in on all the weirdness the squad had encountered down in Eiger base. The burned pressure suits, the abandoned floors, how the one survivor they'd found had attacked them and then killed himself, about the ghost panther and its rampage. She told how the Major had gone loopy, deciding that everybody was in league with his imaginary terrorists, how Denk had disabled him and how Hibbs had assumed command. She explained her belief that the Eiger scientists had created a killer plague that had wiped them out. She pointed out that the entire squad was infected—apparently even Marshall, as evidenced by her zombie hallucinations.

"How could I have gotten infected before I got in here?" argued Marshall.

With a shrug, Gina professed she was a gutter-brat, not a medico. She knew how to fight and kill, not to heal or fathom the nuances of viral communicability. "I'm supposed to fetch a new suit for Denk. Hibbs' orders."

"Then lover boy's screwed," moaned Marshall, "because there aren't any extra pressure suits in the tractor."

"What?"

"There was only one suit and Moss took it. He got free and ran off. I tried to chase him, but things got really weird out there. He reached the bunker before me. He got inside." She waved a hand in an attempt to move the conversation along. "The point is—there's no extra suit for Surge."

"Dammit." Gina's shoulders slumped inside her armor. This was really bad news. With an unknown plague loose in the base, Denk was stuck in his underwear.

She tried to notify Hibbs of this development, but there was only static on her comm-line.

"There's too much solid rock blocking a transmission," Marshall informed her. "You'll have to wait and report to Hibbs face-to-face."

"Then c'mon, let's rejoin the rest of the squad."

But Marshall turned instead to the airlock's sealed outer hatch. She bent to examine the controls, then began fiddling with the mechanism.

"What're you doing?" complained Gina. "Leave that closed."

"I'm not opening it," Marshall replied curtly. "I'm not that stupid."

She drew forth a small device from a compartment in her gauntlet, too tiny for Gina to make out what it was. Moving swiftly—but carefully—Marshall attached the device to the hatch controls. Then she typed a series of command codes into her wrist pad.

"C'mon!" insisted Gina. She glanced at the gore the zombie had left splattered across the outer hatch. Although normally unbothered by carnage, this time Gina's stomach threatened to betray that warrior resolve. It had been Danford she'd just watched be blown away. She'd known Emil, had even bedded him a few times back in the 51 barracks; not that those couplings had established any emotional bond between them. But still… he'd been a fellow Marine. Seeing him die so violently had been disturbing. According to Marshall, he'd already been dead—but he'd still been moving. Recalling the state of his head before the Corporal had shot it to pieces, Gina prayed he'd been dead.

"Unbunch your panties, girl." She stepped back from the hatch. "I'm done."

"Then let's stop wasting time and go."

"I never waste my time," Marshall told her. "I have initiative."

By this point, all Gina wanted to do was escape from the bloodstained airlock. She hurried off down the access tunnel. Marshall followed her.

12

"Get going, girl," rang Hibbs' voice on the squad's comm-line. "That's a direct order!"

The Bombshell grumbled, but she accepted his directive.

Throwing Sergio a scowl of resentful resignation, Scarpetti departed the residential ward.

"Make sure she goes," Hibbs advised Sergio.

"She's already gone," he told him.

"Good. It's too dangerous down here for you as long as you're unprotected, Surge. You stay where you are until she returns with a suit for you."

Sergio fumed. There was danger afoot—and he was stranded up here, unable to help. A wave of uselessness swept over him. This wasn't the way things were supposed to be. Surge Denk belonged on the front lines.

The only thing keeping him from there was the lack of a pressure suit.

He eyed Major Dummheit's immobilized form. *That's a perfectly good pressure suit you got there, Major... and as long as you're out of play, you certainly have no need for it.*

A self-serving smirk traveled across Sergio's face.

There was no easy way to do this. Right now the suit's jammed servos were holding the Major motionless. Removing that suit would grant him freedom to move—to struggle and fight. Sergio could see the rancor in the Major's eyes, the man was furious about the mutiny that had deposed him as the squad's C.O. Sergio had been the one who'd struck him down, so the Major hated him most of all. A scuffle was bound to ensue as long as the Major was conscious.

As soon as Sergio twisted off the man's helmet, the Major began bellowing ugly threats.

"You're way too tense," Sergio advised him. "I think you need a sedative to calm you down." He drew a hypo from the med kit on the belt of the Major's suit and gave the man a shot right in the neck. Within seconds the Major's tirade sputtered off and he slumped unconscious.

Sergio swiftly divested the Major of his armor and suit, donning them himself. He reactivated the suit's comm unit and phased it to work with his earbud.

What to do with you…? He regarded the Major's inert body. The sedative should keep him out for a while, but sooner or later he would wake. Once roused, the Major's rage would climax. Sergio had no desire to have the man, semi-naked or not, running around with a grudge against him and the rest of the squad. Major Dummy needed to be locked up.

It was a simple matter to close the apartment's door and secure the lock from outside. *That'll hold the asshole.*

And off Sergio scampered to join his comrades as they searched the base's labs.

Sergio wasn't about to let his comrades face danger without him at their side.

Ever since that day in Madrid, audacity had become Sergio Denk's outlook. He was always on the lookout for crises, for adventure, for tail.

Everybody thought he was a thrill junkie, but the truth was more pathetic. He didn't think he deserved his nickname. The battle charge that had earned him notoriety had been accidental. Sheer clumsiness had been mistaken as valor. In the aftermath, Sergio had been reluctant to confess this to anyone. He'd accepted his nickname and his reputation without protest. But personally he couldn't abide that his heroic status was based on a lie. Ever since, he'd sought to achieve a moment of true courage that would justify his reputation. His recklessness soon affected his libido, magnifying his sexual appetite to flagrant proportions. Each new conquest got him closer to matching the prestige of his reputation.

This current mission was certainly affording Surge with ample opportunities to prove his prowess.

Hibbs voiced no surprise that Sergio had ignored his orders, or more precisely that he'd found a way around them. By stealing the Major's suit, Sergio was no longer at risk of any contamination. He could join

Hibbs and Doc Holmes as they searched for Eiger survivors.

He took point, leading them into the lab's depths.

In contrast to the radial layouts of the higher levels, the individual laboratories were all arranged along a single corridor. Although each lab was sealed, the Doc had codes to unlock the doors.

The first lab was empty. Jars of chemicals sat neatly on shelves. Pieces of disassembled hardware littered worktables. They found no one hiding under the tables or in the utility closet.

The next chamber was a conference room. A single occupant slumped at the head of the long faux mahogany table. The man's gaping neck wound went with the blade he clutched in his dead hand. Another suicide. A large pool of dried blood stained the table around him.

"Professor Harris," breathed Dr. Holmes.

"A lot of unstable people among the staff, huh?" Hibbs muttered.

"No," she weakly protested. "These people were scientists, learned professionals… none of them would kill themselves…"

"Hate to contradict you, but…" Hibbs gestured at the Professor's cold corpse. "This is the second of your learned professionals who've taken their own lives."

"It makes no sense," she fretted.

Sergio laughed. "None of this makes sense, Doc."

"Of course it does," she spat back. "There's a rational explanation for all of this. We simply haven't figured it out yet."

"Scarpetti's plague outbreak theory is sounding better and better," grumbled Hibbs. "These scientists couldn't face what they'd done, so they committed suicide."

"I told you, there's no plague."

"Let's keep moving," Hibbs urged. "If there are survivors, they better be able to explain what happened."

The next lab offered quite the opposite of survivors. Its perimeter was crowded by medical apparatus—a centrifuge, a spectrograph, a spectrophotometer, an electron microscope, an obviously sophisticated computer array to process data—all of which were battered and broken by savage assaults with a fire ax that lay nearby. The floor beneath this smashed equipment was littered with charred mounds that had once been data chips mixed with shards of what looked to be specimen slides and plastic sheets of the type spat out by the assorted machinery, all fused together in molten globules. At the center of the room stood a row of shiny-topped tables with raised lips. The endmost tables were occupied… by the dissembled remains of a woman. The condition of the body made her age and ethnicity impossible to gauge. Her skin was a landscape of intricate lacerations. Her torso lay on one chromium slab, opened down the front by a clean slice. Her ribcage had been split, the individual ribs pried back until they reared from the gaping wound like the grisly wreckage of a pair of opposing picket fences. Her limbs had been detached, then placed on flanking autopsy tables. Her head had been separated from her shoulders and then cut into lateral halves which had been positioned nose-to-nose, flat ends down, at the head of the table. An effort had been made to drag her internal organs out and hang them from hooks that depended from the ceiling. The result looked like a meatmarket parody of holiday garlands. Considering the extent of the mutilation there was a remarkable scarcity of blood splattered around the cadaver.

Sergio lurched back in horrified disgust.

Doc Holmes spun on her heel and vomited inside her helmet.

Hibbs went closer to investigate.

"The heart's missing," he reported. "So are her privates."

"You're kidding," gasped Sergio.

"Fraid not." Hibbs made a circuit of the med lab, examining the un-bloodied regions. "I don't see the tools that did this. The killer must've taken them with him."

"What about the knife Harris had?"

Hibbs bent down to poke at the woman's bisected head. "You'd need a bigger blade to cut a person's head this cleanly." He stood erect and frowned down at the body. "It's hard to tell for sure, but these cuts look pretty shallow. I doubt they were administered to inflict pain. These carvings are… almost artistic."

Horrification numbed Sergio. He was a combat-seasoned warrior, had witnessed awful atrocities on the European battlefield—but this—*this* was different. No random explosion had torn apart this woman—this dissection had been accomplished with meticulous and deviant skill. This atrocity had been willfully created. The depravity of it all sickened Sergio. The anatomical vandalism was extreme enough, but Hibbs' clinical evaluation was dehumanizing. Lest his disgust raise his own gorge, Sergio fled the desecrated site.

He joined Dr. Holmes out in the corridor.

"You okay?"

"I threw up… in my suit…" she moaned.

Sergio showed her the switch that activated the suit's internal clean sweep. A mild suction collected her spew and ejected it from a nozzle on her suit's collar. Unscrewing her helmet and wiping its inside clean was advisable, but he guessed that the foul-smelling air permeating the research level might cause her further distress, physical and mental. She would just have to endure whatever residue still clung to the inner surface of her headgear.

Meanwhile Hibbs had forged ahead to peek into several more of the laboratories. He returned now, grim-faced and edgy.

"Found a few more vivisections."

Sergio shuddered. He wasn't sure he wanted the details.

"I think you need to see some of them." Hibbs led him to the lab at the end of the hall.

It was another med lab, only here the dissection was more traditional… in so far as an alien dissection could be considered normal. Although it fundamentally possessed a humanoid form, the body on the slab had never been human. That anatomy had been cut apart and neatly folded back to reveal unnaturally configured and wildly hued internal organs. One forearm's muscles and tendons had been peeled away to reveal a single supporting bone.

"Recognize it?"

Sergio had to nod, for he did. Before him lay the thin-limbed gray alien of ancient lore, complete with its big oval head and oversized lidless eyes. All the old UFO stories cast these fellows as space travelers who'd visited Earth to examine human beings back in the 20th Century. Sergio had never put much credence in the old tales, dismissing them as the spawn of somebody's overactive imagination. But here he was, staring down at an actual Gray, or at least the corpse of one. As an additional edge of weirdness, he couldn't shake the feeling that he'd seen this alien corpse before.

It looked old… not wrinkled old but desiccated old.

"So… they're real," he mumbled.

"There's more." Hibbs took him next door, where another Gray lay in mid-dissection. He quickly moved him along to a third lab to show him another alien. This one was wholly unhumanoid. Measuring three meters from end to end, its body seemed to be a shelled slab from which a host of boneless tentacles draped like meaty fringe. The creature didn't seem to have any head or detectable eyes. The torso had been laterally cut open, the crusty shell peeled back to reveal a network of utterly strange organs. Even their pink and purple colors were foreign.

"What the hell…"

"Yeah," snorted Hibbs. "Aliens on the Moon."

"What've you found?" Having recuperated, Dr. Holmes wandered into the room. Glimpsing the bizarre cadaver, she halted with a gasped, "It's true—"

"This is the big secret, isn't it?" Hibbs tossed at her. "This is what Eiger base was doing. Not cooking up killer plagues—but studying aliens."

Dr. Holmes remained silent.

"Yeah, not much point in wasting breath on denials at this stage."

Sergio was still coping with the acceptance of intelligent alien life— more than one species, from the looks of it. He hadn't yet grasped what Hibbs had deduced.

"I didn't know for sure," she offered an excuse. "Nobody did. A few days ago the Eiger staff reported finding evidence of extraterrestrial life— and then the facility went dark. So I convinced Global to send me to find out what happened."

"And we got assigned to be the canaries," Hibbs remarked.

"I guess you could call it that…"

"I don't understand—" Sergio had to complain. "What do canaries have to do with aliens?"

"It's an old mining term," Hibbs told him. "They used to send canaries in cages down into the shafts to see if the air was breathable."

"To know if it was safe…" mumbled Sergio.

"Global wants these aliens, but first they want to make sure there's no threat… like a plague."

"How many times do I have to tell you, Hibbs? The Eiger staff was *not* conducting germ research. They did *not* engineer any killer plague."

"What if the plague came from *him*?" Hibbs gestured to the dissected shell creature. "Or maybe one of the Grays."

"There are Grays?" she gasped.

"In other labs, yeah. A whole smorgasbord of extraterrestrial dead meat potentially teaming with alien microorganisms. Any one of which could've wiped out the staff here… or driven them to suicidal insanity."

A glimmer of realization dragged Dr. Holmes' face into a mask of dread. "An extraterrestrial contagion…"

"Ultimately much nastier than man-made plagues."

"We're infected, aren't we?" blurted Sergio. "That's what's causing all our delusions."

"No, wait—" Dr. Holmes interrupted. "Look at the condition of that body. It's old—ancient—mummified. No microorganism could have survived in it."

"Are you an authority on alien biology?" grunted Hibbs. "Don't think so."

"You and I—we've been exposed to the alien germ." Sergio shook Hibbs' arm. "We could already be contaminated!"

Hibbs gave him a withering scowl. "Rather not be reminded of that, okay?"

But— Sergio panicked. *This means we're gonna go crazy and kill ourselves.*

"We need to search the rest of the labs," insisted Dr. Holmes. "There has to be somebody left alive… somebody who can explain what happened…"

"How can you be so callous about this?" Sergio shouted at her. "You were exposed too when the Major made you take off your pressure suit. All three of us could've picked up this alien virus."

She turned a stoneface on him. "I'm not freaking out because I do not believe any alien virus exists."

"But—the other scientists—something drove them crazy…"

"Chill out, Surge," Hibbs advised him in a calm voice. "If we're infected, that's that. Searching the rest of the facility could unearth something we could use to cure ourselves."

That was a stretch, but Sergio needed something to hold on to, something to restore sanity to this day of weirdness. Any chance, no matter how slim or spurious, was worth consideration.

But he had little faith in finding anything that could help them. If the Eiger scientists had found a cure, they would've used it to save themselves.

At the far end of the corridor a shaft led to deeper realms, regions not contained on the schematics they'd been given with their briefing. The three of them easily fit on the open lift that carried them down the oblique tunnel.

This passage delivered them to an elevated catwalk. A vast cavern spread beneath them. A large shape protruded from the floor of the cave. The exposed portions looked remarkably like a flying saucer. Once more, Sergio had the uncomfortable feeling that he'd seen this all before.

"Now, *this* makes sense," declared Hibbs.

"How so?" Sergio grunted.

"Something had to have brought those aliens here."

Sergio nodded. Yes, that part did make sense. After several decades of exploration, mankind would've found some evidence of these aliens if they were native to the Moon. The discovery of an alien spacecraft was no more fantastic than finding the alien bodies. One came in conjunction with the other. Even so—it was an incredible discovery! Incontrovertible proof of intelligent extraterrestrial life!

"Look at that thing," Dr. Holmes whispered with a touch of reverence. "It's still shiny. At this depth, buried so far beneath the lunar surface, it must have crashed long ago. It's been here for centuries. And after all that time it's still shiny. This relic could unlock quantum mysteries for mankind. It could give the human race the capability to expand into interstellar regions."

"Or it could be the cause of the madness going on here," proclaimed Hibbs. "Anybody foolish enough to want to go down there and check it out up close?"

"I'll go," Sergio attested.

"Jeez, Surge… this is stupid even by your reckless standards," Hibbs sighed with evident exasperation. He turned to accost Doc Holmes, "And I suppose you're itching to go along with him."

"Of course," she insisted.

"Knock yourselves out." Hibbs stepped back and looked back up the shaft. "I'm heading back to the labs. Maybe I can find some log that'll explain all of this."

"Watch out for that panther," Sergio called out to him, only half in joking.

"What panther?" asked Dr. Holmes.

As they descended the ladder to the floor of the cavern, Sergio told the woman about the phantom panther that had attacked the squad back in the cafeteria. She hadn't seen the thing, and it took a bit of earnest avowal to get her to believe that such a creature existed, much less prowled the secret research facility.

"There's no wildlife on the Moon—and I cannot envision the Eiger staff bringing a jungle cat here to the base," she assured him. "What you saw had to be a hallucination."

He chuckled without humor. "Hibbs, Scarpetti, and I all shared the same hallucination—*right*. Did I mention the cat tore up Hibbs' suit? The thing was awfully feisty for a damned hallucination, Doc. This place is haunted."

"By dead aliens?" It was her turn to laugh. "Why would extraterrestrial beings choose to posthumously manifest as a terrestrial beast? That makes no sense at all, Corporal Denk."

"Not much has today," he grumbled.

Once they were down on the cavern floor, it became apparent how incredibly large the saucer was. Calculating its size from the exposed portion of the discus, the ship had to be over a hundred meters in diameter. The shiny wedge filled the cavern.

The top—at least he presumed it was the saucer's upper face—was tapered at a smooth angle that swept to a rounded apex that was still embedded in rock. The underside was flatter, and appeared to feature a series of domed extrusions. The Eiger staff had ceased their excavation once they'd uncovered the ship's hatch. A scaffolding had been erected so the doorway could be easily reached. That portal stood open.

"Are you really going in there?" she softly inquired.

"Sure," was Sergio's spry response. "I thought you were gung ho to examine the thing."

"I was… but up this close… it's intimidating." Dr. Holmes fidgeted. She regarded the huge ship, her head thrown back as far as her fishbowl helmet would allow. "This thing is an actual interstellar spacecraft. Its inhabitants, its technology—the very materials of its construction—everything about this thing came from an alien world."

"I would think such a thing would thrill your intellectual curiosity."

"It scares me too…"

He laughed. "Considering our present situation, Doc, a little bit of fright is a healthy thing."

But before they could advance any closer to the interred saucer, a ruckus came over the comm-line. Their earbuds buzzed with a string of angry profanities.

Sergio leaped to scale the wire-frame ladder.

Floundering in his wake, Dr. Holmes fretted aloud, "What's going on?"

"Hibbs is in trouble," he advised her. "Stay down here."

He reached the catwalk and ran its length to find the lift not there. Hibbs had ridden it to the top of the shaft. Without hesitation, Sergio scrabbled up the tunnel's incline.

The going was easier than he would've expected. Whatever method had been utilized to bore this shaft had been crude, leaving the walls ragged with a plethora of wedges he could use as foot- and handholds. The low gravity helped increase his climb, too.

"Hibbs!" he commed ahead. "I'm on my way—report your status—"

But Hibbs was too engrossed in whatever was going on to switch from obscenities to explanations. The Corporal's cursing actually grew more vehement as Sergio scaled the shaft. It sounded as if something was attacking him. Could the panther have returned to finish him off? Whatever was happening, it sounded as if battle-savvy Hibbs was having a hard time coping with it.

A ridiculous scenario ran through Sergio's bewildered mind. In it, the dead aliens' ghosts haunted the base. They wanted vengeance for the desecration of their corpses. First they had punished the Eiger staff, but now the angry aliens were going after everyone they encountered. *They're using weird alien mind warp weapons against us... making us experience physical hallucinations... like the panther.*

How do we fight alien ghosts?

But the threat facing Hibbs wasn't supernatural in the least. When Sergio finally clambered from the mouth of the shaft, he discovered the Corporal had been forced into a corner by a crowd of naked people. As he got closer, Sergio realized the mob wasn't attacking Hibbs—they were trying to seduce him. Men and women alike were rubbing themselves in provocative ways and pressing their bodies against Hibbs' body armor. One elderly man was pressing his lips against the outer surface of the Corporal's helmet, trying to kiss him through the crystal bubble. Hibbs was cursing with disgust, not terror.

For a moment Sergio almost laughed. The situation had its amusing perspective: this group of Eiger scientists were way too overjoyed that someone had come to rescue them.

Close enough now to clearly see the figures engaged in seducing Hibbs, Sergio gasped. Horror erupted in his chest like a frigid volcano.

Hibbs' suitors were more than unclothed—they were unskinned. Every square inch of flesh had been removed from these people. Their blood-soaked sinews flexed and caressed and glistened. This wasn't a welcoming committee—more like a lynch mob. Another deviant hallucination to confound the soldiers.

He waded in, yanking assailants from the crowd and flinging them down the lab level's corridor. Their slippery bodies were difficult to grab. Hibbs fought his way free of the group. Both Corporals stepped back into defensive positions.

"What the hell—" gasped Hibbs.

"Why didn't you just fight back?"

"They were normal people at first, Surge. They came from a lab I hadn't examined yet. They were clothed and acting rational and everything—I swear—and then suddenly they started throwing equipment around and mutilating themselves. By the time they swarmed on me, they'd ripped off their own skin." He swiped at the crimson stains smeared across his armor.

"Another hallucination…"

"Funny how the phantoms in this place bleed," grumbled Hibbs. "Oh yeah—and they try to kill people."

Having reorganized, the skinless ones were trying to surround the two soldiers, to pin them against the wall. They snarled and spat with hateful rage, but their movements were jerky, clumsy. They comported themselves as if each step was an agonizing exertion, and considering their flayed condition maybe it was. Hibbs struck two of them down with vicious backswings of his gauntlets. Ramming the butt of his rifle into the face of another one, Sergio sent the hissing wretch stumbling back into his raw accomplices.

"If these bastards weren't the people we came to rescue, we could waste them easy," Hibbs sighed as he kicked one in the stomach.

Sergio swung his weapon, warding back a fresh wave of skinless foes. "It's a quandary, yeah."

"The Doc'll raise a stink if we kill them."

"Probably," Sergio grunted.

"So what do we do?"

"Try a concussion grenade."

"You got one?"

"I did—but you're wearing my suit, so you got it." As he'd learned earlier when transferring himself into the Major's suit, Dummheit carried no weapons or explosives, hardly any tools at all. If danger threatened Major Dummy, obviously he expected his troops to protect him.

"Lemme check." Hibbs stepped behind Sergio and rooted through the armament cache mounted at his waist.

Sergio continued swinging his rifle like a truncheon. So far this had succeeded in holding the skinless ones at bay. They flinched away from the weapon's metal stock as if it radiated scalding heat.

"Found it," chimed Hibbs.

"Okay, hold on, gimme a minute… I'm gonna try to herd them back into that lab." He pointed the rifle at the open door at the rear of the crowd.

Together, wielding their rifles as bludgeons, the soldiers intimidated the skinless mob back into the open lab. The room housed one of the semi-dissected Grays. Once the Marines had gotten them all inside, Hibbs activated the grenade and tossed it in after them. Sergio slammed the lab's door.

The lab was hermetically sealed. Barely a muffled hint of the concussive detonation leaked through its walls. The soldiers relied on sensors loaded in their hardware to verify the blast.

After a moment, they took a peek. Every member of the skinless mob lay inert on the floor. All out cold. The worst they would suffer might be headaches... although after the mutilation to which they'd subjected themselves, headaches would be trivial discomfort.

They grimaced to see that the blast had not been as kind to the alien cadaver. The concussion wave had thrown it from its table, and the brittle corpse had come apart.

"Uh oh," grunted Sergio.

"Don't sweat it," Hibbs remarked. "There's another Gray—and that headless turtle thing. They'll keep the scientists happy enough."

Sergio was more concerned how the alien ghosts would react to this. They'd slaughtered the Eiger staff for digging them up and dissecting them. What would they do to anyone who inflicted additional desecration?

To squelch his fearful worries, he took refuge in black humor: "So happy they're liable to rip off their skin, huh?"

"We're all contaminated."

"You still think it's a disease?" He was leery to mention his suspicion about alien ghosts haunting the installation. Modern man was supposed to be logical, not superstitious. Centuries of science and technology had weaned mankind away from mysticism. Believing in ghosts was ludicrous, even more so for a battle-trained Marine.

"The Bombshell's theory fits the facts, Surge—well, most of them. I suspect what we're dealing with here isn't an outbreak of a designer man-made virus. We're dealing with an ancient alien germ."

"The part I can't swallow is the hallucinations having physicality. If an infection is making us see and do weird things, how come our fever-induced delusions are solid? They rip things up, they bleed, they kill— they tore Corporal Green to pieces topside. How can mirages leave behind visible evidence?"

Hibbs shrugged. "It's an alien disease."

"That's an answer that doesn't tell us anything."

Hibbs grinned. "Hey, I'm a jarhead, not an egghead. Hell, I'm in a borrowed suit because an imaginary panther ripped up my own gear. I'm in no position to be an objective judge of anything."

And I can't shake the feeling that I've seen all this before, mused Sergio. Not that he was about to share this opinion with his comrade. It sounded crazy—almost as crazy as the shit they were facing.

They each had their own conjectures to confound them. Hibbs probably felt more comfortable with his presumptions, just as Sergio was prone to favor his own theories. For all either of them knew they were both wrong. At least they'd both moved past the Major's stupid assertion that terrorists were behind everything.

He wondered what Dr. Holmes thought. In many ways the woman was better prepared to develop hypotheses concerning their quandary. Her knowledge about the Eiger base and the research it'd been conducting still surpassed anything the soldiers had accidentally uncovered. They needed a chance to sit her down and get her to talk. So far, each time Sergio had tried to do so, circumstances had interfered.

Like now.

Standing in the empty corridor, the two soldiers were momentarily lost in their own thoughts. Hibbs was checking to make sure the lab was locked down securely; the last thing they needed was the skinless mob rousing and getting underfoot again. Sergio was trying to raise Dr. Holmes.

"Doc?" he commed to her. "This is Denk. You there?"

Before an answer could come, something struck Sergio across the back of his legs. The impact buckled his knees and sent him tumbling on his butt. As he toppled, Sergio saw the Hibbs had suffered a similar assault.

Dammit—we got too wrapped up in our thoughts—and somebody sneaked up and ambushed us—

Instinct made both of them roll as they hit the deck. The next strike missed them, crashing into the cement floor and peppering the air with concrete chips. Before their attacker could initiate another clout, Sergio and Hibbs had regained their feet and swung their weapons to bear on their assailant.

Major Dummheit!

Dressed in his sweaty underwear, the Major clutched a metal bar (something he'd probably picked up in one of the other labs). His eyes bulged with mania and he shouted at them, "You mutinous turds! Think you can fool me? The terrorists have bought your loyalty, haven't they? You traitorous scumbags!"

How the hell did the asshole get loose? Sergio was certain he had secured the apartment door; he'd even tried to jam the controls that locked down the room. Major Dummy couldn't have escaped on his own. So, who—or what—had come to his assistance?

There was the culprit: crouching just down the corridor. The ghost panther blinked drowsily as it watched the soldiers struggle with their furious ex-Commanding Officer.

"Down the hall," Sergio hissed to Hibbs.

"I see it," Hibbs replied. "The sneaky beast."

Hoisting his bludgeon high over his head, the Major bellowed more invectives and came at his adversaries. As he rushed them, his spectral sponsor released a guttural snarl from down the hallway. Fearing that this growl signaled a dual assault, Sergio and Hibbs fixed a wary eye on the panther, but it remained in the background, smoldering with feline rancor. This momentary distraction allowed the Major to get close and strike with his makeshift bludgeon. He battered away like a maniac, seemingly unmindful that their armor protected Sergio and Hibbs from the brunt of his blows. His frenzied momentum carried the Major into and over the soldiers. He moved without concern for his own safety.

Both soldiers were reticent to fight back with any degree of force, afraid that their armored blows might hurt the man. For all his craziness, he was after all their assigned Commanding Officer. It would be better all around if they managed to subdue him without breaking any of his bones. Consequently they pulled their punches, which only allowed Major Dummheit to maintain his brazen advantage.

He capered about them, hammering their shoulders with his metal bat. He yelled obscenities and spat on them. He stomped his bare feet with barbaric emphasis. He exhibited the agility of a rabid monkey.

"This is ridiculous," Hibbs complained.

"Maybe he'll wear himself out," mused Sergio.

Hibbs narrowly dodged getting batted in the helmet. "Wo!" he grunted. "More likely he's going to land a lucky shot and crack our helmets."

"So—what do you suggest we do?" Sergio stepped out of the way of a backhanded swing.

"Hit the bastard—knock him out." Hibbs shoved the Major away from him.

"You do it. I hit him last time." Sergio pushed him back.

"Don't be childish—"

For a moment they played pingpong with the Major, propelling him back and forth between them. While they were careful to guard their helmets, the soldiers allowed their opponent to whack away at their armor.

"Hey, it's your turn, Hibbs."

Outraged by their snide attitude, the Major attacked with renewed verve. Concentrating on Sergio, he battered the man with repeated blows. "You stole my suit! You left me to die! I always knew you were scum, Denk, worthless scum masquerading as a Marine! And in the end I was right! You're nothing but a cowardly toady for terrorists!"

His armored gauntlets spared Sergio any serious injury, but one of the blows succeeded in dislodging his rifle from his grip.

Sergio lunged to reclaim his gun, but just as his gloved fingers were about to close on the barrel, the rifle was snatched away. *Oh shit—*

Wrapping his hand around the plasma rifle's handle, the Major raised the weapon to point at Sergio's face and tightened his finger on the trigger. There was no time to duck aside. Sergio actually saw the energy blast spark deep within the barrel.

The rifle's death-spewing nozzle veered off at the last instant. The plasma blast barely missed Sergio, roaring right past his head and scorching the outside of his helmet. The shot blinded him. He fell back, suddenly weighed down by an avalanche of relief.

Through the whiteout veil, he heard Hibbs and the Major exchange curses and blows. The Corporal must've jumped the asshole just as he'd fired the weapon. Hibbs had saved his life.

His vision cleared just in time to witness the Major score a lucky blow against his opponent.

The pair were locked in combat. The Major held onto his stolen rifle, but he'd lost the metal bar. For an instant it looked as Hibbs had the advantage, catching the remarkably spry Major in a bear-hug. Pressed chest to chest, the Major squirmed and flailed, but the Corporal's grip held firm. The Major's stolen rifle dangled uselessly at his side. They were too close for him to shoot Hibbs. Swinging the weapon in among their struggling legs, the bastard managed to wedge it in-between Hibbs' thighs and a savage twist destroyed the Corporal's precarious balance.

Hibbs went down on his side, pinning his own weapon beneath him.

Meanwhile the Major made a tactical retreat. Carrying off Sergio's plasma rifle, Major Dummheit took refuge in one of the labs.

Pausing to grin at them, the panther followed the Major. But where the man had used the doorway, sealing it after him, the cat simply strolled through the wall and vanished.

"You let him take your gun?" Hibbs yelled.

Sergio flinched. "Right—I gave him my gun on purpose—to make it more interesting."

"Jeez, I wouldn't put it past you, you adrenaline junkie." Hibbs rushed the Major's sanctuary, but couldn't get the door open.

"What's that supposed to mean?" Sergio snarled back.

"You know damned well what it means, Surge. Now isn't the time to discuss your reckless thirst for danger, okay?" Hibbs edged away from the door. "Major Dummy's got a plasma rifle and we need to get the damned thing away from him."

"Not my fault," muttered Sergio. "Asshole knocked it out of my hand."

"Spare me, butterfingers." Hibbs waved dismissively at him. "Which lab is this? The ones with the aliens are down the end of the hall."

"You checked out more of them than I did…"

"There were a few more vivisections… one with the undissected body of a woman… the conference room where Professor Harris killed himself…"

"This is the conference room."

"You sure?"

Sergio nodded. "Absolutely. It was the second room we investigated." He pointed to the archway that led to the access hatch. "See? Second one in."

"Okay…" Hibbs took up a position next to the door and hefted his own plasma rifle. "I'm gonna give the lock a short burst, just enough to melt it. Then I'm going to burn a hole here beside the doorway. I hope I have enough charge left for this. I expended a lot of shots holding the panther at bay earlier."

"As soon as you burn the hole, I go through the door and rush him."

Hibbs nodded. "I thought you'd like that."

"Keep an eye peeled for that panther."

"Trust me, the instant I spot the cat, it gets fried."

With a nod, Hibbs executed a silent countdown with his fingers. Even though their adversary wore no comm equipment, the Corporal was unwilling to risk any transmissions or verbal utterances that might betray the start of their assault on the lab.

With the lifting of the third finger, Hibbs gave the door lock a fractional plasma burst. He waited two beats, then unleashed a concentrated shot of energy on the wall beside the door. The latter blast vaporized a hole through the plastiform wall. Hibbs kept firing to maximize the distraction inflicted on the lab's surly inhabitant.

Moving with expert finesse, Sergio shouldered the door open and tumbled inside. He rolled to the side away from the enduring plasma blast and deftly regained his feet. He gun, a projectile weapon, swung up as Sergio searched for his target.

The blast had caught the conference table and toppled it. Professor Harris' body had fallen in the process and presumably lay on the floor, blocked from Sergio's view by the slagged table. Figuring the Major had ducked down behind the debris, the soldier quickly crossed the room to bring his gun to bear on the hidden area. The Professor's dead body was crumpled on the floor, his dead gaze pointed at the ceiling, exposing his gruesome neck wound. There was no sign of the panther. Nor was Major Dummheit anywhere to be seen.

"He's gone," Sergio commed Hibbs.

"What?" came the incredulous response. The plasma blast, already sputtering as its battery ran low, abated, and a second later Hibbs entered the lab, boldly stepping through the hole he'd made in the wall.

Once the glare of the incandescent energy beam dissipated, Sergio saw that another hole had been blasted in the far wall. Instantly he guessed what had happened: the Major had used his stolen weapon to burn himself an exit. Dummheit might've been crazy, but that madness hadn't muddled the bastard's cunning. While the Corporals had concocted a plan to catch him, the Major had acted and escaped to the laboratory next door.

Seeing the side hole, Hibbs cursed. He waved at Sergio to go after the Major, then dove back into the corridor to cover that flank.

Initially Sergio wasn't all that keen about this new plan. Armed with a gun that only fired bullets, he didn't like the prospect of trying to surprise a crazyman slinging a plasma rifle.

The neighboring lab was dark, Sergio could detect nobody moving about it the gloom. If he remembered correctly, the Eiger staff had used the room for storage of chemicals and extra machinery. Was the Major sharp enough to cook up a bomb in so short a time? Doubtful; he wasn't that adept with such things, nor smart enough to think of doing so. There was little chance of the Major braining Sergio with any of the equipment. Without battle armor augmenting his strength, there was no way Dummheit could lift any of the machinery.

The best way was to just do it—go through and face whatever consequences awaited him.

Moving cautiously, Sergio stepped through the hole. At once he saw Dummheit. The Major had opened the room's door and was firing at someone out in the hall. His target had to have been Hibbs.

With the Major distracted, Sergio crept up behind him. His first instinct was to jam the nozzle of his gun into the man's back and order him to drop the rifle. But he could not trust Major Dummy to react accordingly. The asshole might take a bullet and jerk around and blast Sergio to atoms as he fell. The most effective way to handle this situation was to brain the idiot without warning. He raised his handgun, positioning its handle to bring it down on the fool's unprotected head.

At the last instant, the Major shifted in the doorway, seeking a better shot at Hibbs outside. Sergio's weapon came down and smacked the Major between the shoulders instead of hitting him atop his blonde mane. The errant impact sent Dummheit staggering out into the corridor.

Sergio rushed after him, eager to deliver another blow that might take him down. His haste worked to his disadvantage. He swung and missed as his target danced about in distress. As Sergio struggled to regain his balance, the Major hoisted the plasma rifle high, clearly intending to use it to bludgeon his attacker.

Gunshots rang out in the corridor.

Major Dummheit recoiled. For a precarious moment he stood there with his arms in the air, his features twisted with embittered bewilderment, then the stolen rifle fell from his hands and hit him squarely on the head. This blow drove the man chin-first to the concrete floor… where he remained, unmoving and finally quiet.

"Damn," came Hibbs' relieved gasp. "The bastard never fought that hard against any enemy that deserved it."

"Did you shoot him?"

"With this?" Hibbs held up his own plasma rifle. "There'd be nothing left of him if I had."

"Then who shot him?"

"That'd be me," came a new voice on the comm-line.

At the end of the corridor, Private Scarpetti stepped from the shadows of the access passageway. A smoking handgun dangled in her grasp. A moment later Corporal Marshall appeared behind her.

"So…" remarked the Bombshell, "Major Dummheit got infected and went crazy."

"We were trying to avoid *killing* the asswipe," Hibbs replied.

"I didn't kill him," she asserted.

"But—" grunted Sergio.

"Tranquilizer pellets." The Bombshell lifted her handgun and waggled it in the air. "Although he really didn't deserve the consideration."

Sergio and Hibbs responded with weak chuckles.

"What the hell is going on down here?" exclaimed Corporal Marshall. "Scarpetti mentioned you guys were having trouble with Major Dummy, but *this* is pretty extreme, don't you think?"

If you think this *is extreme, Marsh, check out the…* But a quick survey told Sergio that the panther was gone. He hadn't seen the beast in either of the rooms in which the Major had sought refuge. The creature had helped him escape, had led him here, but when the Major's assault had failed, the panther had abandoned him.

Capsulizing developments, Hibbs told the two women what he and Surge had found and how the Major had attacked them.

"An alien spacecraft?" gasped the Bombshell.

"What happened to the extra suit you were going to bring back?" asked Sergio.

Marshall explained that there was no extra pressure suit aboard the prospector's tractor. "Moss escaped and took it with him."

"Great," Sergio expelled an unhappy sigh. "So not only am I stuck in the Major's stinky suit, now we have Moss to worry about…"

"If Moss got into the base, did you see him on your way down here?" inquired Hibbs.

The women assured him they hadn't seen Moss or anyone. They'd come directly down. Scarpetti had been eager to see if the Egghead had gotten the research level's entry hatch open.

"Shit—" blurted Sergio. He switched to an open comm-line and called out, "Dr. Holmes—are you there?" With all the fuss of coping with Hibbs' skinless assailants and then the Major's appearance and attack, Sergio had completely forgotten about Doc Holmes.

But she wasn't answering.

"I want to see this spacecraft," Corporal Marshall was insisting.

"Me too," piped the Bombshell.

"Business first, Scarpetti," announced Hibbs. "Help me find a secure place to lock up the Major."

"He's out cold," she complained. "He won't be making trouble for hours."

"We can't trust anything down here," Hibbs asserted.

Sergio muttered, "I locked him in a room up on the residential level, but he managed to get out."

"Give me a hand, Scarpetti."

"Why me?"

"You shot him."

"But I want to see the spaceship."

"It's not going anywhere," he hissed. "C'mon, grab his legs."

While the two hauled the sedated Major out of the hallway, Marshall commed Sergio, "You okay, Surge?"

"I've had better days," he confessed. "But so far I'm still kicking."

"And you're going down in the history books for discovering an alien spacecraft."

Sergio gave a dismissive snort. "We only found what the Eiger staff discovered. They're the ones who dug it up."

"Gina told me most of them are dead. Or did you find any of them alive?"

He cast a nervous glance at the lab where he and Hibbs had confined and subdued the mob of scientists who had divested themselves of their skin.

"So—show me your big discovery."

"Yeah, okay…" He was itchy to return to the excavation cavern and learn why Doc Holmes hadn't answered his call.

But nobody was going below.

The panther was back. Or maybe it had just relocated itself. Now the beast sat on the lift that waited at the mouth of the shaft to the cavern. When the soldiers drew near, the cat paused its preening and issued a seriously hostile growl of warning. Its claws extended, scraping the lift's metal surface.

"Damn—there really is a panther down here!" gasped Marshall. "I thought Gina was… I guess I don't know what I thought… but I didn't really expect there to be an actual big cat…"

"Did she mention how it can walk through walls?' Sergio mumbled.

"But…" Marshall fingered her handgun. She'd reholstered the weapon after rejoining the squad.

"Plasma blasts only seem to tickle the thing, so I doubt bullets are going to bother it much."

"That's impossible…"

"Everything down here is impossible, Marsh."

"What do we do…?"

"What's going on?" Hibbs demanded as he came up behind them. When he saw why they'd stopped, the Corporal grumbled, "Not that thing again."

"It looks as if kitty doesn't want anybody else to see the ship," Sergio remarked half in sarcasm.

"No fair," moaned the Bombshell.

13

The idea that anything could cause Corporal Hibbs trouble seemed implausible to Dr. Holmes. Without question, Hibbs was the most competent member of the mission squad. She couldn't envision any opponent capable of threatening the man… but then her imagination was logically limited to conventional threats. She reminded herself that Eiger base had become a breeding ground for impossible circumstances. As much as it rankled her innate sense of order, Amelia Holmes had to concede that *anything* could happen down here. She'd already witnessed events which violated several basic laws of physics.

Not to mention the Eiger staff's fabulous discoveries. Those finds challenged a host of stodgy preconceived notions among the scientific community. Ever since mankind had become active in outer space, they'd found a complete absence of any evidence of other intelligent life. This had confirmed the proclamations of a number of narrow-minded authorities: humanity was unique and unopposed in the universe.

Amelia had never agreed with that conceited presumption. The universe was much too vast a place to be empty of any other life. Among the billions upon billions of worlds out there, the conditions necessary to produce life had to exist on some of them. And evolution would certainly carry some of those alien organisms to sentience. Even if cosmological accidents or self-destructive temperaments put an end to a percentage of those alien civilizations, some would survive, some would flourish, some would venture off to explore interstellar space. It was arrogant for mankind to believe they were unique, and inefficient to base those beliefs on the slipshod search they'd conducted looking for intelligent extraterrestrial life. The extent of humanity's expansion was minimal beyond their native solar system, their search had been limited to the eight planets circling one sun. Any judgment made from such infinitesimal data was bound to be inaccurate. It was the equivalent of looking for water in a new land by sampling a single spoonful of soil.

Despite the unpopularity of belief in extraterrestrial life, Dr. Amelia Holmes had devoted her life to the subject. For most of her career, the scientific community had treated her like a leper. Association with cranks like her could kill tenure or dry up research grants. Only a few eccentrics shared her passion and were willing to part with the wealth necessary to finance SETI studies. She'd been extraordinarily lucky to have found employment with one of those privately endowed organizations. Once hired, though, Amelia had proven herself to be a valuable asset. In six years she had risen to a position of some authority among SETI.

When the Eiger base's announcement had come in, she had been among the first to learn that possible extraterrestrial evidence had been discovered. She had requested more information and eagerly awaited a response... that had not come. She had immediately requested Global assistance, since SETI certainly possessed no ships nor suitably trained individuals to launch a rescue mission to the lunar installation. It had taken considerable pressure to force cooperation out of the government; some of the tactics she'd employed had been ethically questionable, but she felt these transgressions were justified by what was at stake. The discovery of extraterrestrial life was the most important find in mankind's history. Besides, the base had gone dark, implying the personnel were in trouble and needed help.

Global had sanctioned the deployment of a small squad of soldiers to investigate the situation. One SETI representative would be allowed to accompany the squad. Amelia had promptly assigned herself. Riding a commercial jet to a public orbiting station, she had transferred from there to Station 51, a military outpost located at one of the outermost L5 positions. A shuttle had transported her and the rescue team to the Moon.

It hadn't taken Amelia very long to ascertain that the mission's Commanding Officer was an idiot. Major Dummheit's stupidity was equaled only by his unwavering faith in that stupidity. She was relieved to discover that the idiot's troops were capable of intelligent action. She'd acutely resented the security issues which had prevented her from giving those soldiers full disclosure about the Eiger base.

Would knowing have spared the lives of Corporal Green?

She doubted it. The travails that had plagued the squad since their arrival were a complete surprise. She was as baffled as the soldiers by everything that had occurred since their arrival. She couldn't perceive how knowing about the alien spacecraft would have prepared them to deal with outlandish phantoms. There couldn't be any connection between the two phenomena.

Something was behind the weirdness going on here at Eiger base, but Dr. Holmes couldn't figure out what it could be.

At first she'd had to suffer the Major's incessant prattle about terrorists. Then she'd tried to alleviate the squad's worries about the outbreak of a manmade disease. There were no terrorists, nor had the Eiger staff unleashed any killer plague.

In her heart she'd wanted to believe that the Eiger base had found an extraterrestrial spacecraft, but her mind was influenced by cultural mores that denied such a thing could ever exist. She hadn't properly thought through the whole scenario. The possibility of alien contagion had not occurred to her until the soldiers had mentioned it.

Against her heart, Amelia had to admit that alien contagion might explain the pandemonium they'd faced in the installation. The Eiger staff would've used extreme caution in their work, isolating and studying samples under rigid protective protocols. But even the best precautions were hopeful at best when dealing with unknown situations. The alien ship or the bodies they'd found in it might have presented innumerable contagion risks. Who knew what effect alien germs could have on human physiology.

Something had escaped, something that had infected the entire staff, driving them to suicidal insanity. And now the rescue squad had been exposed to that same rogue poison.

Except... the squad had exhibited irrational behavior *before* they'd gotten down into the contaminated base. It was highly unreasonable to believe that any germ could infect from afar, reaching across distance and through sealed hatches to sicken the soldiers. Granted, Amelia—along with Hibbs, Denk and the Major—had been exposed to the base's air and might've picked up the alien germ then... but the two female soldiers—Private Scarpetti and Corporal Marshall—had remained securely protected by their suits, they shouldn't be sharing in the other's delusions. How could the germ have gotten to them through their pressure suits?

Nothing about the Eiger contagion made any sense.

Furthermore, Amelia had only the soldiers' word about the ghost panther and the animated corpses they'd seen in the cafeteria. She had witnessed none of these outrageous mirages. So maybe she wasn't infected.

Ah, she reminded herself, *but what about the hallucinations I had topside?* Those she *had* experienced firsthand. One of them had killed Corporal Green—and hallucinations were not capable of murder. A particularly vivid nightmare might cause a heart attack, but Green had been physically torn to pieces. And the soldiers had claimed the panther had ripped Corporal Hibbs' suit. If the imaginary cat hadn't been responsible, what had done the damage? Were the soldiers delusional enough to rip Hibbs' suit and blame that vandalism on a mirage?

If any chance of an alien contagion existed, Amelia knew she had to do everything in her power to make sure the bug never got out of Eiger base. Such a rogue disease could wipe out humanity if it escaped. Mankind would have no immunity to a germ of extraterrestrial origin. The medical community might devise some cure, for human beings were tenacious creatures when backed into a corner, but how many people would perish before that happened? Scientific advancement was imperative—but not if it threatened to destroy mankind.

The Eiger personnel had attempted to destroy most of the information they'd gathered regarding their discovery. Why? What radical piece of information had they deemed too perilous for anyone to know? Had the madness overtaken them by that time? Had they tried to save mankind from the disease? Perhaps obfuscate its nature to impede anyone from duplicating the alien contagion? There was no way of guessing how much—if any—data remained to document what had occurred here.

Only one place remained where the data was still intact and whole—and she was staring right at it. The alien ship itself. Studying the spacecraft was the only way to reclaim the invaluable information which the Eiger staff had annihilated.

I have to go in there, she told herself.

Danger aside, Amelia felt compelled to reassemble that information and see that it was transmitted to the world-at-large. A discovery of this magnitude could not be allowed to be kept secret because of any potential contagion. The disease was completely separate from the technical knowledge to be derived from the alien spacecraft.

But she knew how the authorities would react. They'd immediately lock down the facility, isolate any survivors—for their own safety. All knowledge of the contagion—or the alien ship—would be prevented from leaking out to the public. In the course of forestalling widespread panic, the data would become classified and be forever lost in a Global mire of security conventions. Fear could cost humanity valuable knowledge, technologies that might unlock interstellar travel and more. Amelia refused to allow that to happen.

I'm the only one who can salvage the precious alien knowledge.

Her heart struggled with this decision, but her own fear of the space-craft kept her from acting upon her conviction. It was so huge and ancient... and alien. What if the contagion was strongest inside the ship?

I can't, she lamented. *But I'm the only one who cares... the only one who even knows there's something to care about.* The soldiers were more concerned with survival, which was their job. Gathering information fell to her as the sole representative of the scientific community. She would be failing her entire species if she shirked this responsibility.

It took a lot of conscious effort to get her feet moving. Unwilling to expose herself to potential danger, Amelia's body resisted her decision. She rallied all her conviction to overcome her fear and propel herself toward the half-buried spacecraft. Each step was a momentous struggle for her. Amelia's resolve fought against a tide of unreasoning terror. She stared down at her legs, willing them to carry her to the ship.

Looking up from her grudgingly moving feet, she saw that someone stood there beside the ship's open hatch. This surprising sight made her halt.

The figure came forward to the edge of the scaffolding erected outside the alien hatch. It—he—was naked... and younger than she would've expected to find among the base's research personnel. She knew none of them personally, yet there was a familiarity about the man... and that disturbed her.

She moved closer—and finally recognized him. It was Corporal Denk! How had he gotten past her into the ship? And why had he shed his protective pressure suit? This didn't bode well. The only reason Amelia could envision for Denk to have exposed himself was that he'd given himself over to the disease's madness.

She paused, took a backward step.

But he doesn't look crazy...

If anything, Denk appeared remarkably calm, unbothered, composed, almost docile. He squatted on the scaffold and regarded her with a placid expression. Did he even see her?

She waved to him. He lifted an arm and waved back.

She couldn't remember how to activate her external speaker. For a moment she fumbled with her gear, but it was beyond her. She decided to abandon caution. At this point she'd definitely been infected. Either she was naturally immune or her madness simply hadn't manifested yet. Whatever the case, she couldn't undo her contamination. Spared any worry of additional exposure, she unscrewed her helmet and called out to him, "Denk! What're you doing up there?"

The man offered no verbal response. After a moment he rose and retreated into the spacecraft. As he went, he gestured for her to follow him, to accompany him into the depths of the alien vessel. He didn't seem to care whether or not Amelia took him up on his invitation.

"Wait!" she shouted, but already he was gone.

Now she ran, her prior hesitation banished by fervid curiosity. She stumbled across an uneven terrain. The excavation had scattered medium-sized stones everywhere; so excited had they been with their unearthed saucer, the workers had neglected to move any of these obstacles to the side of the cavern. When she reached the scaffolding, she struggled to climb the ladder, for its framework had not been constructed to be used by anyone wearing a pressure suit. She persisted, though, reticent to shed the suit so close to the ship. But when she arrived at the top platform, she found that the alien portal was too small to allow her to pass through it. If she wanted to enter, Amelia was going to have to cast off her protective attire.

It'll be worth it, she assured herself. The armor attached to her suit was hardly as bulky as that worn by the soldiers; even so, it hampered her efforts to quickly peel away the crinkly-but-resilient material of her pressure suit.

Awesome secrets awaited her inside. Miraculous technologies that had been invented lightyears away, then brought all this distance to be discovered by Amelia Holmes.

Technically, the Eiger scientists had been the first to make these discoveries… but they were all dead now, or insane. Amelia had wanted to be the one to rediscover those mysteries, but somehow Corporal Denk had beat her to it. Apparently he was willing to share what he'd found. Ah, but it wouldn't really be "sharing," for Denk was a soldier, unschooled in higher technologies. The understanding, the adaptation, the exploitation would all happen because of Amelia's shrewd mind. She might share historical credit with the man, but the patents would belong exclusively to her.

Rid of the clammy pressure suit, Amelia felt refreshed, liberated. It was as if she'd been reborn, casting off her terrestrial shell to go explore astounding new vistas that would send mankind to the stars.

Her enthusiasm washed away any trace of her prior fear.

She crawled through the portal and peered about with the aid of a flashlight she'd taken from the suit's gear. The immediate chamber served the aliens as an airlock. Another hatch hung open across the narrow cubicle. Through it lay a corridor. She had no need of the flashlight in here, for the walls were decorated by strange luminous patterns, an odd conglomeration of angular and curlicue lines that shed adequate illumination on the passage. The hallway existed at a right-canted angle and followed the saucer's outer curvature. The overall tilt of the ship as it protruded from the lunar rock added to this cockeyed perspective. To maneuver the passageway she had to crawl along its inner wall. Along the way she passed several circular doorways that were securely sealed.

Denk had invited her to join him inside the ship. He wouldn't shut doorways along his path, impairing her ability to follow him. So she was clearly meant to continue along this outer corridor.

For the most part the walls were smooth and cool. Every once in a while she encountered symbols etched into the resilient metal. If these sigils had any meaning they were beyond Amelia's ken. Cryptography was not among the disciplines she had studied. The actual etching fascinated her, though, for metallurgy *was* among her lettered credentials. A shallow gouge (just under a few centimeters deep, she estimated) had been dug into the metal surface. Whatever methodology—heat, scraping, atomization—had made the indention had left raised glossy lips on either side of the trough. The perfect uniformity of these brims indicated they were intentional, not accidental byproducts of the process used to carve the symbols into the metal walls. She wondered whether these patterns were ornamental or some form of public instructions. At this point, with no surviving aliens left to explain things, there was no way of knowing.

This spacecraft had been buried here on the Moon for centuries. None of its crew or passengers could have endured that long without air or sustenance. She knew they were dead, she'd seen their bodies in the Eiger autopsy labs, the flat round creature and the Grays.

Grays! It was remarkable to discover that those old aliens had been more than just urban legends of the last century. Among her inquiries into extraterrestrial life, Amelia had investigated those old tales of alien abduction. They'd seemed so absurd, so fanciful; they'd been so spurious, so unsubstantiated. It was clear that many of the reported cases were nothing but desperate bids for attention or notoriety. As the UFO mania grew, it became fashionable to claim to have seen one. To have been abducted earned one a high place in deviant society. It had always amazed Amelia that the human psyche had cast such a basically innocuous, almost friendly-looking, alien as the wicked invaders. The old tales attributed Grays with dispassionately executed atrocities—painful anal probes and cattle mutilations and teasing jet pilots with the aerial agility of their invisible-to-radar saucers.

Furthermore, the flying saucer motif had never seemed convincing to Amelia. It was a design whose objective involved aerodynamic navigation through atmospheres, not the vacuum of interstellar space. She felt the imagery had originated in cheesy sci-fi films from the 1950s and had crept into the public subconscious over subsequent years during the UFO heydays.

Yet once mankind had embarked on serious expansion into interplanetary space, sightings of UFOs had decreased instead of flourishing, as if the Grays had been too shy to openly deal with humanity. Pilots should have been encountering extraterrestrial spaceships on a daily basis, but that had not been the case. The local regions of space had proven to be devoid of alien visitors. Over time, people had gradually accepted that little gray men from space had been nothing more than urban legends all along.

And now that actual extraterrestrial evidence had been found—it turned out the ship belonged to those gray aliens. They were real, or had been real. Earth had been visited time and again in its past by alien ships. The Eiger excavation was destined to change a lot of things about how humanity viewed the universe.

With Corporal Denk's help, Amelia would be at the forefront of those amazing changes. Even now the man was leading her to some incredible revelation—she knew this with all her heart.

Later, when things had evolved from bad to unmercifully worse, Amelia would recriminate herself for lapsing into an analysis of these deep background aspects... when she should have focused her wonder on how the Corporal had gotten into the alien spacecraft ahead of her. She'd watched him run off to help his harried comrade. Denk had climbed the shaft that connected the cavern with the labs. To have reached the spacecraft, the man would have had to return and sneak past her. And she was certain he hadn't. Maybe he'd found a second route into the excavation cavern...

Right now, however, Amelia was mesmerized by the alien ship. Even the air in here seemed foreign. Beneath the mustiness lingered a tinge of something spicy and exasperatingly elusive, an odor that had no comparison in human experience. *Is this,* she pondered, *the stench of alien perspiration trapped in the air by the ship's ancient recycling system?*

When she finally came to an open doorway, it turned out to be another passage leading deeper into the ship. Here, the corridor adopted a gloomier decor, dark and slimy. Yet the sliminess possessed no moisture, as she discovered running a hand over the glistening lumps. The architecture was starting to exhibit an organic quality to it, curves and contours replacing harsh flat planes and sharp corners.

Ahead of Amelia, she caught a glimpse of Denk waiting for her at a junction of tunnels. Before she could reach him, the naked man had moved on down the right-hand passage. She called out to him, but received no replies. She pursued Denk, clambering faster in the hope of catching up to him.

The tunnel emptied out into a large rotund chamber bisected by a variety of what appeared to be fluorescent support struts... only they weren't made of metal. They felt fragile under her fingers, porous, almost like desiccated bones. At first there seemed to be no order to their placement, but as she crept deeper into the chamber she perceived that the bone struts radiated from the domed ceiling. The struts curled down to join the floor in a ring at the center of the room. The regions just outside that central cluster of pylons were crowded with mysterious shapes whose sharp corners identified them as machines. Denk awaited her within the pylon cluster. There, he stood next to what was inarguably a reclining chair. The thing's contours were configured to cradle a humanoid form—one much larger than the Grays, one designed to hold terrestrial human beings. Manacles dangled from the chair's extremities. Above the confinement couch hung a nasty-looking device. Several needles and vile corkscrews depended from this apparatus, ready to be drawn down to inflict suffering on the couch's occupant.

A shudder ran through Amelia as she recognizing the torture chair from the old abduction tales. According to those ancient accounts, this was where the Grays had conducted their profane experiments on human captives, probing them, dissecting them, implanting nefarious devices in them, terrorizing them. The ones who had been released after these atrocities had not considered themselves fortunate to have survived their experiences. Amelia had always rejected tales of these torture sessions as far too monstrous to be credible. Yet—here one was. They existed... and their existence tended to validate all the old horror stories. The couch and its attendant torture equipment generated a queasy feeling in Amelia, a visceral repulsion. Chances were good that innumerable people had suffered in this seat at some point in the dim past. The Gray aliens had persecuted innocent captives here. Their blood might still stain the floor. Their fear could still linger in the stale air.

Denk appeared unbothered by the couch's horrific nature. He bid her to approach.

"No," she told him. "I'm not going anywhere near that thing."

A smile cracked Denk's handsome face. He urged her closer.

She was near enough now to detect certain anomalies about the man. The Denk she knew had a buzzcut head, while this person had hair. The Denk she remembered had a chiseled physique, one she had secretly appreciated when he'd stripped down to give Corporal Hibbs his suit, but this one lacked any of that appealing muscle definition. And hadn't Denk had tattoos? How could he have grown a full head of hair and lost muscle tone and his tats in so short a time?

"I don't want to see this part of the ship," she insisted. "Take me to the engine room. Show me the propulsion drive."

He pointed with tenacious emphasis at the contoured couch.

"What's the matter? Cat got your tongue?"

Her remark cast a dark scowl across the man's features. Suddenly he didn't look as inviting or friendly.

She drew back, but her muscles responded with clumsy lassitude. Fear closed a vise on her chest. She couldn't breathe. A numbness spread like a cloud across her mind. The input from her senses remained unimpaired, but all outgoing signals from her brain were blocked from transmitting throughout her nervous system. She felt herself sinking to her knees; her palms pressed against the chamber's oblique floor, preventing her from toppling over on her face. Panic overwhelmed her, surging against whatever seditious influence was deadening her thoughts.

Hands plucked Amelia from her spread-eagled crouch. She was dragged toward the torture chair, hoisted up and deposited on to it. Centuries had hardened the cushions, they no longer relaxed into a pliant contour that cradled her form. She stared up at the apparatus that loomed overhead, trepidant that its menacing needles were going to descend and subject her to ancient rituals of alien inquisition.

Instead, Denk leaned over her, and his expression was almost as scary as the deadly machinery. Any signs of human decency were gone, replaced by lines that communicated animosity and disdain. His grimace was almost predatory. There was something wrong with his eyes, his pupils were tightened into vertical slits... like a cat's. A trickle of viscous drool escaped from his agape lips to splatter across her face.

She felt him slip the couch's manacles around her wrists and ankles. A strap was pulled tight across her belly, securing her in place.

Amelia screamed. She tried to struggle, but even though her prior paralysis had passed, now ancient straps immobilized her limbs. She raged and whined and wailed and begged for release.

As he pressed against her, his feral scowl momentarily flickered with tortured angst. He rasped, "She's forcing me to do this." His voice didn't belong to Corporal Denk, it was barely even human.

14

The soldiers were completely befuddled. At this point they had no idea what to do next.

They'd been sent to investigate why the Eiger station had gone dark, then they were supposed to rescue any surviving personnel. As to what disaster had befallen the research facility, no clear explanation had been discovered. And the staff... well, the few scientists whom the squad had encountered were dead or worse. Something had brutalized their minds beyond any hope of sanity before driving them to murder each other.

"So far," remarked Corporal Sergio Denk, "the only things that haven't attacked us are the half-dissected alien cadavers." *And each other,* he added privately. *But who knows how long that'll last.* He eyed the others. Technically, the Major had attacked them, but no one thought of him as a comrade-in-arms. His madness had been inherent, not caused by the interference of any alien ghosts. Were any of the rest of the squad primed to lose it and turn into an enemy?

He trusted Hibbs. He'd slept with Marsh, and wanted to share a bed with the Bombshell. As for Dr. Holmes... he wondered if she were alive or dead.

The squad had tried repeatedly to raise Dr. Holmes on a comm-line, but the woman hadn't answered. Even Marshall and Scarpetti exhibited traces of concern for the missing civilian.

The ghost panther quite rigorously prevented anyone from going down into the excavation cavern to learn what had happened to the woman. So far the beast hadn't attacked them again. Sergio feared the creature was just biding its time before it made its move and wiped them all out. None of their weapons were capable of halting the beast. Bullets were useless, and while plasma beams had proven temporarily effective, Marshall had lost her rifle topside, and the battery in Hibbs' weapon was already nearly exhausted. Sergio held the only full-charged plasma rifle...

not that it would do much to deter the beast. When it finally decided to attack, its talons and teeth would tear them to pieces.

Subsequent discoveries only served to further unnerve the remaining soldiers.

The mob of skinless scientists was gone. Sergio and Hibbs had locked them into a laboratory, but when they'd peeked in to check on the prisoners, the room had been empty. There were no other doors or access panels through which the people could've escaped. The ventilation shafts were barely large enough to fit a person's arm, and those were all sealed with slitted vents that were welded in place. The prisoners had simply vanished.

Marshall and Scarpetti adopted a mute skepticism regarding the escaped captives. They hadn't seen them, they had no reason to believe they existed. For all the women knew, the captives could've been figments of the others' infected minds.

The consensus at this point was that some contagion was behind the mass hallucinations and the madness that had conquered the Eiger personnel. Sergio was still unwilling to share his suspicion that alien ghosts were to blame. Once the Bombshell got to see the alien corpses, she conceded that the disease was probably of extraterrestrial origin instead of some manmade concoction in a biological lab. Marshall, too, was impressed by the Gray carcasses. The flat turtle thing confounded them all.

After an hour, the Major awakened in the closet where Hibbs and the Bombshell had stashed him. He raised such a ruckus that Scarpetti was forced to administer another tranquilizer dose to quell his tirade.

She worried how this was going to look on her record. Relieving Major Dummheit of his command position in the midst of a mission was questionable enough, but repeatedly knocking him out seemed excessive to her.

Hibbs assured her that the video recordings each of them carried in their suits would exonerate the squad's actions. "Once we get back to Station 51, the Major can bluster and rant all he wants, but none of his delusional accusations will match the footage of what actually occurred."

If we ever get back to 51, ruminated Sergio.

Corporal Hibbs announced it was time for them to review their options.

The squad retreated to a room away from the panther's sentry position. Hibbs was hopeful that distance and a sealed doorway would provide them with a modicum of security from eavesdropping pointy ears.

"I don't understand why we're sticking around here," muttered the Bombshell.

"For one thing, Private," Hibbs huffed at her, "we haven't completed our assigned mission."

"There's nobody left to rescue, Corporal. They're all dead!" When he made to interrupt, she plunged on, "And don't give me any bullshit about how we haven't discovered what took out the Eiger personnel. The evidence points to a plague that causes hallucinations and then suicidal madness. That's a good enough answer to take back to Global. Let them deal with the problem."

Hibbs squared his armored shoulders. "According to protocol, Private, if there's a biological contagion here, we have to effect an immediate quarantine." His voice rang with uncharacteristic authority. "From this point on, nobody leaves this installation."

"Begging the temporary Commanding Officer's pardon, but you and Corporal Denk are the ones who've been potentially exposed to the contagion. Neither I nor Corporal Marshall have. *We're* not infected; you are. We can leave without risk of spreading the contagion, sir."

Hibbs shook his head with evident regret. "You're forgetting, Private—you've seen the panther. That delusion marks you ladies as infected as we are."

"But—" Marshall started to protest.

"He's right, Marsh," lamented Sergio. "The delusions are a sure sign of infection. We're all stuck here together."

She flashed him a desolate look.

"We're Marines—all of us," contended Sergio. "We face death every time we go into battle, and we do it with courage and honor. This instance is no different."

"We have to think about the Big Picture," Hibbs insisted. "If any of us leave, we run the risk of spreading the contagion."

"Hibbs is right," warranted Sergio. "It's our job to protect the public."

Corporal Marshall gave a grim nod.

Reluctantly, Private Scarpetti shrugged.

"Our first order of business is to contact 51," decreed Corporal Hibbs. "We have to warn Global about the possible contagion. The problem is: the crazies destroyed the base's radio equipment. And our suit comms aren't strong enough to send a transmission that far beyond the Moon."

"We need to check on Dr. Holmes," argued Sergio. He still felt responsible for the woman.

"I already—" Marshall started to speak.

Hibbs cut her off, "Wait—the prospector's tractor! We can use its radio!"

"Not going to happen," Marshall told him. "Moss demolished the tractor's radio and everything, even the controls to start the motors. But I was trying to—"

"The crazy bastard," fumed Hibbs.

"We need to check on Dr. Holmes," insisted Sergio.

"Excuse me, can I finish a sentence?" Marshall persisted. "I'm trying to tell you: I already warned 51."

Pushing Sergio aside, Hibbs grabbed Marshall's arm. "What? When?"

She shook off his grip, glaring, then resumed her explanation. "When I entered the installation, Gina told me about the weird shit you guys've been facing down here. She mentioned the suspicion that the Eiger scientists had unleashed a plague that had killed most of them. I decided to use a little initiative and send out a quarantine warning."

"How?" he demanded.

"I set up a boost box at the airlock hatch and tuned it to amplify my suit comm's transmissions. The signal I sent isn't strong enough to get all the way to Station 51, but it will reach a satellite in lunar orbit that'll relay the signal to 51."

"I could kiss you, Marshall!" cheered Hibbs.

"We need to find out what happened to Dr. Holmes," Sergio protested. Everyone was so wrapped up in Hibbs' scheme to warn Global, nobody was paying any attention to their more immediate problems. "She's a civilian," he reminded them.

Exasperated by Sergio's constant interruptions, Hibbs turned on him and sternly stated, "In order to search for her, we'd have to get past the panther."

"I think it's safe to assume the Egghead's no longer in the game," commented the Bombshell.

"We don't know she's dead," Sergio protested.

"She's probably better off dead…"

"If she *is* dead," Marshall reminded them, "we might have to worry about her becoming a zombie and coming after us."

Despite their run-in with mercurial corpses in the cafeteria, Sergio and Hibbs had some difficulty accepting Marshall's tale of the reanimated corpses she'd faced topside after the rest of the squad had entered the base.

Scarpetti emphatically corroborated the phenomenon, though. Private Danford's dead body, she claimed, had attacked her when she'd opened the surface airlock and let Corporal Marshall into the base. "And believe me, he was *really* dead." She made a ghastly face to emphasize that point.

"If that's the case," Hibbs conceded, "then we need to do something about Professor Harris' cadaver… and the other bodies throughout this station."

"But first we have to find Dr. Holmes," insisted Sergio, but nobody heeded his frantic reminder.

"The alien corpses?" choked the Bombshell. The prospect of alien zombies clearly scared the shit out of her.

"Yeah, I guess them too, but I meant the other human victims. There's the woman whose head was chopped off and then cut in half… and other bodies we found among the labs, some mutilated, some intact… not to mention Professor Hoek, whose body is (presumably) still up on the residential level…"

"We don't want any zombies bothering us," Marshall avowed.

"If these zombies are hallucinations, why are we worried about them in the first place?" countered Scarpetti.

"Because one of those hallucinations killed Corporal Green," Hibbs growled.

"And another murdered Danford," added Marshall.

"Then they're not hallucinations," the Bombshell asserted.

"Semantics won't make them any less lethal, Private," remarked Hibbs.

"Then let's get to it," chimed Marshall.

"Okay," Hibbs gave an authoritative grunt. "Our first order of business is to gather the dead and lock them up."

Considering how the skinless mob had vanished from a sealed room, Sergio harbored little faith in the squad's ability to contain any potential threats. But he chose to leave his concerns unvoiced. Although Sergio still felt that finding Dr. Holmes should be their priority, he had to admit that Hibbs was right. They needed to take proactive steps to protect themselves from the outlandish threat of zombies.

He wondered if their feline warden would allow them to freely move about the underground facility so they could collect the various corpses.

Before they could embark on their corpse gathering duties, the squad discovered the panther no longer guarded the lift. While they had held their private conference, the beast had departed… if it actually had been there in the first place.

"Now we can go find what happened to Doc Holmes," proclaimed Sergio.

"You've really got a boner for the Doc, haven't you, Surge?" Marshall teased him.

Sergio scowled. "I abandoned her when I came to Hibbs' aid. She's just a civilian; I shouldn't have left her alone. If something has happened to her, it's my fault."

"Okay, okay," Hibbs interceded. "Christ, Surge, you can be a pain-in-the-ass sometimes. You're so hot to find the Doc, you go look for her. The rest of us will work our way through the levels, gathering the dead."

"*I'm* going with him," insisted Marshall.

"Yeah, me too!" the Bombshell chirped. "I want to see the alien spacecraft!"

For a moment Hibbs tensed, visibly disgruntled that his orders were being challenged.

Sergio spoke up: "C'mon, Hibbs. It's only fair. We've seen the ship, they deserve to see it too."

"Fine. We'll all go look for Dr. Holmes' body."

She better not be dead, Sergio bemoaned as the lift carried them down the shaft to the excavation cavern.

The girls' reaction to the cavern was a replay of Sergio's first encounter. In fact, the awe hadn't worn off. Standing here on the shabby catwalk and viewing the half-buried spacecraft left him breathless once again. It was so huge… and so undamaged by time or its interment.

"It's a flying saucer!" Marshall exclaimed. "Just like in all those old movies."

"Are you sure it's real?" mumbled the Bombshell.

With a furrowed brow, Hibbs commented, "Look at all this, Private. Awfully elaborate for a fake, wouldn't you say? Hell—the hoax even comes with its own alien infection. Talk about authenticity."

"But it's preposterous," asserted Scarpetti. "A *flying saucer*? It's straight out of every cliché urban legend. Doesn't it bother you that those old stories turn out to be true?"

"Why should it?" grunted Sergio.

"It wouldn't be the first legend to turn out to have been built around a factual kernel," Hibbs observed.

"Did you check it out?" pushed Scarpetti.

"No…" Sergio admitted. "The Doc and I were about to when Hibbs got attacked."

"I don't see her," remarked Marshall.

"She must've gone ahead to explore the ship on her own," Hibbs suggested.

Although Sergio nodded, he wasn't fully convinced of this. Doc Holmes had been overtly uncomfortable about entering the spacecraft. Despite her intellectual curiosity, the woman had been unable to rally the courage to even approach the ship. What had changed that would've driven her into the saucer?

On the other hand, she had to be somewhere. There didn't seem to be any other exit from the chamber. In fact, the cavern wasn't included in the schematics that'd been included in his briefing files.

"Maybe she's hiding behind the spaceship," muttered Marshall.

All during their descent into the shaft, Sergio had doggedly tried to raise Holmes on their comm-line. The woman hadn't answered, and when he called out to her from the catwalk, using his suit's external speaker, he still got no reply.

One by one, they carefully climbed down the rickety ladder to the floor of the cavern. Anxious, Sergio jumped down, relying on the low lunar gravity to soften his landing. He used this momentum to carry him across to the excavation site in long floating leaps. The others followed at a conventional stroll. The women chattered to each other, their wonder escalating the nearer they got to the saucer.

By the time they arrived at the ship, Sergio had already clambered up the scaffolding to examine the open portal. Before climbing aloft, he had peered around behind the half-buried ship. He saw no sign of Dr. Holmes anywhere.

"Anything?" Hibbs called up to him.

"No," he replied. "And that can't be right."

"She must've gone inside."

"She wouldn't have fit." Sergio explained how the alien hatch was too small. No armored pressure suit could fit through the narrow threshold. It was scaled for Gray anatomy, not human. "If she went in, she'd've had to take off her pressure suit."

"You don't think she would've done that," ventured Hibbs.

"No. And even if she did strip off her suit—where is it? She would've left it here, but there's no sign of it."

"She has to be in the ship," insisted Marshall. "There's nowhere else she can be."

It certainly did look that way. The missing suit annoyed Sergio. Could she have taken it with her? There didn't look to be enough room inside to carry around the suit and all its accompanying gear. So... what had happened to it?

"Maybe the panther took the suit," Marshall jested.

"Maybe the Egghead was just an hallucination all along," laughed Scarpetti.

Ignoring their taunts, Sergio started peeling away his armored plates.

"What the hell are you doing, Surge?" Hibbs' stern voice rang in Sergio's earbud.

"I'm going in after her," he avowed.

"You don't have to do this..."

"You know I do." He unscrewed his helmet.

"Yeah, I guess you have to."

"Are you two crazy?" protested Marshall. "You can't allow him to expose himself again—"

"I'm already infected," Sergio reminded her. "What harm can another dose do me?" He wriggled out of his suit and lowered the empty attire from the scaffolding platform to the others below.

"Take a weapon," advised Corporal Hibbs.

"I plan to."

Unfamiliar with the nuances of the old UFO mythology, Sergio experienced no thrill from the weird architecture through which he moved. He wasn't awestruck, but neither was he blasé. He knew it was an incredible experience, a human aboard an actual alien spacecraft, but it was foremost in his thoughts that he was here looking for Dr. Holmes. Gawking and enthralled curiosity would have to wait until later.

The passageways were distinctly claustrophobic, narrow and tilted at an awkward angle because the entire vessel was stuck that way in the lunar rock. It was remarkably chilly, too, a stark and uncomfortable reminder that he was half-naked far beneath the lunar surface.

The place had an odor to it that could only be described as… different. Not that there was anything rank about the fragrance. It was a wholly foreign smell. No terrestrial comparisons came to mind—but how could they? It was an *alien* bouquet, a product of extraterrestrial chemicals. No human nose could possibly codify the olfactory essences in this air. If anything, it vaguely reminded him of the smell of his grandmother. This wasn't meant as any insult to the woman's legacy. He'd been a young child the last time he'd visited her and thus unfamiliar with what he later came to recognize as a medicinal effluvium.

Besides his Smith and Wesson .45 handgun (a model specially adapted for use in airless environs), Sergio had brought along a portable light source, but that lamp was unnecessary once he got inside the ship, for he found that the walls were inlaid with glowing lines which provided lighting that was dim but satisfactory for his purposes.

At first he wondered how he was going to track the Doc through these bizarre corridors. He had no desire to conduct an exhaustive reconn of the entire ship.

A trace of pheromones helped guide his search. Being a staunch lothario, Sergio was finely attuned to female scents. Traces of her fragrance lingered in the passages, as detectable in the alien aroma as a neon trail through absolute darkness. As long as he caught hints of this smell, he knew he was following the right course through the ancient spacecraft.

Her scream proved to be a more helpful beacon. Hearing it put a burst of speed to Sergio's cautious pace.

Something had frightened Doc Holmes.

No—there was more than base terror in those shrieks, they were the screams of someone in mortal danger. Something was attacking the woman.

What the hell could be attacking her in here? Everything in the alien spacecraft had been dead for centuries. *The panther? Is this where it went?*

As far as he could recall, Dr. Holmes had heard tales of the beast but hadn't actually encountered the creature—until now. No wonder she was screaming her head off.

Scrambling along strange passageways, Sergio followed her outcries.

They led him to a large chamber which seemed out of place after the labyrinth of cramped corridors. Here, claustrophobia was replaced by a more visceral trepidation, as if some deep racial memory drenched with irrational apprehension had sprung forth from his unconscious to chitter in the dark inside his skull. At the same time, there was that annoying feeling that he had been here before—but he hadn't, he knew that quite well.

There was no time to analyze this innate uneasiness. Doc Holmes' screams compelled him into selfless action. He surged on the incredible tableau he found at the center of the oversized spooky chamber.

There was a weird-looking couch, and Dr. Holmes was strapped to it. A naked man leaned over her, his ominous posture advertising his menacing intentions.

Sergio caught the Doc's captor and threw him from her side. The assailant tumbled away, too startled to do more than squawk.

And Sergio saw that the man wore his face.

What the hell—this is a new hallucinatory wrinkle...

His replica clambered to his feet and advanced on Sergio. That familiar face was twisted with outraged fury.

Moving with curt efficiency, Sergio flipped his revolver in his hand and bludgeoned the replica smartly on the forehead. A second blow was necessary, but eventually the man crumpled to the floor.

With the hostile down and unconscious, Sergio turned his attention to Dr. Holmes.

She too was unconscious. The woman's frenzied fright had driven her to pass out. She lay slack on the contoured couch, held in place by crusty manacles. Wearing only underwear, there was something erotic about her helplessness. For a moment he appraised her with a wholly unprofessional eye, appreciating the taut curve of her belly, the roundness of her breasts as they settled against her chest in the low lunar gravity. Unconscious as she was, her face was completely relaxed, and, as he'd expected, she was an attractive woman without her haughty attitude.

She was really out cold. His most brusque efforts couldn't rouse her.

"I found her," Sergio commed the others. No reply came, but that didn't surprise him. The ship's alien metallurgy probably blocked any transmissions.

Not that it mattered. His inability to contact the others would have no impact on his circumstances. He was the man-on-the-scene, it was his responsibility to deal with the situation.

Find and rescue the Doc. Check.

That left her assailant to be dealt with. And explained, too. For this physical hallucination had stolen his identity. That was uncool.

Leaving the Doc where she was, Sergio crouched to examine his puzzling replica. It had to be another material phantom. Sergio didn't like the idea that the hallucinations were starting to mimic members of the squad. If that were the case, though, this one was an imperfect copy. The hair was too long, and the replica lacked Sergio's tight muscle tone. Nor did this version have any service tattoos. If Sergio didn't know better, he might have thought he was looking at his twin brother.

But that was ridiculous. What would Riccardo be doing here?

Sitting back on his heels, Sergio peered around at the gloomily-lighted chamber. The place's creepiness made it difficult for him to concentrate on his circumstances. He didn't like the look of the machinery that hung above the couch. In fact, there was something unsavory about the entire chamber—its vast dimensions, the thin, glowing columns that curved down from the rotund ceiling, how this expansive area seemed to focus in on the padded couch with its bindings. The entire chamber inspired shivers along his spine. At one point he thought he spied a pair of luminous feline eyes watching him from a dark recess of the big room. But when he directed his lamp in that direction, the beam revealed only barren wall. The eerie locale was making him jumpy.

He wanted to get out of this unholy place.

"Time to go," he announced as he rose to his feet. "You first, Doc. You're the reason I'm here."

Jamming his gun and lamp into the waistband of his shorts, Sergio unbound the woman. He slipped his arms in the crook of her knees and under her back, then lifted Doc Holmes from the alien couch. Her skin seemed awfully warm considering the overall coolness of the ship's environs. She weighed almost nothing in the lunar gravity, this would make his task easier.

He set her aside for a moment and hoisted his replica to take her place on the couch. He strapped the copy in. "I'll be back for you," he advised the still-unconscious man. "You better be here."

Carrying Dr. Holmes, he left the horror chamber.

It was difficult going, and they both incurred a variety of bruises along the way, but Sergio managed to drag the Doc back through the maze of tunnels.

Marshall and Scarpetti waited outside the exterior hatch. They took the limp woman from him and conveyed her down from the scaffolding.

When Sergio turned around to go back inside, Hibbs demanded, "Where the hell are you going?"

"There was somebody else," he remarked. "Some guy was attacking the Doc. I knocked him out. I should go back and bring him out." Sergio held back how the Doc's assailant wore his own face.

"One of the missing scientists?"

Confining his response to an ambiguous shrug, Sergio returned to the alien labyrinth before his acting C.O. could offer any further commentary. There would enough of a fuss over the assailant's stolen identity once Sergio dragged the replica's ass out here; he wanted to avoid a premature inquiry. In truth, he wasn't looking forward to the questions the assailant would inspire in his fellow soldiers. They would expect him to have some insight, but he was as much in the dark was they would be. Nothing made any sense anymore.

He retraced the route to the large spooky chamber by following the scrapes in the dust where he'd hauled Dr. Holmes along the narrow passageways. He moved cautiously, his gun held ready with the safety off. No specific threat made him apprehensive; by now he'd learned to expect the unexpected. The Eiger base was a snakepit of nasty surprises. Sergio was tired of getting caught unprepared.

But fate wasn't done toying with him.

The alien couch was empty. The Doc's assailant was gone. The replica had escaped... or maybe he hadn't existed in the first place.

I hate this place, he grumbled.

Before he rejoined the squad, Sergio searched the chamber for any signs of the missing man. He didn't expect to find any, nor did he. The room was unpleasantly strange. The walls felt greasy. At one end (being round, the chamber had no actual corners), he found a pile of objects... or possibly trash, alien trash. Trying to be objective, he reasoned that alien machinery would not resemble human technology in any way. What he perceived as spooky was simply foreign. Even so, the equipment made him uneasy.

He studied the array of apparatus which hung poised over the empty couch. It reminded him vaguely of a dentist's equipment, although most of this gear appeared to have been designed for bolder evisceration. Although Sergio had heard of the old legends of UFOs piloted by Gray aliens, his knowledge on the subject was sketchy. He failed to recognize the notorious torture couch, but its ghastly purpose was not lost on him.

There were two other exits from the large chamber. He examined them with his lamp, but saw no tracks in the ancient dust. The replica must have left by the doorway Sergio had used to get here. He'd seen no sign of anybody hiding along the route. It was as if the replica had vanished like a ghost.

Okay, he warned himself. *Enough of that. The bastard was real. He felt solid when I hit him. He wasn't a phantom. He was real. So... where did he go?*

The mystery assailant could be hiding anywhere inside the alien spacecraft. Sergio had no desire to get lost searching for him. All things considered, Sergio wanted to be out of the ship. The place's utterly alien nature disturbed him.

His departure was hasty.

"What do you mean—he's 'gone'?"

Corporal Hibbs' skepticism was understandable. Supposedly Sergio had captured the Doc's attacker and tied him up inside the ship. But when Sergio returned, he was alone. How had the captive gotten free?

All Sergio could do was shrug. He had no explanations.

"More weirdness," grumbled Hibbs. Even he was getting used to things turning bizarre in this hellish place.

"He was real," Sergio asserted. "He wasn't some hallucination who faded away."

"Sure, whatever you say..."

Somehow it seemed important that he convince Hibbs of the assailant's existence. Still, he was reluctant to mention the man's stolen face.

"He attacked Doc Holmes," he insisted. "She was strapped into a chair in there, and I seriously doubt she did that herself. I fought with her assailant. I used this to knock him out." He lifted his gun to expose the handle. "I strapped him into the chair before I left."

"So he should've been there when you went back."

"But he wasn't."

"You think he had an accomplice who set him free?"

Again Sergio shrugged. That possibility hadn't occurred to him. He shuddered as he wondered if the accomplice also wore Sergio's face.

"Where's everybody?" he asked as he started climbing into his pressure suit.

Hibbs jerked a thumb in the direction of the lift shaft. "They took the Doc upstairs to recover."

Sergio nodded.

"So," asked Hibbs, "what's it like in there?"

"Cramped... and creepy."

"Feel up to doing it again?"

Sergio gave him a what-the-hell look.

"At some point, we should search the ship for this assailant and his accomplice."

"Well, it isn't going to be now," Sergio told him. "And it isn't going to be me."

Hibbs shrugged. "I suppose I can understand your unwillingness to go inside again. For all its cliché appearance, the thing *is* an alien spacecraft. The idea of crawling around inside it would make anyone's skin itch, even the hide of a combat-seasoned soldier."

Hibbs helped Sergio don his armor.

"While you were inside, I checked over the rest of the ship out here," remarked Hibbs.

"Find anything interesting?"

Hibbs shook his head. "Nothing really. No markings or other openings. Not even a trace of seams or welding."

"Their technology is obviously more advanced than ours."

"It made me wonder about that big flat creature's cadaver."

"Huh?"

"The other alien corpse we saw in the dissection lab. How did the scientists get it out of the ship? It's way too big to fit through that hatch."

Wearing a new frown, Sergio glanced up at the open portal in the side of the ship. He paused to consider Hibbs' dilemma. It was a valid question—how had the Eiger staff gotten the turtle thing out through that tiny hatch? But upon consideration, Sergio decided this mystery was too trivial to waste time worrying about it. The squad had more crucial concerns.

They decided to close the hatch, trapping the mystery assailant and his hypothetical accomplice inside the alien ship. Hibbs felt it was the smartest move until they were ready to flush out the vermin and incarcerate them.

Hibbs was eager to search the entire base. Sergio agreed, but first he wanted to check on Dr. Holmes.

"I should never have left her alone down in the excavation cavern," he remonstrated himself.

15

"How's she doing?"

Marshall and Scarpetti had taken Dr. Holmes to one of the empty apartments on the residential level, where they could make her comfortable in a bed and find clothing for her.

Hibbs and Surge loitered in the doorway.

As far as Hibbs could tell, the Doc looked pretty shell-shocked. She had every reason to be, if Surge's account of her attack was credible. (There was still some doubt in Hibbs' mind that any assailant existed, otherwise Surge would've brought him out of the ship.) She was just a civilian, after all. She lay on the thin foam bed, her hands raised to clutch at her own head.

Corporal Marshall stood at the Doc's bedside.

Private Scarpetti sat on the edge of the bed next to the woman's reclining form.

Dressed as they were in their pressure suits, they looked like attendants in a quarantine med lab tending to a sickly patient.

"Awake but still shaky," Marshall informed them in an unnaturally terse voice. Striding over, she edged the men back into the corridor. She closed the doorway behind her, then turned to confront them.

"Did she tell you what happened?" asked Corporal Hibbs. "Where's her pressure suit? She's going to need it."

A fury burned within Corporal Marshall; Hibbs could see it in her eyes. And it seemed to be directed at Denk.

Surge noticed it too. "What's the matter?"

Out of nowhere, Marshall gave Surge a double-handed shove that sent him staggering back across the hallway. "You bastard! You couldn't keep it in your pants, could you?"

"Hey—" protested Hibbs. "What's going on?"

"She claims Surge attacked her!" Marshall snarled with a stern hissiness.

"What?" grunted Surge.

"She says you strapped her down to some alien torture chair her!"

Oh shit, Hibbs privately groaned. Something like this was the last thing he needed right now. The squad had enough to worry about without adding sexual harassment charges to the nasty mix.

Denk's reputation as a philanderer was renowned around Station 51. Ever since Madrid, the man had become obsessed with bedding every woman he met. They didn't seem to mind, for no one ever heard rumors of complaints from any of Surge's conquests. Consequently, Hibbs couldn't imagine Surge forcing himself on any woman. Moves like that just weren't in his nature.

But then, today was a bad day for everybody. Could the alien contagion have warped Surge's normally courteous amorous behavior into uncharacteristically brutal lust?

"I never touched her!" Surge's outcry resounded with indignity.

"That's not *her* story, you scumbag!" Marshall yelled at him. "I can't believe you pulled a stunt like this here—with all the strange shit going on—how could you?" She kicked at him.

"Cut it out, Marsh," complained Sergio. "It wasn't me—I saved her from the real assailant!"

"Back off, Marshall," Hibbs warned her. "I'm the acting C.O., and I'll deal with this."

He pushed his way past Marshall and barged into the recovery room. Going over to stand at the foot of the bed, he stared down at the woman with fierce authority. "I understand you've made some serious accusations, Dr. Holmes. Would you mind repeating them for me?"

Denk and Marshall had followed him into the room. Standing near the bed, Marshall positioned herself as a barrier between Surge and his accuser. Scarpetti remained seated on the foam mattress, but she glared up at Surge with overt hostility.

Cowering on the bed, Dr. Holmes looked torn between tears and intimidation. Her haunted eyes flickered from face to face among the soldiers gathered around her bedside.

"Someone attacked me," she moaned. "He lured me into the ship… and then he—" She broke down into gasping sobs.

"She claims *Denk* did it," snarled the Bombshell. She didn't look all that hot right now, though. Anger had transformed the buxom pixy into a fuming gutter-punk.

"No," Dr. Holmes interjected. "The man who attacked me looked like Corporal Denk, but it wasn't him. Denk showed up and rescued me from the madman. I saw that right before I passed out."

"But..." sputtered Scarpetti. She seemed disappointed that Surge was guiltless in this matter—much less that Dr. Holmes was naming him as the hero.

Marshall took the news much better. It must have been tough for her to have her lover accused of attacking the Doc. Now she was gratefully embracing the possibility that her Surge was innocent.

"Then where is this attacker?" demanded Scarpetti.

"He got away," Surge mumbled.

"How convenient," she sneered back.

"I want to hear this from Dr. Holmes," Hibbs proclaimed. He nodded to the woman. "Start at the beginning."

Composing herself with some strain, Dr. Holmes told them, "We went down to the cavern together... but then Corporal Denk ran off... he told me you were in trouble... he climbed the shaft... he left me alone... I decided to check out the ship on my own... but then—choke—then I saw he'd come back and gotten to the ship ahead of me... I thought it was Corporal Denk, but it only looked like him... he lured me inside... he promised to show me the ship's secrets... but he took me to the ship's torture room..."

"There's a 'torture room' in the ship?"

She nodded meekly. "It matches descriptions of the chamber UFO abductees claimed the Gray aliens used to conduct experiments on humans they captured."

"And what happened to *you* there?"

"He—choke—he attacked me... he forced me into the alien ship's torture chair..."

"Corporal Denk, you mean."

"No—it only looked like him," insisted Dr. Holmes. She reached a thanking hand toward Surge. "The real Corporal Denk showed up and stopped him."

"How do you know which Denk was the real one?" the Bombshell wanted to know.

"The one who saved me looked more like the real Denk," Holmes declared. "The other one had longer hair and his eyes—they weren't human."

"But he looked like Corporal Denk," Hibbs remarked. He threw Surge an inquisitive look.

Surge fidgeted, then contributed, "Yes, the attacker I saw looked like me."

"And you failed to mention this piece of information *why*?"

"It was... creepy. It felt strange seeing one of the hallucinations wearing my face."

"But before," Hibbs reminded him, "you asserted the guy was real."

"He must've been one of the physical delusions... like the skinless mob and the panther..."

"Which would explain his disappearance." Hibbs nodded. "All these phantoms keep coming and going."

"Right..."

"So... our phantom adversaries are copying us now." Hibbs gave a disgusted grunt. "Unless you have a twin brother you've never mentioned..."

16

"Umm…" As a matter of fact, he did. An identical twin brother named Riccardo. Sergio hadn't thought of him in nearly a year. Ever since Riccardo had denounced their father as a fascist and stormed off, the family had disowned the spoiled brat. According to rumor, the runaway sibling had spent two months abusing the high life on the Riviera before his personal funds had run out and he'd dropped off the party scene map. "Actually," he mumbled, "I *do* have a twin brother."

"No shit?" Hibbs looked honestly surprised.

"Anyway, he can't be on the Moon. Look, I'm not comfortable discussing my family."

"What would your brother be doing here anyway?"

Exactly. How could a penniless Riccardo have gotten to the Moon? This was the reason Sergio had given no credence to the possibility that the replica had been his twin brother. The odds of him showing up here at Eiger base were too astronomical.

"It couldn't have been Riccardo," Sergio declared.

"But what if it was?" countered Hibbs. "It makes more sense than the attacker being a physical phantom. Why would the hallucinations start using your face?"

"Why would Riccardo attack the Doc?"

"If he's here, he's infected like everybody else. The madness must've already set in."

"All this is ridiculous. It was just another phantom, only this one copied my face. It wasn't Riccardo."

"I'll bet he came here with Moss," exclaimed Marshall, "in the prospector's tractor."

"What?"

"Remember how Moss was ranting that 'Denk' had beaten him up?"

144

"The man was clearly crazy," muttered Hibbs.

"Suppose a Denk *did* attack Moss. If it wasn't Surge—and we know he couldn't have done it, he was with us in the transport shuttle en route from 51—it might've been his brother."

A reflexive denial snagged on Sergio's tongue and hung there, unspoken. Marshall's theory was disturbingly plausible. It tied together several circumstances into a fairly credible tale.

Lunar prospecting had a reputation as a get-rich-quick profession, exactly the type of "work" that would appeal to lazy Riccardo. He could have partnered with Moss. They could have come hunting valuable mineral deposits, but they'd found something else buried beneath the lunar soil. With Riccardo's impatient temper, Sergio could see an argument breaking out aboard the tractor. Suddenly the prospector's weird claims that he'd been "beaten up by Denk" made sense.

"So," Hibbs remarked, "Dr. Holmes made the same mistake. When your brother attacked her, she thought it was you—until the real you showed up."

"Corporal Denk saved me," Dr. Holmes insisted.

"What happened to your pressure suit?" Hibbs inquired. The matter of Surge's twin being the Doc's attacker was potentially a nasty subject. Clearly he wanted to draw the conversation to more constructive topics.

"The evil one lured me into the ship. I had to take off my pressure suit to follow him inside."

"But he fit through the alien hatch…?" Hibbs probed.

"He was naked."

"And what did you do with your suit?"

"I left it on the scaffolding platform."

"There was no suit there when we reached the ship."

"What happened to it?" she moaned. "Did he take it?"

"We'll find it," Sergio assured her.

"Dr. Holmes, you've suffered a traumatic incident," Corporal Hibbs' tone had lost its authoritative edge and now he spoke with sympathy and respect. "We'll talk again later, after you've gotten some rest."

"But—what about Denk?" gasped Private Scarpetti. "Aren't you going to do something about what he did to her?"

Jeez, reflected Sergio. *Why is she so determined to blame me?*

Hibbs cast a stern look at the Bombshell. "According to Dr. Holmes' own testimony, Corporal Denk is innocent. Her assailant just looked like him."

"You can't blame Surge if the villain has good taste in faces," Marshall gave a forced chuckle.

Glaring, the Bombshell showed no appreciation for this feeble joke.

"For now, we've locked her assailant in the alien ship," Hibbs told them all. "Whoever he is, we'll deal with him later."

Sergio could tell that Hibbs wasn't happy with how this inquiry had gone; neither was he. Despite the Doc's testimony, Scarpetti was blatantly unsatisfied with the outcome. For some reason, she seemed to *want* Surge to be guilty.

This tension among the ranks was bad. As long as the squad was stuck here in Eiger base, they needed to be a tight-knit unit. Any latent animosity could threaten all their safety if it reared its head during an attack. Order—social and military—needed to be restored. This was Hibbs' responsibility now, and he wasn't managing things as well as he should. But then, Hibbs was a fighter, not a leader.

"I think it's time we conducted a full reconn of this installation," announced Hibbs.

"We need to gather the corpses," Marshall concurred.

While Sergio harbored sensible doubts about the need to worry about the dead coming back to life, he was unsettled enough to play it safe and see the corpses collected and locked up. The squad was being plagued by improbable dangers—why was one more impossible threat less credible?

Anyway, this would keep them busy.

"Right," Hibbs decreed. "Marshall, you stay with Dr. Holmes. Surge and Scarpetti, you come with me."

17

The darkness pressed in on Riccardo Denk, stranding him with his thoughts.

He felt terrible. The bitch had forced him to do an awful thing. Knowing he would refuse, her familiar had hijacked his body to do her bidding. Riccardo had been a helpless prisoner in his own mind, watching as his body had assaulted the woman he'd lured into the ship. At the last minute, Riccardo had succeeded in regaining control of his body.

But then someone had arrived to stop him from torturing the woman. Someone who looked just like him. This anomaly had confused Riccardo, loosening his resistance and allowing the cat to regain its control of him. There'd been a struggle and the intruder had succeeded in knocking him out. When Riccardo had come awake, everyone was gone—the woman and the intruder. Only the cat had remained, glowering over him as he lay strapped to the torture couch.

The cat had freed him. And then he'd fled., to hide among the spacecraft's maze of corridors.

Hiding only postponed the inevitable, for he knew her cat would find him.

For a while, Riccardo blamed Moss for all this. If the prospector hadn't turned out to have been a crazy son of a bitch, then he wouldn't have driven his tractor all the way out into the uncharted regions looking for his dead family. And Riccardo wouldn't have ended up stumbling into this abandoned underground installation and meeting the place's hellish mistress.

But then, he realized the blame went back farther than Moss. If Daddy Denk hadn't treated Riccardo like a secondhand child, maybe the boy wouldn't have grown up so full of resentment. But no, Daddy Denk had lavished all his paternal affection on Riccardo's brother. *What's so special about Sergio?* fumed Riccardo. *My God—we're identical twins!* That feeling of inadequacy had driven Riccardo to abandon his uncaring family, to seek his own destiny out in the world. And that search had brought him to the Moon... where Riccardo hadn't made the fast fortune he'd imagined he would. If he'd never come to the Moon he'd never have fallen under the bitch's spell.

Sometimes he blamed others, like the girl who had spurned him in Costa Rica. Sela had shown no interest in him once she'd learned of his impoverished condition. Only a rich Riccardo was worthy of her affection, so he'd decided to leave the Earth and seek a fortune on the Moon. It was *her* fault he was here now.

He never blamed himself. Riccardo Denk was always the hapless victim of every circumstance.

And he *never* blamed his tormentor. The bitch was too scary.

18

The squad planned to start their reconn at the top of the installation and work their way down, examining each room for bodies or anything that might come in handy.

"Remember," Hibbs cautioned them as they climbed the stairs, "be careful to determine whether anybody we encounter is hostile before you start shooting them. According to Marshall, that prospector—Moss—got inside the base; he's hiding down here somewhere. He's a crazy coot, but we have to treat him as a noncombatant unless he gives us reason to act otherwise. And there still might be Eiger staff left alive—we don't want to harm them, either."

"What do we do with them?" asked Scarpetti. "If we run into anybody like that…"

"We lock them up in a separate room," decided Hibbs. "Preferably one on the residential level."

"Where do we stash the corpses?" Sergio inquired.

"One of the dissection labs should make a suitable morgue."

It was clear that Hibbs had thought this out. This was good, for stress had taxed Sergio's nerves beyond their limits. He could react to external stimuli, but his cognitive faculties were currently unavailable to process complex matters. *Tune in later,* he advised himself. The idea that Riccardo was here—that his brother had attacked Doc Holmes—it was too much to handle. His brain simply refused to accept this data. For now, Sergio was comfortable being a follower.

In his current confused state of mind, Sergio had abandoned his suspicion that alien ghosts were behind this mess. Superstition had no place in a Marine's mind. Despite her irrational predilection to blame him for attacking the Doc, Sergio had to admit that the Bombshell's alien plague theory was a more logical explanation.

The squad's experiences at the underground lunar base had put everyone's nerves on edge.

He wondered if this was how the madness would hit the soldiers. Creeping up on them, undermining their solidarity with sordid suspicions, until each of them became a human bomb waiting to explode.

The evidence indicated this was what had happened to the Eiger staff. Once the alien contagion had run rampant through the installation, the scientists had started exterminating each other. And—he shuddered to recall—done terrible things to each other. Vivisections and mutilations and unspeakable atrocities. To each other and to themselves. Professors Hoek and Harris had killed themselves—out of guilt or more madness?

The prospect of following in their bloodstained footsteps frightened Sergio.

Thank God somebody's *holding it together.* Hibbs was clear-headed and full of ideas.

"I think it might be a wise move to send 51 a follow-up message," proposed Hibbs. "Marshall was smart to get out a quarantine warning when she did, but at the time she didn't know the details of our predicament. Every piece of information we can relay to Global will aid them in deciding on a course of action."

"Bah," Scarpetti grumbled. "We're going to die here, all of us, and you know it."

"51 won't let Global abandon us."

"No one gets left behind," Sergio instinctively recited the Marine credo.

"Who knows," quipped Hibbs as they moved along the corridor that led to the access shaft, "maybe Global will send a med crew that'll cook up a cure for us."

"Weirder things have happened," Sergio remarked. Today had been a day for weird things."

"Get real, you guys," growled the Bombshell. "We're talking about an alien plague, dammit. People—especially politicos—are going to shit themselves when they hear about it. And the instant Global realizes this contagion might be an extraterrestrial plague, they're going to nuke this place. But that really won't matter much to *us*, will it? We're already doomed. We're infected. So far our symptoms have been mild, just outrageous delusions. Sooner or later, though, we're going to lose it... just like the Eiger staff did... and we've seen what they did to themselves."

Sergio scowled at her, but he was unable to offer any hope of a rosy salvation. Her assessment was harsh… but basically accurate. The members of the squad *were* all doomed.

"None of us are getting out of this place alive," she predicted.

Hibbs was quick to rebuke her fatalism. "If unleashed, Private, this contagion could wipe out the entire human race. Just because *we're* doomed is no reason to take everybody with us. This plague has to be contained."

"But—it *is* contained," she asserted, "confined to the base."

"And we need to keep it that way."

They had reached the top floor.

"You're really going to do this…" whined the Bombshell.

"Marshall already did it," he reminded her. "I just want to give Global a better idea of what's going on here. Tell them about the spacecraft and the alien bodies… and how the Eiger staff killed themselves…"

"And the panther," Sergio chimed in. "We have to tell them about the panther."

They moved along the passageway, past the locker room with its pile of torched pressure suits, toward the elevator shaft that would deliver them to the outer airlock where Marshall had installed the boost box. The Corporals exchanged comments with such aplomb it sounded as if they were discussing which restaurant to go to. The Bombshell followed them, radiating a surly discord concerning every part of their plan.

"The delusions," Hibbs nodded. "Yes, we should warn them about that symptom."

"Don't forget to tell them how the delusions killed Danford and Green," sneered the Bombshell. "That'll really help your credibility."

Hibbs paused a few steps from the elevator door. "You have a point, Private. Maybe we shouldn't mention the panther just yet… or the other physical hallucinations…"

Sergio bobbed his head inside his fishbowl helmet. "If you think so… you're in charge."

The elevator didn't come when they summoned it.

"When did this break down?" grunted Hibbs. He examined the control panel, but it confounded his rudimentary tech skills.

Sergio shrugged. "Maybe Scarpetti can hack it open." She'd certainly shown a talent for bypassing security systems when she'd cracked the lock at the upper end of this shaft.

With a theatrical sigh, the Bombshell elbowed her way past the men and bent over to examine the small control panel. "This is such a bad idea," she muttered to herself over the open comm-line.

"But it's the right thing to do," offered Sergio.

She gave him a harsh *harrumph* and continued to fiddle with the door's mechanism.

"Well… it *is*…"

A moment later her handiwork generated a spark—and the elevator door slid open.

What they saw made them all exclaim "What the shit—" or variations thereof.

Not only was the elevator car not there, nor was the shaft. The open doorway revealed a facade of solid rock. The elevator shaft was gone… as if it had never existed.

Hibbs extended a hand and touched the stone mass. It was solid. It was real. "This shit is wrong," he mumbled.

"The whole shaft's caved in," yelled Scarpetti.

Sergio just gaped, stunned speechless by the incredibility of this new twist.

"I wish it were that simple. Look close—" Hibbs slapped the palm of his glove against the rock. "This isn't made up of chunks that fell down to fill the shaft. This is a solid wall of stone. It's as if the shaft never even existed."

"But of course it existed. We rode the elevator when we came down into the base hours ago." Had it only been hours ago? It seemed to Sergio as if they'd been stranded here for days.

"It was there when Marshall and I came back from the surface," insisted the Bombshell.

"Well, it isn't here now," Hibbs snarled.

"But—where the hell did it go?" she wailed.

Sergio muttered, "Somebody sure doesn't want us getting out of here."

"Nobody I know has the power to do this," remarked Hibbs.

"What's that supposed to mean?" Scarpetti moaned.

Hibbs issued a slow sigh that reeked of despair. "It's almost as if the base itself doesn't want us to leave."

Resigned that no second warning was going to get sent, the squad resumed their original task.

The uppermost floor offered no corpses, nor anything useful. The cartons in the storage room contained canisters of chemicals which were only valuable to the dead research scientists. The devastation subjected to the pyre of melted pressure suits had been too extreme, offering no chance that a single suit might be cobbled together from intact pieces. Doc Holmes was stuck in her underwear for the time being, as was the Major.

They spent some time rooting through the junk thrown into the drained swimming pool on the second level. They found a few items that might have been of interest—had they been intact. A personal laptop had been bent into an inverted V; when they pried it open, they discovered the harddrive had suffered a similarly fatal fate. There were pieces of equipment that had come from the base's communications system, but these too had been brutalized until they were no more than rubbish. At first they thought they'd unearthed another staff member's corpse, but the body turned out to be a plastic dummy; its markings identified it as a medical mannequin. They did puzzle, though, over the dummy's mutilated condition—someone had hacked a hole in its chest (as if searching in vain for a heart that wasn't there) and cut off all its fingers.

They searched the dusty apartments and found nothing new. No cadavers hung from meathooks in the cafeteria; Sergio didn't know whether to feel relief or anxiety about this disappearance. He stared at the junglescape wall murals for long minutes, but spied no sign of the ghost panther lurking among the two-dimensional shrubbery.

They stopped to inform Marshall and the Doc about the sealed elevator shaft. While Dr. Holmes expressed disbelief in what they told her, Marshall accepted the news with weary composure.

"It just keeps getting weirder and weirder," Marshall muttered to Sergio on a private comm-line.

"We okay?"

She gave him an inquisitive look.

"You were pretty mad at me earlier, Marsh."

"Because I thought you'd attacked Dr. Holmes," she insisted. "But now we know it was your brother…"

Do we? Sergio was still unconvinced that Riccardo could be here in the Eiger installation. The odds were too wild for such a coincidence to occur. But he had no desire to argue with Marshall regarding his lazy brother's guilt. Right now Sergio was more interested in making sure she didn't hate his guts for something he hadn't done.

"So—we're okay."

She nodded and gave him a warm smile.

"C'mon, troops," Hibbs called on the squad's comm-line. "Let's finish our clean-up."

"Do I have to stay with Dr. Holmes?" moaned Marshall. "Let Gina baby-sit her for a while."

Standing over the Doc, Hibbs inquired after her health. "How are you feeling, Dr. Holmes?"

"I've recovered," she informed him.

"I see you found some clothes."

She nodded, self-consciously fingering the baggy jumpsuit she now wore. "Corporal Marshall went through a few dressers and gave me this. It's a little big on me… but it's better than running around in my underwear."

Sergio could have contested that judgment—he'd enjoyed the view of the Doc's surprisingly tight bod—but if being dressed helped her confidence, he was all for that. The Eiger base was scary enough without the added stress of facing it partially naked.

"Feel up to joining us?" Hibbs asked. "We still have to reconnoiter the office level and the labs. The extra hands will speed the work."

She readily agreed to offer what assistance she could.

The four of them set off to finish going through the installation.

Marshall was eager to help, but the Doc's squeamishness around dead bodies made her more of a nuisance than anything. Scarpetti was conscripted to watch over the retching woman as she lagged at the periphery of the rest of the squad's search. Dr. Holmes' nausea grew so extreme that Hibbs ordered the Bombshell to escort the civilian back upstairs to the residential floor, away from the carnage.

Sergio and Marshall took Professor Hoek's corpse down to the lower laboratories, locking the body in with the woman whose head had been severed into two halves. Hibbs had chosen this room to serve as a morgue for all the potential zombies, since nobody had the stomach to gather the woman's scattered parts and move them elsewhere. The other mutilated bodies were fetched from the other labs and relocated to this room.

After discussing the matter, they decided to store the alien carcasses in another room, segregating them from the human dead. The two Gray cadavers were moved to the room that held the turtle thing, the latter being too large for the soldiers to move. Again, Hibbs voiced his wonder at how the Eiger scientists had gotten the creature out of the alien ship in the first place. Marshall seemed more impressed by this puzzle than Sergio was.

Once all of the cadavers, terrestrial and otherwise, had been secured, Marshall suggested setting up monitors in both rooms. Equipped with motion sensors and an assortment of surveillance protocols, these devices would alert the squad if any of the dead started getting restless.

While Hibbs didn't openly scoff at such foolishness, Sergio knew him well enough to catch traces of the Corporal's intrinsic skepticism which lay beneath his veneer of polite acquiescence. Hibbs was an old-school pragmatist. It would take more than hearsay to make him believe in zombies. Even Sergio had his doubts.

Notwithstanding his personal opinion, though, Corporal Hibbs let Marshall install her sensors in the twin crypts. And despite his own doubts, Sergio privately applauded this move.

During their base-wide search, the soldiers came upon no signs of the skinless people.

"They can't have just vanished," muttered Hibbs. "They have to be somewhere."

"Unless they never existed in the first place…"

"Of course they existed. You helped me fight them off. Did they seem unreal to you?"

Sergio confessed that the mob certainly had seemed tangible at the time. "Now, though… I dunno…" As their predicament grew more and more unbelievable, it became increasingly difficult to shrug off things as delusions or hallucinations or phantoms or whatever word one chose to label these impossibilities. Reality was supposed to adhere to set rules of physics and logic, while dreams and delusions were free to violate such basic principles. The physical world and delusions were not supposed to share traits. Sergio was having a hard time dealing with irregular reality.

"There's something hinky about this entire situation," he mumbled with rote conviction.

"No shit, Surge."

"He's right," claimed Marshall. "Alien or not, diseases can't pass through a pressure suit's material. And hallucinations don't fight back."

"Today they do."

"We done gathering the dead?" Sergio was weary of this existential argument. They were limited to data availed them by their perceptions— the same perceptions that impaired their ability to codify everything into a nice little explanation. Judgments became highly unreliable when the facts were inherently dubious. Any attempts to fathom what was going on was equivalent to chasing their own nonexistent tails.

"Yes," came Hibbs' weary reply.

"I suggest we hose ourselves down before we rejoin the others," Marshall remarked.

"Grossed out, Corporal?" sneered Hibbs.

"No, but the Egghead sure was. If we show up covered in blood and gore, she's liable to have a nausea relapse."

Against their better judgment, the soldiers couldn't bring themselves to leave the Major locked away in a closet on the laboratory level. If any of the corpses started getting feisty, he would be in harm's way. Dummy or not, Major Dummheit didn't deserve that. So they hauled him upstairs with them.

"We can lock him in a closet in an empty apartment," Hibbs proposed. "He'll be safe there—at least, as safe as anybody can be in this place."

Sergio had no argument with that. He'd suffered enough of the Major's ranting to last him a lifetime.

Hoisting the man's still-sedated body over the shoulder of his armor, Sergio followed the others as they climbed the stairwell.

After dumping him in a closet down the hall, he met up with everyone in what had previously served as the Doc's recovery room.

"I'm sorry," groaned Dr. Holmes. "I've never been around... dead people before. I had no idea it would be so... gruesome..."

Corporal Hibbs advised the woman there was no shame in her reaction. "Atrocities are supposed to make you nauseous."

Marshall added, "They almost made *me* sick."

"So," grunted Scarpetti. "What do we do now?"

"What can we do?" muttered Marshall.

Not much, Sergio ruminated. *All we're good for is sitting around and waiting for the contagion to drive us crazy.* But he kept quiet. Fatalism would only undermine the illusion that the squad could master this outlandish crisis.

Turning to Dr. Holmes, Hibbs inquired, "How many people were stationed here, Doc?"

"Seventeen," she responded.

"That matches the tally in our briefing," Marshall added.

Hibbs nodded solemnly. "We collected ten corpses—Professor Hoek, Professor Harris, and eight more bodies."

"That leaves seven people still unaccounted for," moaned Dr. Holmes.

With a cavalier shrug, Scarpetti snorted, "Maybe the panther ate them."

"Funny..." muttered Marshall.

Sergio didn't think so.

"We must search for them!" Dr. Holmes insisted.

"Most likely," commented Hibbs, "those seven individuals represent the mob of crazies who attacked me and Surge. Everybody's dead, Doc."

The missing individuals obviously accounted for the skinless mob. But when Sergio conducted his own mental tabulation, he thought he remembered there had been eight people in that group. His count must have been wrong.

But, refusing to believe in this mob, Dr. Holmes demanded the squad find the missing seven scientists.

"Maybe," supposed Marshall, "the madness drove some of them to go topside without their pressure suits."

"We just scoured the entire installation," Hibbs declared. "If they were here, we would have found them, Dr. Holmes."

"They must be hiding…"

"Where?"

For a few beats nobody spoke. They stood around staring at each other, wondering which one of them was going to state the obvious.

Taking the initiative, Dr. Holmes proclaimed, "In the alien spacecraft."

"If they're hiding down there in that thing, they're already crazy," remarked Sergio. "Leave them there."

"Which brings us right back to my original question," the Bombshell chirped. "What do we do now?"

"As long as we're stuck here," announced Corporal Hibbs, "I suggest we make the best of our situation by trying to find some evidence we can pass along to Global concerning the contagion."

19

Busy work, Gina grumbled to herself. *Idle hands and all that bullshit.* Drawing another case from the filing cabinet, she gave it a shake. Each of the slim plastic boxes she'd checked so far had been empty, so she'd adopted the shake-first habit to spare herself the hassle of fumbling open the cases to discover they contained no data chips. Her fingers were normally remarkably dexterous, but her suit's protective gloves reduced her nimble digits to clumsy sausages. This time, though, something clattered about in the case she held.

Rather than interrupt the rhythm she'd achieved, Gina set the occupied case aside for later examination and continued to remove new cases from the cabinet. She gave each one a curt shake, then dropped it back into the drawer. All empty.

When Private Scarpetti was done rooting through the rows of cabinets, all she'd found was one box that needed to be inspected closely. While tormented by the effects of the contagion's mind-altering effects, apparently the Eiger staff's efforts to destroy all of the base's data chips had been quite successful. One miss out of several hundred cases—that was a rather commendable purge considering the self-destructive impulses the scientists must have been fighting off at the time.

For Gina, however, the scientists' competency left her very little to show for her own efforts. Corporal Hibbs wasn't going to be pleased.

Aw, bugger High-and-Mighty Hibbs, she fumed. The man had really changed since he'd relieved Major Dummheit of command, changed in a bad way. The power had gone to his head. He'd immediately started ordering everybody around, forcing them—mostly *her*—to do the menial labor. *Go fetch a new pressure suit from the topside tractor.* Oh yeah, *that* chore had been really vital to everyone's survival.

And now this stupid busy work, searching the base for any data chips the staff might have missed in their widespread destruction of all information involving their findings. As if there was anything to find. And even if she did discover an intact data chip, the chances were slim that it would be helpful in battling the alien disease.

If the Eiger staff discovered anything relevant to the contagion, they'd've used it to save themselves. But they were just archeologists digging up a buried alien spacecraft. What would they know about alien diseases?

By this point, Gina had seen the entire installation. There'd been no bio-labs, invalidating her suspicion that the contagion was manmade. The disease, though, *was* real. It had to have come from somewhere—and the half-dissected alien cadavers were the likeliest origin.

That realization had convinced Gina right away: what she needed to do was get out of this hellhole. But the damned elevator shaft was filled-in—Fagen only knew how *that* had happened—so nobody was going anywhere. Mysterious forces had sealed all of them in the facility.

Gina couldn't shake the feeling that unseen villains were watching the squad, studying their every move and cataloging each of their reactions to the alien infection. *With the Eiger staff all dead, we've become lab rats in some forbidden experiment.*

Paranoia was hardly a new outlook for Gina Scarpetti. As a Chi-town gutter-brat, she'd lived with mistrust her entire life. It was a survival tool for her. Time and again, extravagant caution had saved her ass on the street, from seedy flesh predators, from fellow gutter-brats, even from the well-meaning but intrusive attention of the police.

Gina's childhood had been a nightmare. The Chicago gutters were a terrible home for an orphaned girl. She'd spent years living in the cracks... until she literally outgrew those crevices. With puberty had come a whole new level of potential victimization for the young girl. Her early and curvaceous blooming had made her the target of all kinds of scum. Teenage Gina had been forced to escalate her savagery in order to survive. Such intensity was difficult to maintain alone. The gutters offered no one she trusted enough to even call an acquaintance. She had no allies. And when the police had caught her napping one day and dragged her off to protective custody, there'd been no one to step forth to champion her plight. She'd spent six months in an orphanage before her records had declared her eighteen and she'd been tossed back onto the street. When the chance had come to enlist in the military, she'd joined in a second. The Marine Corps had promised to clothe and feed and house her, to train her, to make her a valuable warrior… to put a gun in her hands. *That* had been the real lure: guns. Being a soldier was a means to an end. Her primary concern was always her own survival, and Marine training had taught the gutter-brat many new skills to take care of herself.

For her entire life, Gina had trusted no one but Gina. And now… her time at Eiger base had made her doubt even her own perceptions… leaving her with nothing but zealous distrust for everything.

Even her current squad-mates had proven their unreliability.

Danford had gone and gotten himself killed. Although their coupling had involved no deep emotional bond, she'd enjoyed the distraction he provided. But now the stupid stud was gone.

For a while Gina had entertained the possibility of using Denk as a sexual replacement for Dead Danny-Boy. She'd had no objection when Denk had pranced around in his underwear. She'd enjoyed getting an eyeful of the man's buff physique. But during her topside run, Denk had disappointed her by commandeering the Major's suit and putting an end to the meat parade. Later, when Dr. Holmes had accused Denk of attacking her, Gina's casual interest in Denk's body had been squelched by the supposition that this potential lover had turned into a rapist. If they'd let her, she would've castrated him on the spot.

She still couldn't believe how everybody had decided he was innocent. Well, upon reflection, maybe she could.

It was no secret that Denk and Marshall frequently shared a berth in carnal delight. Clearly that relationship had motivated Marshall to defend him—much to Gina's vivid distress. She'd thought the woman had possessed more independent spunk than that.

And Hibbs—the Corporal had a bad case of hero worship for Surge; the letch could do no wrong in his regard. Yes, Hibbs had turned out to be a real disappointment.

Why Dr. Holmes had refused to finger Denk as her assailant befuddled Gina. His attack couldn't have been *that* satisfying. Even the Egghead had fallen short of Gina's hopes. Besides, with all her scholarly intelligence, how could Holmes refuse to credit the true cause of their problems?

While Gina believed in the alien contagion, she had no faith in the hallucinations she'd seen, nor their physical accomplishments. As far as she was concerned, the delusions possessed zero physicality. Their tangibility existed only in the deluded minds of the infected parties. Heart failure or strokes had killed Danford and Green, not invisible monsters or zombies. Nor was the panther real; it hadn't torn Hibbs' original pressure suit to shreds, *he* had done the actual damage during a delusional fit. The idea that any of the dead were going to come back to life and attack the squad—it was ridiculous. But the others believed they would. The zombie Danford she had seen and destroyed topside had been only another phantom, a product of her deluded mind.

Despite her rigid skepticism and distrust, however, Gina found herself filled with dread every time she thought of the panther. She knew the creature was purely an illusion, a product of brain fever caused by the alien disease, but that knowledge did nothing to defray the fear she felt for the panther. She was terrified of the beast, afraid it was going to pounce on her and tear her to pieces. The fear was, she suspected, some residue of the mortal wariness she'd been forced to live by in the Chicago gutters where feral cats and dogs and alligators could be waiting in every sewer shadow. She knew she was here, on the Moon, not back in her childhood haunts—but that reassurance still allowed the fear to leak through and flood her mind every time she thought of the beast. It was a knee-jerk reaction, and she admonished herself for it with every irrational shudder.

Scared of some stupid overgrown pussy cat that doesn't even exist, she scoffed. *You're no better than a chem-tard or a tourist.*

Lifting the single case she'd found, Gina fumbled it open. The box contained numerous slots designed to hold an array of data chips; only one slot was occupied. She plucked the solitary chip from the case and gave it a cursory review. Looking at the thing would tell her nothing. Even the labeling code was gibberish to her.

Let's hope this has something to offer, she sighed. *For that matter, let's hope we can find an unbroken piece of equipment that will allow us to access the data stored on it.* The Eiger staff had been remarkably thorough in their destruction of the installation's machinery.

She turned to take her search to the next office—and stopped dead in her tracks. A hoarse curse escaped her lips before they compressed with abject terror.

Sitting in the office's open doorway, the panther stared at her with half-closed eyes. The creature looked drowsy, but her gut knew that was not the case. The beast could spring into action at any second. Claws would unfurl, lips would draw back to expose fangs, and all of them would dig themselves into Gina, shattering her plates of battle armor, penetrating the reinforced mylar of her pressure suit, piercing her flesh, gouging deep into her muscles, snapping bones and ripping meat from her body.

She couldn't move… and she couldn't stop shuddering.

The beast's tongue darted from its mouth to caress its lips and cheek. Yellow teeth were revealed, each as big as one of her own fingers. The panther's stare smoldered with animosity. Humans were nothing but food for this imaginary creature.

It's not real, she reminded herself. But that avowal did little to diminish her acute dread.

Her hand dropped to the rifle slung at her side; it closed on the handle, but Gina was unable to muster the strength to lift the weapon to bear on the beast. She stared wide-eyed at it, struggling to unclog her throat. Her head filled with near-hysterical moans she was too afraid to utter aloud.

Then—suddenly—the cat raised its haunches and stood erect. Its evil red eyes never left Gina as it moved... until it turned and trotted out into the corridor.

Even though the monster was gone, Gina remained frozen by fright for another minute-and-a-half.

When she did move, she instantly bellowed a war-cry and rushed to the doorway with her weapon finally drawn. Embarrassment goaded her to recklessly storm out into the hallway.

It was empty. No panther, real or imaginary.

A moment later, Corporal Hibbs peered from an office at the far end of the passageway. "Something the matter, Private?"

"N-nothing," Gina managed to rasp out.

She wasn't about to share her lapses of sanity with him.

I thought I saw something... but I was wrong... there was nothing there... even though I know I saw it...

Denk and Marshall and the Egghead were searching the laboratories. Hibbs had assigned Gina to help him inspect the offices.

"Did you find anything?"

His question roused Gina from her post-hallucinatory distress. "What? No, nothing." Fear of the phantom panther had occluded any recollection of the single data chip she had found.

Hibbs was about to duck back into the office he'd been searching— when he suddenly swung up his own rifle and pointed it in Gina's direction. "In-coming! he shouted.

Her reflexes were sharp this time. She flung herself to the floor and to the left, against the wall. *What the hell—* she raged. *Hibbs has gone crazy!* His gunfire zipped past her. And then she realized that other shots were ricocheting along the walls... and most of them were coming from the other end of the corridor.

An attack? She wrestled her weapon around to bear on the mystery attackers. Who the hell could it be? Had the rest of the squad lost it and come to slaughter them? For an instant so fleeting she hardly noticed it, Gina hoped it *was* her fellow comrades attacking her. She ached to put a bullet between Denk's beady eyes—*that smug turd.* But no—they appeared to be strangers. Were they real? Or was she firing at figments of her infected imagination?

If these invaders were hallucinations, their bullets weren't. The slugs chewed up the hallway. Debris pinged off Gina's helmet. An enemy shell hit her in the chest; it hardly chipped the veneer of her tempered armor, but she felt the impact as if someone had jabbed her in the bosom with a broom handle.

Oh, who the hell cares who they are, she decided. They were shooting at her—and she was going to defend herself.

And maybe vent a little of her frustrated rage in the process.

20

When Corporal Hibbs saw the figures step from the stairwell, he didn't stop to wonder who they were. They clearly weren't Global troops, which made them potential threats.

The group halted. As soon as they caught sight of Hibbs and Private Scarpetti in the corridor, the intruders lifted the weapons to point at him and the Bombshell. Hibbs could tell they were half-a-second away from firing.

So he fired first. Battle-honed reflexes brought his own weapon to bear on the men, and he blasted away without hesitation.

"In-coming!" he warned Scarpetti. She expertly dove out of the way. *Good girl.*

For a protracted moment, a madcap exchange of gunfire echoed in the corridor. Seconds into this din, the Bombshell added her own shots to the pandemonium. Hibbs had to turn down his external sensors to prevent the noise from deafening him.

Eventually questions regarding the attackers' identity strobed through Hibbs' mind as he stood there blasting away.

Who the hell are these guys?

The surviving Eiger staff? Where would they get guns?

Did 51 dispatch a rescue team? If so, why are they shooting at us?

But Global wouldn't send a rescue party. Marshall had sent a quarantine warning. Would Global sent troops to wipe out all infected personnel? No, the figures he saw wore raggedy pressure suits, they were unarmored, wielding only projectile rifles. There was no chance these men belonged to an official military team.

Who the hell are they?

And—*how the hell did they get past the filled-in elevator shaft?*

The *who* didn't seem as important to Corporal Hibbs as the *how*. They were shooting at him—that effectively established them as adversaries.

How they'd gotten into the installation, though—*that* was information Hibbs deemed to be quite relevant to the squad's current circumstances.

The invaders were backing off. They took refuge in the stairwell, but continued to fire upon the Marines from this shelter.

Scarpetti charged down the hallway.

Godammit, she's as bad as Surge. Hibbs felt a modicum of relief that Sergio wasn't around right now, or Hibbs would've had two candidates for Idiot of the Day. One rambunctious rookie was more than enough to handle under fire.

"Get back here, Private," he ordered her. "Where do you think you're going?"

"We have them on the run, sir!" came her breathless response.

"Fall back!"

But she kept on going.

Clearly, military discipline wasn't going to override the girl's reckless enthusiasm.

By the time she reached the doorway to the stairwell, the intruders had fled up the stairs. She pursued them without pause.

Knowing full well the utter stupidity of doing so, Corporal Hibbs followed her.

What else could he do? The idiot girl had fire in her blood and a lot of tension that needed to be released. If she was going on the offensive, he couldn't leave her to do it alone. He was all the back-up she had right now.

Stupid little punk, he growled to himself. *You're going to get us both killed.*

Up ahead of him, he saw the invaders, then the Bombshell, dash through the doorway of the residential level and disappear from view. *Why would they take refuge there… instead of fleeing all the way out of the base?* When he reached the landing, he learned why.

It was a surprise, but one that he should have expected.

The stairwell ended at this level. Where the steps had once continued upward, now there stood a solid rock wall. Exactly the phenomenon that had sealed the elevator shaft.

Gunfire from the residential floor reminded Hibbs he had more immediate worries than another impossibly walled-off passageway. He raced after Scarpetti.

Fueled by blind zeal, the Bombshell had made it several meters down the right-hand corridor before enemy fire had forced her to seek shelter in an open apartment. From that doorway she exchanged salvos of bullets with their foes.

Her exuberance provided Hibbs with covering fire, allowing him to safely reach asylum in a doorway on the opposing side of the hallway. As he commenced matching her show of force, firing long bursts of armor-piercing ammo, Hibbs thought he caught a glimpse of their enemy as shadows scurried for cover down the corridor.

Were they real or more hallucinatory chimeras?

They looked human, but that meant nothing in this place.

The bullets they fired at him seemed real. Those slugs tore holes in the plastiform walls and gouged tracks in the cement flooring and shattered light strips mounted on the ceiling… but again, that damage had little bearing on whether or not the men were real. The panther had been a phantom, yet it had ripped his pressure suit to shreds. It was a terribly disorienting state of affairs when mirages packed as much of a punch as actual foes.

"Private!" snarled Hibbs over the squad's comm-line. "What the hell do you think you're doing?"

"Forcing them back along the corridor, sir," she cackled with earnest bloodlust.

"Get the hell back to the stairwell! That's an order!"

Ignoring him, Scarpetti plunged into the hallway. She ran fast and laid down suppressive fire as she moved. She gained the next apartment doorway on Hibbs' side of the passage.

"C'mon, Corporal," she called to him. "We can trap them in the cafeteria!"

"A 'corporal,' eh?" a new voice rang in Hibbs' earbud. "So you are a military team."

The enemy had hacked into the squad's comm-frequency.

"That's right, whoever you are," Hibbs responded crisply. "This facility is under Global protection. I advise you to put down your weapons and surrender."

The foreign voice chuckled as if he'd spent a lot of time studying villainous cackles from old adventure videos. "I do not think so, corporal. The stakes, they are too high, eh?"

Stakes? What was the man talking about?

"I must insist that you—" Hibbs started to demand.

The other interrupted him with a menacing intonation: "You are the ones who would be advised to surrender, corporal."

Hibbs let the moment stretch out without a reply.

The other's voice had a strange accent that Hibbs couldn't easily place. Mid-European? Or was it Slavic? Ever since the European collapse, languages had become so jumbled together that accents and tongues ceased to have any meaning when it came to identifying a person's origins or allegiances.

The enemy continued, "The odds of your survival do not look good, corporal. There are two of you—and our scouting party numbers five. Soon the rest of our group will join us and overwhelm you."

Still, Corporal Hibbs remained silent. He prayed that Scarpetti would keep her mouth shut, too. Any response to threats only served to validate those extortions. This was standard training. Would the Bombshell adhere to it? Or would she rise to the snide bastard's bait?

Okay, Hibbs ran a speedy logic chain in his head: *I think it's safe to assume that these guys aren't a military rescue team. They're trigger-happy and they're after something... They must be criminals... scavengers looking to loot the installation... Somebody picked up the base's distress transmission... and they've come to grab what they can.*

"Look, I'm sorry to disappoint you," Hibbs announced, "but there's nothing worth stealing in this place. The staff went crazy and trashed everything."

"Do not waste your last moments with lies, corporal. We know what the Eiger base discovered."

Oh... right... the alien spacecraft.

But how could they know about that? Had that information been part of the distress signal the scientists had sent? Why would that information be included in a distress call?

Assume they know about the ship, but admit nothing. They're here to snatch the ET technology.

"If you're after the ship," Scarpetti taunted the scavengers, "you're wasting your time. It's half-buried in rock. It isn't going anywhere."

"Zip it, Private," Hibbs ordered the cocky girl. But she was too wired up to censure her outbursts. Now that she'd named the prize, all the cards were on the table. *You ballsy bitch, you've signed our death warrants. If they can't steal their prize, then they'll have to take over the base... and kill us.*

"The ship and everything connected with it *will* be ours," the pirate coldly informed them.

"Over our dead bodies, vowed Hibbs. "And eventually, yours too."

The scavengers had no idea they had charged into a contaminated zone. For a minute, Hibbs debated whether to warn them or not. His sense of common decency won out over expediency. They probably wouldn't believe him; they'd scoff at his outrageous attempt to drive them off. But he had to try.

"It's important that you know something," he told the hiding pirates. "There's been a biological outbreak. The entire base is contaminated. The longer you remain here, the higher the chance that you'll get infected." *And share in the rampant chaos. Craziness leading to self-destruction. It'd serve them right.*

"Nice ploy," the pirate spokesman commed back. "Trying to use the alien plague to scare us into leaving."

"It's no ploy," insisted Hibbs. "I'm telling the truth."

Hold on—how did he know it was an alien *plague? I never mentioned that.*

"I know you are, corporal. I believe the plague exists. It is, after all, what we came for."

What they came for...

Newsflash, Jack: these bastards aren't scavengers looking to steal some ET technology—they're maniacs looking to steal the alien virus! To use—or to sell to someone who will *use it!*

"You're *terrorists...*" Hibbs gasped. Hysterical laughter burbled in his throat, aching to be released. The squad had scoffed repeatedly at Major Dummheit's obsessive belief that terrorists lurked around every corner. And here they were, real and troublesome. His terrorists had finally shown up. Hibbs wasn't sure which irony was more painfully hilarious: that Major Dummy's delusion had actually become a reality, or that the poor fool was locked in a closet where he'd never see them.

"That is such a vulgar word, corporal," the pirate spokesman retorted with a touch of resentment. "We prefer 'proactive lobbyists.' It is so much more accurate."

"Terrorists!" Hibbs heard Private Scarpetti swear over the comm-line. "Dirty terrorists!"

All during this exchange (one could hardly call it "negotiation"), Scarpetti had persisted in firing off sporadic bursts at the enemy.

Outraged by the intruders' identity, the Bombshell dashed forth from her hiding place and stormed the hallway. Now both of her guns issued continuous salvos.

Hibbs wanted to yell "No no no! Fall back, you idiot!"... but he didn't. No longer was a tactical retreat the prudent action. Terrorists had invaded the installation with the intention of stealing the alien contagion and using it against society. As a Global Marine, it was Hibbs' duty to stop these villains.

Scarpetti's brazen charge actually bullied the pirates back into the cafeteria. Her firepower was relentless. Her sheer tenacity intimidated the otherwise overconfident villains.

Go with the flow, Hibbs advised himself. Against all odds, the Bombshell had succeeded in trapping them in the dead-end room. If she or Hibbs could get close enough to shut the hatch, they might actually manage to lock up these bastards.

"You think you have us boxed in," proclaimed the terrorist spokesman. "But soon our compatriots will arrive—and you will be stuck, corporal, between them and us." He laughed, again excellently capturing the mania of some adventure movie villain.

With a mighty war cry, Hibbs launched himself down the remainder of the corridor. His rifle barked with savage recoils as he sprayed the doorway with bullets, warding the pirates even farther into the trap. He was within a meter of the hatch when the screams started.

At first they resounded in Hibbs' earbud, but the shrieks quickly leaked out into the air and were picked up by his suit's sensors. Their unbridled terror made the Corporal's stomach churn. One by one, the wailing voices cut off, each cessation marked by a gurgly timbre.

By the time Hibbs stumbled forward to gape through the hatch, most of the terrorists had been rendered into scattered lumps of meat. Tattered body parts and twitching limps littered the floor.

He felt Scarpetti come up behind him just in time to watch the bloodied panther drag the last survivor into the wall mural. The beast and its hysterical prey disappeared into the two-dimensional jungle.

"Holy shit," rasped the Bombshell.

"There's nothing *holy* about it," Hibbs whispered.

Hibbs sealed the cafeteria hatch. He knew the futility of the measure, but leaving the door open was just asking for trouble.

When he and the Private returned to the stairwell, Hibbs was not surprised to find the upward way was no longer sealed off by a solid wall of rock. The anomaly had occurred to redirect the terrorists' flight onto the residential floor... to herd them into the cafeteria... so the panther could have its way with them. Now that they were gone, so was the barricade.

"They were terrorists!" moaned Scarpetti.

"Apparently..." Corporal Hibbs muttered.

"They want the alien virus!"

"Yes, I know..."

"We have to stop them."

"The panther beat us to it, Private."

"But there are more!" she wailed. "He told us, remember? Coming any minute!"

She was right. And now that the stairwell was unblocked, those terrorist reinforcements could freely enter the base—and gain access to the virus.

"Guard the stairs," Hibbs instructed her. He knew he didn't have to tell the Bombshell what to watch for. Still wired up from chasing the other villains into the cafeteria, Private Bloodlust was liable to shoot at anything at this point. "I'll be back."

"Me?" she chirped, her voice tinged with apprehension. "Alone? Against them all?"

"You can handle it, Marine," he advised her.

Without awaiting her acknowledgment, Hibbs scurried down the stairs. He was going to fetch his own reinforcements.

21

"Get topside, troops," Corporal Hibbs' voice crackled in Sergio's earbud. "We have company!"

Sergio immediately dropped the palmpad he'd been examining. He whirled and dashed from the gloomy laboratory. Marshall reached the hallway at the same time as he did. Their eyes met for a brief instant, exchanging looks of "Oh shit!", but neither of them paused. They raced in synchronized steps down the corridor.

"Terrorists are trying to breach the—"

Before they reached the security hatch that segregated the lab level from the rest of the complex, a klaxon went off, drowning out the rest of the Corporal's warning.

"What the—" Sergio grunted.

"That's the morgue monitor!" exclaimed Marshall.

The alarm could mean only one thing, but Sergio refused to believe it was actually happening.

As she turned to gawk at the lab in question, that door suddenly exploded open and something reached through to grab Marshall. An instant later, she was gone, dragged from the hallway by a misshapen limb.

"Marsh!" Sergio's rifle leaped into his hands as he rushed the busted portal. He was ready to blow away whoever had grabbed her.

He dashed through the doorway and shock momentarily muddied his resolve. He kept moving, but his next few steps were made on automatic while he gawked at the abomination that had Marsh in its clutches.

To call it humanoid would've been accurate, but only in a vague sense. The monster stood half-again as tall as a human being. Its heads scraped against the ceiling as it shambled across the lab. Its *heads*—it had *three* of them... but each one seemed to be a haphazard melange of pieces from different faces. A woman's lips writhed below two melded-together noses,

171

mismatched eyes scowled. One head recognizably belonged to Professor Harris—except for the fingers that wriggled from the barren eye sockets. The creature had several arms, most of which were busy manhandling Marshall. These limbs were lumpy with unfamiliar musculature. Its torso was horribly bloated trying to contain two broken ribcages and what appeared to be a plethora of shredded internal organs. The latter slushed about in the thing's bulbous belly like a swarm of squirming puppies trapped inside a balloon. Five legs scrambled to support this monstrosity. It was naked.

Of course it's naked, Sergio told himself. *The thing's a composite of parts from the dead people we gathered and stashed down here.*

How had this bonus-sized zombie assembled itself?

It had to be another aberrant fever dream.

Before Sergio could react, though, the beast barged past him, carrying Marshall out into the hallway. The impact sent Sergio staggering back. Scraps of flesh came loose from the creature as it collided with him. It took Sergio a moment to regain his balance, then he rushed after the thing.

It had already made it halfway down the corridor.

Throwing off his horror, Sergio opened fire on the beast. His shots tore holes in its deformed shoulders and patchwork heads. Even with pieces missing, the faces were gruesome. No wound, though, appeared to daunt this monstrosity. It continued to drag Marshall down the passageway.

Sergio's relentless firepower succeeded in disabling the creature. He shot three of its legs to pieces. The zombie was too cumbersome to be held up by only a pair of legs. It crumpled under its own ghastly mass. And took Marshall down with it.

The woman's armor protected her from her comrades' shots.

As obstinate as it was ugly, the beast floundered on the floor, but refused to release its captive. It clutched wildly at Marshall, deviant sinews bulging along the disfigured arms. So far, its pawing was clumsy, inflicting no appreciable damage to her gear. Even so, she fought back as best she could, kicking and screaming.

Everybody was screaming.

The alarm still wailed on the squad's comm-line.

Sergio howled with horror.

Marshall had good reason to scream.

Even the awful monstrosity bellowed away with its four mouths, each one issuing a different raspy voice.

Utilizing some maneuver that the scuffle hid from Sergio, Marshall managed to twist free of her captor's multitude of arms. She rolled aside, allowing her comrades' gunfire to fully strike the beast. It had been using her armored body as a shield against the barrage of bullets. Marshall speedily regained her feet and added a second salvo to the fusillade.

The combined firepower tore the zombie to shreds. The grotesque body had so many arms and legs that, as it came apart, each portion ended up with its own limbs, allowing the pieces to scrabble around with a shade more lively activity than dismembered anatomies should have been able to exhibit. One piece clambered for Marshall; she immobilized it by shooting up its leg and arm, leaving a chunk of torso twisting on the floor. The soldiers' salvos forced the other body parts back toward the shaft. One by one, the zombie chunks fell into the open pit.

Standing at the edge, Sergio watched the pieces tumble down the shaft. Marshall came up behind him.

"A super-zombie," she gasped. Her voice was hoarse from all the screaming she'd done. "How did it…?"

"How does any of this shit happen?" Sergio cursed. "I hate this place."

"Hibbs needs us topside," muttered Marshall. "Let's get moving before any more weirdness attacks us."

While Sergio desperately wanted to follow her advice, he had to disagree. "We have to destroy that thing."

"We just did, Surge."

"No… all we did was break it down into smaller pieces."

"Pieces that won't be bothering us," she insisted. "C'mon—"

"The corpses were mostly pieces to begin with—but *something* put them together into a big body and animated it. What's to stop that *something* from repeating the process?"

"That…" Marshall floundered. "That can't happen…"

"Neither can most of the attacks we've faced down here—but impossibility doesn't seem to have stopped any of them from happening."

"But…"

He glanced at her and saw how terrified she was. *With good reason,* Sergio realized. The monster had grabbed Marshall and assaulted her; her encounter with the thing had been up close and dangerously personal. She was loathe to go anywhere near the monster again, dead pieces or not. After all, the pieces had been dead to begin with. Their being dead had no bearing on their ability to attack her… or him. Did Sergio *really* want to chase the pieces down into the excavation cavern?

It has to be done, he fretfully asserted. When he told her that, Marshall only shook her head—not in disagreement, but expressing her inability to help him do it.

"Stay here, Marsh. I'll deal with it…"

No no no, his self-preservation instinct bellowed in his head. *Leave it be—go topside—get the hell out of here—*

Ignoring that hysterical guidance, Surge's sense of duty forced him to step onto the lift. He activated its motor. As the lift started its descent, Marshall called after him. He looked up in time to snatch from the air the ammo pack she tossed him.

He rode the lift down toward his abominable duty.

The walls of the descent shaft were decorated with splattered zombie blood and viscera. Sergio tried to avoid staring at the gore.

Most of the chunks had fallen all the down into the cavern. Only one lone piece had lodged on the catwalk. It was already twitching with post-humous revitalization. The animated piece was small, looked to be just a section of a ribcage, but its movements sickened him. He stomped the meat to goo, crushing the bones under his servomechanical boot.

Once again not bothering with the ladder, Sergio jumped down from the steel-mesh catwalk. He landed in the lunar cavern amid the rest of the super-zombies' pieces. All of them were spasming with undead life. Repulsed but fascinated, Sergio gaped as the twisted remnants began to crawl toward each other. As he watched, the pieces came together to fuse into a new monster.

Exactly as he'd feared.

Right about now I could really use my plasma rifle, he moaned to himself. But the Major had stolen it from him earlier, and in all the flurry of action, Sergio hadn't reclaimed it. Meanwhile, his rifle was running low on ammo.

Unslinging Marshall's ammo pack, he rooted through it for something that might put an end to this madness. Most of the high caliber ammunition was already gone, but there, buried under a cache of tranq shells, were bricks of C4. He prayed *they* would do the job.

Moving with as much haste as he could muster, Sergio approached the reforming monster. He commenced shoving the slabs of plastique into the coagulating body. Now he had to attach each brick to a detonator. It was gruesome work, hampered by the pieces' thrashing convulsions. The thing's anatomy was viscous, more like rotted food than human remains. He gagged back vomit, determined to set the charges before the zombie achieved its reassembly. As he finished the monstrosity grabbed him by the leg. He kicked it off, danced back from it; the lunar gravity elongated his impulsive retreat and he landed three meters from the newly reborn zombie.

He drove his thumb down on the detonator button.

The explosion threw him across the cavern. His battle armor protected him from the brunt of the blast. As he quickly scrambled back to his feet, he saw that the detonation had vaporized the unholy creature. All that remained of the zombie was liquefied residue covering a small crater like a grisly coat of paint.

As chunks of rock fell around him, Sergio realized that the blast had weakened the cavern's stability. Portions of the nearby wall were crumbling. A series of wicked-looking cracks crawled across the ceiling.

Oh shit— he panicked. The whole cavern was threatening to come down on him. Sergio had no interest in being entombed alive on the Moon. He started for the entrance of the descent shaft. As he bounded, he threw a glance at the half-buried spacecraft—and what he saw made him stumble as he landed from one of his extended leaps. He fell and slid on his belly, too stunned to competently halt his plummet.

When he and Hibbs had left the alien saucer, they'd closed and secured its entry hatch. That portal was open now, and crouching on its threshold was—him!

As Sergio struggled to lift himself to his hands and knees, his external sensors caught a voice shouting to him. His normal hearing would never have been able to pick it out amid the cave-in's bedlam. What he heard was more shocking than anything so far.

"Lucy! Help!"

A maelstrom of perplexed synapses fired off in Sergio's brain.

No one knew his middle name was Lucio, no one outside the Denk family. Yet here was someone shouting its familiar abbreviation at him. And only one person had ever called him that. Riccardo.

Dr. Holmes' assailant hadn't been a delusion with a borrowed face—it had been Riccardo! Sergio's twin brother was here on the Moon, down in the Eiger base, crouching there in the open hatch of the alien spacecraft—and about to be buried in a cave-in.

Sergio had to save him.

22

When unconsciousness rolled back and released Harold Moss, he found himself still immersed in darkness. He curled into himself, fearful that another maniac waited among the murky surroundings, waited to torment him, waited to hurt him, waited to punish him for his undying love for his lost family.

Gradually, his eyes adjusted somewhat to the pervasive gloom. Not enough to grant him vision of any clarity, but good enough for him to discern shadowy shapes amid the denser darkness. A pair of eyes peered at him from these stygian depths. There was something odd about those eyes.

Squinting, Moss realized they were feline, not human. Green with a subtle crimson underglow. Periodically they blinked, the lids languidly closing then reopening, as if the creature possessed momentous patience—or confidence.

It was the cat! Presumably the one who had guided Moss through the kidnappers' lair.

"I thought you were trying to help me find my family," Moss croaked at the beast. "You took me to that room, but when I got it open, my wife and children weren't inside. Just that crazy man in his underwear. He attacked me! You let him hurt me..."

The cat's inscrutable stare remained constant, unflinching.

"How can I trust you now?" moaned Moss.

A dull radiance blossomed behind the cat. Tendrils of blue light swirled in the darkness. These filaments coalesced, weaving limbs and a torso and finally a head. From that cranium streamed an expanding web of blue tresses. A human figure was taking form, the threads converging into internal organs and a skeletal structure, more tendrils molding muscles onto that anatomical nucleus. The figure's hourglass physiology identified it as a woman. When she opened her eyes, a dazzling effulgence flooded forth, banishing the gloom and blinding Moss. Before the white-out completely conquered his vision, the woman's luminosity briefly revealed a cat sitting at her feet like some occult idol.

When his vision cleared, Moss recognized the woman. It was his wife. He wailed with a mixture of relief and anguish. He pledged his eternal devotion to her. He swore to destroy Denk for having captured her.

"Help free me," she whispered. So deep was Moss in her thrall, he never noticed how her voice sounded like autumn leaves being crushed underfoot.

23

As soon as the shaft had swallowed Surge, Marshall turned and fled down the hallway.

It wasn't fear that drove her. Corporal Hibbs had summoned them. Somebody had to let him know why they hadn't responded. Besides, as acting C.O., Hibbs should know what had happened. Whether he believed any of it was up to him. Even though it had happened to her, Anne was still in shock about the horrific circumstances. Half of her couldn't accept the reanimated dead thing, her other half loudly protested, *Are you frigging crazy? Of course it happened, girl—you've got the bruises to prove it!*

She planned to only go as far as the stairwell that rose through the installation. From there Anne assumed she could reach Hibbs on the comm-line and brief him on these latest developments. Then—regardless of what Hibbs ordered her to do—she intended to return to wait for Surge's return. She refused to leave him behind.

As she neared the end of the corridor, deja vu engulfed her.

Another alarm went off and a doorway was flung open.

Her dread intensified as she realized what lab it was. In there the squad had gathered the dissected Grays and that big turtle cadaver. In the stress of battling off a super-zombie cobbled together from the pieces of the human corpses, Anne had completely forgotten about the alien remains. But suddenly, rampant terror swept through her. If the human corpses could come after them, why not the alien ones, too?

But the figure that shambled forth wasn't some grotesque conglomeration of alien anatomies. It was Moss, the crazy old prospector. Not that identifying him defrayed Anne's anxiety, for the mad man wielded a pair of Gray limbs as bludgeons. He charged her.

As far as weapons went, the alien arms were pretty pathetic. They fragmented upon impact as Moss battered her with them. Their desiccated pieces rained about her like aberrant ash.

Screeching over the loss of his ghastly truncheons, Moss flailed Anne with his fists. He kicked her. He danced around her, pummeling her from every direction. His blows were like useless breezes against her battle armor.

She hit him in the gut with the butt of her rifle. He crumpled like a wet doll.

Her attack had been basically a reflex maneuver. The majority of Anne's mind was still locked in horror at the possibility of alien zombies. That overwhelming panic started to abate when no travesties lurched from the open lab. At first she was relieved—then she tensed up again, for a monster could appear at any moment. Just because none had so far didn't mean something wasn't biding its time, waiting to ambush her the instant she turned her back.

The only guarantee she had that such an assault wouldn't occur was to go in there and destroy the alien corpses before they could come after her.

Surge is right, she fretted to herself. *I hate this place.*

It took her a moment to rally the courage to enter the alien morgue. She used the delay to reload her weapons. She wished she hadn't lost her plasma rifle during her topside misadventures. That weapon would dissolve anything she might encounter. As it was, though, she was stuck relying on bullets to destroy any adversaries. *Could be worse, girl,* she cajoled herself. She might've been reduced to hacking at foes with knives. The thought of chopping up alien corpses was not a pleasant one.

Holding her rifle ready, Anne strode into the alien morgue.

With the exception of the arms Moss had appropriated, all of the alien carcasses were as they should be: dead and dormant. To make sure, she fired a short burst at one of the Gray bodies. It twitched from the impacts, but manifested no other responses.

Maybe whatever reanimated the human corpses can't affect alien tissue...

Although she was no xenobiologist, Anne liked the sound of that hypothesis. This way, she didn't have to worry about alien zombies. But then, maybe the resurrection process took longer with inhuman biology.

The only solid prevention Anne could think of was to destroy the alien cadavers... but doing so would certainly win her the rancor of any true scientist who learned of her wanton devastation. Without the Gray bodies to study, mankind would never discover what made these aliens tick. The

Eiger staff had examined the cadavers, had undoubtedly compiled a vast amount of data on the bodies—and then they'd demolished all of it.

In the end, Anne found herself unable to destroy the alien corpses. The knowledge those remains could teach humanity was potentially invaluable—especially when it came to trying to figure a cure for the alien virus. She didn't like leaving the chance that alien zombies might attack her or the squad at some later point, but she decided she—and the other soldiers—could deal with that attack if it happened.

Resetting the monitor, she locked the lab behind her.

Standing in the deathly quiet hallway, Anne debated whether to continue on to the stairwell in order to send Corporal Hibbs a briefing… or to go check on Surge's status.

She decided that Sergio was more than capable of defending himself from a pile of blown-apart zombie pieces.

Moss' inert body lay sprawled on the floor. Anne could see the man was out cold. He wouldn't be causing any trouble for a while. Even so, she took the precaution of locking him in the human morgue.

Then she headed for the security hatch that was the only exit from the laboratory level.

Behind her, the door she had just secured clicked open, but the sound was too small for her external sensors to notice it.

In the stairwell, she commed Corporal Hibbs.

But got no reply.

Maybe the signal can't get past all the floors, she mused. But that suspicion seemed less credible in light of the fact that Hibbs had commed them earlier. His transmission had penetrated down into the installation to successfully reach her and Surge. Anne's own signal should've been able to reach him in return.

Unless he had left the base…

No, she told herself. *Hibbs has a real bug up his butt against unleashing the alien contagion.* The only way anybody could leave the base was over his dead body.

Now she was worried.

Had something happened to Corporal Hibbs? And what about Private Scarpetti? It boded ill if neither of them were responding to Anne's signal.

She rushed up the stairs.

Originally, Hibbs and Scarpetti had been searching the office level for any clues the Eiger staff might have overlooked in their data purge. But they weren't there now. However there *was* ample evidence of a firefight.

Hibbs had warned that "company" had arrived. He'd summoned Marshall and Surge topside… that would be where he awaited their arrival.

She continued up the stairs.

The trail of pockmarks in the walls led her up and onto the residential level. The door to the cafeteria was locked, but she risked a peek and saw the grisly body parts strewn everywhere. The pressure suits—or scraps thereof—which she saw hadn't belonged to any Marine, they were bargain basement gear. And there was no sign of battle armor. Whoever these victims had been, they weren't Hibbs or Scarpetti. Anne relocked the hatch.

She checked on Dr. Holmes. After the Egghead's exposure to the base's gory corpses, Gina had been forced to heavily sedate the woman. She should be soundly sleeping… but she wasn't in the room where they'd left her. Maybe the woman had joined Hibbs and Scarpetti.

She checked on Major Dummheit. At least he was where he was supposed to be: languishing in a narcotic slumber.

Returning to the stairs, Anne headed up.

En route to the top, she searched each subsequent floor, but found no sign of Hibbs or Scarpetti. Anne periodically sent out comms, but never got an answer.

They weren't guarding the base's entrance. The elevator shaft was no longer filled-in. She rode up to find the airlock empty. Hibbs and Scarpetti had completely vanished.

She couldn't believe that Hibbs would have violated his own obsessive rule and left the installation. Gina, she knew, objected to the entire quarantine. Gina wanted to evacuate the base—but Hibbs would never have allowed her to do so. So where the hell were they?

Activating the exterior camera, she looked outside and saw no sign of the missing soldiers. What she *did* see, though, changed her priorities.

A vessel had landed out there. It was parked near Moss' tractor. Figures milled about in the moondust.

It was *not* a military ship. Nor were the men she saw wearing Marine armor. In fact, the ship looked like a luxury space yacht. And the pressure suits worn by these men looked to be commercial attire.

She remembered that Hibbs had mentioned something about terrorists trying to breach the base. Now she could guess whose bodies were strewn about the cafeteria downstairs. And, here were more invaders. She counted seven of them. They carried weapons. They intended to break into the contaminated base.

"Not on my watch," growled Marshall.

Nobody gets in or out, had been Corporal Hibbs' decree. Anne basically agreed with that decision. Even though it stranded her in here, she understood the incredible danger posed by the alien contagion getting out. It was her duty to guard against that happening.

Meanwhile, if these intruders were terrorists as Hibbs had claimed, there was no damned way Marshall was going to let them in. Terrorists would just love to add a killer plague to their arsenal.

Patching into the airlock controls, she programmed the hatch to permanently stay closed. No hacker could break the access code—because none existed. The hatch's ability to open had been entirely deleted from its system.

"They'll have to blow it open," she chuckled to herself.

Unfortunately, they might try to do that. The airlock was a standard affair, not especially armored. A moderate blast would blow the hatch from its frame.

A backup barricade was needed.

Retreating from the airlock, Anne considered her options.

Sticking around would be futile. The seven intruders outgunned her. She would put up a good fight, but inevitably they would overpower her and gain access to the installation.

She could lock the elevator, but it too would succumb to explosives.

Oh, if only the shaft was still filled-in. That would keep the invaders out. But no—whatever mysterious force had been behind that phenomenon had unsealed the vertical tunnel.

For an instant, she considered resealing the shaft… but then she remembered that her C4 was in the ammunition pack she'd given Surge. She had no explosives with which to close the elevator shaft.

Marshall refused to let the intruders in.

She just couldn't think of a way to keep them out.

24

Corporal Hibbs had no intention of traveling all the way down to the laboratory level to get Surge and Marshall. Leaving the Bombshell to guard the head of the stairs, he descended a flight of steps. From there he planned to summon the others via their comm-line.

"Get topside, troops," he broadcast. "We have company!"

As an afterthought, he added, "Terrorists are trying to breach the installation." That would get them scrambling.

Speed seemed essential to Hibbs. He had no idea how long the terrorist reinforcements would take to show up. Nor how many of them there would be. He wanted time to post his troops in optimum defensive positions. It did not daunt him that, at this point, his "troops" numbered four individuals—they were Global Marines, worth a throng of grubby terrorists.

It was very possible that the spokesman had been bluffing, that no reinforcements existed. Lies were an integral tool for most terrorist organizations. But Hibbs was reluctant to put his entire faith in their dishonesty. If a slim chance existed that more enemies were coming, he couldn't afford to get caught unprepared.

He and the rest of the squad were all that stood between the installation's security and the terrorists getting their nasty hands on the alien contagion. These valiant Marines were mankind's only hope of survival.

A tingle of annoyance teased his lips into a frown.

Why aren't they replying?

He ventured further down the stairs, and after another flight he discovered the reason for that silence. The way was blocked by another solid rock wall. Even if his transmission had gotten through to them, they couldn't join him now.

Whatever force was behind all this madness had efficiently separated the squad. *Divide and conquer,* fumed Hibbs. *But screw with us first.*

Play with our heads until we don't know what's real and what's a mirage. Privately, Hibbs had to confess: it was an effective strategy. *A few impossible twists, throw in a ghost panther—and you've dumfounded an entire squad of battle-seasoned Marines. We're still armed and dangerous, but we don't know what to shoot at.*

None of the things occurring at Eiger base were possible. But that didn't stop them from happening.

By now Hibbs had moved beyond blaming everything on the alien contagion. The delusions were too strategic, each one designed to hamper the squad's ability to do their job. Once, maybe twice could be a coincidence; this constant interference had to be intentional.

Something was orchestrating their problems. Something was forcing everybody to suffer the same delusions.

Something had driven the Eiger staff to kill themselves.

Something wanted the squad trapped here in the base.

Something wanted more people to come and share in the misery.

Something was *enjoying* all this.

What was it Professor Hoek had told them before he'd ripped out his own throat? *"She doesn't want to kill you! She has more fun with living playtoys!"* But the man had been insane, Hibbs could put no credibility in Hoek's babble.

What's next? A plague of locusts? A swarm of rabid wolverines? Why not a full-scale devil, breathing fire and wielding a pitchfork?

This enemy was capable of making an elevator shaft vanish as if it had never existed. Why did it bother attacking them with phantoms? Why didn't it just defeat the soldiers by liquefying their bodies? Or escalate the insanity to the point that each member of the squad was at each other's throats?

These were frightening mysteries… and Hibbs wasn't all that sure he wanted to know the answers. More specifically: he wasn't sure he could cope with those answers. If the effects were so outrageous, the cause had to be equally inscrutable.

Damned obstacle, Hibbs snarled to himself. *I need the rest of my troops.* He banged his fist against the barrier. It was solid, it was real. Nobody was getting past it.

What the—

The wall had moved! Its coarse rock surface pressed against the palm of his gauntlet. He pushed against the wall—and the thing pushed back! He put his full weight behind his arms, both of them now. The barrier continued to advance on him. He watched it swallow a step, then another. It drove him up the stairs, steadily forcing him into retreat.

He was being herded topside.

He didn't like it, but resistance was pointless. The rising barrier resolutely impelled him up the stairs.

The only action left him was to turn and flee from the advancing stone wall. His stomping gait propelled him several steps with each footfall.

He hit a landing, rounded to the next flight of stairs—and ran right into someone. They both tumbled back and sprawled on the landing.

"Hibbs!" buzzed his earbud.

"Scarpetti?" he growled. It was the Bombshell. "What are you doing here? I told you to—"

"It's gone!" she responded. Flailing, she crawled from on top of Hibbs. "It chased me away—"

"What are talking about?" he snapped a her.

And then he saw.

Another solid wall of stone was descending the stairs. The Private hadn't abandoned her post, she'd been driven off by an impassable obstacle... exactly like the one that had forced him up the stairs.

Exactly like the one that forced me up here...

Scrambling to his feet, Hibbs peered down the lower flight of steps. The barrier that had chased him off was still there, still coming.

"Oh shit!" he gasped.

He staggered back, collided with Scarpetti.

"We have to flee downstairs," she insisted.

"Can't," grunted Hibbs. "There's—"

Scarpetti pushed past him—and came to a halt at the edge of the landing. She wailed, "There's another one blocking the stairs!"

She retreated from the rising barrier until she bumped into Hibbs. "There's no way out!" she moaned.

If they had plasma rifles, they might have been able to blast their way out of this trap... but Hibbs' batteries had been drained long ago, expended uselessly against the ghost panther. And being a Private, Scarpetti hadn't been issued a plasma weapon. The pair had explosives, but any detonation in this confined space was liable to kill the Marines, too.

"We're really screwed this time," screamed the Bombshell.

The upper wall reached the landing first. It continued unabated, gradually, steadily moving along, swallowing the floor, the side walls, the ceiling. There was no visible disturbance to mark its progression. The walls didn't crumble as the barrier came on, they disappeared behind it, seamlessly, impossibly.

The lower barrier climbed to the landing and kept coming.

If the walls continued to advance, they were going to crush the soldiers between them. Hibbs and Scarpetti were running out of room. The barriers marched in on them, pressing them back-to-back. Within seconds, both of them were fighting back, pushing against the advancing walls.

A wild impulse made Hibbs shout, "Go ahead—kill us—you'll only spare us any more torment—"

Rushing in, the walls engulfed them.

And they spilled into the most astounding hallucination yet.

The gray corridor of the stairwell landing was gone, replaced by a day-lit pasture. Trees, grass, a blue sky peppered with wispy white clouds. The meadow rippled as a soft breeze rolled across the landscape. In the distance, lively birds flittered among the verdant foliage.

Laying where he'd fallen, Hibbs gawked at this extraordinary apparition. At his side, the Bombshell did the same.

It took a few moments for either of them to verbalize their shock. They'd been staring death in the face. They'd fully expected to be crushed to a pulp between the advancing walls. A transformation from that death-trap into a terrestrial pasture had stunned the pair of Marines.

"What the hell—" growled Hibbs.

"Holy shit!" exclaimed Scarpetti.

Hibbs looked around. Pastures and woods as far as he could see; blue skies above. All trace of Eiger base had vanished.

"This is another delusion, right?" Scarpetti gasped. "I mean, this can't be real... it has to be an..." The Bombshell's voice trailed off, wonder deadening her ability to rationalize.

"If this is a delusion," Hibbs remarked, "it's mighty widespread. All of the others were limited to phantoms moving about in the real world—but this..." He shook his head, momentarily unwilling to finish his statement. But he had to: "This is an entire environment onto itself. And a remarkably detailed one at that." Each blade of grass was perfectly defined; there were even insects scuttling about in the dirt.

"Is this supposed to be an attack?"

"All the other hallucinations were hostile," Hibbs reminded her. "So we should assume this one is no different."

"What—" Scarpetti released a burst of near-hysterical laughter. "You expect the trees to try to eat us? Look at this place—it's beautiful!"

Few locations were left on Earth which could claim beauty like this. Overpopulation had spread concrete towers everywhere, forcing nature into scarce wildlife preserves. Not to mention: the sky hadn't been that color for over half a century. It *was* beautiful... and that worried Hibbs all the more.

"Look," chirped Scarpetti. She pointed to their right.

A trickle of smoke rose from beyond the woods.

"A settlement," grunted Hibbs.

"Or a forest fire."

The Bombshell's mounting hysteria was clouding her outlook with negativity. Hibbs needed to distract her, to find her something to do— otherwise the woman would lose it.

"Let's check it out." Hibbs started off in that direction.

"Wo!" she yelled. "We could get lost in the woods." She peered around with sudden fear. "Panthers can hide in the woods."

"It's too beautiful for panthers," announced Hibbs. "Besides—what else are we going to do? Stand around and wait for all this to fade away?"

"That's not a bad idea..."

Hibbs snorted at her reticence. "C'mon."

After a moment, she scurried after him.

Together, their boots swishing through the tall grass, the soldiers crossed the meadow.

25

The noisy surf woke Dr. Holmes.

Sitting up, Amelia ogled at the ocean. The ground was soft and loose beneath her; lifting her hands she stared at the sand that trickled through her fingers. The salty air stung in her nostrils. Overhead hung an azure sky unlike any she'd ever seen.

This has to be a dream, she told herself.

The last thing she remembered was vomiting. The corpses scattered throughout the Eiger base had been too much for her. It hadn't just been the sight of dead bodies, *that* she could've handled. What had ultimately empowered her nausea had been the corpses' mutilated condition. To her, murder was abhorrent enough, but the atrocities visited upon these bodies had been *inhuman*. None of her analytical resolve had kept her from being sick. She had thrown up. She'd swooned. And in the end, one of the soldiers had escorted her back to a room on the base's residential level. There, the soldier—Private Scarpetti—had been forced to sedate Amelia.

I'm sleeping... so this is just a dream...

A pleasant dream, too. Some kind of self-generated psychological reward for her recent horrific experiences.

How much of what she remembered was real? Much of it seemed so preposterous—could all of it be just another dream, a nightmare that had preceded this one. Maybe she had fallen asleep in the military shuttle en route to the Moon, and her anxious expectations for reaching the Eiger facility and seeing the extraterrestrial artifact they had unearthed had spawned this horrific nightmare in her slumbering mind.

Lying back on the beach and squinting at the noon sky, she decided to not kill her buzz with such worries. She was going to relax and enjoy this pleasant dream while it lasted. The sun was warm on her face. Her muscles unbunched. She nestled into the beach's sandy embrace. She felt her tension evaporate away.

Entranced by the tranquillity of these somnambulant environs, her mind wandered. The discovery of an alien spacecraft would change everything, not just for her but for mankind, too. Humanity would finally know they were not alone in the universe; they could abandon their arrogant egocentricity and join a galactic commune of civilizations. And Amelia would be at the forefront of this fantastic new age. She would reap fame and glory—but more importantly her belief in extraterrestrial intelligence would be vindicated. She had spent so much energy striving to convince the world that she was right, a difficult endeavor armed as she'd been with only ancient rumors and farfetched extrapolation. All those who had scoffed at her eccentric dedication would be forced to admit their mistake. Their narrow-minded arrogance would pale before the facts, and Amelia Holmes would rise to prominence as a voice of authority. After so many years of being the butt of everyone's pity and scorn, she desperately coveted this respect.

Something made her open her eyes. The sky was still there, blue and clear and full of wispy clouds. Impossibly blue, impossibly clear, full of clouds that were wispy instead of muddy with a hundred years of toxic pollution.

She sat up and an ocean spread before her. A languid surf carried waves toward the shoreline. The beach around her was white and clean, no rubbish, no trash.

There should be shantytowns, Amelia thought. *Where are all the people? The sea shouldn't be an open expanse, it should be crowded with industrial platforms. And the sky—I shouldn't even be able to* see *the sky.*

This wasn't the Earth, at least not the Earth she knew.

Twisting around, she peered behind her. The beach stretched up to a bundle of scrub—no, it wasn't scrub—the vegetation was green and healthy. Beyond this shrubbery lay woods, robust trees topped with mounds of leafy growth. Amelia's breath caught in her throat as she saw birds and animals dispersed throughout the scenery. Suddenly she became aware that the air around her wasn't empty. A fog surrounded her, but it wasn't a cloud of noxious chemicals. Each particle was moving, buzzing randomly about. They were alive—insects!

Something moved beyond this immediate cloud. Her eyes refocused and she saw that the forest wasn't a solid wall at the edge of the sandy beach. There was an opening, a clearing where the foliage didn't grow as thick as elsewhere. A man stood in this gap in the woods. His garb was strange… but then everything around her was strange.

The man lifted an arm and waved it above his head.

She waved back.

The man took a step toward her—and he came apart. It was an odd coming apart. His limbs didn't detach, his clothing didn't tear, his flesh didn't flake away. A more accurate description was: his body separated into small colorful pieces that fluttered into the air.

Butterflies! she realized. She'd seen pictures of them in old textbooks. A species of insect… that had been extinct since before she was born.

Her amazement took on a horrified edge as each one of the butterflies burst into flames. In seconds the beautiful swarm was gone.

The terrible immolation brought Amelia scrambling to her feet. She ran across the beach, screaming incoherent denial. But when she arrived at the clearing, there were no traces of the man, nor of the butterfly swarm.

No, that was imprecise. There were *traces*. A set of footprints showed where someone had stepped from the woods, but the barefoot impressions in the dirt ended at the edge of the beach… as if the person had ceased to exist… or had been whisked away into the air. Amelia scanned the sky, but saw nothing hovering up there except impossibly clean clouds. At her feet were more *traces*. Tiny smudges of ash… as if a swarm of small airborne things had been incinerated and their ashes had fallen to the ground.

"They *were* real!" she told herself. "I saw them! The man waved… and then he turned into butterflies… that burned up…"

Listen to yourself, girl. Do you realize how preposterous that sounds? Of course you do, or you wouldn't be questioning any of this.

This had to be a dream. How could anything in a dream be real? Yet, she knew the man had been real, not some dreamscape character.

Now you're just talking crazy. How can he have been real if this is a dream? Even I'm not real here. All of this is a figment of my sleeping mind…

Her perspective was far too rational to cope with this quandary. Amelia lived by scientific logic. Everything was explainable. Anything that wasn't explainable was simply fantasy. Her dreams were whimsies of her head; nothing in them was real.

Conflicting synapses confounded her and panic set it.

She plunged into the woods, following the trail that led off from the clearing.

Her fervor petered out faster than she would've expected. She'd barely run twenty meters before she found herself staggering. Depleted of stamina, the majority of her hysteria bled off into the humid afternoon air. Falling against a tree, she dug her fingers into its craggy bark to keep herself aloft. Her grip failed and she sank to her knees. A sob escaped her lips.

I should never have left the beach...

The placid beach with its warm sand and salty breezes, but that refuge was lost to her. There was no turning back. No do-overs. No reprises... only reprisals.

Better than anyone else, Amelia knew her personal history was littered with bad decisions.

She'd spent six grueling years studying an administrative curriculum. Her ambition had been to land a corporate position that promised lucrative promotion options. But when the time came, she chose to work for SETI... all because she had wanted to please Gregory.

Handsome Gregory had been another misstep on Amelia's life path. He'd been so dashing, so smooth. Unable to resist his charms, she'd given herself completely to Gregory, body and soul, ultimately allowing his interests to supplant her own goals. It was Gregory's preoccupation that mankind was not alone in the universe... so it became hers. She studied the myths of extraterrestrial contact until she became an expert in such alleged encounters. Upon graduation, she had abandoned her corporate aspirations and had used her economics doctorate to seek employment with SETI. A month later, Gregory had run off with a waitress.

Suddenly alone, Amelia had made her next bad decision and had thrown herself into her job with an all-consuming passion. The promotions she had dreamt of as a college student had been realized, but they'd lacked the high salaries and luxury perks. Instead, all she'd reaped had been the estrangement of family and friends, none of whom could comprehend her new beliefs. Her dedication had earned her the reputation of an adroit negotiator. Her contacts had spread through the strata of high society and government officials. A pity the things she'd negotiated for had been held in such public scorn.

When SETI had detected the Eiger base's distress call, Amelia had been quick to seize the opportunity and bully her way into a rescue mission. She'd coveted the chance to be part of the discovery of evidence that might certify the existence of intelligent extraterrestrial life. Another faulty decision.

If there'd never been a Gregory, Amelia Holmes wouldn't be here now. It was *his* fault she was stranded on the Moon, infected by an alien contagion and wallowing in a fever dream.

When I wake up, she lamented, *I'll still be trapped in Eiger base, still be contaminated and delusional.* Staying here in the dream seemed less stressful.

Crawling her way to her feet, Amelia wiped the tears from her face, straightened her borrowed clothing. She lifted her head to start off along the woodland trail—and gasped.

A man stood among the shrubbery. A half-naked man. As she gaped, he stepped out from behind a tree. He wore a breechcloth. A knife and a small pouch dangled from a string looped around his waist. His skin was bronzed by the sun. His facial features were flat, angular. He stared at her with stoic curiosity. His hair was jet black; it fell from his scalp in twin braids that reached all the way to his well-defined pectorals. A necklace of what appeared to be animal teeth hung on that sculpted chest.

An American Indian?

Before Amelia could pursue that awestruck train of thought, a loud sound rang through the woods. A gunshot.

Dread tied a knot in her throat. Gunfire meant violence. Violence would inevitably lead to death.

Dammit—why does my dream have to be filled with death?

Pushing past the Indian, Amelia stumbled along the trail. Although she knew this was another bad decision, she ran in the direction of the shot.

26

If Sergio stopped and thought about it, the collapse of the excavation chamber seemed rather extreme. He'd only used two bricks of C4 to destroy the regathering pieces of the super-zombie. He was no expert on the structural strength of lunar rock, but really... that certainly didn't seem enough to bring down the whole cavern.

But Sergio didn't have the time to stop and think about such factors. He was caught in the collapse and needed to dodge the boulders falling about him. His armor would protect him from the smaller debris, but some of the chunks raining down around him could do him serious damage. He needed to be spry and alert—focused. There was no time to question reality.

Besides, Riccardo was also trapped in the cave-in. As if Sergio didn't already have his hands full, now he had to rescue his stupid brother. Considering the severe rubble that tumbled down around him, Sergio seriously doubted his ability to save even himself.

None of which stopped Sergio from scrambling to Riccardo's rescue. His mind could examine circumstances and evaluate consequences all it wanted, but duty drove Surge into motion. He wormed his way through the bulky downfall, crawling at points where rubble had already piled high to block his progress. His entire psyche was devoted to getting him safely through the collapse—so he could grab his brother and drag him all the way back through the bedlam to reach the shaft. The shaft was the only way out of here.

If only Riccardo would use his head and come to meet Sergio half-way. But no, Riccardo was too lazy, too pampered, too cowardly, too dependent on others for his own survival.

When he finally caught sight of his brother, Sergio was barely meters away from the half-buried spacecraft. Riccardo crouched in the open hatch, waving him on.

"C'mere, you fool!" Sergio broadcast on his suit's external speakers. "Let's get out of here!"

Riccardo just urged him closer.

Maybe he can't hear me over the ruckus...

By now, the rockfall had accumulated in the cavern. The rubble was piled so high it buried nearly the scaffolding. Dodging additional falling chunks of rock, Sergio clambered up to the hatch.

He tried to grab Riccardo, but his twin pulled back, retreating into the alien ship.

"No!" Sergio yelled. "Get back here, you idiot!"

But Riccardo was gone. The only way Sergio was going to get him now was to go in after him.

"Damn you!" he cursed.

It was too late to go back through the collapsing cavern. He'd never make it to the shaft before the rubble covered it. Even the servos in his suit wouldn't help him dig his way through that much tonnage of rock. He was trapped where he was. And within minutes he, too, would be buried under the deluge of boulders.

Unacceptable as it was, there was only one way to survive this present crisis. *Take shelter inside the ship.* He rankled at the notion of using the alien saucer as a sanctuary. His prior visit to its inscrutable depths had left him with an intrinsic aversion for ever going in there again. But he really had no choice—it was go inside or die.

Making matters worse: his armor and his suit would have to be shed, for his gear was too cumbersome to fit through the small Gray-scaled entry hatch. He would be near-naked, exposed to whatever weirdness lurked within the profane vessel.

If I'm going to do it, I'd better do it now. The cavern's collapse wasn't going to wait for Sergio to conquer his loathing. Stripping off his armor and suit took time—if he didn't hurry, the cave-in would bury the hatch before he was small enough to fit through it.

Oh God, he fumed. *I hate this place!*

Now that he was safe inside the alien spacecraft, Sergio started to question the wisdom of his impulsive actions. As the rubble built up and buried the entry hatch, he realized this was no more than a temporary sanctuary. Safety in here would only last as long as the air trapped in the spacecraft. He—and idiot Riccardo—were entombed in the ship, deep beneath the lunar surface. There was no way out.

He couldn't even comm for help. His transmitter was outside, crushed under all that rock. Anyway, he knew from experience that comm signals wouldn't penetrate the saucer's alien hull.

He had no illusions that Hibbs and the rest of the squad could dig him out. Even with the Major's help (and that'd be one highly unlikely alliance, all things considered), there were only five of them. They lacked the brawn and the tools to re-excavate the collapsed cavern.

He was trapped in here with his stupid brother and whatever monsters waited to make matters worse.

I'm screwed, he grumbled. *But—before I go down, I'm going to get some answers. And I know exactly what my first question's going to be.*

Poking his head out of the alien airlock, Sergio spotted his brother down the circumference tunnel. Riccardo waved to him.

"What the hell are you doing here?" Sergio shouted.

Instead of replying, Riccardo used gestures to implore him to follow him down the corridor.

"No," snapped Sergio. "Whatever you want to show me can wait. First I want some answers. Are you really Riccardo? Or just another delusion?"

"I could ask you the same thing," Riccardo retorted. "What the hell are *you* doing here?"

For a while, it was an existential standoff. Neither Denk could accept the other's presence here. One of them *had* to be a hallucination, for they both knew *they* were real.

Sergio was forced to explain that a squad of Global Marines had been dispatched to discover why this research base had gone dark. Sergio Denk had been among that group of soldiers.

"I came here with Moss," exclaimed Riccardo. "That crazy prospector drove all the way out into uncharted territory, but he wasn't looking for a score—he was hunting his dead family. I came into the base to escape him. If I'd known what lay in here, I'd've stayed on the surface—asphyxiation would be better than this place's madness!"

Only after comparing intimate childhood tales did the two Denks convince each other that both of them were real.

"Why didn't you let me rescue you?" Sergio remonstrated his twin. "Now we're trapped in here."

"I can't leave the ship."

"What?"

"She won't let me!" blurted Riccardo. "You have to save me, Lucy."

"Don't call me that," Sergio snapped. Only Riccardo had ever called him that, and he'd never liked the nickname. "She who?"

"She won't tell me her name!"

"You don't mean Dr. Holmes…"

"Who's that?"

"The woman you assaulted earlier. Remember? You'd strapped her to that alien torture chair. I stopped you from doing something to her."

"That was you…? *You* stopped me…"

"Yes, that was me, not some hallucination."

Riccardo sobbed to his brother. "You stopped me! Thank you! I couldn't stop myself—her cat forced me to attack that woman."

"Cat? You mean the panther."

"Panther—ha!" Riccardo expelled a coarse laugh. "It wants you to see it that way—but that form is a sham—a disguise!" He was ranting. "The thing is just a cat—a small black cat!"

"Easy, Ricky," Sergio spoke softly to calm him down.

"But the beast is *more* than that!" Riccardo hissed with fevered urgency. "So damned much more! It's a devil—a demon from hell!"

That damned panther brings the crazy out in everybody, reflected Sergio. *Something about the creature scares everybody to the breaking point. Even me.*

Throwing an obviously fearful glance at their murky surroundings, Riccardo clutched at Sergio. "This passage is too accessible We need to hide… or it will find us." He pulled Sergio along the corridor.

Rather than pique Riccardo's mania, Sergio let himself be dragged deeper into the alien spacecraft than he really wanted to go. As he joined his twin in flight, Sergio caught glimpses of some of the ship's chambers.

A honeycomb of massive proportion covered the walls of one room. Each cell was large enough to fit a full-grown dog. But wait, the aliens were small… they might've fit into those honeycomb pods. Was this some sort of sleeping barracks?

Another room featured a conglomeration of tubes, all tangled into a knotted morass that filled the compartment.

While another chamber was filled with large flat slabs that jutted from the walls at erratic angles, forming an angular maze through which no one, human nor Gray, could have squeezed. At first Sergio suspected these slabs might contain machinery, perhaps even the storage medium for the ship's computer systems. But then he saw that one was broken, presumably by the Eiger scientists during their examination of the saucer's interiors, and that broken stump revealed that the slab had a solid core of inert matter. Sergio couldn't begin to imagine how a machine could function without internal mechanics.

Eventually Riccardo brought them to a tiny room, little more than a glorified niche, where he apparently believed they might be safe from detection.

"Did I hurt your Dr. Holmes?" Riccardo was suddenly lucid. "I didn't want to do any of that—the damned cat forced me!" But just as quickly he degenerated into frightened babble. "You have to believe me—I would never hurt anybody—" He flung himself on Sergio, his arms clasping the two estranged siblings together.

"She's okay," Sergio assured his trembling twin. "I stopped you before you hurt her."

For a moment, Riccardo sobbed against Sergio's chest.

Then Sergio probed, "What did the cat want you to do to her?"

"It wanted her body—"

"You mean in a sexual way?" Sergio couldn't picture the panther having any carnal impulses toward a human female.

"No—it wanted to take her soul—so her body would be empty—"

"Empty for what?"

"For *her!*"

"Her… the same her you mentioned before… Is she the beast's master?"

"She calls it her familiar."

"Like a witch's familiar?"

Riccardo nodded spastically against his brother.

Sergio tried to suppress an anxious sigh. Without question, Riccardo was infected. The madness had utterly warped his outlook. He was seeing witches and monsters… just the same way the squad was seeing panthers and zombies.

The problem was: the panther and the zombies were physical delusions. They'd already proven their capacity for causing trouble. Did that mean that Riccardo's witch was another hallucination given flesh?

Sergio threw a wary glance at the slanted corridor beyond their hiding place.

As if I didn't already have enough to worry about…

27

They tracked the smoke to its origin: a rustic cabin's chimney.

From the safety of the woods, Corporal Hibbs studied the settlement. Five cabins were clustered in a clearing. The structures were primitive, their walls comprised of logs held together with dried mud. This crude architecture marked them as pre-industrial constructions. While goats and chickens roamed freely near these abodes, there was no sign of the settlement's human inhabitants.

An assortment of agrarian artifacts were scattered around the cabins. One, a stone wheel mounted in an upright frame, might have been a device to sharpen blades. Most of the stuff was so primitive that few modern people might have been able to fathom their purpose.

As a child in Gettysburg, Jack Hibbs had grown up surrounded by an antediluvian military presence. Several locales in the region had been preserved as historic monuments. Consequently young Hibbs had developed a fascination with the American Civil War. Back then there'd been no electricity, no cars, no solar heating, no indoor plumbing, no internet, no stem cell medical procedures. Life had been hard and being a soldier in those colonial days had entailed legitimate valor. His keen interest in the military had sprung from those studies and ultimately had led him to enlist as a Global Marine in his early twenties.

Although rustic and primitive, this settlement didn't seem all that strange to Hibbs. This was, he knew, the way people had lived in those ancient times. From a flintlock rifle propped beside a doorway, he guessed this tableau might belong to an era older than the 1860s.

He had to wonder from what remote corner of his brain this scenario had been dredged. But then, if it had been derived from his memories, it should have been a Civil War setting. Could it have come from the Bombshell's mind?

198

"Is this place familiar to you, Private?"

"Hell no," she snorted back at him. "Why should it be?"

It had to come from somewhere. The delusions couldn't be concocting themselves... could they? No, there had to be some force behind all this, some conscious influence dedicated to tormenting the soldiers.

"It's ancient, isn't it?"

He nodded, then realized she wasn't looking at him to see his physical response. She stared with utter fascination at the cabins; and probably a little touch of disgust, too. To a gutter-brat like her, this settlement must have seemed prehistoric, something built by Neanderthals.

"Very old," he commed to her. "Two, three centuries..."

"Why did you think it was familiar to me?"

He saw no point in explaining his confusion. She barely believed in the hallucinations in the first place. Applying deductive reasoning to them would be a joke to her. He chuckled to himself. It was a waste of time trying to analyze any of this.

You're never going to understand any of this, he chided himself. *That's why they call insanity—it has no rhyme or reason.*

His job, Corporal Hibbs had to remind himself, was to keep the base quarantined... for as long as he could. Sooner or later, the madness would overwhelm him and he would no longer be capable of responsible deliberation or action. Then the burden would be somebody else's worry.

Until then, he had to keep a clear head and insure his survival.

Which brought him back to their immediate circumstances. *What should we do? Do we investigate this settlement? Or avoid it like the plague?* His choice of words made him wince. Unintentional or not, he didn't like being reminded of the root of their problems.

"If people live here, where are they?" muttered Scarpetti.

"There's smoke coming from that cabin's chimney," Hibbs pointed out, "so *somebody* has to be around." Caution was called for, at least until they determined whether the settlement's inhabitants were friendly or not. But then, so far all the other delusions had been hostile. There was no reason to expect this one would be any different.

"Although I guess it doesn't really matter," she remarked caustically. "After all, none of this real."

"It's real for us." He really wished she would drop this rigorous pessimism and remember she was a Marine.

She shrugged. "That's your opinion, sir. Not mine."

"It was real enough for Green. And Danford, too."

Her eyes narrowed. He'd hit a nerve; he wondered which one.

"If there *are* people here," Hibbs mused, "maybe they can provide us with some answers."

"And if they attack us?"

"Eh?"

"What do we do if they attack us, sir?"

What difference does it make to you, girl? You don't believe any of this is real.

"Attack us with what, Private? Wooden sticks and antique flintlocks? Put a little more faith in your battle armor."

He led the way, edging out of the woods. She followed.

They'd barely stepped from the shrubbery when the door of the cabin with the smoking chimney swung open. A dazzling light spilled from the abode's interior.

Hibbs halted, immediately wary. What could be inside the cabin that would outshine the noon sun?

The answer burst forth and dashed across the yard. It was a man—and he was on fire! His wail filled the afternoon air. He thrashed as he ran, waving his aflame limbs above his head. As he drew near, Hibbs could see the flesh melting from his face.

A loud *crack* momentarily drowned out the burning man's outcries—in fact, the noise put an end to his agonized yelling.

In midstep the burning man spun about as if hit by something. Then he crumpled spread-eagle in the dirt. The flames continued to dance from his now-inert body.

"What the hell happened?" snapped Hibbs.

The Bombshell grunted, "I shot him."

"Why?"

"He was attacking us, sir."

"He was on fire!"

"He could've been a suicide attacker," she grumbled.

My God, she really has turned into Private Slaughter.

"We'll never know now..." muttered Hibbs as he nudged the smoldering carcass with his boot. He had to wonder: *Why was the man burning in the first place?* Had he set himself aflame? Was he indeed a suicide assailant? Or had someone else set him on fire?

But when he went to look, the cabin was empty of anyone else. It was a one-room interior, with a primitive kitchen sink, wooden cabinets, and a rustic dining table on the left, a rickety bed on the right. Unless the firestarter had fled through one of the unpaned windows, the burning man had ignited himself.

"Hibbs!"

He stepped back outside. Her urgent tone had brought his rifle into his hands. "What?" And then there was no reason for her to reply. The reason for her agitation was plain to see, impossible though it was.

At first it looked as if the burning corpse was melting, but then Hibbs realized that the black stain oozing across the dirt wasn't a liquid—it was a swarm of ants! He stared, aghast and confounded. Soon the ants had dispersed, leaving behind only a scorched humanoid-shaped patch on the ground to mark that a body had been there.

"What the hell—" he gasped.

"I don't like this place," muttered Scarpetti. "I want to wake up now..."

"I hate to break it to you, Private," spoke a new voice, "but this isn't your dream."

Recognizing the voice, Hibbs advised the Bombshell to stand down. He lowered his own weapon and looked about for Dr. Holmes.

The Doc emerged from an opening in the woods. She was dressed in the baggy jumpsuit Marshall had found for her, but her attire was damp, as if the woman had gone wading in it. Her appearance in this ancient history tableau was surprising enough, but walking along beside her was a half-naked man. His dark features and primitive attire identified him as an American Indian. What was Dr. Holmes doing in the company of an indigenous inhabitant of this era?

Hibbs had to order Scarpetti to lower her weapon again. She'd raised it and brought it to bear on the Indian as soon as the man had stepped into view. Killing the burning man had left Private Slaughter trigger-happy. She was ready to shoot anything.

"What's she doing here?" complained Scarpetti.

"Why do you think I'm here?" the Doc laughed. "It's *my* dream."

"It's *nobody's* dream," asserted Corporal Hibbs. "This is real—as real as any of the other delusions have been."

"I heard a shot," Dr. Holmes remarked. "What happened?"

Hibbs gave a snort. "Private Scarpetti overreacted to a bit of weirdness." He strode over to confront the Doc and her companion.

"What do you mean it isn't a dream?" whined the Doc. "I'm asleep in a room on the residential level. The Private gave me a sedative."

"We're *not* sleeping, Dr. Holmes." Hibbs made a gesture that included himself and Private Scarpetti who'd come up to stand beside him. "A nasty bout of weirdness brought us here."

"But…" She shook her head. "I woke up on the beach…"

"Who's your friend, Doc?" he inquired.

The Indian cocked his head and gave the Corporal an inscrutable look, as if he knew Hibbs was talking about him.

"I met him in the woods… on my way here." Her explanation was dismissive, as if the matter had no real significance. She was peering beyond the soldiers.

Great, Hibbs mentally sighed. *Private Slaughter doesn't believe any of this is real—and the Doc thinks it a dream. I wonder what the Indian's opinion is…*

"This is a settlement!" Dr. Holmes exclaimed. "I thought it was all wilderness…"

"You recognize this place?" asked Hibbs.

"No… not specifically. But it's obviously a settlement of some kind, albeit an old one."

"But you're familiar with places like this," he probed.

"Only from history texts…"

Aha, Hibbs grunted to himself. *So the culprit behind all this plucked this scenario from your brain.*

"Is there anything significant about this settlement?" He urged her to examine the cabins.

As she moved off to study the rustic structures, the Indian caught Hibbs' attention. The brown man swung his arm in an elevated sweep that encompassed the cluster of cabins. He spoke, "Roanoke." His voice was husky, extremely masculine.

Hibbs arched an eyebrow. "You speak English."

"English, yes." He lifted his hand and held his thumb and fingers a few centimeters apart. "Little."

How convenient, reflected Hibbs.

"Where are the people?"

"All dead," announced the Indian. A frown furrowed his noble brow. "Witch."

"A witch killed them."

The Indian nodded gravely.

"A witch…" Hibbs puckered his lips with skepticism. "You mean a woman who can do magic spells—that kind of a witch." He wanted to confirm the Indian's grasp of the specific terminology.

"Witch and her devil cat."

A cat—the panther?

Before he could inquire about this feline coincidence, Dr. Holmes approached to inform him that she saw nothing out of the ordinary about the settlement. "Besides the absence of any settlers, that is," she qualified her assessment.

"All dead," the Indian insisted. "Burned by witch."

"Burned?" grunted Hibbs.

"I saw a burning man," Dr. Holmes declared. "On the beach. He turned into butterflies and they burned up as they flew away."

Hibbs tried to ignore the Doc's contribution to the ongoing weirdness, but before he could speak Scarpetti blurted out, "There was a burning man here too!" She pointed to the spread-eagle char mark in the clearing. "He melted into a swarm of ants that crawled off."

"All burned by witch," expounded the Indian.

"A what?" the Doc piped.

"Everybody calm down," insisted Corporal Hibbs. "We're finally getting some answers here." Not that they were rational answers. He addressed the Indian, "This witch had a cat? A black cat? A big black cat? A black panther, maybe?"

The Indian treated Hibbs to a perplexed look. "Little cat."

"What are you babbling about?" cried Dr. Holmes. "Witches and black cats—are you crazy? Witches aren't real—"

"Neither is any of this," the Bombshell muttered. With her overall disbelief in these circumstances, she was content to stand back and watch the others embroil themselves in the latest fantasy.

"As long as we're *here*," countered Corporal Hibbs, "we're subject to this place's conditions. It might be helpful for us to understand the local rules."

"But—*witches*—?" the Doc protested.

"A witch is no stranger than ghost panthers and zombies," he reminded her. "I mean, look at us! One minute we're in an underground lunar installation—the next we're in a colonial American settlement from a few hundred years ago. We left the realm of sanity behind us when we got infected."

"Ride it out," suggested Scarpetti. "That's what I'm going to do. You mentioned a beach? That sounds nice. I'd like to get out of this suit and stretch out on a nice sandy beach, catch a few rays, relax. Sooner or later we'll all find ourselves back in Eiger base. We might as well take advantage of this delusion." She turned away from them. "Is it this way? This path leads to the beach?"

"You're not going anywhere," barked Corporal Hibbs. "We need to stay together."

"Why?" she scoffed. "It's all a big elaborate hallucination."

"Dammit—remember what happened to Green and Danford," he replayed his earlier remark. It had the same stifling effect on the girl, throwing doubt across her sultry features. "Get back here. You want something to do? Check the perimeter, Private, Be on the lookout for the panther. Panthers like to hide in the woods, *remember*?" His added jab sent her scuffling off in a surly mood.

The Doc was arguing with the Indian. "You're just a superstitious savage! There's no such thing as witches!"

Elbowing her away, Hibbs confronted the Indian. "Where is the witch now?"

The Indian gestured around them. "Here."

"Hiding in the woods?" Hibbs pointed at the trees.

The Indian expanded his gesture until it included the entire environment. "All here."

"She conjured all this," guessed Hibbs. He mirrored the Indian's gesture. "Witch made all this?

The Indian nodded.

Hibbs was getting information, but none of it made any sense. How could a witch be to blame for their predicament?

Scarpetti walked up and asked, "What's 'croatoan' mean?"

"Eh?"

"Somebody carved the word into a tree over there." She gestured to the woods.

"What was the word?" gasped Dr. Holmes. She didn't wait for an answer, but scurried over to investigate the trees for herself. "Oh my God," she eventually squealed. "It *is* 'croatoan.' That's incredible…"

"What's the matter?" Hibbs called to the woman.

She waved them over to show them all what she'd found. The bark of one tree had been scarred by a blade. Someone had carved the word "croatoan" in the wood.

"So?" grunted Hibbs. "What's it mean?"

The Indian thumped his palm on his bare chest. "Name of my tribe."

She babbled, "This place isn't imaginary—it's real… or at least it was… back on Earth in the 1580s—…"

"Want to share something with us, Doc?"

She wandered off, gazing with fascination at the cabins. "That's why there's no settlers—they're all gone."

"Burned by witch," insisted the Indian.

Paying no attention to the savage's remark, she continued: "This place was an ancient American settlement! Sir Walter Raleigh made three attempts to establish a British colony on an island on the coast of North Carolina in the mid-16th Century. All of them failed. The third one—all the people vanished! Nobody knows why. A supply ship arrived after being away for a few years—it was delayed by British bureaucracy—and they found the settlement empty... no bodies... no sign of violence... meals on the table..." She turned to face the soldiers and declared in a voice tinged by more than a little hysteria (or was it fanaticism?), "Everyone disappeared, men and women and even a few children, including Virginia Dare, the first British child born on American soil—and nobody knows what happened to them! The lost Roanoke colony is a famous unsolved historical mystery!"

Hibbs jerked a thumb in the Indian's direction. "That's what he called it—Roanoke."

"For a long time, people thought 'croatoan' was a clue to what happened to the missing colonists, but it turned out to be just the name of a local native tribe. The Croatoans weren't to blame—in fact, they were friendly, helped the colonists cope with the wilderness."

Hibbs nodded. From his knowledge of early American history, he was familiar with how the government had tried to vilify Native American Indians, casting them as villains who preyed on early American settlers—when in truth the Indians had been the victims of the white man's dogma of manifest destiny. It took hundreds of years before history would correct this inaccuracy and vindicate the Indians as a peaceful people abused by white greed.

"The lost Roanoke colony..." Dr. Holmes was hyperventilating. "This is amazing! We're on Earth—five hundred years in the past!"

"So... why are we here?" Hibbs pondered aloud. "What connection is there between this Roanoke colony and the Eiger lunar base?" They were getting closer to some kind of explanation, irrational as it might seem. Hibbs could feel it. But a profound bit of information was still missing. *Ha*, he thought, *There's more than a single crucial factor missing from this puzzle, the gaps are big enough to drive a truck through.*

"Get a grip, Egghead," Scarpetti chided the Doc. "We're on the Moon, not Earth. It's 2098, not the 1580s."

"How do you explain all this?" rebuked Dr. Holmes.

"*This*," the Bombshell laughed at her, "is just a delusion instigated by the—" She never got the chance to finish her declaration.

Bursting from the woods came a swarm of people, all of them ablaze and screaming. Flames leapt from their flailing arms to the leafy boughs. The conflagration spread briskly among the trees. Within seconds, half of the clearing's circumference was a raging inferno.

Hibbs' battle reflexes immediately kicked in. He dove to shield Dr. Holmes from the fiery mob's charge. His armor would protect him, her jumpsuit would not do the same for the woman.

Private Slaughter's instincts were quick to spur her to action, too. She abandoned cajoling the Doc and brought her rifle to bear on the mob. Her shots shredded a portion of the burning human tide.

A number of the survivors converged on the Indian. He tried to fight them off, but there were too many of them. They bore him down, piling their flaming bodies on top of the man. Their flesh bubbled and oozed into a gruesomely greasy mound. The half-naked savage didn't last long beneath this human pyre.

Before fire entirely consumed the mob's clothing, Hibbs saw they were dressed in colonial garb. This fact spawned a host of puzzles. Were these the rest of the missing Roanoke settlers? Why were *they* attacking the soldiers? Much less, why had they made dispatching the imaginary Indian their priority? The Marines were the ones with the guns.

Almost by accident, Hibbs spotted the panther. He'd been scanning the woods for a possible second wave of attackers. The beast crouched amid the as-yet-unburning foliage. It watched the melee with obvious glee. When flames encroached on its position, the panther retreated from view.

It's afraid of fire, Hibbs realized.

A few ablaze stragglers took mindless refuge inside the cabins. Soon, tongues of fire were consuming the log structures.

The entire settlement was ablaze by now. The inferno had swept through the woods, encircling the squad in a ring of fire.

Scarpetti didn't relent until she'd shot each and every burning colonist. Her firepower only put them down, though, not out. The clearing was littered with figures who refused to die. They thrashed and shrieked, but no relief came to end their suffering. They continued to grope about long after their sinews had shriveled into char. The squad was surrounded by hideously animated skeletal remains.

It was only a matter of minutes before the ring of fire closed in and consumed the clearing… and everything in it.

28

Securing the base's outer hatch had been a temporary reprieve. Corporal Anne Marshall knew that, but it was the best she could do under the circumstances.

If she stayed and fought when the terrorists broke in, she'd be one against a crowd. Those seemed like suicidal odds to her, so she withdrew.

She needed to find the others. One Marine would be hard-pressed to oppose an incoming tide of invaders; three—four, if Surge had survived his encounter with the super-zombie's reanimated pieces—would change the odds. Together, they might stand a chance of repelling these invaders.

Having seen no sign of Hibbs or Scarpetti or Dr. Holmes during her search of the installation, Anne resolved to get Surge's help.

By now he should have dealt with the super-zombie's remains and rejoined her. Where was he? Had the undead monstrosity overpowered him?

I should never have let him go after the thing, she remonstrated herself.

Lost in her thoughts, Anne hurried down the stairwell half-oblivious to her surroundings. Consequently, she ran right into Moss without even seeing his threatening advance up the steps. She didn't even notice his fierce tirade until he knocked her back.

"—pay for tormenting my family—" he bellowed, "—you murderous whore—you can't deceive me—I know you're guilty—*she* told me so—"

Anne sprawled on a landing, dazed and confused.

Before she could recover, the prospector was hacking at her with a fire ax. (*Lord only knows where he got the thing.*) Luckily her armor protected Anne from his manic chopping. She pushed him away. As she struggled to regain her feet, he hit her again. Her balance was precarious; his chubby mass sent her on her ass.

She was given no opportunity to wonder how the crazed prospector had escaped from the locked room down on the base's research level.

This time, ridding herself of Moss proved to be more difficult. Although he'd lost his ax, now he assailed her with his fists and feet. He clambered on top of her, wrapped his arms and legs around her. She couldn't dislodge the mad man. He continued to yell and curse and promise to eviscerate her. He was too tightly clutching her. She couldn't squeeze between them and pry him from her.

She rolled. The maneuver smashed Moss against the wall. His pressure suit might have been shabby, but it served to cushion him from the jolt; or maybe he was too far gone by this point to feel pain. Rocking back, Anne repeated the move, again and again, until finally the impacts loosened Moss' hold on her. She quickly scrambled away from his stunned figure. This time, she got to her feet scarcely seconds before he came at her. She caught him with an elbow to the chest. This blow stopped his rush. She swiftly followed up with a shoulder butt to his torso. He staggered back from her. Before he could rally his fury, she delivered a savage kick that sent him flying from the landing. Flailing and cursing and bouncing from step to step, Moss disappeared down the stairwell.

Anne took a few seconds to gather her wits.

Then she dashed down the steps. It wasn't Moss she was worried about. When she came to the prospector's inert body. she hopped over the corpse and continued on her way. She barely noticed the man's broken helmet or the severe tilt of his head on his misshapen neck. He was nothing more to her than a troublesome obstruction.

Concern for Surge drove her down into the installation's depths.

The lift was still below. Sergio hadn't ridden it back to the laboratory level.

He's still down there, Anne fretted. *In the cavern... with the zombie.*

She jumped into the open shaft and slid down the tunnel.

The cavern was empty. She saw no sign of Surge. A small crater yawned at the base of the catwalk that led down to the cavern. The surrounding ground was stained red. She hoped this was the zombie's residue and not his.

"Surge!" she called on the comm-line.

He didn't answer. No one did.

Perhaps he'd been forced to battle it out with the reassembled zombie before blowing it up. He might have gotten wounded. He could have crawled off into a corner where he now lay unconscious.

She searched the chamber, but her hunt did not find him.

The entry hatch to the excavated alien spacecraft was sealed shut. That was how Hibbs had claimed they'd left it, locking Dr. Holmes' attacker inside the ship. Had Sergio taken shelter in there?

Shelter from what?

Her hand slid to her waist and readily hugged the grip of her revolver. She warily surveyed the region, but saw nothing. Of course she saw nothing; she'd already examined the cavern and found nobody hiding here.

Wait—if Surge had gone inside the ship, where was his armored pressure suit? The hatch was too small for him to fit through wearing that gear. Having found no discarded suit, Anne knew he wasn't in the alien saucer.

So where the hell are you?

Frustration drove Anne to conduct another thorough sweep of the base, hunting for signs of Sergio or anybody. This was starting to become a habit, scouring the base for dead hostiles or dead allies. She had mixed feelings about finding none of the latter. Okay, her comrades weren't dead—but in this place missing was no better.

She *did* find dead hostiles, though.

Shredded corpses were strewn through the higher regions of the stairwell. A trail of gore proceeded down the corridor of the recreational level, culminating in a poolside last stand. There were no survivors. In fact, there weren't enough pieces left for a mother to identify. Anne knew who they were, though, for she recognized the shards of privateer armor that were scattered among the entrails. The terrorist reinforcements had gotten past the sealed topside hatch and into the base... only to be massacred by something. Something fierce and bestial.

The panther?

Or another monstrous zombie?

She took heart that these cadavers were too minced to give her any posthumous trouble.

Moss' corpse had vanished, too, but Anne doubted the dead prospector was responsible for this widespread evisceration. His carcass had revived, but instead of coming after her, it had fled.

Fled from whatever had ripped the terrorists to pieces?

None of these findings boosted Anne's confidence.

Everybody's vanished, she bemoaned, *and left me alone with something capable of slaughtering a troop of armed terrorists.*

A shudder ran along her spine as Anne realized that her only available ally was... Major Dummheit.

No—I'm on my own...

29

The blaze got frightfully close... before it vanished in a negative flash.

"What the hell—" swore Scarpetti.

Corporal Hibbs let his arms drop from protectively encircling Dr. Holmes. He stared at the incinerated landscape, but somehow the fire's sudden disappearance didn't unduly surprise him. Death had been imminent—too imminent. But death wasn't the enemy's ulterior goal.

"She's toying with us," Hibbs muttered.

"What?" choked Dr. Holmes.

"She doesn't want to kill us," he declared. "She can't scare us if we're dead."

"What are you babbling about?" growled Scarpetti.

"That's what all this is about—terror. The witch is feeding on our fear."

"You're not buying this witch story, are you, sir?" she scoffed.

"I'm adapting to the delusion's rules, Private. As long as we're trapped here, we're subject to its conditions. So we need to act accordingly."

"You forget that all of this is an hallucination brought on by the alien contagion, Corporal," muttered Dr. Holmes. "But how can—"

"Disease-induced hallucinations or a spell cast by a witch—does it really matter which is the real delusion? Which came first, the chicken or the egg?" Hibbs flipped a who-cares hand at their surroundings. "Whether we're here in 1580s Roanoke or back in the Eiger base on the Moon in 2098—either way, we're stuck dealing with it."

"Witches are make-believe," Dr. Holmes insisted.

"*All* of this is make-believe!" scoffed the Bombshell. "Delusions in our head."

A blackened countryside surrounded them. The inferno had scorched the immediate clearing. The colonists' cremated remains blended with the singed grass. The wooded landscape had suffered more severe damage. For as far as the eye could see, the terrain had been transformed into a graveyard of charcoal monoliths. What had once been trees were now splinters rising from the charred earth. The scene was ominously surreal.

Hibbs saw no sign of the panther, but then the beast could be anywhere out there, its black pelt undetectable against the black countryside.

As lifeless as it looked, Hibbs expected that danger lurked everywhere. There was no telling how it would manifest. Logical causality was no longer in play. An attack could appear out of thin air. Or the charred trees might turn into a stampeding herd of buffalo. By now Hibbs had learned to expect the unexpected.

The others believed the danger was delusional, but he knew otherwise. The danger was all too real.

It was distracting having to worry about guarding Dr. Holmes from whatever absurdities might pop into being and throw themselves at the squad. As long as she remained vulnerable, his attention would be divided between protecting her and defending them all. So far, Private Slaughter had displayed ample battle skills, but he couldn't expect her to master each threat alone.

He began to strip off his armor.

"What the hell are you doing?" grunted the Bombshell.

Hibbs addressed Dr. Holmes, "You're going to wear my suit and armor."

"I can't—" she choked back.

"I disagree, Doc. You're going to put this suit on if I have to stuff you into it. I'll be able to better defend us if I don't have to worry about your safety."

"But then you'll be unprotected," complained Scarpetti.

"I'm a Marine. I can handle myself. She can't—she's a civilian."

"You're crazy." The Bombshell turned away to scrutinize the landscape.

Hibbs hurried the Doc into his pressure suit, then he attached the armored plates. He kept the rifle and a pair of knives, leaving her with the revolver so she had something with which to defend herself. Once the woman was securely attired, the Corporal approached Scarpetti. He assured her he would be okay.

"It's your funeral," snorted the Bombshell. "Sir."

"We're ready to roll now," Hibbs announced.

"Going where?"

He shrugged. "Good question. We could wait here for something to happen, or we can find a more defensible position to fight off whatever happens. I favor the latter."

"Your call, sir."

Scanning the horizon, Hibbs saw no trace of the beach Dr. Holmes had mentioned. He wasn't keen on the option of finding himself in a fight with the ocean at their backs. High ground would be best, but the territory appeared to be mostly flatlands. The fire had devastated the forest in every direction. The inferno had been intense, but hardly big enough to cause this much damage. Yet a forsaken vista of charred woods stretched as far he could see. The radius of the blaze was definitely unnatural.

"What's that over there?"

He peered in the direction indicated by Scarpetti's raised arm. There was something out there. Her sensory gear showed it to the girl, but it was too remote for his unaided eyes to be able to identify it as anything more than a lump in the incinerated landscape.

"It'll do," he proclaimed. He set the Bombshell on point and escorted Dr. Holmes away from the ashes of the Roanoke settlement. He stuck close to the Doc, planning to use her armor as a shield against unpleasant surprises.

Nothing bothered them as they strode across the scorched earth. For the most part, the landscape was static. Even the infrequent breezes failed to disturb the ashen remains of the forest.

The only noise other than their footfalls was the sizzling of dying embers all around them. Periodically, trees crumbled into ash. The first collapse spurred Private Slaughter to pepper the fallen tree with a volley of gunfire; she exhibited more restraint when subsequent trunks fell to pieces.

A stench of char permeated the air. Every breath Hibbs took coated his throat with soot. There was another stink lingering beneath the incinerated residue, but it was too faint, too elusive, for him to identify it.

They marched for quite a while, but the sun never moved from its zenith. Nor did their target destination get any closer. The dark hump remained on the horizon. When Hibbs glanced behind them, he discovered the charred log cabins appeared to lay only twenty meters in their wake. For all the time the squad had walked, they'd traveled only a small ways. The witch was distorting distance, he suspected.

He decided against bringing this to the attention of his companions. The news might panic the Doc, while it undoubtedly would fuel the

Bombshell's argument against doing anything. The phenomenon had to abate sooner or later. Until then, they would just forge ahead in defiance of the witch's spatial dilation spell.

It took more hours than Hibbs thought credible before they reached the hump.

A while ago he'd stripped off his undershirt and wrapped it around his head so that it draped over his shoulders, minor protection from the unmoving sun, but better than nothing. His bare feet hadn't fared well traveling across the scorched terrain. He was dehydrated and achy by the time they stood before the dark structure.

The thing was a mound of blackened branches. A stout and equally charred stake rose from the center of the pile.

"A bonfire?" grunted Scarpetti.

Hibbs muttered, "Back in colonial times, they used to burn witches, didn't they?"

"Yes," gasped Dr. Holmes. "They tied them to stakes and burned them alive."

"Okay, I'll play along," jeered the Bombshell. "So, if they burned the witch, why is she still around?"

"Excellent point," Hibbs agreed.

"Shouldn't she be dead?"

"According to the mythology," offered Dr. Holmes, "burning witches at the stake was the way to kill them."

"So—if she's dead, who's screwing with us? Her pet cat?"

"They weren't pets, they were called familiars. They were supposed to be demons, pipelines between the witch and their font of satanic power."

"You know an awful lot about witches," commented Hibbs.

"No more than average," Dr. Holmes' reply sounded defensive. "Every teenage girl goes through a phase of fascination with magic."

"I didn't," asserted the Bombshell.

"You—"

"Enough," Corporal Hibbs barked. "Let's try to focus on our current situation."

"Our current hallucination, you mean," scoffed Scarpetti.

Ignoring the Bombshell's snide attempt to reemphasize her own personal outlook, he gestured to the heap of burned sticks. "What do your sensors tell you about this?"

She gave a derisive snort. "Nothing much. It's a pile of burned branches. Carbonized cellulose, if you want to get technical."

"Any human remains?"

"No…"

"No bones."

Scarpetti paused before replying, obviously checking her scanners' readouts. "No."

"If somebody got tied to this stake and burned alive, then where are their bones?"

"Ahhh…" came Dr. Holmes' burgeoning exclamation.

"That only proves there was no witch," chirped the Bombshell.

"Don't you see what he means?" Dr. Holmes contested. "*Somebody* was burned here—that much is obvious—but there's no body."

"Yeah, well…" she grumbled. "It wasn't a witch. They don't exist."

"You're missing the Corporal's point. What happened to the burned-up body? Where is it?"

"Whoever burned them took the body away."

Hibbs sighed internally. Sometimes Scarpetti's stubbornness blinded her to the obvious. Give her something to shoot at and her aim was reliably accurate. But the girl was incapable of thinking outside the box—even when she found herself stuck outside the box.

"Why would anybody haul off a pile of charred bones?" Dr. Holmes persisted in trying to get the Bombshell to understand.

During their exchange, Hibbs had stepped back to survey the horizon. The first thing he noticed was that the settlement was gone; the torched ruins had finally moved beyond the squad's immediate vicinity, out of sight, in fact. Again, the countryside was a blackened prairie of ash punctuated by the charred remains of innumerable trees.

"Let's go," he proclaimed. No answers would be gained remaining by the pyre. It had provided the group with a respite, but now they needed to resume their trek.

While the terrain had originally appeared flat to Hibbs, time revealed that perception to be deceptive. Rolling hillocks comprised the landscape, but none of them were extreme enough to be readily apparent. In the distance (to what Hibbs presumed was the west) the horizon was gray with what he took to be mountains, probably the Appalachians. He wondered if the scorched earth stretched all the way to the mountain range.

From one hilltop, he spied a stream winding through the charred debris. He headed for it, hopeful that its water might be uncontaminated and could offer some succor from the oppressive heat of the eternal noon.

His companions showed little interest in the stream. Protected by their suits, they'd been spared dehydration. He, though, was parched and drenched with baked perspiration.

Sinking to his knees beside the stream, Hibbs scooped some of the water to his lips and tested it. The clear liquid was indeed untainted by the inferno that had consumed the countryside. He gulped the water down, relishing its crisp tang. Collecting more in his cupped hands, he splashed it on his face. At first the moisture stung his sunburnt skin. He ignored this and continued to douse himself, washing away hours of accumulated sweat from his body. If the stream had been deeper than a few centimeters, he would have jumped in and immersed himself in the refreshing liquid.

With his thirst slaked and the grime washed from his blistered skin, Hibbs rose and joined the others. During his indulgence, the Doc and the Bombshell had wandered thirty meters or so upstream. There, they loitered at the edge of a hole. Well, technically, only Dr. Holmes stood there; an indifferent Scarpetti had wandered off a bit to stare off into the blackened distance.

This pit measured three meters in diameter and descended several meters into the ground. The stream flowed into this small grotto, trickling down the rocky escarpment like a miniature waterfall. The pit must have connected with subterranean depths, for the water failed to fill the well, creating a shallow pool at the bottom of the burrow. It was an unremarkable geological formation, notable only for the fact that it deviated from the rest of the scorched landscape.

"Feel better now?" Dr. Holmes inquired of him.

"Some," he admitted.

There was something about a section of the mouth of the grotto that seemed odd to him. It took him a minute to recognize the nature of that anomaly. While the rest of the pit remained unscarred by the inferno, an area of the precipice was scorched. A chunk appeared to be missing from the rim, and upon closer examination he found that the stone seemed to have been melted away. It puzzled him, but not enough to warrant more than a moment's consideration.

He had more immediate concerns, bigger mysteries and dangerous adversaries to worry about.

Climbing a nearby rise, Hibbs surveyed the territory. Still nothing but an incinerated landscape.

No, wait—he thought he saw something, another lump in the northern distance.

"What's that?" He pointed at the far-off topological irregularity.

Dr. Holmes joined him atop the hill and squinted in the indicated direction, but Scarpetti obstinately refused to look.

"Private!" snapped Corporal Hibbs, employing his authoritative voice. "Use your suit's scanner. What is that out there?" While his own vision was augmented by implants, whatever the object was lay beyond his enhanced range. The suit's equipment was far more acute. He doubted the Doc knew how to operate Marine combat gear, so he needed Scarpetti to do it.

Grudgingly, the Bombshell trudged up the slope and peered in the designated direction. After a moment she grunted, "Something sticking out of the ground... a boulder, maybe..."

"Our next destination," he decreed.

Scarpetti was quick to complain. "How long are we going to trudge around this desolate place?"

"Until we find something useful," Hibbs informed her.

Off he went. The Doc promptly followed him. The Bombshell eventually trailed along.

It took another proverbial age to reach this new oddity.
As before, very little changed in their environment. The scorched forest still predominated the terrain. The sun continued to hang in its near-noon position. For the longest time it appeared that, no matter how long they marched, they never managed to leave the bonfire behind. Then suddenly it was gone. And the squad's new destination came rushing into their proximity, advancing twenty meters for every step the group took. It was weird, but Hibbs was used to weird by now.

The new oddity was a real surprise. For here, planted in the middle of this limitless burned woodlands, was the alien spacecraft from the Eiger digs. The saucer protruded from the ground just as it did in the lunar cavern. The alien metal showed no trace of the inferno that had devastated the surrounding territory.

"How did this get here?" gasped Dr. Holmes.

"Looks like it crashed," Scarpetti scoffed, unable to suppress her contemptuous amusement at the Egghead's inability to see the obvious.

"But it crashed on the Moon. It shouldn't be here on the Earth, much less back in the 1580s."

"Neither should we—but *that* part doesn't bother you."

"Oh, it bothers me," mumbled Dr. Holmes.

Hibbs let the two vent their confusion in debate. He understood their psychological need to express themselves. Dr. Holmes needed to voice her confusion, otherwise it would boil up and explode. Meanwhile he hoped the Bombshell would exhaust her stubbornness arguing with the Doc; depleted of her rebellious spunk she might be more receptive to follow his orders.

He examined the spacecraft. Its presence here was indeed a quandary—but what he found on the other side of the ship raised a whole new snakepit of bewilderment. Standing against the saucer's tilted flank was the scaffolding they all knew from the lunar excavation.

This was the same ship from the Moon. Not an earlier version that had crashed on ancient Earth. It was the *same identical* alien spacecraft. The half-buried vessel from the lunar excavation had been supplanted here to 16th Century Earth. Or transplanted into their mass delusion, as Scarpetti would put it.

The entry hatch—the one he and Surge had closed and locked shut—stood open.

Was this some deranged roundabout way of herding them into the spacecraft?

Was this the squad's way back to the lunar base?

Did they want to go back there?

By the time he rejoined Dr. Holmes and Private Scarpetti, their debate had almost brought them to blows. Hibbs was forced to physically intervene.

"Your disbelief in all this isn't going to prevent it from being hazardous, Private!" he growled. "You're stuck here, so you'd better adjust to the damned environment. Stop obsessing on killing and think about survival. Otherwise your sloppiness is liable to endanger the rest of us. Even a rookie knows to adapt to unexpected circumstances."

Then he wheeled about to chastise Dr. Holmes. "And you—*you're* supposed to be the rational one here! Stop and think for a second, Doc—if an intellectual like you can't understand all this, imagine how screwy it looks to jarheads like us. Cut us a break. Stop expecting us to have the answers and try to figure out some for yourself."

His tirades cowed the two women.

He'd expected no less of Dr. Holmes. Confusion had weakened her will. His accusations served as a sharp slap to her professional pride, jolting the woman from her arrogance-spawned rancor.

He was somewhat surprised (and personally relieved) that Private Slaughter could be verbally smacked back to reality. It was a good sign, though. Scarpetti's denial of the situation was every bit as delusional as the mirage she believed everything to be. She needed to remind herself that she was supposed to be a Marine. It wouldn't have counted if anyone else did the reminding; the insight had to be internally generated for it have any effect on the pugnacious gutter-brat. Marines didn't quit. They didn't throw down their toys and go home when things failed to go their way. There were no time-outs for a soldier.

While they were still acquiescent, Hibbs ushered the women around to the far side of the half-buried saucer. He wanted them to see the scaffolding that gave access to the open entry hatch.

"But..." gasped a puzzled Private Scarpetti, "this is the way it was in the lunar cavern..."

"Exactly the way it was," he agreed, then took the deduction a step farther: "Exactly the way it is."

"The answer—it's in there, isn't it?" Dr. Holmes whispered.

"I think so."

The saucer's alien metal gleamed in the high sun. While the surrounding terrain was blackened, no scorching showed on the spacecraft, nor on the scaffolding. The contrast forced Hibbs to squint when looking at the ship.

The Bombshell scoffed, "There's nothing in there but the source of the alien contamination."

"Why should that scare you, Private?" taunted Hibbs. "You're already infected. We all are."

"I'm not scared of a delusion," Scarpetti grumbled.

"You think there's a cure!" exclaimed Dr. Holmes. "That it's in there!"

In all honestly, Hibbs wasn't sure what he thought about any of this. But he had a gut feeling, and it was spurring him into the ancient spacecraft. He couldn't understand what was going on, but he suspected this was their way out of the 1580s. This scorched landscape wasn't real, but the saucer was. It was a common element between this place and where they belonged. That *seemed* logical... didn't it?

Hibbs was reticent to confess his uncertainty, for doubt would make him look weak. As the squad's acting Commanding Officer, he had to feign confidence if he expected to maintain his authority. So he lied and assured them that he believed a cure lay within the spacecraft.

"I can't go in there," Dr. Holmes choked out. She waved a hand at the ship, as if the gesture might ward off the alien vessel and the unpleasant memories it held for her. Her prior experiences inside the saucer still lingered in her mind with all their traumatic associations.

"We must," he announced.

"You're not getting *me* into that thing, either, sir," muttered Scarpetti. Her bravada faltered as she peered up at the ship. For all her battle-lust, Private Slaughter was frightened by the alien ship.

Recalling Surge's account of his own time spent inside the dead ship, Hibbs wasn't all that keen about going in there. But it was their only way out of this desolate wasteland. If they didn't take it, they might end up stranded back here in these imaginary 1580s.

"Would you rather stay here?" He waved both arms to indicate their burnt surroundings. "Build a little cinder hut and live off cooked grubs?"

"I can't—" moaned Dr. Holmes.

As she took a step back, Hibbs grabbed the Doc and wheeled her around to face him. He unscrewed her helmet and cupped her face in his sunburned hands. "You have to, Dr. Holmes. We don't belong here. We have to get back to Eiger base. Our only way home lies inside the ship."

"It... he... that other Denk—he's in there..." she blubbered. "He'll assault me again..."

"That was then—this is now." He gave her arms a confident squeeze.

"This is crazy," muttered Scarpetti.

"You have to be brave, Doc," Hibbs instructed her. "You won't be alone, we'll be there to protect you."

Dr. Holmes gave him a reluctant nod. Hibbs helped her out of her pressure suit. When they were done, he turned his attention to Scarpetti, who'd been pacing back and forth, muttering to herself the entire time.

"Do you need to be coddled, too?" he snarled at the Private.

She flashed him a daggers-look, but grudgingly shook her head.

Leaving her to strip on her own, Hibbs gathered some gear from the discarded suit. He took the shoulder strap from his rifle and looped it around his waist, then attached an assortment of equipment to it. From Surge's description of the ship's interior, Hibbs figured the rifle would be an inappropriate weapon in such cramped quarters. His handgun, a long bladed knife, a few other items would have to suffice as his defensive arsenal. Finally outfitted to the best of his capacity, he helped the Doc climb the scaffolding.

"I'll go in first," he advised the Doc. "You wait to follow me until I signal you. Don't worry, you'll be sandwiched between me and Scarpetti. Nothing's going to get you..." *Unless it takes us out first,* he privately finished.

He waited until the Bombshell had shed her cumbersome attire and clambered up to join the Doc on the scaffolding. She had followed his example, collecting some key gear she would carry along with her. Once Private Scarpetti was in place to watch over the civilian, Hibbs took a deep breath and ventured into the open hatch.

30

Major Dummheit was furious.

He came awake slowly as the sedative's numbing influence ebbed from his system.

They drugged me! he raged. *Those swine mutinied—they stole command from me—and they drugged me!*

It was dark, and his movements were restricted.

Those bastards tied me up and threw me in a closet!

He couldn't believe his troops had turned on him. But then, they were despicable scum, rebellious lowlifes who had no respect for authority. Here they were on a rescue mission, but apparently they'd decided to go rogue and loot the research base for their own profit. Knowing Dummheit would oppose such nefarious deviltry, they'd overpowered him.

They'd actually drugged him, tied him up, and thrown him in a closet!

Their audacity astounded the Major. Did they think they could get away with this? They would pay for their diabolical antics. He would see them all court-martialed, shot as the traitors they were.

Corporal Hibbs was the ringleader, of that Dummheit was certain. For a long time, the Major had pegged Hibbs as a troublemaker. He was a career soldier; he thought that made him better than everybody else. He habitually disobeyed orders, escaping reprisals as situations unfolded in ways that made it look as if his contentious actions had been justified. An entire drawer in the Major's office was filled with the meritorious commendations he had refused to pass along to the arrogant Corporal.

And Denk was another bad egg. From the very beginning, there had been something about Denk that had rubbed the Major the wrong way. Denk was so handsome and dashing and courageous—all qualities Dummheit coveted. Denk was a hero—big deal—Dummheit could be a hero too if he wanted to act reckless. The lowlife's amorous exploits were another bur in the Major's shorts. He felt that wanton sexual activity undermined the discipline of the troops under his command. The Major disapproved of his soldiers befriending each other, and he actively prohibited them from engaging in sexual liaisons—for all the good that did. He went to great lengths to regularly shuffle the soldiers among different barracks to prevent them from establishing any relationships. He firmly believed that emotional attachments impaired combat skills. And Denk was an unrepentant transgressor, bedding everything in reach. It was a good thing that Dummheit's wife was so frigid, or the cuckold would've harassed her too.

Corporal Marshall was too full of herself. She knew her computer skills made her a valuable asset—and she never passed up the opportunity to snidely rub that in the Major's face. He despised her expertise. When the time came to falsify records to cover the mutineers' tracks, she would be the one they would turn to.

While Private Scarpetti was another full-of-herself bitch. Prancing around like a sexpot all the time, the hot little tramp undoubtedly believed that made her special... exempt from the rules. Well, she was in for a big surprise when the Major brought the hammer down on their seditious uprising.

Private Danford was a smug little prick, too new to the Corps to have established any solid loyalty to the greater good. A wad of tax-free cash had probably bought his allegiance. Profiteers like that were, in the Major's eyes, no better than felons.

Corporal Green had been a career Marine. No amount of money or lies would've swayed him from his duty—so they'd made sure he was the first to fall. The poor patsy.

And Dr. Holmes—that bitch had been a nuisance from the start, challenging his authority and flaunting her extended knowledge of the Eiger facility. Civilians were like that, imagining they were better than military personnel. That kind of logic was a classic mistake, dating from eras before terrorists had replaced unfriendly governments as the enemy. These days, civilians were nothing more than enemies who hadn't been recruited to the dark side—or worse, dupes who unwittingly helped terrorists accomplish their destructive plots. The Holmes bitch was a prime candidate for the latter type. It was the Major's job to spot such weak-willed individuals and make sure they never got the chance to cause trouble.

For all he knew, they were all in league with terrorists. That would explain their criminal activities. Terrorists were everywhere, no one knew that better than Major Dummheit. He was constantly vigilant for seditious activities. Granted, he had yet to uncover and foil a terrorist plot, but not for lack of trying. So far, the terrorists had managed to elude him. The word had probably been circulated to avoid him like the plague. The terrorist leaders knew better than to tangle with someone of Major Dummheit's caliber. But finally they'd made a fatal mistake. This time they had relied on lowlifes to set the stage for their scheme.

They'd never have overpowered the Major if his guard had been up. But his attention had been distracted by the rescue mission, and the scum had blind-sided him. He'd known the troops under his command were slackers, but he'd never suspected that any of them would sink so low as to turn traitor. Surliness and unsquelched initiative were undesirable traits among jarheads, but these bastards had allowed their misanthropic attitudes to mutate far beyond acceptable limits.

Each one of them was guilty. They deserved the utmost penalty for their actions. If any of them happened to get caught by stray gunfire, their deaths would only spare Global the cost of a court-martial, or a military tribunal in Holmes' case. The Major wouldn't shed any tears over their accidental demise.

But first, he had to free himself and regain control of the situation.

The Major struggled to liberate himself, but his restraints were too secure. Operating in the cramped and dark confines of a closet didn't help, either. He was confident, though, that he would succeed, for he was the only authorized agent of the law on the scene. There were no allies who might come to his—

The door opened. Light spilled on the Major; he squinted in the sudden glare. Someone stood there, probably one of the traitors.

They've come to drug me again, he realized. *That's the only way they can hope to pull off this betrayal, for once I'm awake they know I will stop them.*

But once his vision cleared, the Major saw that this figure was not wearing a Marine combat suit. This pressure suit was shabby, assembled from discarded scraps that bore countless repair patches. There was something odd about the man's posture, too, as if he suffered from some congenital spinal defect.

A terrorist! Dummheit gasped to himself. Already the traitors' associates had arrived at the Eiger base.

The man reached for him. Responding defensively, the Major kicked out, catching the stranger full in the unarmored crotch. But the man did not crumple under this punishing blow; hell, he didn't even flinch.

A terrorist who's had their pain receptors disabled—diabolical.

The Major fought like a wolverine, but trussed up as he was all he succeeded in doing was bruising himself as he flailed about. The terrorist leaned in and threatened him with a knife. A gasp caught in Dummheit's throat. He ceased struggling. If this man killed him, the Major would never bring them all to justice. He cringed back, loose-limbed but fearfully tense.

Don't kill me, he tried to get past the cloth that gagged him. *I'm just an officer, I have no combat skills.*

To the Major's surprise, the terrorist cut the plastic loops that bound his wrists and ankles. The man stepped back to allow Dummheit to crawl from the closet.

He tore the gag from his mouth and blurted, "Thank you!" As he clambered to his feet, the Major struggled to concoct a story that would assure this man to trust him. Coming erect, he confronted the man. He glimpsed the face inside the bubble helmet and what he saw made him gasp, in surprise and in revulsion.

He knew this man. His savior was the prospector they'd caught topside; the Major couldn't recall his name. What was he doing down in the base? Clearly Dummheit's original suspicions had been correct—the lunar prospector was in league with the terrorists.

There was definitely something wrong with the man. His head was tilted at an awkward angle. The features of his face were slack, devoid of expression... devoid of life. His eyes were clouded, unfocused. The man looked dead.

The Major came instantly alert. What bizarre game were the terrorists playing now?

"What's going on?" he asked the leaden prospector.

The man offered no verbal response. He shuffled back and lifted a limp arm. The Major turned to see—

To see an awesome sight that stunned the Major's over-critical soul.

Arcs of electricity radiated from the wall, converging on a foggy morass that hung in the corridor. As the Major watched, that cloud writhed and unfolded into a cosmic doorway, revealing a figure of breathtaking beauty. She was statuesque, her limbs well-muscled yet still voluptuous. Her breasts were enormous—just the way he wished his wife's were—and bouncy in the lunar gravity. Her face spurred his heart to race, for he saw there a conglomeration of every woman he had ever lusted after, old girlfriends and acquaintances and media starlets, all swimming together into a highly tempting gestalt. A swarm of silken blonde tresses surrounded that enticing facial fusion, the strands wavered in the air as if they were living tendrils.

The woman emerged from the vaporous portal, crossing a barrier between worlds to stand before him. Her arms raised and encircled the Major's neck, pulling him close. Her lips brushed his cheek, then settled into amorous contact with his own. Her tongue pried its way into his mouth. She ground her naked body against him. Sexual desire blossomed in Dummheit, a stirring that was most uncommon for the Major who had long ago sublimated all carnal lust and devoted his energies—physical, emotional, social, even private endeavors—to the promotion of his military career. But this fairy beauty inspired in him fervent urges that transcended his normal self-restraint. His own arms lifted to embrace this siren. He hugged her and sent his own tongue out to probe her rosy mouth… but her tongue blocked his way, denying him access to her own warm cavity.

In fact, the beauty's tongue was surging past his lips, filling his mouth, burrowing down his throat. He couldn't breathe. The Major tried to push her away, but he couldn't break her hold on him.

Beside him, the prospector had slumped to the floor as if he'd been a puppet whose strings were now cut.

Marshaling his strength, the Major fought to disengage himself from the beauty's embrace. His muscles proved insufficient to the task. She clasped him tight. And her tongue forced its way his throat, blocking his breathing passage. Now his exertions grew frantic as panic set it. He twisted and contorted, to no avail. He fought to push her away from him, but they remained compactly pressed together.

No—pressing together was only the beginning. The woman's body was merging with his! Her supple breasts flowed into his masculine chest, her pelvis superimposed itself on his privates, her arms sank into his shoulders.

He tried to scream, but his face was already immersed in her flesh, his mouth swallowed by her own maw.

Before the merger was complete, frantic panic had driven the Major's mind into dark submission.

31

Fear rendered Riccardo Denk relatively useless. What little information Sergio could pry from his brother was mired in superstition and foreboding. Sergio was uncertain how much credence to give even the few scarps of data he got.

Sergio had a small lamp, his handgun, and some extra ammunition clips stashed in the satchel Marshall had given him. He wasn't all that sure how much these things were going to protect them from the hallucinations spawned by the alien virus. He took a few pills from his med kit and fed them to his brother; they were designed to calm without fuzzying perceptions. This seemed to be the best he could do: keep them alert and sane… until he could figure out what to do.

What the hell can *I do?* he reflected. The cavern had collapsed on the spacecraft, burying it and them inside the saucer. There was scarce likelihood of digging their way out. And even less chance of finding extra air and food cached inside the alien vessel to keep them alive until a rescue crew could get to them. There'd be no rescue crew; Sergio knew that. The base was under quarantine, locked down to prevent the contagion from escaping. *We're here for the duration…* Which was a tactful way of saying: *This is where we die.*

But Sergio refused to let fear settle in his own mind. Once let in, its effects would be impossible to supersede. He needed to remain calm, cool, cautious. His own hide was no longer the only one at peril. Now he had to safeguard his estranged twin as well as himself.

Despite their identical genetics, the twins possessed numerous readily visible differences. Both were swarthy skinned with angular features, although Riccardo's indulgent lifestyle had rounded out his face and physique with chubby padding. Riccardo's hair was shaggy, while Sergio's was buzz-cut. Sergio had a number of tattoos, mostly military in nature; Riccardo's flesh was pallid and undecorated. Years of stimulant abuse had given Riccardo's voice a whiny edge. Even their individual posture expressed extreme variations: Sergio was tense with readiness, Riccardo slumped with trepid defeatism.

After so long apart, the Denk brothers experienced no desperate need to hug and gush over each other. It had been many years since they'd been close. Long before Riccardo had flown the family coop, the twins had drifted apart—or more accurately, Riccardo's selfish attitude had isolated him from anyone who cared. Each brother had grown to maturity separated from the other's influence. Sergio had joined the Global Marine Corps, while Riccardo had sunk into high society debauchery. In truth, Sergio's reflex to protect the brat was more rooted in his military discipline than in any familial loyalty.

At least his brother's presence here explained Sergio's recurrent feeling of deja vu. Ever since he'd reached Eiger installation, Sergio had repeatedly encountered strange things for the first time, and yet he'd been tormented by the elusive impression that he'd seen them before. Now he knew why. It was because Riccardo had seen them. Despite the conscious alienation that had developed between them, the twins still were connected on a psychic level; what one saw, the other knew about. Riccardo's sensory stimuli had impinged itself on Sergio's mind, but in too subtle a fashion for him to recognize as external input. Riccardo had entered the base first, descending into its depths hours before the Marine squad had arrived. He'd seen the horrors and the astonishing weirdness, so that when Sergio came upon these surprises he had the vague feeling that *he* was not seeing these fantastic things for the first time. While Sergio basically harbored scarce belief in such mystic rubbish as psychic connections, he could not deny the evidence of personal experiences. Ever since they'd been young, the Denk kids had shared each other's lives in this strange manner. Sergio had been somewhat pleased when Riccardo had deserted the family and gone off on his own, for the connection had faded with distance, leaving Sergio's head unbothered by extraneous sensations. Now, though, the brothers were in close proximity again, and the psychic connection had reappeared. Until he'd accepted Riccardo's presence here, Sergio had not identified his signs for what they really were.

And now Sergio found it difficult to ward off his brother's hysterical despair. Confusion and fear flowed from Riccardo, drenching Sergio's mind in these counterproductive moods. This emotional pollution interfered with Sergio's determination.

When he tried to assure his brother that everything was going to be all right, Riccardo launched into a rambling diatribe that blamed a series of other people for his social downfall. It came as no surprise to Sergio to hear how everybody else was to blame for the mistakes Riccardo had made. After a few minutes, Sergio tuned out the tirade.

His training urged him to scout the territory. As long as they were trapped in here, it seemed wise to reconnoiter and familiarize himself with their prison.

The niche Riccardo had chosen as a hiding place was no bigger than a closet. No door shut it off from the passageway. A beveled ridge formed a prominent jamb that ran all the way around the threshold. With the aid of his lamp, Sergio discovered the walls of the niche were covered with intricate traceries etched into the resilient alien metal. A tapestry of curlicue lines surrounded him; it made him uneasy, although he couldn't ascertain exactly why. This ominous premonition finally succeeded in rousting him from hiding to go investigate the rest of the ship.

Of course Riccardo protested vehemently. He pleaded with Sergio not to leave him. There was too much danger. What if her cat came while Sergio was gone? The beast would do terrible things to Riccardo. He shuddered like a palsy victim as he begged Sergio to stay.

"I'm a soldier, Ricky. Hiding isn't my thing, it's yours. If you want to stay here, be my guest. But *I'm* going to check out the ship." It might harbor something that could be used to their advantage. More likely, though, Sergio would find nothing but alien weirdness, artifacts and machinery utterly beyond his comprehension. But even that was preferable to listening to Riccardo's poor-me rant.

Actually, Sergio was conflicted regarding whether or not he wanted Riccardo to accompany him. While protecting his brother was the honorable thing to do, Sergio was loath to be burdened with the sniveling pest. Riccardo would slow him down, annoying him with his endless complaints, requiring him to keep one eye peeled on his twin's safety. If anything did show up to threaten them, Riccardo's hysterical presence would hamper Sergio's defensive aptitude. Besides, as long as they stayed together, Riccardo's angst was fouling up Sergio's ability to think clearly. If only his own resolve could vanquish Riccardo's frightened bias, but the brat's fear ran too deep. Separation might alleviate that unwanted fog of psychic influence. But then, leaving Riccardo behind was foolish. He was bound to panic and run off to hide elsewhere, forcing Sergio to track him down in this claustrophobic labyrinth. Sergio had no desire to waste his final hours searching for his brat of a brother. Keeping them together was the thing to do, despite the downside of doing so.

All things considered, though, Sergio knew the futility of trying to compel Riccardo to follow his advise. Riccardo was too willful, especially when it came to his own misguidance. In many ways, he and Major Dummheit shared several behavioral traits. Guile would bee required to force Riccardo to abandon his stubborn sequestration.

"If her cat shows up," he intentionally taunted Riccardo, "give me a yell." He stepped from the hiding niche. Choosing left on impulse, Sergio started off down that corridor. The hallway's severe tilt made it difficult for him to move with any degree of aplomb, but he strove to maintain a nonchalant air. He stumbled and ultimately found it easier to maneuver on his hands and knees.

A moment passed, then fear of losing his protector drove Riccardo to pursue Sergio along the corridor.

It soon became apparent there was no hope of searching the entire spacecraft. The passages were bewilderingly circuitous. Sergio tried to chart his route but soon lost his bearing. The corridors twisted and turned contrary to common sense. A few times he suspected the hallway had looped back on itself, yet the path eventually delivered him to different destinations. He decided to ignore these impossible contortions and concentrate on exploration. More than once he came upon the same confounding location… or maybe he kept encountering chambers whose differences were too subtle for his human senses to discern.

So much of what he saw was completely beyond his understanding. Geometric configurations abounded, but when it came to discerning the functions of these shapes his imagination failed him.

There appeared to be two diametrically contrasting architectural styles inside the alien spacecraft. While the outer regions were angular and cramped, deeper into the ship things became more spacious and almost organic in countenance, as if these infrastructures had been grown instead of fabricated. Peculiar textures adorned these vacuolar passages, spiraling along the walls and feathering out into circular fractal patterns. The cold light given off by these luminous ribbons made everything glisten as if it were soft and moist, yet in actuality the surfaces were hard, metallic to his tactile senses.

Their course took them through a region of these tunnels, past chambers too creepy to comprehend, and finally Sergio found himself once more crawling along the narrow angular byways. Had he penetrated the ship's innermost depths and reached the far outer edge of the buried saucer? Or had he gotten lost and doubled back on his original path? It was all too foreign to provide him with any memorable landmarks.

On a few occasions, Riccardo's grumbled complaints had escalated into urgent laments, expressing inarticulate warnings against venturing into certain cavities, but Sergio ignored his twin's apprehensive advice. He had no intention of bypassing pertinent aspects of the ship's interior—although when Sergio stumbled upon the torture chamber where he had rescued Dr. Holmes, he shared his twin's visceral reluctance to revisit this repulsive locale. Afterward, Sergio tended to heed his twin's inarticulate counsel and avoided examining certain rooms.

An oppressive silence surrounded the Denk brothers as they moved through the ship. The walls seemed to absorb stray noise like a sponge, muting the rasp of Sergio's breathing and leaving him with a soundtrack comprised solely of the throb of blood coursing through his head. Even Riccardo's low moans were dampened.

When Sergio finally heard something, the anomaly immediately put him on his guard. The sounds were too muffled, though, for him to identify them. He proceeded with stealth, his handgun drawn and ready. Each portal and juncture was approached with utmost caution. Apprehension instilled him with the expectation that he would round a corner and find himself nose-to-nose with the ghost panther. He hoped this prospect was as unreasonable as he thought it was.

Even so, he extinguished his lamp, concerned that its beam might betray his presence. The phosphorous strips lining the walls provided enough illumination for him to spot anything threatening.

After a while he paused and squinted. The end of the passageway shimmered with a more pronounced glow. What could it be? As far as he remembered, the panther hadn't given off light. It had to be something else causing this eerie brilliance.

He prayed that the alien contagion had spawned no new hallucinatory monstrosities.

His hand tightened on the grip of his weapon. His fingers trembled on the trigger; he had to consciously restrain himself from prematurely squeezing it. It wouldn't do to start blasting away before a target came into view. Sweat beaded on his brow, trickling down to sting his eyes. He lifted his arm and wiped away the salty moisture. And when he blinked to clear his vision, he found the end of the corridor ablaze with a fierce glow. Murky shapes lurked behind that dazzle.

"What the hell—" a human voice echoed along the passage. "Surge?"

Sergio snapped on his own lamp, but its beam was weaker than the other and failed to show him any details that lay beyond the oncoming glare.

Then that stronger light turned its beam to the floor, and a familiar face was revealed in the gleam of his own lamp.

"Hibbs?" he gasped.

"What the hell are you doing in here?"

He could—and did—ask his comrade the very same question.

They swapped tales.

Sergio learned about their incredible ordeal—how the walls had closed in, herding them into a death-trap that had transported them to 1580s Earth instead of crushing them to a pulp. Hibbs explained how they'd found themselves in a verdant forest, how they'd discovered a human settlement, how Dr. Holmes had appeared with an Indian companion. Dr. Holmes related the grotesque fate of the missing Roanoke colonists, telling how the blaze had spread to devastate the entire woodland countryside. Hibbs clarified that they'd marched for endless hours, only to find the alien spacecraft half-buried in the scorched wasteland. The extent of Private Scarpetti's contribution to these tales was a curt assertion that "None of this is real."

In turn, Sergio told them how he and Marshall had tried to respond to Hibbs' comm that had called them topside to help defend the base against invasion by terrorists, but the corpses of the Eiger staff had reanimated and merged into a super-zombie that had attacked them. The two soldiers had succeeded in blasting the monster to pieces, then Sergio had pursued those pieces into the excavation cavern to prevent them from reassembling. He'd used some C-4 to blow the congealing cadavers, but the explosion had collapsed the cavern. He'd been forced to seek shelter from the cave-in inside the alien spacecraft. There, he'd found his twin brother. He gave a condensed account of how Riccardo had gotten here, for some of those details were still hazy in Sergio's understanding. He pointedly skipped his sibling's irrational ramblings, for he saw no importance in these superstitious explanations for the weirdness.

"So now we're all trapped in here," Scarpetti complained. "Great. We can all suffocate together."

Despite the prevailing dire circumstances, Sergio had to admire the Bombshell in her underwear. She really was a hot little thing. The lunar gravity did amazing things for her bosom. Her legs displayed excellently contoured sinews. Her hips flared with junoesque zest. Her belly looked tight enough to bounce bricks off it. He regretted not having noticed her back in 51's barracks.

"Unless her cat gets us first," moaned Riccardo.

"What?" Hibbs grunted.

Now Sergio had to describe his brother's delusions.

"A witch's cat, eh?" remarked Hibbs. Sergio had expected the Corporal to scoff at this fantasy, but instead Hibbs revealed: "The Doc's Indian companion warned us to beware of a witch and her feline familiar. At the time, I didn't take him seriously. But now..."

The Bombshell gave a contemptuous snort. "It doesn't matter if it comes from an imaginary Indian or Denk's crazy brother—it's all just preposterous trash."

"What happened to this Indian?" Sergio asked Hibbs.

"Lost in the fire."

"Ah. No chance then of getting any more information from him about this supernatural enemy."

"Oh, come on, you guys," Scarpetti chided them. "You don't really believe any of this, do you? It's all—"

Ignoring the Bombshell's denial, Hibbs conferred with Dr. Holmes. "What do you think, Doc?"

"It's highly implausible that two independent sources would concoct the same wild explanation for all this..."

"Unless both of them were telling the truth," Sergio finished her evaluation.

"The truth as they knew it. After all, we're talking about an imaginary Indian and..." She threw a suspicious glance in the direction of Riccardo Denk. "...and *him*." Her voice bore a trace of animosity, for her prior experiences with Sergio's sibling had not been very pleasant.

"I told you," Sergio quickly defended his twin, "he was under the witch's spell. He tried to resist, but was powerless to stop."

"So he says," she snarled.

"It's not very fair to believe this witch exists and then blame Riccardo for the things she forced him to do."

Throughout this debate, Riccardo cowered behind Sergio. His fear was too generalized, though, not spawned by the Doc's animosity. He was simply out of it.

"Let's assume for a minute that this explanation is an accurate one," muttered Hibbs. "What do we do about it?"

The others looked at the Corporal as if he'd suddenly sprouted wings from his temples.

Scarpetti laughed, "What *can* we do about it?"

No one seemed to have a practical suggestion.

So Sergio voiced the obvious: "We find her and waste the bitch."

"You mean waste the witch."

Sergio gave a curt nod.

"You guys are crazy—" The Bombshell's cackle abruptly cut off in mid-beat. It was replaced by a raspy out-gust of breath that endured until she had emptied her lungs. Her eyes, previously a'twinkle with scathing derision, clouded with dumfound vacancy, then glazed over with a feverish urgency.

Nearest her, Sergio frowned and wondered if she was having some kind of fit.

Something jerked Scarpetti away from the group where they all crouched in the narrow alien corridor. This movement restored sound to her lips, as if motion had somehow revitalized her vocal chords. She issued an ear-splitting shriek.

Lunging forward, Sergio grabbed her arm.

Hibbs moved to shield Dr. Holmes from whatever was going on.

Releasing a wail, Riccardo withdrew into a catatonic ball.

Scarpetti's hands clutched at Sergio. Her fingers gouged skin from his forearms. Her eyes widened with a vivid declaration of shock/horror/pain.

Past the struggling Bombshell, the radiance cast by everybody's dropped-in-startlement lamps revealed a tawny black form in the process of savaging the girl. Talons and fangs flashed. Blood sprayed against the narrow walls, adding runny graffiti to the alien patterns. Scarpetti's mouth contorted with aggravated verbiage that degenerated into fierce squeals of agony.

While the squad had discussed their predicament, the ghost panther had crept upon them and attacked the youngest member of the herd.

Sergio held on, refusing to let go of her. He strained to drag her back from the beast's attack—and suddenly she came loose. He tumbled on his back and she fell atop him, her full breasts pressing against his chest, her screaming breath warming his cheeks, her flailing hands plucking at his shoulders. A viscous dampness drenched him.

Dr. Holmes screamed with abject terror.

Even Hibbs gasped with disgust.

Only the Bombshell's upper half had come free from the panther's clutches. Her torso squirmed against Sergio. Her blood and entrails spilled out across his waist. He embraced her, horrified but unwilling to release her. These were undoubtedly her last minutes, he refused to let her endure them alone. She died in his arms.

32

While Scarpetti expired in Sergio's embrace, Corporal Hibbs flew into action. Protecting Dr. Holmes had been instinctive—guard the civilian—but now the threat had killed one of his troops. For all her bloodlust, Private Slaughter had fallen victim to one of the very hallucinations she'd refused to believe in. To insure the safety of everyone else, someone must engage the enemy. Surge had his hands full. The Doc was no fighter. And the Denk twin had gone catatonic.

Ever since he'd entered the alien spacecraft, Hibbs had been alert for signs of the panther. The creature had a predilection for showing up at the worst possible moment; he doubted it could resist tormenting them once they were crowded into the ship's narrow passages. On prior occasions, his expectancy had been flavored with dread, but this time a flood of confidence instigated the Corporal's reaction. This time he was armed with a strong conviction that he knew the beast's weakness.

He advanced on the panther, brandishing his long knife as his other hand rifled through the pouch he carried. He slashed at the beast, but the wounds he inflicted with the blade seemed to be nothing more than minor distractions to the great cat. Even so, the panther abandoned the Private's lower extremities and recoiled from the blade. The beast snarled at him, baring bloodstained teeth. He continued to slash at the creature, driving it back down the passageway.

His other hand finally closed on what he wanted. He wrenched it from the pouch and thumbed the stick alight. The flare erupted, producing a brilliant blaze that crackled and hissed with as much hostility as the angry panther. The beast flinched from the burning magnesium.

You're afraid of fire, Hibbs silently accused. Back when the forest fire had just begun to spread, Hibbs had noticed how the cat had shied away from the advancing flames. The fire had driven it into retreat. This weakness defied logic, for the beast had shrugged off blasts from the soldiers' plasma rifles. If quantum energy couldn't scorch the creature, why would elementary flames intimidate it? Perhaps it had something to do with the cat's primal fear of fire. Hibbs hadn't bothered to over-analyze the matter, lest criticism undermine what little faith he had in his speculation. If fire didn't work, he was no worse off than before.

It worked, though; oh, it worked superbly.

Hissing and growling, the panther cringed away from the heat. Wielding the flare like a mystic talisman, Hibbs chased the beast down the corridor. His route was calculated, and he succeeded in herding the beast into a small room with no other doors. Hibbs had to act fast before the creature pulled its walk-through-walls trick and escaped him. He dove for the beast, jamming the flare into its face. It thrashed with savage rancor, snapping at him but unable to close its terrible jaws on his arm past the flare's blazing tip. Hibbs dragged the stick along the length of the panther's body, smearing the smoldering magnesium across its flank and effectively painting the beast with fire. The beast twisted and flailed, biting at its flaming haunches. Hibbs didn't relent; long after it was entirely engulfed in flames, he continued to jab the tormented creature with the burning flare. It screamed. It contorted. But it couldn't escape, nor could it extinguish its fiery flesh. It threw itself against the walls, but did not pass through them. Beleaguered by its intense torment, the beast was unable to marshal its occult abilities. All it could do was scream and thrash and burn.

Stepping back, Hibbs watched the fire consume the beast. It curled into a fetal clench. Its flesh withered and peeled. Its sinews bubbled and melted to reveal something concealed beneath this feline facade. This hidden shape writhed like a compressed bulk of dark worms. Tendrils reached out, only to char in the flames and disintegrate into ash. Whatever monstrosity lurked within the panther's molten residue was too abnormal for Hibbs to identify. It possessed no form which his human mind could grasp. It looked like a morass of black jelly, but he knew it had to be more than that, much more, something profane and not-of-this-world. Somehow Hibbs realized that the shape was not just extraterrestrial in nature; this classification was far too limited. The oily apparition did not belong to this universe. It was an abomination that had swaddled itself in panther meat to hide its perverted identity.

Eventually, even that unholy aberration melted away, exposing the body of a small house cat. Silhouetted within the concentrated inferno, the cat underwent its own dissolution. Its hide vaporized. Its sinews shriveled and flaked away. Its guts boiled and ruptured and sagged into a bubbly lump. Its bones disintegrated to ash. Soon, even the glutinous residue was ravaged by the fire.

"Gotcha, you bastard," declared Hibbs.

With nothing left to fuel itself, the fire sputtered out. All that was left was a scorched mark on the floor.

This victory made Corporal Hibbs yearn to howl with primitive satisfaction. He had vanquished an invulnerable adversary. The beast's demise seemed to warrant a more primal commemoration of his superiority. Giving in to a bestial urge, Hibbs urinated on the char mark. The act proclaimed his dominance over his defeated foe, over anything that dared to oppose the soldier.

Now *he* was the invincible one.

When he rejoined the others, Hibbs found:
Surge seethed with anger over Scarpetti's murder.

Sight of the Bombshell's eviscerated corpse had plunged Dr. Holmes into nauseated withdrawal.

Surge's brother was still lost in his own hysteria.

"I wasted it," Hibbs told Surge.

"The thing killed her."

"I know. And now it's dead, too."

"For real?" His skepticism was understandable.

"I burned it." He held up the flare. It sputtered, almost spent.

"Fire!" gasped Dr. Holmes. She rallied a pretense of composure and exclaimed, "Fire kills witches. The beast served her, so only fire could slay it."

"But—" Surge started to ponder aloud.

"It worked," advised Hibbs. "Don't question the stuff that works—especially when it's to our advantage."

"It's dead?" The catatonic twin had thrown off his stupor. He gaped at Hibbs with almost reverent awe. "You really destroyed her beast?"

Hibbs shook the flare at him. "Burned to a cinder."

Instead of relief at news of the beast's destruction, a look of desolate panic swept across Riccardo's face. He covered his head with his arms and collapsed to the tilted floor, wailing, "Now *she* will come after us!"

"No, she won't," snarled Hibbs. "Because we're going to find her first and burn her ass."

"Yeah," Surge snarled in concurrence.

"How can we find her?" moaned Dr. Holmes.

Surge turned on his twin and hauled him from his fearful cringe. "You know where she is, don't you, Ricky? You've known all along, but you're too afraid to admit it."

Cowering in Surge's grip, Riccardo hid his face and refused to meet his brother's accusations.

"You sniveling wretch—where is she?" Surge raged. "Where's the bitch hiding?"

"She's everywhere!" blurted Riccardo. "This is *her* realm, we're nothing but toys for her wicked amusement."

"The tables have turned," Hibbs announced. "Now *we're* the hunters—and she's reduced to being the prey."

"You'll never overcome her," moaned Riccardo. "She's too powerful. Her power—it's incredible! You thought her cat was a monster—*her* power makes the beast seem like an insect."

"I beat the cat," Hibbs reminded him.

"You'll never beat her!" With that, the twin's mind shut down. He slumped in his brother's grasp, escaping his incarnate dread by fleeing into a coma.

"I *will* beat her."

"Will you?" Dr. Holmes asked in a hesitant whisper.

"Yes!" decreed Hibbs. The adrenaline of victory still pervaded his blood. He was intoxicated with superiority. He felt imbued with the zealous fortitude of every champion who had ever conquered a dangerous enemy. Nothing could oppose him.

The ship's labyrinthine interior stymied their determination. They searched, examining each chamber they encountered, but found no trace of the witch's hiding place. The weird apparatus they saw confounded the two soldiers. Dr. Holmes exhibited an insatiable curiosity with this foreign machinery, postulating functions with feverish verve, as if her remarks were intended to convince herself most of all. The accuracy of her presumptions was impossible to confirm.

Still catatonic, Riccardo was hauled along as so much dead weight.

Undaunted by their consistent failure to unearth the witch's hidden lair, Hibbs and Surge forged on. They moved with military efficiency, weapons ready and senses alert. Hibbs let Surge take point. His present state of agitation made it unwise for Hibbs to contest the man's self-proclaimed right to be the frontline. It was his thing, let him have his way. Their aggression should be reserved for their prey, not wasted on squabbles among the ranks.

With each chamber, Surge entered and ascertained that no apparent threat existed therein, then Hibbs would join him in a detailed search of the room. They probed for removable panels that might conceal hidden recesses or crawlways, but if any existed the men never found them. Once their examination was completed, Dr. Holmes would hurry in and study each resident mystifying facet. Her results were no more fruitful than the soldiers'. Her voiced guesses held little interest for them. They sought prey, she was more concerned with fathoming alien technologies.

Their frustration mounted with each subsequent failure, but that emotion only served to strengthen their resolve, compounding their hostility into a fury of epic proportion. Hibbs still rode his adrenaline high, while Scarpetti's death fueled Surge's fervor.

After a while, however, defeatism began to gnaw at the edges of their tenacity. They had searched what seemed like every chamber within the alien spacecraft, but had found nothing to indicate the presence of their prey. More than once, they were sure they'd examined a chamber before, but they scoured its contents all the same, unwilling to take a chance of overlooking some clue they might have missed on their first pass... or their second or third... Time became elastic and hours seemed to stretch into days.

But that was impossible, for there couldn't have been days worth of air trapped with them inside the alien vessel. Sooner or later, the air had to run out, and asphyxiation would bring their hunt to a disappointing end.

Hibbs started to wonder if they might be hunting an imaginary foe.

For some time, he had suspected that a diabolical intelligence guided the weirdness. The squad's tribulations had been too well-timed, too poignant, too nefarious. Something had to be orchestrating their problems. When the witch theory had come along, it had satisfied his need for someone to fill that role. Granted, witches and sorcery were superstitious bunk, but so were zombies and ghost panthers. However crazy it was to believe, a witch was no more fantastic than the atrocities which had harassed the soldiers.

But their comprehensive search had uncovered no evidence of this villain, no trace of anything terrestrial hiding in the alien spacecraft. With such negative reinforcement, the existence of a witch began to seem more and more questionable. Doubt crept in to dampen Hibbs' conviction.

Was there really a witch behind their sufferings? Or were they simply entering a new level of mania induced by the alien contagion?

33

After much deliberation, Corporal Marshall decided to settle down in the apartment that had served as the Egghead's recovery room. It seemed to Anne that this spot had become the soldiers' rendezvous point. They had left Dr. Holmes here, sedated and sleeping. Sooner or later, the rest of the squad would return here, if only to check on the Doc's safety.

But they won't find her, Anne sighed to herself. *All they'll find is me, confused and alone. I won't have any answers for them… and they probably won't have any for me, either.*

Ludicrous things happened here. The Eiger facility had become a nexus for the impossible. Here, the dead walked. Here, a ghost panther prowled the installation, lording over everything with its deadly wrath. Here, passages sealed themselves off, then reopened again without rhyme or reason. Here, the laws of physics had been reduced to obsolete suggestions. Here, causality was subject to fluid variations, all of which apparently devoted to inflicting suffering on anyone who dared to intrude upon these gloomy halls.

There was no way to escape this horrible place. And if she did succeed in breaking out, then she ran the risk of spreading the alien virus to others. As much as she valued her own life, she couldn't condone saving herself if her salvation would condemn mankind to extinction. That price was too high.

She repeatedly contemplated putting herself out of her misery. Suicide would end her torment. Untimely though her death would be, it would guarantee she wouldn't infect anyone else. But it would also leave the contaminated base open to rediscovery. She must stay alive to guard against anyone venturing into the facility.

Besides, the madness had driven the Eiger staff to suicide, and she knew from experience how effective that solution had been. She had no desire for her dead body to become reanimated and pitched against her comrades.

Corporal Green had died and then been used to attack the squad. Then Private Danford had suffered a similar fate. She'd been forced to destroy them both. She dreaded that Surge and Hibbs and Gina—and even the Egghead—might return as zombies, that she would have to destroy them to save herself.

Who am I kidding? she chided herself. *Saving myself is a selfish goal. My primary concern has to be keeping the alien contagion contained here in the base.*

Only by remaining alive could Anne preserve the integrity of the quarantine.

As the only one left, that duty fell to her. Whether anybody might enter by accident or with bad intentions, the prospect of intruders posed a viable danger, one she shouldn't ignore. She should post herself as a topside sentry.

But then, Anne reminded herself, *so far the base has proven to be quite adept at protecting itself against invaders. It doesn't need my help.* The contaminated installation could close itself off if it so desired, and the phantom panther was here to slaughter any intruders who were unlucky enough to breach the base.

On the other hand, what else was there to do? Sitting around waiting for the rest of the squad to reappear might be wishful thinking. For all she knew, they were dead, and she would grow old waiting for their return.

As long as I'm stuck here, I might as well do something useful.

With a resigned sigh, Anne climbed to her feet and crossed the dreary apartment. She wasn't really paying attention as she thumbed open the door. The panel slid aside, and she stepped out into the corridor. She turned and headed for the stairs.

Something hit her from behind.

Anne's armor protected her from the first blow. Before she could spin around, though, someone jumped on her back. She saw hands fussing about in her peripheral vision. Her suit was too bulky, she was unable to reach around and dislodge her assailant from her back. By the time she thought to just smash her foe against a wall, the bastard had managed to unseal her helmet and twist it off. A battery of fists assailed her head, beating her down into a darkening pit.

Before losing consciousness, Anne thought she glimpsed her attacker… but she must have been mistaken. It couldn't be him, he was…

Darkness truncated her surprised reaction.

34

"Enough," Hibbs finally grunted.

"What?" Sergio peered up from the alien apparatus he was groping. He was sure this manifold should come free, there were seams and even obvious clasps, but the affair resisted his manipulation.

"This is getting us nowhere. She's not in here... if she even exists in the first place..."

Reluctant to lose the object of his wrath, Sergio protested, "The bitch is here—we just have to find her, then we can—"

But Corporal Hibbs was adamant, "We're wasting our time in here. We need to get out of the alien ship and continue our search throughout the installation."

"How many times have we conducted thorough sweeps of the base, Hibbs?" Sergio had lost count. "And we never found anything except the mutilated bodies of the Eiger staff?"

"Would you have known a stranger among those bodies?" inquired Dr. Holmes.

"They weren't all mutilated," Hibbs mumbled.

"It doesn't matter," Sergio yelled. "We're trapped in here. The ship is buried under thousands of tons of lunar rock. It—"

"The cave-in could have been another delusion," suggested Dr. Holmes.

Sergio had set off the explosives that had brought the cavern down. He's seen it collapse. He'd barely escaped alive. How could he convince them of the veracity of his perceptions?

For that matter: how confident was he concerning the reality of what he'd experienced? With hallucinations so rampant in this place, no perceptions could really be trusted. Had the cavern actually collapsed? Or had the contagion just screwed with his mind?

He glanced over to assure himself that Riccardo was still there. His twin's presence here was too implausible; if anything was a delusion, it was Riccardo. But Ricky still lay catatonic, a burden the others would have to drag through the ship's passages to reach the outer hatch. He was awfully true to form, a constant nuisance, to be a fever dreamt mirage.

Hibbs would brook no dissent. He had decided they were leaving, and that was that. Arguing with him was pointless, Sergio new that. Unless he wanted to challenge his friend's authority, Sergio was just going to have to play along.

Anyway, the Doc had planted the seed of suspicion in Sergio's mind, and now he found himself questioning his own convictions. For all he knew, *all* of this could be an elaborate delusion. The alien ship, the mayhem the squad had faced inside Eiger base, even identifying a witch as their adversary. That last bit was pretty farfetched.

Witches and magic weren't real. *Neither are zombies and ghost panthers,* he reminded himself. But how wise was it to believe in witchcraft just because the other phantoms had proven their lethality?

After all, the sources of the information they'd used to base their belief in a witch were an imaginary Indian and Riccardo's babbling. Neither of which seemed all that credible to Sergio. He knew from personal experience how disreputable Ricky could be. And an Indian? How reliable was an imaginary character the others had encountered in a bigger mirage?

Hibbs had claimed to have defeated the ghost panther, the witch's supposedly invincible familiar… but Sergio had seen no corpse, no evidence to prove the Corporal's allegation. Under normal circumstances, Sergio would never distrust Hibbs, but these were far from normal circumstances. Maybe Hibbs had imagined his victory over the devil beast. It could still be out there somewhere, waiting to attack them.

These ruminations were making Sergio's head hurt. He was no master of existential philosophy. Without concrete evidence, he doubted everything. The problem was: here, every experience was suspect. Sergio had no idea what or who to trust. Even his own eyes and ears were rendered untrustworthy by the damned alien contagion.

Was *that* even real?

Too many quandaries. Sergio was a jarhead, not a scholar. That was Dr. Holmes' job, and the woman had repeatedly shown her inability to live up to her qualifications.

For now, Sergio was willing to just follow orders. Let Hibbs take over and guide them to whatever goal he had decided was viable. Sergio appreciated the respite from having to worry about things.

It took them a while to find the exit hatch. Despite their repeated circuits of the ship's interior, the passages were too convoluted for the human mind.

What warned them they might be close was Riccardo's sudden tantrum. Rousing from his coma, the twin threw a fit. He wailed and protested that they couldn't leave the ship. It was not allowed. *She* wanted them right where they were.

"We must be getting near the hatch," observed Hibbs.

"Yeah." Sergio had to agree, for there was no other reason for his brother's hysteria if they weren't about to stumble upon the exit. Riccardo's fear of crossing the witch was an excellent barometer for the soldiers.

"There it is."

They advanced along the narrow corridor. Sergio dragged a kicking and screaming Riccardo with them.

After a moment, Sergio hauled off and punched his brother in the side of his head, silencing his annoying histrionics.

"Thank you," Hibbs muttered as he examined the sealed portal. "Couldn't even hear myself think with all his caterwauling."

"He's really your twin brother?" Dr. Holmes asked Sergio.

He nodded. For all that Sergio wished he was an only son, denying his relation to Riccardo was foolish under the present circumstances.

"But—what are the odds of him being here?"

Sergio shrugged. He had no desire to drag himself through a discussion of this bizarre turn of events. He'd already exhausted himself with internal reflections of the mystery. Even the best explanation he could think of was too ridiculous. Sharing his bewilderment with the Doc would only exacerbate his frustration. "You're the egghead. You tell me."

"You're sure he's *real*?"

"Right about now, Doc, I'm not all that sure *I'm* real."

35

"I can't figure out these controls," grumbled Corporal Hibbs. "Where's Marshall when we need her..."

"You worked them before," remarked Corporal Denk. "When we locked the Doc's attacker in the ship."

"Unfortunately, these are entirely different from the outer controls."

"Let me see them." Dr. Holmes edged forward, but waited until the Corporal had withdrawn before she approached the panel set into the tilted wall beside the sealed hatch.

Although hardware was not her forte, Amelia had learned by now that her capabilities with technology, human or otherwise, outclassed these two men. True, Corporal Marshall possessed skills that eclipsed them all, but the woman wasn't here right now. After all the years Amelia had spent obsessed with proving the existence of intelligent extraterrestrial life, she felt embarrassed that when she finally found herself in the presence of alien hardware, it confounded her.

The inset panel was shaped like an angular hourglass, akin to a pair of triangles joined at the tips. Each plate featured a series of tiny triangular buttons decorated with inscrutable symbols. There were sixteen of these tabs in the upper triangle, fifteen in the lower plate—so it was doubtful that they represented a numeric sequence, certainly none she knew of. If the Gray aliens used a different base system of numerics, which was it—base fifteen or sixteen? Thirty-one? That seemed more like an alphabet, but if that was the case, why were the symbols separated into two sections?

Whatever the case, Amelia had no idea what to do with the control panel. She studied the thing, initially too intimidated to actually touch her finger to any of the small buttons.

Behind her, the Corporals were engaged in a whispered conference. Probably reviewing their options. Maybe they were proposing that they could shoot their way out—an automatic military solution. But no, that assumption was unfair. Private Scarpetti had been the trigger-happy one; so far the men had practiced a more rational outlook than what Amelia thought of when she envisioned the average soldier. They'd been quick to employ violence when it was necessary, but only in self-defense, fighting the panther and zombies. She shouldn't assume the worst about Hibbs and Denk. They were decent guys. Without their protection, she would never have survived this long.

This was her chance to contribute something, but she wasn't able to do so. The hatch's controls baffled her. The soldiers kept alluding to her academic intelligence, but when the time came for Dr. Holmes to apply that superior intellect, she had nothing to offer.

Out of frustration, she began pushing the tiny buttons. Her selections were random, more angry pokes than judicious choices.

"Have you got it?" came Corporal Hibbs' inquiry.

"Not yet..." mumbled Amelia. But as she spoke, the hatch slip aside with a hiss, a surprisingly soft one considering the mechanism's advanced age. Something she had done had triggered the portal's release. "There," she stated the obvious. She felt petty taking credit for the hatch's opening, but couldn't face the men knowing that her success had been wholly accidental.

Light spilled through the portal.

Had they returned to the 1580s scenario? Or was this illumination from the lamps installed in the excavation cavern?

Before she looked, the lack of a scorched stench told Amelia what lay outside the alien spacecraft.

"The cavern," grunted Corporal Hibbs.

"It didn't collapse..." Corporal Denk remarked.

The two men clambered through the hatch. After a moment (presumably spent determining whether any immediate threats were present outside), Denk helped her climb out onto the scaffolding. Hibbs was nimbly descending the ladder.

It was indeed the lunar cavern, exactly as she'd last seen it. No, wait—a blackened crater lay across the expanse near the access shaft. *That* hadn't been there before. Looking down, Amelia saw a pair of combat pressure suits piled on the floor of the cavern... the same suits they had left outside the ship back in the 1580s burnt forest. But now the suits were here... transported to the Moon along with their displaced occupants.

Clearly this proved that none of them had ever left the lunar base, that their entire Earthside ordeal had been confined to their own warped perceptions. How the three of them—herself, Corporal Hibbs and Private Scarpetti—had shared an identical hallucination was still a mystery, though.

These developments certainly gave credence to the suspicion that the 1580s tableau had been no more than a dream. But if that were the case, how could they place any faith in clues learned while they'd been immersed in that delusional realm? The idea that a witch was behind all of this had come from the Indian she had encountered en route to the abandoned Roanoke settlement. Believing the Indian's explanation seemed foolish if he himself had been nothing more than a prop in the overall mirage. Corporal Denk's twin brother had corroborated the witch tale, but his sanity was patently dubious, making his validation equally spurious.

Looked at logically, the entire account was absurd. How could a witch from the 1580s end up on the Moon five hundred years later?

They were chasing ghosts... but then, they were being harassed by imaginary phantoms. All of which was easily explained away if one introduced an alien virus to the equation. But... if the zombies and the panther had been delusions, then how had these insubstantial illusions managed to physically harm corporeal human beings? Private Scarpetti's openly professed disbelief in the panther hadn't prevented the beast from murdering her.

None of the events here at Eiger base made any sense.

Her economics background refused to accept this blanket excuse. The universe operated by a set of quantum rules. All circumstances could be boiled down to values that adhered to logic. That the goings-on at Eiger base failed to match any known criteria only implied there was something missing from the equation.

Of course, their minds might no longer be adequately operational. The alien virus could have disturbed routine cerebral functions to the point where she and the soldiers were just raving lunatics, plagued by delusions so vivid that any imagined injuries became manifest enough to kill the dreamer.

But if that were the case, neither Amelia nor the surviving soldiers exhibited any signs of insanity. If anything, they were striving to rationally explain their travails. They certainly weren't behaving in a suicidal manner like the Eiger personnel.

Conversely, embarking on a witch hunt wasn't exactly a good example of rational behavior. So, not all of the group's thinking was patently sane.

Dr. Holmes was reminded of a theorem put forth by a person who might have been one of her ancestors—had he not been a fictitious character. "When you have eliminated all possible explanations, whatever remains, however improbable, must be the truth." She had read that in her teens and later in life the doctrine had helped justify her belief in extraterrestrial intelligence. Now that Amelia found herself mired in a situation that embodied wanton illogic, though, she derived no solace from the theorem.

A weary smile tickled her lips. If she, the scholar, was unable to explain anything that had happened to them since they'd arrived at Eiger base, then she could imagine the fretful despair of her plebeian companions' attempts to understand any of this.

No wonder they had so readily accepted blaming a witch for their troubles. When logic failed, all that remained was superstition.

In this miasma of implausible factors, Amelia recalled a piece of advice Corporal Hibbs had offered them. So long as they were stuck in this predicament, if they didn't adjust to its prevailing rules, they had no hope of surviving it. His assumption sounded so pat, so simplistic—and yet so far, Hibbs was still among the survivors. Private Scarpetti's adamant skepticism hadn't protected her from the fangs or claws of the imaginary beast that had slaughtered her.

And if the witch was nothing more than a delusional culprit, then destroying her would have no real effect their plight. They'd be no better—or worse—off. For now, though, it gave the group something on which to focus their energies.

In the end, Amelia felt that the Corporal's outlook was probably the most advantageous one to adopt. When in Rome (went the old adage), act like a Roman. When trapped in a delusional situation, go with the delusion's flow. Swimming against the current would only exhaust you so that you drowned all the quicker.

Either the group would find the witch and slay her, ending all this tyranny… or they'd continue scurrying about until the madness spurred them all into self-destructive outbursts.

When she climbed down from the scaffolding, Corporal Hibbs insisted she don Scarpetti's suit and armor. He would tolerate no dissent. "You'll be safer that way."

Meanwhile, Corporal Denk had dragged his unconscious sibling from the alien ship, then carried him down to brusquely deposit him on the floor of the cavern.

"You take my suit," Hibbs directed Denk. "It's a fair turnabout, since I borrowed the thing from you when the panther shredded my own suit."

"What about you?" worried Amelia.

Hibbs assured her that he could take care of himself.

Denk offered no argument. Nor did he suggest that his brother should wear the remaining suit. There was no gallantry involved between the two, their relationship was clearly steeped in bad blood. Ever since his twin had shown up, Denk had shown very little concern for his kin. Instead, Denk had openly treated him like a troublesome nuisance. But then, from what Amelia had seen, Riccardo Denk *was* a troublesome nuisance. Granted, her feelings for him were colored by resentment for the mistreatment she had suffered at his hands. He claimed the witch's cat had forced him to assault her, but that excuse left her conflicted. On a cerebral level she could understand the extenuating circumstances, but her emotions refused to let Amelia think of him as a victim.

Apparently Corporal Hibbs shared Denk's lack of concern for Riccardo's safety, for he offered no suggestion that the remaining suit should be put to use protecting the other civilian.

As soon as he'd helped Amelia into the pressure suit, Hibbs set off across the cavern, headed for the exit. She followed him at a respectable distance, so that if anything happened she wasn't caught in the thick of things. Hoisting his brother over his now-armored shoulders, Denk brought up the rear.

They skirted the new crater. Amelia couldn't help but notice that slimy gore was sprayed around the explosive indentation. According to Denk, he had used a few C-4 bricks to destroy a composite zombie that had been trying to reassemble itself.

The blast had damaged the ladders leading to the catwalk. At first, Amelia was stymied how to climb up to the rickety platform, hampered as she was by the bulky combat suit. Denk showed her how easy it was to jump to the catwalk in the low lunar gravity. Although he made it look easy, even burdened as he was with his brother's inert body, it took Amelia several leaps to accurately land on the platform. Meanwhile, Hibbs had scaled the struts that supported the platform. By the time the rest of them reached the elevated position, Hibbs was already waiting on the lift.

As they rode the lift up the shaft, Amelia had the distinct impression that Corporal Hibbs was *eager* to get back to the installation. She couldn't imagine why.

36

When the lift reached the laboratory level, Sergio automatically took point. He dumped Riccardo on the floor, then ventured into the corridor.

A ghostly silence dominated the area.

Where was Marshall?

"Dammit," he grumbled.

"What's wrong?" came Hibbs' inquiry.

"Marshall's supposed to be waiting here," announced Sergio. Her absence troubled him. He'd been gone a while. Had she given up hope of his return? Or had something driven her off? Hibbs had mentioned a group of terrorists who'd invaded the base, only to get slaughtered by that damned panther. Had more of them gotten into the installation and surprised her down here? Or had another unsavory hallucination shown up to harass her?

"She'll be around somewhere." Hibbs climbed from the lift and stepped over Riccardo's snoring lump. Dr. Holmes followed with evident reluctance; she stuck close to the Corporal.

Activating his suit's comm-unit, Sergio called out to the missing woman.

When no reply came, Hibbs shrugged. "Probably waiting higher up in the facility."

"I'm going to go look for her," declared Sergio.

"She can wait," Hibbs advised him. "First we have a witch to burn."

At their feet, Riccardo moaned in his sleep, as if their discussion had somehow penetrated the foggy veil of his withdrawal.

"Marsh could be in trouble," asserted Sergio.

"We're all in trouble as long as the witch survives," Hibbs proclaimed.

"Believing in witches is just juvenile, Corporal," complained Dr. Holmes. "And witches on the Moon—that's simply ludicrous."

"You haven't figured it out, Doc?" Hibbs remarked. "I would've thought a smart lady like you would have put the pieces together already."

"What pieces?"

Before Hibbs could respond, Sergio caught movement at the end of the corridor. A shadow stirred in the security tunnel that connected the research level with the rest of the installation. The Bombshell would've started blasting away as she swung the weapon up to bear on the far portal, but the connection between reflex and bloodlust wasn't that strong in Sergio. His hand tightened on the gun, but he held his fire. "Marsh?" he commed. "Is that you?"

It wasn't; at least he hoped it wasn't her. Whoever belonged to the shadow was armed and fired a hostile volley of bullets down the hallway.

Most of the shots spent themselves on the body armor worn by himself and the Doc. Luckily, Riccardo lay behind the lift, out of harm's way.

As Sergio squeezed off a return salvo, he saw Hibbs double over and crumple to the floor. "Doc!" he shouted. "Get Hibbs to cover!"

The woman shouldn't've been hiding behind Hibbs. As the one with the armor, she should've been out front. But civilians weren't the type to stand as a frontline, they ran and hid at the first sign of trouble. Which was exactly what Dr. Holmes was doing now. Instead of coming to the Corporal's assistance, she went scrambling to dive behind the manifold that housed the lift's mechanical winch.

"Dammit, woman!" he snarled. There was no opportunity for Sergio to help Hibbs. A concentration of enemy firepower erupted, the slugs ricocheting along the corridor and gouging into the plastiform walls. Sergio rushed forth to block the passage with his bulky suit. His own combat armor would have to provide his fallen comrade with a modicum of cover.

He heard a raspy voice over the comm-line: "Get 'em, Surge. I can—choke—take care of myself—" Relieved to hear that the surprise attack hadn't taken out Hibbs, Sergio focused his attention on dealing with their new adversary. He sprayed the end of the hallway with bullets, hoping to force the gunman back into the security airlock.

"Traitors!" a voice bellowed over the comm-line. A familiar voice that Sergio was utterly stunned to hear.

"Major Dummheit?" he gasped. "Cease fire, sir—it's us, your troops."

A bark of contemptuous laughter preceded a fresh fusillade of enemy gunfire.

"Of course I know who you are, you treacherous scum! Why do you think I'm shooting at you?"

"Major—we're on the same side—"

"What side would that be, asswipe? The side that mutinied against their legally appointed Commanding Officer? Are you saying I helped you overpower and drug me? I suppose I locked myself in a closet!"

Oh shit, fretted Sergio. *This is bad*—really *bad.* Somebody—or some*thing*—had let the Major out. He was armed now—*where the hell did he get a weapon?*—but worse, the man was gunning for the ones who had usurped his command. There'd be no chance of talking him down. Major Dummy was livid and looking for revenge—or "justice," as he presumably saw things.

"Stop this!" came Dr. Holmes' outcry over the comm-line. "You were acting irrational, Major, endangering us all."

Sergio wished she would shut up. Dummheit was already majorly pissed off, and he'd never appreciated any recommendations offered by the Doc. Her advice would only further infuriate him.

"I knew you were in on it, bitch," growled the Major. "You're all in league with each other—and you're going to pay for that treasonous conspiracy."

"There is no conspiracy, Major," she shouted back. "You're not thinking clearly. The alien virus is screwing with your mind. You—"

"Ah, an 'alien plague'—what a convenient excuse for your mutinous behavior. A pity that I don't believe in your plague. I know you for the traitors you really are!"

Hoping to take advantage of this exchange, Sergio moved forward. He restrained from firing until he got closer. Ammunition was limited, he couldn't afford to waste it on suppressing fire.

But apparently the Major had no concern over the wealth of his arsenal. He blasted away with murderous fervor, filling the passageway with a cloud of high velocity projectiles. Although the shots posed no direct danger to Sergio in his armor, the barrage forced him to pause and shield those behind him with his bulk. He sneaked a quick glance over his shoulder.

Hibbs was crawling for cover. He was moving slow, but with determination. So far, he'd made it halfway to the lift's encased winch. A smear of fresh blood documented his course across the dirty floor.

Crouching behind the winch cowling, Dr. Holmes continued to try to talk sense to the madman attacking them.

"Desist this madness, Major!" she urged. "The same dangers that threaten us threaten you too!"

The Major wasn't going to stop. Sooner or later, another of his shots would catch Hibbs, maybe even Riccardo (not that Sergio really cared about the latter). It was time for some unexpected mayhem to distract the madman's homicidal concentration.

Flinging wide his arms to provide more cover, Surge rushed down the hallway, face-first into the hail storm of slugs. He conserved his ammo, but bellowed loudly over the comm-line, "You stupid son of bitch! How a moron like you ever got out of boot camp alive is a complete mystery! Whoever gave you your commission should be tossed out an airlock! Here I come—your worst nightmare, you limp dick!"

Initially, the Major showed no reaction to Sergio's madcap charge, but as he drew closer, stomping along and waving his arms like a lunatic, the enemy gunfire abated. He caught a glimpse of the Major's shadow retreating into the recesses of the access passageway. This goaded him to run faster, to boldly cross the portal's threshold—

And a rifle butt caught him squarely in the gut. Although his armor defused most of the impact, Sergio stumbled, floundered momentarily. A second blow hit him on his right shoulder, driving his suit's collar into his neck. His temple slammed into the inside of the helmet. He sank to his hands and knees. As he knelt there, stunned, the Major pounced on Sergio and unscrewed his helmet. Before Sergio could regain his wits, the Major was hammering his head with the butt of his rifle. The blows threatened to plummet him into an abyss of oblivion.

He collapsed, rolled on his side. Blood seeping from his head wounds clouded his vision… but he saw the Major stand over him, leering down and sneering, as the bastard shifted the weapon around in his grip so that its barrel pointed directly into Sergio's face.

Not only was Major Dummy wielding a rifle, he was wearing an armored pressure suit. Where the hell could he have gotten that gear? An answer stirred in Sergio's mind, but it took a moment for him to shove aside the waves of pain and access the appropriate synapse. *Marsh!* he gasped. Now Sergio knew why she hadn't been waiting at the top of the lift. The bastard had attacked Marshall and stolen her suit and weaponry!

"Always the smartmouth, eh, Denk?" snarled the Major. "Well, none of your terrorist buddies can help you now, you scumbag. This base belongs to *her*, not your treacherous gang."

Groping feebly, Sergio tried to ward off the rifle's imminent barrel. His head still thick with disorientation, he thought the Major was referring to Marshall. "What did you do to her, you bastard?"

Dummheit threw back his head and cackled. "You stupid jarhead—I let *her* in! And she's helping me punish all of you for your seditious actions."

It seemed highly dubious to Sergio that Marshall would willingly help the madman do anything… except maybe return to a drugged coma. The Major was just raving.

Keep him raving, Sergio advised himself. *Buy me time to strike back at him…* But when he shifted his position, prepatory to springing erect, a swamp of disabling pain flooded his skull. His resolve lost its cohesion. He sank back on his side, staring up at the muddled image of the Major which his wobbly eyes transmitted to his brain. "You hurt Marshall," he gasped.

"Screw Marshall!" barked the Major. Then he cackled anew with derisive scorn, "But then, you already have, haven't you? You have to stick it to every woman you see, don't you, you slimy stud. Big dick and a petty mind running it."

"I nailed your wife," Sergio choked out. Anything to blow the bastard's cool.

"You—" The Major's eyes flared wide with a mixture of denial and rage. "Don't you dare talk about my Tara!"

"Stealing your command was her idea." *Keep piling it on, build his fury to the point where he gets sloppy…*

"Lies!" howled Major Dummheit. He squared off and re-aimed his rifle at Sergio's head.

Uh oh—pushed him too far—

Rallying vitality that didn't exist, Sergio flung himself aside at the last instant.

"Surge!" his earbud buzzed. "Report!"

The rifle barked and spat shells that zipped past Sergio so close that the trajectory of one of them singed a scar across his left temple.

Coming out of nowhere, a naked figure tackled the Major. Assailant and victim went down in a flailing tumble before Sergio could identify whoever had come to his rescue. Gunshots quaked in Sergio's hearing, drowning any outcries issued by the clash.

Straining to exploit this sudden reprieve, Sergio concentrated on purging himself of incapacitation. He willed the vortex of agony that frothed within his head to subside, failing that to at least diminish slightly, enough for him to transmit practical mandates from his shell-shocked brain to his uncooperative limbs. It was a momentous struggle, yet for all the herniating exertion he applied his arms barely trembled. He embellished his laborious deliberation with nondenominational prayers, beseeching a generic deity to cast off his confusion, to help him bully his way past the misery and achieve mental clarity. Violent tremors plagued his coordination. He succeeded in goading movement into his arms, but that animation was crude, too callow to perform the physical realignment he needed. Zealous though they were, his efforts only managed to roll him onto his stomach, where he lay wheezing through clenched teeth and wincing from the fierce headache incited by his futile labor.

Dimly aware that a flurry ensued nearby, Sergio caught hints of a chorus of grunts and meaty thumps just beyond the range of his immediate hearing. A scuffle—a fight. Whoever had come to his rescue was getting the crap kicked out of them.

He twisted to bend his arms and plant the palms of his gloved hands against the floor. He struggled to push himself up... but his muscles refused to cooperate. All he did was intensify the hurricane roaring inside the confines of his skull. Flashes of light occluded his already blurred vision. His peripheral view closed in as gloom dampened those ocular flares. He felt his arms tremble, then give way.

The floor rushed up and smashed him in the face.

Categorical darkness swallowed him.

37

Dammit, Corporal Hibbs groaned to himself, *that's the last thing we need right now.*

He didn't bother wondering how the Major had gotten free, or where the bastard had found a weapon. These developments were par for the way things went in this place. If anything could happen to make matters worse for the squad, it happened—and at the worst possible moment.

Because, he knew, there was nothing circumstantial about these haphazard travails; they were intentional and quite strategic.

At least the witch hadn't improved Major's bad aim. Hibbs' shoulder hurt like someone was jabbing it with a red hot poker, but he could tell it was a superficial injury. If he could reach Dr. Holmes, he could grab a med-patch from her suit's first aid kit and stop the bleeding. A stim shot would abolish the pain and get him back on his feet.

Major Dummy was nothing more than a distraction. By this point, Hibbs had fit the clues together in his head. He knew the witch was to blame for everything. He knew where she was, and he knew how she'd gotten there. And just as firmly he knew that only by dealing with her could they stop these relentless attacks... and restore peace and quantum order to the Eiger installation.

Surge could deal with Major Dummy, Hibbs was fairly confident of that. Sergio was armed and armored. He would rush the bastard and take him out.

Hibbs hoped that Surge would employ some restraint in that beatdown. So far, the squad was only guilty of relieving Major Dummy of his command. Enough video evidence existed to prove Dummheit's incompetency, so they would be exonerated of any mutiny charges. That verdict would change if somebody wasted the asswipe. The Big Brass tended to frown on enlisted men killing officers.

Someone ran past Hibbs. He twisted about, but his shoulder wound protested about that sudden contortion. An explosion of pain momentarily blinded Hibbs.

For a moment he worried that foolish valor had suddenly overwhelmed Dr. Holmes, spurring the civilian to dash to Surge's help.

Then someone grabbed him and dragged him behind the cowling that covered the lift's winch machinery. And he saw it was the Doc.

So—who ran off?

Simple mathematics gave Hibbs his answer. It had to be Surge's twin. The nuisance had woken up and gone to his sibling's assistance. The fool: naked, unarmed and untrained. Hopefully Surge would disable Major Dummy before his brother got hurt.

"Are you all right?" the Doc was whining. Her oversized glove fumbled against his wound in a clumsy effort to stem his bloodflow.

He reached past her arm and engaged in some fumbling of his own. Maneuvering by touch, he located the first aid kit and rooted through its contents until his fingers came upon the flat pliant rectangle he wanted. Brushing aside her arm, Hibbs tore open the med-patch and applied it to the hole in his upper torso. Next, he fetched a stimulant pod and injected the chemicals directly into his carotid artery.

Seconds later a wave of vivid clarity blossomed in Corporal Hibbs. He sat up, then drew back into shelter behind the winch manifold. The exchange of gunfire had ceased, but, unprotected as he was, Hibbs had no desire to take another bullet if this lapse was only temporary.

"Surge!" he commed. "Report!"

No answer.

"Watch out," he called anyway. "Your brother's incoming."

"The alien virus has driven Major Dummheit insane," fretted Dr. Holmes.

There is no mind-bending alien disease, Hibbs reflected. *Major Dummy has always been an asshole.* But he didn't vocalize any of this for the Doc. He had no time to waste on explanations. Action was called for—immediate and lethal.

Grabbed the woman by both her shoulders, Hibbs sternly advised her, "Stay here. Whatever happens, don't move from this spot." Releasing her, he snatched up the satchel he had loaded and raced off down the corridor.

Speed was essential at this stage. If the witch had her psychic hands full right now manipulating her Dummheit puppet, she might not notice Hibbs coming.

But as he reached the doorstep of her secret lair, the witch proved her ability to multitask.

Everything went blurry when Hibbs' hand touched the door to the laboratory.

He opened the door and stumbled into a full-blown inferno. Fierce pain danced along his exposed limbs. The raging heat made him recoil. Momentarily blinded, his stride broke.

It has to be an illusion, he told himself. The witch wouldn't start a blaze this huge so close to her remains. *Fire is her enemy, she'd never use it to defend herself. She's trying to project her own worst fear against me. This blaze is imaginary, no more than a spell she's cast to ward me off.*

Mustering his resolve, Hibbs strained to disregard the flames and the agony they inflicted. These sensations were extremely difficult to ignore. Fire was a universal terror to all living things, the impulse was rooted deep in his psyche. When you stuck your hand in a fire, you didn't consciously decide to yank it back out, it was a reflex action. Overriding that automatic response took an enormous amount of concentration.

Leaving him undefended against the witch's next wave of attack.

Suddenly the scalding flames became slithering snakes. A solid wall of serpents closed in around him. The creatures wound themselves around his arms, his legs, his torso, his neck, his head. A vehement spasm traveled through his body, expressing another deep-rooted revulsion common among human beings. The serpentine enclosure tightened on him. He felt several bites across his body, but ignored them.

Just like the flames, these snakes weren't real. Reality was defined by the stronger will-power. The witch wielded ancient skills, but Hibbs was a Marine. His determination was inviolate, ideally impervious to interference. She could throw anything she wanted at him, but it wouldn't work.

The panther had possessed substance because it was a physical manifestation of her familiar. The zombies had been reanimated dead bodies. These weapons had been real.

Granted, the witch had achieved a high degree of tangibility with such tricks as walling off the installation's passages, but that had been before Hibbs had identified that the changes were illusionary and depended on the subjects' ignorance. But he knew better now.

The snakes became wolverines, gnawing and tearing at his flesh.

Ignore them.

The wolverines scattered into insects, buzzing and burrowing into his skin.

Not real.

The insects dissolved into acid, sizzling and smoking and dripping from his unbothered body.

After the fire, that *almost tickles.*

The corrosive flood evaporated, leaving behind not even a hint of its caustic stink.

Hibbs stood in the dingy laboratory where the squad had gathered the human remains from the rest of the base. At the time, they'd believed those cadavers had belonged to the Eiger personnel who had suffered mutilation and suicide. One body, though, was not a citizen of the 21st century: it had, in fact, died over 500 years ago.

Presently, most of the Eiger staff corpses no longer resided in this impromptu morgue. Various body parts had been used to assemble the super-zombie Surge had fought. What remained were for the most part scattered pieces. Except one intact cadaver that lay in a corner.

"There you are," growled Hibbs.

From the carcass' withered condition, the squad had assumed this person had been burned during the staffers' mass madness. The atrocities inflicted on the other bodies were more severe, so had merited more horrified attention. They had seen nothing extraordinary about this woman's corpse. But now that he knew what to look for, Hibbs saw how ancient the cadaver truly was. Its crispy condition was due to decomposition, not immolation. All along, the witch had been hiding out in plain sight. Her mummified remains had been mistaken by the squad as just another dead research scientist.

"You can't fool me now," Hibbs informed her.

He half-expected the carcass to sit up and curse him. But the witch remained the inert calcified mass which time had made of her. No movement stirred her desiccated limbs. No ghostly light twinkled in her empty eye sockets.

Instead, a shimmering mist rose from the mummified corpse. It hung there, seething and roiling like an angry living cloud. Eventually, the airborne quagmire extended itself into a figure of bipedal configuration. Legs fell from the ball of radiant gas to dangle centimeters above the floor. Arms depended and lifted in defiance. The central mass reconfigured into a curvaceous torso. Large breasts formed. An emergent lump bubbled and became a head. Its exterior flowed like liquid, adopting approximate human features. Within seconds that crude facade had fashioned itself into a seductive face with sensuous thick lips and heavily lashed enormous eyes. The forehead was high, the chin pointed, the cheeks plump like a devilish pixy. Tendrils sprouted from her cranium and swiftly spun into filmy strands of hair. These tresses undulated around her like an animated shroud. Deep within that flowing veil glowed a pair of rancorous scarlet eyes.

Corporal Hibbs stood his ground, refusing to flinch or to show any fear.

"*Thee be of no use to me,*" the specter intoned. The voice sounded like sand spilling across corrugated metal. In no way did it match the erotic persona she wore.

"Good," he grunted back at the phantom.

"*Bring unto me thy womenfolk. One of them will serve as a viable host for mine spirit.*"

"Not going to happen."

The specter bridled with indignity. "*Now!*"

"You don't scare me, bitch," declared Hibbs.

He was beholden to Dr. Holmes for the crucial pieces of the puzzle which she unwittingly had provided earlier. The familiar had been the witch's connection to whatever demonic force fueled her sorcery. The substantiality of her spells had relied on an energy boost from the cat. Without her familiar, the witch's power was restricted to phantasms. Her magic had lost its venom.

"Go ahead," he goaded the malicious spirit. "Try something."

Wisps of ectoplasm ebbed from her accusatory fingers. The tendrils unfurled out, reaching for him and mutating as they came. A conglomerate of bestial heads emerged from the ethereal filaments, bulging forth and snapping their deformed jaws. Worms sporting toothy maws sprang from those slavering mouths, all writhing in Hibbs' direction.

Remaining steadfast, he swatted these chimera aside. The passage of his hand disintegrated the monstrous strands as if they were made of smoke. He sweetened his victory with a caustic chuckle.

The witch's gaze flared with an acrimonious dazzle.

Enough of this, Hibbs cautioned himself. After all the nightmares this bitch had inflicted on them, it was satisfying to see her fume with impotency. But... he could not afford to overplay his advantage. *Strike now—before she figures out some way to stop me.*

He reached for the satchel that hung from his waist. It contained the tools that would bring about the witch's annihilation.

The ground gave way beneath Hibbs. He fell and pitched down an incline of tall weeds. Clambering to his feet at the base of the hill, he recognized his surroundings. The Roanoke settlement spread before him, restored and unburned. This time the tableau was populated; people in colonial attire wandered among the log cabins. Several of them stopped to stare at the near-naked man who had just fallen from the hill.

"Nice try," Hibbs muttered under his breath. "But I know this is just an illusion."

He didn't flinch when a few of the colonists charged him. The pitchforks and blazing torches they brandished didn't intimidate him in the least. They assailed him with their weapons, growing increasingly exasperated when their hostility failed to have any effect on him.

Ignoring these phantoms, Hibbs strode down into the settlement. The colonists scattered at his advance, as if fleeing from some devil.

According to his calculations, the witch's cadaver was located a few meters ahead of him... back in the makeshift morgue. Here in the imaginary village, that put her position just inside the nearest cabin.

He kicked down its rustic door and entered. He drew a magnesium flare from his satchel. In the other hand he held a bulb of napalm.

In the cabin's shadowy interior, he spied the witch. She stood hunched over a table whose surface was littered with occult accouterments. A bowl vented a cloud of foul smoke. A selection of animal bones were decorated with runes. Several jars of noxious powders sat within her reach. In this incarnation, she stood devoid of any voluptuous pretense. This, Hibbs suspected, was what the witch truly looked like—had looked like when she'd been alive. She was a middle-aged woman, prematurely wrinkled, with straggly gray hair, a crone with spindly limbs and an overlong neck. Astringent was the only word for her pinched face. Not even an earnest smile could transform that visage into something that would fail to frighten a child.

"Nay," she spoke. "Tis yee whom are the illusion here."

"Shall we test that?" chuckled Hibbs. He crossed to her in a single lunar bound. En route he thumbed the flare alight. Up close now, confronting the witch across her makeshift altar, Hibbs squirted napalm in her face.

She recoiled in horror. Clearly she had believed herself immune to anything he could do. That she felt the dose of chemical gelatin came as quite a shock to her, not to mention its painful sting against her weathered flesh.

"Surprise," crowed Hibbs.

Reaching out, he drove the flare's sputtering tip into the witch's screaming mouth. For a second her luminous eyes fixed on his, communicating a near-palpable blast of hate, then they narrowed as her nervous system carried a rush of pain from the lining of her mouth to her brain. She spat out the flare, but too late. The incendiary magnesium kernel had ignited the napalm with which he had doused her. Blue flames spread down the woman's neck and across her jellied dress.

Hibbs stepped back to watch her fire dance.

She beat at herself in a futile effort to extinguish the flames, but she only succeeded in transferring the blaze to her hands and arms. Her rat's-nest hair vanished in a puff of combustion. She thrashed about with unaccustomed anxiety. Until now, the witch had perpetrated her villainy long-distance, protected from reprisals by the fact that no one even suspected she existed. Now she was face-to-face with an adversary who knew she existed—and had deduced her weakness.

Her frantic paroxysm knocked over the table. The strewn powders spread the fire throughout the room. Soon, the entire cabin was ablaze.

Amid this inferno, the witch twisted and contorted and cursed and shrieked. After a while, she started to shrivel up. Pieces flaked off her. Her contracting muscles drew her arms into a tight self-embrace. Her mouth yawned in a lipless lament. She sank to her knees, then fell to shatter into blackened cinders across the dirt floor.

"Gotcha, bitch," Hibbs proclaimed. His tone lacked any trace of jubilation. His statement was made with cold certainty, not gloating glee.

Before he could back out of the burning cabin, the structure disappeared. The mirage melted back into history as the witch's environmental alteration slipped away.

On the floor of the laboratory-turned-morgue, flames engulfed the witch's napalm-drenched mummified remains. Hibbs' aim had been true in both worlds.

Little else in the lab was flammable, which drastically limited the fire's ability to spread to the rest of the installation.

Although the witch's corpus no longer had a mouth or throat to generate more outcries, the psychic ether was thick with her dying wrath. Intangible waves saturated Hibbs as he stood over her burning carcass. Her mental screams lambasted him. Not expecting the outburst to last, he endured the acute discomfort.

He was wrong.

The witch's rage overwhelmed him. It became a genuine heat that scalded his mind with pain which rivaled that produced by her earlier illusionary inferno. The agony drowned him, crushing his consciousness beneath its cosmic weight. He felt his mind crumple under the psychic pressure.

For an instant the witch's persona became superimposed over Hibbs' personality. In that flash, a series of memories forced themselves upon the soldier's mind.

Her name had been Millicent Pruitt. Born to pauper parents in 1546 Leeds in old England, she had been tutored in sorcery by an old woman who'd lived alone in the woods. By the time she was in her mid-twenties, Millicent had enthralled a suitably prosperous husband for herself in London.

She never expected to actually fall in love with him, but she had—only to lose him to cholera less than two years into their chaste marriage. His death darkened her spirit, instilling her with a savage loathing for everyone and everything around her. For a while she derived minor solace from the torments she doled out to neighbors and local merchants, but their suffering failed to compensate for her loss.

When she heard that Sir Raleigh was organizing a third group of people to populate his Roanoke colony in the New World, Millicent recognized this as her chance to escape the bad memories that came with living in London. She conjured herself onto the colony's short-list and left England far behind.

In Roanoke, though, she was an outcast. She didn't fit in, but more so: she was dramatically intolerant of frontier life. Colonial existence was harsh and spartan, devoid of even the simplest pleasures. To maintain her own luxurious comfort in this wilderness, she cast spells and appropriated supplies for herself from everyone else's larders.

Her neighbors soon resented her inexplicable prosperity. Gradually, this resentment blossomed into outright hatred. The settlement was small; it was inevitable that sooner or later someone was going to discover Millicent's witchcraft. She denied their public accusations, but knew that her sorcery would not indefinitely stifle their suspicions.

Later that night, aided by her hellcat familiar, Millicent Pruitt cast a spell that sent every last colonist into oblivion. Now no one would bother her peaceful life.

Or so she thought.

The devil ship came one autumn evening as she slept. She never saw it, but learned the details of its arrival from her familiar who had witnessed the vessel's descent from the sky. According to Pyewacket, it had been sau-cer-shaped and flew without wings or the support of any hot-air balloons. Penetrating the clouds to hover directly above her cabin, the saucer had bathed the area with lights that had been eerie even to the demonic cat. The familiar had sought shelter from this unearthly radiance under its mistress' bed—and had thereby shared in her abduction.

Millicent Pruitt, last surviving member of the lost Roanoke colony, awoke in unfamiliar surroundings—unfamiliar and extraterrestrial, al-though she had no way of identifying them as such. To her, the chamber was strange and obviously not-of-this-earth—so she presumed it to be of satanic design. She further deduced that some devil had been presumptuous enough to claim her soul before her time. Neither the witch nor her enraged familiar would tolerate such nefarious deceit. By harvesting the souls of hundreds of colonists for her diabolical masters, Millicent had bought herself an ex-tended existence on Earth. She refused to be prematurely damned.

When the devil's minions, spindly gray creatures with bulbous heads, came to fetch her, Millicent had, with Pyewacket's aid, burned them with a hellfire of her own. She then proceeded to search the rest of this strange, metal-walled place, hunting down and incinerating each gray minion she encountered. She found only one window, but its view revealed to her a dismal darkness outside; starlight twinkled in that black abyss, and an enor-mous ashen globe loomed in that absolute gloom. (Schooled in sorcery, not astronomy, the witch failed to recognize the celestial body as the Moon. Having no knowledge of the UFOs of 20th century urban legend, she had no idea that she had been abducted by aliens in a flying saucer. The Hibbs portion of the psychic gestalt knew these things, though.) *As she watched, that gray globe became a stark horizon; then a lifeless landscape rushed up and swallowed the devil ship. The impact threw her wildly about the narrow passageway, breaking several bones, among them those in her spine. For all its demonic attributes, her familiar suffered similar brutalities. Both were dead within seconds of the saucer's lunar crash-landing.*

(Again, Hibbs understanding of things provided the dying witch with a rudimentary comprehension of what actually had occurred. By slaughtering the Gray aliens—and their large turtle-like servants—the witch had left no one to navigate the flying saucer. Without a pilot, the spacecraft had fallen prey to lunar gravity and crashed on the dark side of the Moon.)

Physical death did not put an end to Millicent Pruitt, however. Her satanic pact had endowed her with exceptional longevity. Her spirit lived on, trapped in her broken body. She spent untold years in this horrible prison. (More like five hundred years, Hibbs informed her.) And then—people dug her up.

(The witch's pre-industrial outlook was incapable of fathoming a technology that could carry man beyond the Earth, into outer space—having been born in an era in which everyone believed the world was flat, she didn't even know what "outer space" meant. If the notion of traveling all the way to other planets ever occurred to her, it would have required an extreme variety of astral projection.)

As far as she was concerned, frontiersmen unearthed her saucer-shaped coffin. The colonization of the New World had continued west until it had finally reached the barren gray territory where the devil ship had crashed. They were strange folk, these far-western pioneers. Their language was difficult to follow even for someone who eavesdropped on their thoughts. From their minds she plucked astounding images: gigantic metal birds that swallowed people and carried them across vast distances without digesting these passengers; windows that were thresholds to different worlds; inert chunks that could mutate into edible food with the application of water; tiny devices that held miniature orchestras prisoner inside themselves. These people busied themselves with tasks that were beyond her ken. Their tools seemed more like magical talismans to the ancient witch. These frontiersmen were great wizards.

Enslaving them would win the witch a retinue of servile magicians. She would resume her life in the lap of unbelievable luxury. Maybe she would even tame one of those metal falcons and travel to see exotic lands.

Just as Millicent's consciousness had endured the ravages of centuries, so had the dark spirit of her familiar. Together, they schemed to conquer these "scientists" who had dug her up.

It seemed to take these scientists an unduly long time before they found her corpse within the devil ship. Their pursuits were mesmerized by the vessel itself. Discovery of the gray minions' cadavers sent these people into an intellectual frenzy.

Impatience drove Millicent to intrude upon their minds. Her intent had been subjugation from within, but the subjects' mentalities were too foreign to the witch's antediluvian perspective. Instead of bending their volition to her will, her psychic influence deranged their sanity. They became violent, self-destructive; after ages of dormancy, the witch approved of this bloodshed, even encouraged it. There were those among the scientists whose minds retained residual independence, who rebelled against her psychic domination. They endeavored to thwart her ambitions of conquest, so she authorized a glut of butchery that swept through the "Eiger base," as they called this excavation site. Before she realized that her fun was depriving her of subservient slaves, the Eiger scientists had nearly wiped themselves out. The "survivors" turned out to be too unbalanced to be of any use to her. None of them would provide her ancient spirit with a healthy new host.

She was on the brink of despair when outsiders arrived at the remote installation.

Sensing the approach of the lunar tractor, Millicent reached out her psychic persuasion to lure the prospectors down into the subterranean base. Her siren call tipped Moss from latent instability over the line into full-blown mania. With Riccardo Denk, her temptation was more effective; he left the tractor and willingly entered the gamut of her enchantment.

Greed and confusion made Riccardo especially receptive to her guidance. He followed her ethereal supervision deep into the underground base, paying no attention to the wreckage through which he passed. Without question, he pledged himself to the witch, body and soul.

(Her glimpses into Riccardo's psyche offered Hibbs a basis for him to understand Surge's attitude toward his estranged sibling. Although they were identical twins, the two couldn't have been more different as far as their personalities were concerned. Where Surge was honorable and brave, Riccardo was a craven opportunist. While a well-rounded ass might turn Surge's head, the barest hint of convenient fortune was all that was needed to bait Riccardo through the gates of hell.)

With the advent of the squad of Marines, Millicent turned dominion of Riccardo over to her trusted familiar, so that she could personally monitor the soldiers' approach. She tormented them with their own worst fears in an attempt to weed out any unsuitable individuals. The one with the strongest mindset had fallen to her spectral gauntlet, leaving only the weak-willed to enter.

(It came as no surprise to Hibbs that Corporal Green had been a strong-willed individual. But Hibbs was disturbed to learn that the rest of the squad had been deemed easy targets for the witch's subjugation. He certainly thought of himself as a person of staunch personal convictions... but apparently he was not as stalwart as he'd believed, for he too had been victimized by the witch's telepathically induced illusions. Things had changed, though. Coping with those tribulations had fortified Hibbs' determination to the point where he had been able to successfully oppose the witch and defeat her.)

The witch concentrated her psychic interference on the weakest members of the group.

Major Dummheit's pomposity was monstrous, but it turned out to be a thin shell that hid an emotional vacuum that was easily influenced—no surprise there.

Normally, Hibbs would never have considered Surge to be weak-willed, but Sergio Denk became the witch's prime target. His carnal appetite was a severe character flaw in the regard of the witch's Elizabethan morals. Besides, a link existed between Sergio and his twin. With Riccardo already bewitched, she found she could use him as a conduit to facilitate her efforts to screw with Surge's mind.

Not that the witch ignored the others. Each of them carried their own psychic defect that allowed her to warp their perceptions so vividly that a cut suffered during their delusions would bleed in the real world.

For all her intelligence, Dr. Holmes harbored superstitious tendencies, chiefly manifested in her fanatical belief in UFOs.

Corporal Marshall shared Surge's immorality, thereby condemning her in the witch's puritanical evaluation.

For all her gutter-brat bravada, Private Scarpetti harbored a deep-rooted insecurity that provided the witch with an open backdoor into her mind.

While Hibbs—his rigid pragmatism was his weakness. By adhering to protocol and practicing strict logic, he was inherently incapable of accepting things that contradicted the norm.

The witch's ultimate goal was to steal a new body for herself. Her obvious choices were Dr. Holmes, Corporal Marshall, and Private Scarpetti, for Millicent had no aspirations to explore cross-genderization. Marshall's sexual promiscuity intimidated the witch, as did Scarpetti's built-for-sex anatomy, so Holmes became the primary target. While Holmes was no virgin, the extent of her licentious activities hardly rivaled the soldiers' quenchless immorality. Before the witch could transfer her spirit into the woman's body, though, the occupant soul needed to be destroyed.

While Millicent Pruitt concentrated on her psychic interference, her familiar acerbated the squad's overall stress level by providing them with tangible threats. The reanimation of corpses was easily achieved through sorcery, further adding to the group's tribulations. The higher the tension, the more receptive the subjects became to the witch's influence.

But when Dr. Holmes was finally isolated, Riccardo Denk had resisted the witch's commands to debase his captive. Before measures could be initiated to completely suppress his independence, his twin intervened and res-

cued the woman. Afterward, the group guarded Dr. Holmes too well. The witch was forced to redirect her assault, invading Holmes' dreams and relocating the woman to a fabricated Roanoke tableau where Millicent hoped to destroy her soul and leave her mind open for a new occupant.

It had been a mistake to exile Hibbs and Scarpetti to that imaginary countryside. The witch hadn't expected the soldiers to find Dr. Holmes. The witch's attempts to panic them into dispersal failed; the fire spurred Hibbs to protect the woman.

By leading them to an earthbound version of the crashed devil ship, the witch hoped to gather them all together in a doomed position. She planned to amplify their paranoia to the point where they might start taking each other out. She underestimated the resolve these individuals could muster under pressure, especially the Marines.

Leaving Pyewacket to harass the group now trapped inside the devil ship in the lunar cavern, she shifted her focus to Corporal Marshall. Using Moss' reanimated corpse to free Major Dummheit, the witch assumed control of the deposed C.O. for the purpose of disabling Marshall and making her ready to host Millicent's hungry spirit.

She might have succeeded, too, had it not been for the sudden destruction of her familiar. This was an unprecedented development, horrifying in its implications. Corporal Hibbs had actually struck a crippling blow against the witch's domination. Outrage overwhelmed her. Hibbs had to be punished—and promptly, before he could win any more victories against the witch. She redirected her Dummheit puppet to go slaughter this impudent nuisance.

But—contrary to the witch's desires, Hibbs eluded annihilation. A single bullet caught him, inflicting a painful but minor wound. In succession, the Denks rallied to challenge the Major's attack, allowing Hibbs to reach the witch's so-far hidden-in-plain-sight remains.

Incarnate hate and loathing were the witch's response to Corporal Hibbs' triumph over her. The man's resolve defied her diminished mesmerism. Nothing she threw at the battered soldier slowed him down. It was as if he knew the nature of the foe he faced—a fact she now confirmed, learning from Hibbs' ambient consciousness how he had assembled clues given to him by the imaginary Indian and gotten secondhand from Riccardo's hysterical babbling. Clearly, she had underestimated the Corporal's cognitive and physical prowess—finally paying for that mistake with her own destruction.

But even as she perished, Millicent Pruitt refused to let this nemesis survive.

These revelations flooded Hibbs' mind with the same proprietary ease that his own thoughts resided in the synapses within his head. As the witch's spirit ebbed from her desiccated cadaver, her consciousness merged with Hibbs', not fusing into a single gestalt but rather coexisting as separate memories.

This was the witch's final bid for survival. If she could establish a connection with the man, a chance existed that she could bully him out of his own skull and usurp his body. Although she had been loathe to consider a male host, the wretch's surprise victory over her had left the witch no choice. Unless she commandeered his meat, Millicent Pruitt was doomed to imminent damnation.

Their psychic union was a double-edged sword, though. Just as his mind became an open book to her, the converse was equally true. The connection revealed the witch's heinous scheme to the soldier, enabling him to resist her invasion. While she possessed more skill with telepathic matters, recent insights had matured his resolve into an impenetrable barrier that did not even buckle under her devastating assault. The witch battered her psychic wrath against his volatile determination... to no avail. She couldn't connect with any of his neurons and secure herself in his cerebellum.

This ultimate failure sent her rage into a final explosive spasm.

Unable to burrow into a niche within his mind, she scrabbled to latch onto some part of his consciousness. Any part would suffice, for all she wanted to do now was dig in her psychic claws and hold on like a spectral vise.

Death pulled at her spirit, a force that could not be ignored or shaken off. Death's hold on her was immutable. There was no escape.

If the witch was headed for hell, then she was going to take her nemesis with her.

Death's own pull would yank Hibbs' soul from his body and drag it along with her down into the abyss of eternal damnation. He would share in her forlorn fate.

All she had to do was get a grip on the man's consciousness... but her vicious assault failed, scraping its psychic talons against the perfectly smooth barricade of his resolve. Even her death's-door frenzy couldn't scratch that potent shield.

Unfortunately the experience was just as traumatic for Corporal Hibbs. Maintaining the integrity of his confidence in the face of the witch's last-gasp zeal was an exhausting accomplishment, especially for someone illiterate in the nuances of psychic warfare. She had volumes of abominable expertise, while he was a callow novice in matters like this. She should have had her way with him, tearing apart his mind with brutal glee... but somehow he rallied the fortitude to resist her exorbitant onslaught. Somehow Hibbs suffered the agonizing pressure exerted on his consciousness. He not only fought to remain in control, he fought to maintain his sanity. The pain was unbearable. It felt as if hot knives gouged at his brain. But he held firm, refusing to relent for an instant.

He fought to defend mankind. If the witch beat him at this mental duel, she would usurp his body. He would die, she would survive. And she would find a way to leave this underground installation, to go out and enslave humanity. *That,* he could not allow to happen. The witch was evil and crazy and vindictive and malicious and sadistic, a selection of traits made even more repulsive with her sorcery backing them up. Hibbs' own life was immaterial in this struggle. Honor drove him to fight for the Greater Good.

It was *this* selfless motivation that empowered Hibbs' resolve to ward off the witch's dying scramble.

She slipped away, drawn into a void beyond the material world.

Once she was gone, he didn't relax. He trusted nothing in this battle. Even victory could explode in his face if he prematurely celebrated. He remained stiffly standing over the witch's ashes, his mind stayed locked down like a nuclear powered steel trap.

Minutes passed and no trace of the witch flickered among the psychic ether. She was gone. Dead... finally dead.

Just to be certain, Hibbs stomped on her remains. He pulverized her cinders into loose soot. He erased any physical evidence that she had ever existed.

Five hundred years after her death, Millicent Pruitt had finally passed on.

Standing in the doorway of the smoky morgue, Hibbs surveyed what had been a laboratory level but had turned into a battleground for the future of mankind. The walls, floor and ceiling were scarred by gunfire and stained with blood—some of it his own, most of it from undead splatter. Clots of viscera were randomly distributed around, residue of the Eiger staffers whose corpses had been conscripted to become the super-zombie which Surge and Marshall had destroyed. Several of the doors hung open, revealing the murky depths of labs that madness had converted into modern torture chambers. Next door to where he stood lay the alien morgue; those remains had been ignored by the witch who had possessed no racial affinity with those extraterrestrial cadavers.

Noises came from down the hall, but they didn't prompt Hibbs into a defensive mode. These sounds were wholly human and tinged with emotional relief. Everyone was recuperating from the witch's final puppet attack.

Now that the witch was gone, the group's struggle for survival was over. Hibbs had defeated their real enemy, but he knew how difficult it was going to be to convince them of his victory. They'd never really believed in the witch in the first place; an alien contagion made a more acceptable explanation for the mayhem they had all suffered. If he hadn't battled the witch face-to-face, their minds united in an unholy merger, he too would have found his tale hard to swallow. The idea of a 16th century witch on the Moon was ludicrous.

Global was never going to accept the true explanation of what had occurred here at Eiger base. Modern civilization was ruled by science and logic. Superstition had no place in a culture on the cusp of the 22nd century.

A flurry of consequences swirled in Hibbs' head. None of the repercussions he envisioned boded well for anybody. No matter how it played out, he wasn't happy with the outcome. Someone had to act to prevent this impending doomsday.

Turning away from the sounds of his comrades, Hibbs went to implement the only answer which, in his opinion, might save humanity.

38

Upon regaining consciousness, Sergio opened his eyes and stared up at his own face in a mirror. No, that wasn't him. He hadn't had hair that long in over a decade, and his face had *never* been that chubby. It was Riccardo, his twin brother. who bent over him.

"Finally back with us, huh?"

"What are you doing here?" grunted Sergio.

"Nice," sighed Riccardo. He twisted his mouth with reproach. "I come to your rescue—and that's the thanks I get."

"What 'rescue'?" But then Sergio sat up, took in his surroundings… and he remembered where he was, what had happened, and from whom he had needed to be rescued.

Major Dummheit lay across the cramped tunnel. From the slack posture of his body, one might've thought he was dead, but the man's raspy snoring belayed that assessment. He was just unconscious.

"You took out the Major?" gasped Sergio. "How the hell did *you* disable a Marine officer in battle armor?"

With a sly smirk, Riccardo confided, "I fought dirty."

Sergio's curiosity regarding how his brother had overpowered the Major was short-lived. Other concerns rose to the forefront of his mind.

Clambering to his feet, Sergio demanded, "Where's Marshall?"

"Who?" his twin replied with innocent bewilderment.

That's right, Sergio realized. *Ricky doesn't know Marsh.*

"The Major stole Marshall's suit and her weapons. I need to find her."

Riccardo turned away and shouted down the passageway, "Hey, are you Marshall?"

A moment later, someone came to the mouth of the security tunnel. Smears of blood decorated the person's pressure suit. Sergio instantly knew it wasn't Marshall.

"Dr. Holmes," blurted Sergio. "Have you seen Marshall?"

"Corporal Marshall? No, I haven't seen her."

Dammit! Worry welled in Sergio's gut. Despite Major Dummheit's normal surly attitude, the man wasn't a violent individual. But fired up by his delusional conviction that his troops had turned against him, he had attacked them, had actually tried to shoot Sergio in the face. When the Major had ambushed Marshall and stolen her gear—had the bastard just knocked her out? Or had he killed her?

"Marsh!" he called on the comm-line, but he didn't really expect an answer. Ever since the squad had gotten to the base, the rock walls had interfered with their communications links. She could be a single floor up and never receive his transmission. He had to go look for her.

He grabbed up his helmet and screwed it back in place. Snatching up his rifle, Sergio made to dash off.

"Where are you going?" Dr. Holmes moaned.

"To find Marshall," he called back to her as he raced along the tunnel. Through the access hatch he went, then up the stairs. He would search each floor for her, every closet and cabinet, if he had to. He would find her!

And if the Major killed her? He ground his teeth together. *She's all I have left.* God help the bastard if Sergio found her dead.

He suppressed his rage; it would only muddy his concentration. He must remain sharp, alert for delusions that could pop up to prevent him from finding her.

His boots clomped on the steps, the echoes bouncing ahead of him up the stairwell.

Realistically, Marshall wasn't *all* he had left. There was Riccardo. Granted, for a long time he hadn't counted his brother among the people he cared about, but he might just have to reevaluate that disregard now. *Ricky jumped the Major, stopped the bastard from putting a bullet in my head. That has to count for something.* Maybe the estrangement between twins had run its course, bringing them full circle, back into each other's lives. Sergio couldn't deny that it had taken guts to tackle the Major. Riccardo had been naked and unarmed, yet he had managed to overpower the armored Major. Even more astounding: his normally lazy coward of a brother had put himself in harm's way to protect Sergio. *That* was entirely unlike the Riccardo he knew. Something had changed him, changed him for the better.

When this was over, Sergio would give him a big hug, and they would sit down and have a beer and get to know each other. They might become as tight as identical twins were supposed to be. But that would be later.

Right now he was worried about Marshall's safety. That anxiety etched creases across his forehead and generated an acid hole in his stomach. His heart ached with the prospect that he would find her murdered body—or worse, that he would find *no* body, that the weirdness might have snatched her away.

When he found her, Sergio behaved like a lovesick teenage girl. He sank to his knees and sobbed. Once he had checked Marshall's pulse and determined that she was alive, he scooped the woman up in his arms and crushed her limp body in an earnest embrace.

She's safe. She's okay. The bastard didn't kill her. I found her, and she's alive.

Unwilling to wait until she awoke on her own, Sergio fished a stim shot out of his suit's med kit. Within seconds of giving her the injection, Marshall stirred in his arms.

"Wha—" she choked out.

"It's okay, Marsh." He hugged her to him. "You're okay."

"The Major—" she blurted. "The asshole got loose and—"

"I know. It's okay. You don't have to worry about him now."

Looking down at herself and finding she was dressed only in her underwear, Marshall gasped, "He took my suit! The scumbag attacked me and stole my suit!"

"Calm down," he urged her. "Everything's okay."

"Where is he?" she snarled, scrambling to her feet. "I want my suit back! I feel exposed without it."

He gave her an intimate smile. "Hey, I've seen it all before, honey."

"Dammit—*exposed* to the alien virus!"

"Oh. Well, we don't think there is an alien virus, never was one."

"Then what the hell's been screwing with our heads? You're not going to tell me the panther and the zombies were *real*, are you?"

"Hibbs thinks a witch was to blame."

She stared at him with fierce disbelief. "A what?"

"A witch. And the panther was her familiar."

"That's crazy. The virus has scrambled your brain."

"Hibbs can explain it better than I can," Sergio told her.

But when they rejoined the others downstairs, Corporal Hibbs wasn't available to conduct any explanations.

"What do you mean: he's gone?"

But that was the extent of the information Dr. Holmes could supply. "Back when the Major was shooting at us, I saw him go into the room where you guys stashed the human bodies, but he's not there anymore. He's not in any of the labs. And the lift is still in place, so I don't think he went down into the excavation site."

Riccardo added: "Hibbs is the other soldier? He never came past us."

The access tunnel was the only way out of the research section.

"He couldn't have gone far," the Doc remarked. "He was wounded."

No mere wound would slow Hibbs down, Sergio knew that. If he had vanished, it had to have something to do with the witch. Maybe Hibbs was chasing her down.

Meanwhile, Marshall was stripping her suit from the Major, returning it to its rightful owner: herself. While so engaged, she kept throwing suspicious glances at Riccardo. She'd been separated from the group during the time Sergio had found his twin inside the alien ship; he was a stranger to her, albeit a stranger with a very familiar face.

Condensing events into a few curt sentences, Sergio brought her up to speed on the presence of his twin brother here at Eiger base. She quickly pieced things together, remembering how Moss had claimed to have been attacked by a Denk, realizing that Dr. Holmes must have been assaulted by Riccardo—she was a quick-witted lady.

"It wasn't my fault," Riccardo moaned. "The witch's cat had control of my body."

"So," scoffed Marshall, "the virus has *everybody* seeing witches now."

"Oh—she's real! So's her damned cat, too!"

"Hibbs killed the panther," Sergio interjected.

"What?" gasped Riccardo.

"Back in the ship," he replied abstractly. "You missed that. You were out of it."

"But—the thing was so powerful..." Riccardo's voice whistled with shock. "How could anybody... kill it...?"

Suddenly, catch-up explanations didn't seem all that vital to Sergio. The hairs at the back of his neck tingled. Something was wrong. He couldn't figure out what it was, but the feeling of *danger* was an itch he couldn't ignore.

"What room was it that Hibbs went into?" he asked Dr. Holmes.

Ignoring Riccardo's on-going prattle, Sergio followed the Doc as she took him to the lab-cum-morgue. As he left the security tunnel, he saw that Marshall was back in her gear; she was securing a new set of plastic loop-ties to the Major's wrists and ankles.

Not that he doubted the accuracy of the Doc's account, but Sergio wanted to review the morgue for himself. In his defense, he detected aspects that had escaped her assessment. As expected, most of the bodies had been cannibalized to build the super-zombie, leaving organic flotsam littering the room. The scorch-mark on the floor was new, though.

The way to kill witches was to burn them. Had Hibbs found the witch and set fire to her here? If so, the enemy had been defeated. Then where had Hibbs gone afterwards? Without an armored suit, he was at risk. Or was he… After all, if he'd burned the witch, then there should be no enemy left to menace anybody.

The irritation at the back of his neck warned Sergio: there was still danger afoot. Although it appeared likely that Hibbs had found and beaten the witch, a threat still remained. Had Hibbs defeated the witch? Sergio was only presuming his friend's victory over the sorceress. What if she had beaten him? Did the soot stain constitute her remains?—or *his*?

He didn't like the idea that Hibbs had failed. That would mean the witch was still on the loose. If that were true, then why had the delusions ceased? Was the bitch playing games, trying to lull the squad into a false sense of security?

He kept these suspicions to himself. From the beginning Dr. Holmes had shown intense skepticism regarding a witch as the one behind the troubles that had assailed the Eiger installation. Sergio had no desire to give her reason to challenge his logic. He needed to keep a clear head if he was going to figure out what had happened.

Stepping back into the corridor, Sergio gazed uneasily along the passageway. Had the witch moved her hiding place? Somebody needed to check the other labs… and search below. He was reluctant to reconnoiter the cavern—and he was definitely unwilling to venture inside the alien ship again.

Coming up beside him, Marshall caught his attention and cocked an eyebrow.

He shook his head. There was no point in elaborating the reasons for his uneasiness. Marshall had made it quite plain that she harbored no belief in the witch. His worries about the witch's survival would be met by more scorn. Sergio decided it was best to leave his misgivings vague. "Something's wrong…" he told her.

"Would Hibbs go back into the excavation?" she pondered aloud.

Sergio lifted his shoulders in a shrug.

"You're going to go investigate, aren't you?"

He nodded. "Has to be done."

"And I get to baby-sit everybody, huh?"

"Afraid so." He gave her a rueful frown, "Can't have the Major getting loose again and stirring up more trouble."

"Go," she sighed. She knew him, and understood the futility of trying to dissuade Surge Denk from rushing headlong into potentially hazardous situations.

As Sergio moved off, Marshall called after him, "By the way, don't freak out if we're not here when you're done. I'm going to move everybody upstairs. I want to find some clothes for your brother."

Glancing back at her, Sergio voiced a token guffaw, "Looking to avoid temptation, Marsh?"

"Don't worry, Surge. He might've been born your twin, but he's not my type. I prefer my men to have better muscle-tone... and a spine." She waved him to embark on his search. "Besides, relocation isn't entirely self-serving. There'll be less gore upstairs to bother the Egghead. And a fresh closet to stash the Major."

Something made Sergio return to her side. There, he removed his helmet, then hers, and planted a lingering deep kiss on her mouth.

"How nice," she whispered when their lips unlocked. "A reward for fidelity."

He smiled, letting her think that.

In truth, Sergio wasn't all that certain he was ever going to see her again. The itch had expanded from the back of his neck, escalating into a tingle that plagued his entire head. He had the distinct impression he was headed into a desperate and deadly situation... one that could very well turn out to be the last chapter in Sergio Denk's autobiography.

None of the other rooms on the research level offered any trace of Corporal Hibbs. While that didn't surprise Sergio, it didn't make him happy. Now he was going to have to examine the excavation cavern, possibly even go back inside that alien vessel.

Standing beside the lift, Sergio stared into the access shaft's depths. *If Hibbs went down there, he would've used the lift... right?* The tunnel *was* awfully slimy with undead gore. If the man lost his footing and fell, he would've broken his neck. With no suit or armor, he wouldn't maneuver the shaft unprotected.

Still undecided what to do, Sergio's eyes nervously wandered. An open panel in the wall at the end of the hallway caught his attention. *That* was new. He hadn't noticed it during any of his previous visits to this point. He wondered where it went.

That answer was easily furnished by consulting the base's blueprints that had been included in the mission briefing. He called up the schematics on his ocular display and clicked his way deep into the installation's layout until he reached the lowest level. The panel was there; it marked the location of an access crawlspace which led down to the nuclear reactor that powered the facility.

Why would anyone want to go down there?

Well now, that depended on *who* had pried open the panel. If it had been the witch, then she might have been seeking a new hiding place. Sergio could think of no reason for Hibbs to go down there. The only way to tell, though, was to follow them into the duct.

At least this offered Sergio an alternative to revisiting the excavated spacecraft.

An immediate problem presented itself: the crawlspace was too small to accommodate Sergio's armor. He could only gain access if he stripped down to his skivvies, just as he'd been forced to do to enter the alien spacecraft. Venturing that close to a nuclear pile without proper shielding didn't exactly thrill Sergio… but he didn't seem to have any other choice.

Resigned to the inevitable, Sergio reluctantly unclipped his armor. If he detached his backpack, he could leave his pressure suit on. At least he wouldn't be going down there half-naked; that would've played havoc with his already-raw courage.

At this point, Sergio's confidence was rattled. He'd survived countless delusional attacks, fighting off creatures that couldn't be killed because they were already dead—or didn't exist in the first place. Now that the enemy was supposed to have been conquered, he found himself heading face-first into manmade peril. The danger never stopped; it just kept changing its configuration, like some paranormal chameleon.

I hate this place.

Hewn through the lunar rock and bulwarked with sheets of metal, the crawlspace descended at an angle that began shallow but that slope increased the deeper it went. According to the schematics Sergio carried in his head, the shaft wasn't longer than a hundred meters, but the darkness—and his present anxious state of mind—made it seem as if it took him almost an hour to travel that distance. His internal clock told him, though, that his descent only endured for fifteen minutes.

The lights mounted on his suit showed him the end of the tunnel long before he reached it. That hatch hung open, more evidence that he was on the right track. Someone had passed through here ahead of him.

When he reached the threshold, he peered through the portal, cautious but alert. Alas, all he saw was another crawlspace positioned perpendicular to the entry tunnel. This inner passage curved away in both directions, encircling the buried reactor and presumably providing access to its controls. No consoles were visible in the immediate proximity of the access portal, although a faded sign advised that admission beyond this point was hazardous unless one was suitably protected against radiation.

Technically, besides providing hermetic protection for a vacuum, military grade pressure suits were designed to insulate the wearer against a variety of cosmic radiation that might be encountered in outer space. He was unsure if that protection extended to the savage gamma rays given off by the reactor's nuclear core. But it was too late to worry about that, too late to turn back.

Now that he'd reached this inner passageway, Sergio saw more proof that he was not alone in here. Ahead and to the left a dim glow illuminated the tunnel. He headed in that direction, his weapon drawn.

"Hibbs?" he commed. "Is that you?"

He knew his inquiry was moot. If it wasn't Hibbs, the intruder had no earbud and wouldn't hear his transmission.

He followed the curving tunnel, and eventually the light became more defined and revealed a figure crouching ahead of him. It was Hibbs. A degree of stress ebbed away from Sergio. He'd dreaded coming face-to-face with the witch in these cramped and deadly circumstances. But Hibbs was no threat; he was a fellow jarhead, a comrade, a friend—more than that, for their survival of the ordeals offered by Eiger base had definitely established an even deeper bond between them.

"What're you doing?" Sergio asked over the comm. "Why didn't you answer?"

"You shouldn't be here, Surge," came Hibbs' terse response.

"I saw the scorch-mark," he confessed. "Back in the morgue. There was a witch, wasn't there? You found her... and burned her."

"For what it was worth."

"If you beat her, then the crisis is over."

"Purely a temporary measure. I'm working on a more permanent solution."

"What? Shutting down the reactor?"

Hibbs laughed—and Sergio didn't like the nasty edge lurking in that guttural expression of mirth. "The opposite, actually."

"What?!" Sergio leaned forward.

And Hibbs raised a handgun. He aimed the weapon at Sergio and gave it a warning waggle. "No—back off."

"Are you crazy?"

"Don't try to stop me, Surge. I know what I'm doing."

"Why the hell would you want to blow up the base? You can't intend to eradicate the alien virus—you proved it didn't exist once you found and beat the witch."

"You wouldn't understand."

"If you're threatening to vaporize the base—and *us*—you could at least tell me why."

Hibbs stopped working the controls and gave a sober nod. "Yeah... I guess you deserve an explanation. It's the witch. I defeated her, burned her corpse—and now I must make sure that she stays dead."

"But—if you burned her, she's dead. Right?"

"All of the powers of modern technology don't stand a chance against sorcery, Surge. The very existence of magic violates a score of physical laws. Mankind can't cope with that much of a cultural upheaval. If anybody reports on what happened here, Global will learn all about the witch. Sooner or later, some research department will try to unlock the witch's sorcery, to duplicate her miraculous achievements. Nothing good will come of such experimentation. No one can ever know she existed."

"So lobby for us to leave the witch out of our reports, Hibbs. We can blame the alien virus for all the madness. Okay, we'd have to trash all of our video records, and that would leave us with no justification for relieving the Major of his command... but c'mon—be sensible about this. We don't have to die. The others don't even believe in the witch. Hell, you're the only one who actually saw her."

Hibbs met Sergio's pleading gaze with a brow wrinkled with worry. "I have to make certain she doesn't come back. I think I felt her corrupt soul being dragged down into hell... but it could've been another trick... she's a crafty bitch... If I blow the reactor, the blast will atomize her ashes, absolutely eradicating her. She'll never come back from that."

It dawned on Sergio that Hibbs couldn't be talked out of his suicidal scheme.

"At least give us a chance to get out of here..." mumbled Sergio. That option had its problems, though.

"You know that isn't going to happen. There's six of us left and only three pressure suits. Half the group can't possibly safely leave the facility."

"We can figure out a solution," he insisted.

"Sorry, Surge," announced Hibbs. "I have to do this." He lifted the gun again. "Can't take the chance that somebody might spill the beans about the witch. Our silence is necessary."

"You know I have to try to stop you," Sergio advised his friend.

"Go ahead. I'll shoot you, though. Don't think for a second that I won't. The fate of mankind trumps our friendship, Surge."

The two remained motionless, watching each other, gauging their own readiness and the faculties of their opponent. Sergio had no desire to battle his friend, but he knew he had to do so. Hibbs was the better fighter, plus his gun was already pointed at Sergio. In the tight confines of this crawlspace, Sergio doubted he could dodge any shots at such close range, much less the slugs would ricochet and create secondary hazards. For the same reasons, he was reluctant to fire his own weapon; his shots would rebound and potentially injure him as easily as his target. Should he hesitate and let Hibbs make the first move? Could he afford such honorable reluctance? More than likely, Hibbs was waiting for Surge to live up to his nickname.

As if confirming that suspicion, Hibbs remarked, "Looks like we have a standoff." Lifting his free hand, he resumed tapping away at the controls.

If Sergio waited much longer, Hibbs would finish setting the reactor to blow. He had to act now if he had any hope of stopping the man's mad intentions.

Giving in to an impulsive notion, Sergio lowered his rifle and released a sigh that he packed with a demonstrative dose of grudging failure.

Hibbs paused at this gesture, but his gun remained pointed at Sergio.

"I don't want to fight you," Sergio proclaimed.

"Then don't," chirped Hibbs. "You'd be wasting your—"

Firing a short blast at the floor, Sergio swung the rifle butt around and toward Hibbs. His swing twisted him to the right, hopefully beyond Hibbs' immediate aim. In that manner, he escaped Hibbs' initial shots.

Meanwhile, his own blast sent bullets ricocheting from the floor, spraying across Hibbs' front. Unfortunately, Hibbs had engaged in his own evasive maneuver. He flattened against the control-bearing wall. Sergio's blast scored no hits—but he hadn't intended it to do so; its true purpose had been to startle his adversary. Pressed as Hibbs was to the side, Sergio's jab with his rifle butt missed, too.

Hibbs drove an elbow into Sergio's ribs.

Sergio retaliated by driving his rifle butt into Hibbs' back.

Neither opponent allowed the pain to daunt their combat.

Spinning in place, Hibbs lifted his leg and kicked at Sergio.

Sergio recoiled to avoid the arcing kick, but Hibbs' foot still caught him in the side. The impact point was located centimeters lower than the earlier elbow jab, acerbating the pain that throbbed along that flank. Of more concern: continuing on in its swing, Hibbs' foot struck Sergio's fore-arm and loosened the rifle in his grasp.

A follow-up punch sent Sergio's weapon flying from his clutches.

Sergio responded by blindly striking out. His fist caught Hibbs in the shoulder, directly on the bandage the man wore.

As Hibbs crumpled in pain, Sergio kicked the revolver from his hand.

Both were disarmed now. The battle could proceed limited to ana-tomical bludgeons.

Fists flew, knees were applied to stomachs, elbows dug into unde-fended flesh, kicks were extended and feinted, bodies smashed into the close walls, gruesome *thwacks* resounded in the crawlspace. Both of these men were skilled in combat techniques.

They continued to exchange blows, savage and swift.

Even with his injured shoulder, Hibbs was proving to be the superior combatant. Sergio had more agility, but his speed gained him no advan-tage over Hibbs' fanatical strength. The man's blows came hard and left bruised muscle. A topography of pain spread across Sergio's body. His aching ribs made each breath a labor. A fiercely delivered blow fractured the bones in his left arm, rendering that limb useless as a weapon. Only Sergio's helmet prevented him from suffering any knockout concussions.

All he had succeeded in doing so far was distracting Hibbs from initiating the reactor's self-destruction. Eventually, though, exhaustion was going to interfere with Sergio's capabilities. Already his stamina was flagging.

For a moment, Hibbs forced him back with his own flurry of fists. Sergio struggled to fend off this torrential assault.

I'm pulling my punches, he chastised himself, *avoiding lethal blows—because he's my friend. I need to fight like my life depends on it—because it does.*

He threw his fist at Hibbs' face, blocking a counterattack with his numb forearm. Before Hibbs could recover, Sergio brought his elbow down on his adversary's wounded shoulder. As a groaning Hibbs fell back against the wall, a breathless Sergio drove his knee into the man's exposed gut. Although his own head pounded from the relentless exertion, Sergio gave no quarter. He pummeled away, battering his friend's head until Hibbs' features were a bloody pulp. But Hibbs refused to stop fighting.

Dammit—why won't you stay down?

Planting his feet squarely against Sergio's torso, Hibbs mustered a mighty thrust that sent Sergio tumbling along the curved passageway. He landed in abject disarray. His lungs strove to replace the air the impact had driven from them. He lay there until he finally managed to gulp a fresh supply of oxygen down his throat.

When his head cleared, Sergio became aware that someone was laughing... and he knew it wasn't him.

A few meters along the crawlspace, Hibbs had sunk against the wall. Shaking with weak laughter, he made no move to push off and resume their battle. Nearby, the controls he had been fiddling with earlier were now blinking.

"I win," Hibbs rasped past his swollen lips.

"What did you do—?" choked Sergio. But the flashing panel needed no explanation; the numbers on display were counting down from an hour. "You fool—"

Punctuated by gurgling chuckles, Hibbs revealed that he had finished setting the reactor's self-destruct sequence minutes ago. He'd only been fighting to keep Sergio from entering a cancellation order. Now it was too late. The countdown was locked; it would continue all the way to zero. "Then..." He brought his palms together, then apart with fingers spread. "—boom."

"You didn't have to do this!" wailed Sergio. He crawled to his feet and stumbled along the tunnel to examine the control panel. Unfamiliar with the mechanism, he pushed buttons at random. His fumbling failed to affect the countdown.

"Had to..." Hibbs spat out blood and a tooth. "Destroying the base... only way to insure witch stays dead..."

"She's already dead, you damned maniac!"

"Dead… but not gone." Hibbs reached up to feebly tap his bruised temple. "Put herself in here… if I don't die, she'll come back…"

"Dammit—you could've put a bullet in your head! You didn't have to kill all of us!"

"Everything has to go, Surge… it's only way to be sure…"

Sergio muttered, half to himself, "An hour… I have to warn Marsh…"

"No!" A bloodied and broken Hibbs launched himself at Sergio. This time, though, his vitality was not as robust it had been. Sergio's beat-down had dampened the Corporal's gusto and nearly crippled his indefatigable physique. Hibbs' leap floundered into a stumble that brought him crashing to the floor at Sergio's feet. Disregarding his ignoble prostration, Hibbs reached out to try to snag Sergio.

Capering back, Sergio easily eluded the man's frantic grasp.

"Everyone has to die," rasped Hibbs.

"That's not for you to decide," Sergio snarled at him. But then, Hibbs had already made that decision—and had backed it up with deadly action. Machinery had been set in motion that would annihilate the base. An hour—less, now, as seconds ticked away—remained before a nuclear explosion vaporized the Eiger research facility and anyone unlucky enough to be trapped here. Sergio had to warn Marshall.

As he started to leave, Sergio paused, turned back to regard his friend on the floor. He was loath to abandon him, but did he have any choice? Hibbs would definitely resist any rescue effort. He was dead set upon his suicide. Time spent fighting to save the man against his will would be precious moments wasted. It was a deep-rooted Marine doctrine to leave no man behind. But if Sergio tried to save Hibbs, the ensuing delay might condemn everyone else to nuclear death. Jarhead ethics and personal friendship struggled against the dire facts of the circumstances.

Hibbs was an adult, a battle-seasoned soldier. His resolve was unquestionable, it was his sanity that was dubious at the moment. But—he had made his decision, had acted to guarantee his mad scheme, would definitely contest any attempts to undo that plan or rescue him from the doom he had instigated. If this was what Hibbs wanted—truly deeply wanted—then it was futile to oppose his choice, no matter how self-destructive it turned out to be.

Sergio's primary concern had to be the safety of the others. Dr. Holmes and Riccardo were civilians. It was Sergio's duty to protect them from danger. As it was, that salvation was going to be nigh impossible to accomplish… and every second he wasted in debate increased the chances of his failure. He had to act now, leave Hibbs to his self-appointed extinction, and apply his energies to finding a means of saving the others.

"I'm sorry, old friend," he whispered over the comm-line. "I wish you hadn't done this… but now I have to do everything in my power to prevent the others from dying along with you."

"I did what I had to do," came Hibbs' unhealthy reply. "Now it's your turn."

Moving with vigorous haste, Sergio fled the reactor pit.

As he raced to rejoin the others, Sergio's thoughts calculated his chances for success. They weren't very good.

With the witch and her familiar gone, at least evacuating the base wouldn't be hampered by phantom obstacles. But there were other inescapable problems to overcome.

Not counting Hibbs, whose mania had subtracted him from the equation, there were five members of the group left, but only three pressure suits that could be used to protect them from the airless lunar environs outside the underground installation. Two people were doomed to remain behind.

Marshall had her own suit, and the Doc was wearing a borrowed suit—at this point Sergio couldn't even recall whose. If he forced Riccardo to wear his suit, then at least the two civilians could be spared from tasting the nuclear inferno. Fate had dealt Sergio and the Major the short straws.

This was one time that Surge Denk wouldn't be living up to his reputation.

"Marsh!" Sergio commed as he burst upon the residential level.

Down the hall, Marshall leaned from a doorway. "Yo."

"Where is everybody?"

"In here."

As he drew near, she saw his bloodied face through his clear helmet and gasped, "What the hell happened to you?"

"Later," he grunted. "No time right now."

She stepped back and allowed Sergio to hurry into the apartment.

Perched on the bed, Dr. Holmes peered up at this brusque entry. "What's happened?" Her now-haggard face arched with worry.

Riccardo stood nearby. True to her word, Marshall had found him clothes: a shirt and pants a tad undersized for his chubby anatomy.

The extra pressure suit spread out on the apartment's desk was a complete surprise.

"What—" gasped Sergio. "Where'd that come from?" Had they found one of the missing suits? No, this one was grungy, patched and old, definitely not military grade.

"I found Moss down the hall," Marshall explained. "He's dead. I took his pressure suit. I thought we might have more use for it than he would at this point."

Okay, Sergio calculated. *Now we're only one suit short.*

"C'mon, everybody up," Sergio shouted. "We're heading topside."

"Why?" piped Dr. Holmes.

Ignoring the Doc's valid inquiry, Sergio turned to Marshall. "Where's the Major?"

"The closet."

Sergio fetched the unconscious Major from his makeshift confinement and threw him over his shoulder. He directed Marshall to collect the unoccupied suit, then herded the rest of them out of the room and down the corridor. "Move! Fast, c'mon, let's go!"

En route to his rendezvous with the group, Sergio had decided to refrain from explicit explanations right away. He wanted to avoid any discussions that might slow down their exodus. News about the Eiger base's latest hazardous surprise was bound to send the civilians into a panic. And Marshall was no dummy, she would immediately identify the flaws in his escape plan and argue with his decision.

It was getting progressively more difficult for Sergio to stay alert. His clash with Hibbs had taken a drastic toll on his resources. He ached all over, but those discomforts he could ignore. His left arm felt as if the broken bone had been replaced with a wolverine that was ravenous gnawing its way to the surface; *that* pain was not easily shoved aside. His stay at Eiger base had depleted his stamina. Too many unnatural confrontations, flooding his system with constant stress and confusion. Marines were trained to endure extreme adversity—but the ordeals he'd suffered here were far beyond combat conditions. He was prepared to face a mob of enemies, but not undead foes, not phantom panthers. No amount of training could prepare a soldier to cope with such outrageous calamities. He would keep going, for that was what a Marine did, but with every passing moment his efficiency was deteriorating.

He had to hold it together, just a little while longer. The others would never escape this hellhole without his help. He was the only one who really understood the doom that threatened to destroy everything. His resolve was vital, for the others would have to forced save themselves. They would object to what was needed, and there just wasn't time to debate the wisdom of his choices. He needed to bully them into evacuating the base before the reactor went critical and vaporized the entire installation.

They were all weary, he could see that.

Trudging up the steps with the extra suit tucked under her arm, Marshall's determination appeared undaunted by her exhaustion. The base's madness had eaten into her reservoir of endurance, but she didn't show it. She was a dynamo, and he envied her pluck. But it couldn't last forever.

Considering that she was a civilian, Dr. Holmes was holding up surprisingly well. Her spunk impressed Sergio; he wished he'd had the chance to taste her amorous ferocity. It was probably her obstinate adherence to logic that kept her so stoked. All along she had contested the delusions, refusing to believe the empirical evidence and holding steadfast to her disbelief in the impossible. If she'd had to face undead mobs and murderous panthers, then maybe her opinions would be more open to shock, but she had been spared any face-to-face confrontations with these deadly threats. Her knowledge of them was purely secondhand, allowing her to reject the stress that came with facing such horrors. But being a civilian, her stamina was finite. Even now she moved with a lethargy that advertised her waning strength.

Riccardo was completely out of it, incapable of even his normal brand of uncooperation. He was like a gigantic rag doll. You could move him, but keeping him moving required constant guidance. The Doc was forced to steer him up the steps, adding to her own exhaustion.

Thank God the Major was unconscious. Dealing with his antics right now would've tipped the scales and sent the group plummeting into a delay that would have cost them all their lives. Sergio was sorely tempted to dump the bastard and continue on without him. He wasn't getting out of here, so did it make any difference whether he died topside or down here? Alas, honor bound Sergio to leave no man behind, not even an asshole like Major Dummheit.

While Sergio stumbled along, fighting off waves of despair and dizziness. He wondered if his fatigue was entirely attributable to his overall enervation. The time he'd spent in close proximity to the reactor was guaranteed to have poisoned him. How long would it take the radiation to start leeching his strength? He shook his head, in negation and to clear it. *I'll be dead long before the effects of radiation poisoning can kick in.*

"What's going on, Surge?" Marshall nagged him.

He urged them on.

No weirdness interfered with their flight up the stairs.

He got them as far as the upper level before Marshall's impatient wheedling forced him to reveal why they were on the run.

"The reactor core is ticking down to overload."

Turning from doctoring the elevator's controls, Marshall gasped, "What?"

"How did that happen?" Dr. Holmes demanded.

Stunned by his brother's announcement, Riccardo gaped with bugging eyes and slack mouth.

"There's no time for a lengthy briefing," Sergio proclaimed. "You have to get out of here."

"Leave the base?" protested Dr. Holmes. "But—that will risk spreading the contagion!"

"There is no contagion," he insisted. "The witch was behind it all."

"The witch," scoffed the Doc.

"But she'd gone now. Hibbs took her out."

"Where is Hibbs?" queried Marshall.

"He didn't make it." Sergio had given the matter much thought during his race through the facility, and he had decided that nobody needed to know about Hibbs' culpability in setting the reactor to blow. Not that Sergio put much credence in Hibbs' reasons for what he'd done, but if he was determined to perish, then Sergio intended to see to it that everybody believed he'd died a hero. He owed his friend that much.

Marshall's hacking opened the elevator, and the door slid aside to reveal the cubicle, not a wall of solid rock. More evidence that the witch's influence no longer reigned in the installation.

Sergio hurried everybody into the car. "Let's get moving—now!"

"But—how could the reactor become so unstable?" moaned Dr. Holmes. "Did someone tamper with the settings?"

"I have no idea," Sergio lied.

By this point, shock had made Riccardo into a pliant automaton. He went were he was pointed, but offered no sign of cognitive awareness.

"Okay, Surge—if the reactor's about to blow, escaping from the installation is our only chance to survive," acknowledged Marshall. "But—"

He cut her off, "I know."

"What? You're not telling us everything," accused the Doc.

Sergio met Marshall's eyes. "There's no other way, Marsh."

The aching look she gave him told Sergio that she understood. For all her vehement regret, she knew there was no other recourse.

39

The stim in his bloodstream had worn thin, leaving Corporal Hibbs plagued by a plethora of unpleasantries.

He had to give Surge credit. He'd put up a good fight. A thousand pains wracked Hibbs.

His thoughts were a seething snake-pit of conflicted emotions.

Hibbs was glad he had succeeded in distracting Surge long enough for the reactor's meltdown sequence to initiate. There was no turning back now, no stopping things.

Hibbs wasn't all that keen on dying—but that was part of the deal. The base had to be destroyed to eradicate all trace of the witch and her sorcery. For the selfsame reason, Hibbs must die, too. The witch had touched his mind. He couldn't risk her using him as a doorway out of Hell. Under no circumstance could Millicent Pruitt be allowed to return.

Hibbs felt no animosity for the rest of the group. He wanted them to save themselves—but at the same time he felt their deaths were integral to hiding the witch from mankind. His heart and mind were not in agreement on this matter. He was torn between common decency and the need to extinguish all knowledge of the witch. She posed too great a threat—everyone who knew about her had to be silenced.

Hibbs hated this mental duel.

In all fairness, the others hadn't really put much faith in the witch's existence. They believed she was nothing more than another delusion induced by the alien contagion. As far as they were concerned, the zombies, the panther, the blocked passageways, the witch, all the weirdness that had tormented them—everything had been an hallucinatory byproduct of the alien infection. Their perceptions had been faulty. There'd been no monsters, only imaginary phantoms.

The others are no threat, he told himself. *If they mention the witch, no one will put any credence in their outrageous claims.*

It was okay to hope they might escape.

Hibbs didn't see how they were going to pull it off, though… not without help.

40

By the time Sergio had gotten everyone topside, the mathematical inequity had become apparent to Dr. Holmes.

"But," she blurted, "we all can't escape—there aren't enough pressure suits!"

Sergio commenced stripping off his own suit.

"Riccardo is going to wear my suit," he declared. "And he Major will wear Moss' suit. That way four of you will get out of here."

"But—what about you?"

"I draw the short straw. I stay behind and take my chances." *Ha—what chances?* "You four run."

"You can't!" Dr. Holmes lamented. "You won't survive!"

Sergio shrugged his unarmored shoulders. "You can't argue with the basic math, Doc. Four suits, five of us—somebody isn't going anywhere."

He started getting Riccardo into the suit. His brother was still in shock; it was like dressing a dummy.

A mute but sulky Marshall started stuffing the Major into Moss' raggedy pressure suit.

"You'll have to go back down into the base before we can open this inner hatch," she muttered to Sergio. "I secured the outer hatch against the terrorists—but they blew it open. So the airlock technically isn't an airlock anymore. This passageway will have to serve as an airlock now. Once I open this hatch, all the air in here goes out the door. So... you need to go... if you're not coming with us..."

He wearily shook his head. "You know I can't come along. You've got to get the Major and these civilians out of here."

"What are we supposed to do once we get outside?" Dr. Holmes wailed. Her disgruntled confusion escalated into misplaced panic. "The meltdown will destroy the entire base and the surrounding terrain. We can't possibly outrun the blast."

"Calm down," Sergio told her. "You can use the prospector's tractor."

"No, we can't," remarked Marshall. "The tractor's entirely disabled— even its motors wouldn't work."

Dammit, Sergio cursed to himself. That was right. He'd forgotten about that.

After all the tribulations they'd faced, it was unfair to get this far and suddenly have fate deal them a losing hand. Why couldn't they get a break?

"You'll have to hide in the tractor," he mumbled.

"That antique will come apart like tissue paper in the blast," insisted Dr. Holmes. "We're going to die!"

Grabbing her by her upper arms, Sergio gave the Doc a savage shake. "Calm the hell down!"

Let me think, he fretted. *There has to be a way to get them away from the base...*

"There's another vessel out there," Marshall announced.

"What?"

"Remember the terrorists that broke into the base? They came here in an aerial vessel. Presumably it's still parked out there. We could use *that* to escape."

In his anxious haste, Sergio had forgotten about the terrorists. If their ship was still outside, the three stood a good chance of outrunning the blast.

"See?" He released the Doc. "You're going to make it. Pull yourself together, okay? Riccardo is completely useless as long as he stays near-catatonic. Marsh will be busy carrying the Major. I'm depending on you to help get my brother to safety."

She gave him a slow nod. Her features softened as terror lost its grip and ebbed from her nervous system.

He turned to Marshall. Their eyes met; that had to suffice as a good-bye. Seconds were fleeting, the three needed to be on their way. There was no time for a maudlin or sappy farewell, not even for a last lusty kiss. At least he'd gotten one earlier.

With a solemn nod, Sergio took his leave and hurried down the passage. There was no hatch at the lower end of the tunnel. He would have to get into the elevator and descend into the base.

If he wanted to survive...

For—he consulted his internal clock—another thirty-six minutes. Was it worth it? What could he hope to achieve in a measly half-an-hour?

While Sergio Denk wasn't much of a religious man, he faced his imminent demise with a stoic calm. He'd made his peace with that inevitable doom. Stretching out his dwindling minutes seemed pointless, almost cruel.

Nevertheless, he entered the elevator and punched the down button. For all his existential reflection, his survival instinct ran things from a fundamental vantage. He could ruminate all he wanted about the futility of another half-hour of life, but his involuntary reflexes were proactively on the case. Nobility and self-sacrifice were cerebral concepts; self-preservation was a gut response, a knee-jerk reaction, impossible to curtail or suppress.

When the elevator reached the bottom of its journey, Sergio stepped from the cubicle.

And bumped into someone!

Sergio immediately adopted a battle stance, ready to defend himself against whatever new threat had been choked up by this unholy place.

But it wasn't some fresh monster—it was only Hibbs. Smeared with blood and mottled by bruises, he did look somewhat horrific.

Burdened as he was, though, Hibbs wasn't about to attack anybody. His arms held a bundle of silver material. A loose glass bubble surrounded his head, he had another helmet tucked under his arm.

"There you are," Hibbs grunted.

"Come to try to stop anybody from leaving?" snarled Sergio. He maintained his combat posture. "You're too late."

"I thought these might come in handy." He deposited the helmets and other gear at Sergio's feet.

With a quick glance, Sergio ascertained the nature of the pile. "The missing suits!"

"The witch had the panther steal the Doc's suit when she went inside the ship the first time. The other one probably belongs to your brother."

"This is a trick, right?"

Hibbs shook his head.

"I thought you were all hyped up that everybody had to die…"

"Changed my mind," remarked Hibbs.

"You should've done that before you set the reactor to blow."

"The base has to be destroyed, Surge. Me too. But no reason the rest of you have to die… as long as you make me one promise…"

"Which is?"

"Don't tell anybody what really happened here." Hibbs adopted a serious scowl. "If you have to mention the witch, she was just another delusion caused by the alien virus."

"The virus that doesn't exist."

"Lucky for mankind the reactor's meltdown will destroy all trace of the contagion, huh?"

Sergio gave a slow nod. "I can live with that."

"Not if you don't move it and gear up."

As he clambered into one of the pressure suits Hibbs had brought, Sergio explained how Marshall had found an extra suit for the Major. "You can use this other one."

"I have to stay," intoned Hibbs.

"You're sure about this?"

"She forced her memories on me, Surge. I had a ringside seat to her lifetime of villainy. I know what she's capable of. Can't risk the chance she's in here." He tapped a finger to his temple. Then he gave a wry smile. "This is the way it has to be."

They stood facing each other over the remaining empty suit.

Sergio considered knocking his friend unconscious, stuffing him into the last suit, and dragging him to safety. He didn't want his friend to die. But... he also had respect for Hibbs' conviction. Of all of them, Hibbs was the one who truly understood what had happened here. He had gone face-to-face—mind-to-mind, if his account was accurate—with the witch. Hibbs knew the extent of her powers better than anyone. If he believed she was *that* dangerous, even after her posthumous defeat, then Sergio had to honor that judgment.

"You cheat at cards, you son of a bitch," Sergio told him.

"Yeah, well, nail the Doc for me." Hibbs stepped back. "Get moving, soldier."

They traded salutes.

As Sergio dived back into the elevator, Hibbs retreated to the depths of the doomed installation.

The topside tunnel was cold, dark, airless—none of which bothered Sergio now he wore a pressure suit. He raced along the tunnel.

As Marshall had predicted, the outer airlock was a gaping hole. The terrorists had blown off the entire hatch. Sergio easily leapt across the threshold. He bounded down the ravine and out across the lunar landscape. His hurried progress kicked up tufts into the vacuum.

And there—just as Marshall had guessed—sat the terrorist's ship. It wasn't at all what he'd expected. He'd pictured the terrorists using a grungy relic, something they might have scrounged from an old scrapyard—not this surprisingly sleek vessel. Its tapered hull gleamed silver in the lunar gloom. It looked more like an expensive toy than a transport for rabble-rousing activists.

"Marsh!" he commed. "Hold on—one more passenger coming!"

"Is that you, Surge?" came her stunned reply. "How the hell—"

"Tell you later… but only if you wait to blast off until I'm aboard, honey."

"Well, hurry it up, you bastard."

He crossed the terrain in fervent leaps. By the time he reached the ship, a hatch had opened. His last jump took him right through the portal. He tumbled into the tiny airlock. The hatch closed behind him.

Once the airlock had filled with air and the pressure had equalized, Sergio opened the inner hatch and staggered into the ship. He didn't wait to catch his breath, for he knew there was no time to waste on self-con-gratulation. He ran through corridors that were as sleek and shiny as the vessel's exterior. The extravagance puzzled him. Opulent decor like this was normally reserved for high society. He headed in the direction he took to be the prow, where he expected to find the ship's control booth.

Actually, it turned out to be more like a control auditorium. The room was incredibly spacious and stylish. Rows of spectator seats oc-cupied the chamber's back area. Past that, a succession of tiers elevated the command section. A lavishly contoured control array spread beneath a large display screen that showed the lunar terrain outside the ship. Several chandeliers hung from the high arched ceiling. Everything was lustrous chrome.

Riccardo, still catatonic, was slumped in a spectator seat. Still wear-ing Moss' shabby pressure suit, a still-unconscious Major Dummheit had been dumped nearby; someone had sensibly bound his wrists and ankles with plastic restraints. Across the chamber, Marshall was hunched over the control panel. An agitated Dr. Holmes hovered behind Marshall, ca-joling her with fretful urgency.

"What's the problem?" Sergio grunted.

"She can't turn the ship on!" wailed the Doc.

"With a ship this flashy, you'd expect the equipment to be just as expensive—but these controls are antiques," Marshall complained. "I'm having a bit of a problem hacking into the system—the damned thing is positively primitive."

"C'mon, Doc—" Sergio pulled her away from Marshall. "Let Marsh concentrate."

"We're going to die!"

"No—*we're* the ones who are gonna live!"

"Wow—where'd you get the Lynx200?" Suddenly conscious, Riccardo was sitting up and gawking at his chromium surroundings.

"You too, Ricky," Sergio cautioned his brother. "Give Marsh some quiet to—"

"Wait," exclaimed Marshall. She whirled to accost Riccardo, "You recognize this ship?"

"This specific ship?" Riccardo frowned. "Well, no. But the general model—hell yeah. The Lynx200 is a classic luxury yacht," he laughed. "I had one years ago—what a sweet racer it was."

That would've been before Riccardo had renounced the family, back when he was still spending Dad's money as fast as he could. The spoiled brat had indulged in numerous extravagant pastimes, none of which had interested Sergio. It actually surprised him to learn that Ricky had dabbled in interplanetary racing. The sport was practiced only by ridiculously wealthy idiots. For all their sleek design, most speedster yachts were notorious deathtraps. Stable construction apparently interfered with high velocity, so safety was a counterproductive concern. Clearly, Riccardo had been far more reckless than even Sergio had suspected.

"You *had one*?" gasped Marshall. "You actually flew it?"

"Sure."

"Get the hell over here and fire up this baby," she ordered.

"Why? What's going on?"

"Big explosion about to happen—we need to get out of here—fast!"

"Oh… okay." Riccardo hastened across the spacious command deck.

As if this mission already hadn't been overtly weird, things had taken a distinctly surreal turn. Here they were, trapped, sitting atop a ticking timebomb, and their only hope for a timely escape lay in a skill Riccardo had acquired during his high society lifestyle. This salvation rankled Sergio's sense of propriety, but then he couldn't afford to be picky. When the difference between life and death relied on someone whom you knew to be a habitual screw-up, you swallowed your pride and prayed for a miracle.

Standing aside, Marshall allowed Riccardo to survey the control panels. He spread his hands over the array, fluttering them back and forth a few centimeters above the switches and dials. From across the command deck, Sergio could hear a low tone of satisfaction trill from his brother's throat.

"Well?" she grunted at Riccardo's elbow.

"Give me a minute," he mumbled back at her. "It's been a long time…"

"Kind of time sensitive, Riccardo," she reminded him. "Deadline bearing down on us, y'know."

"Deadline—" cackled Dr. Holmes.

Sergio gave her a curt shake to quell her rising hysteria. He had little faith in Riccardo's ability to save the day, and the Doc's panic wouldn't help his brother rally his dubious expertise.

"I'm not too sharp on take-offs," Riccardo grumbled. "Once we get in flight, though, I can make this baby soar…"

"Just get the ship started," urged Marshall. "I can handle things from there."

Reaching out, Riccardo flicked a series of toggles, then pulled a red lever toward him. "There… that should do it…"

She brusquely pushed him aside and took his place. Her fingers flew across the controls, pressing buttons and adjusting dials.

The yacht shuddered as its motors powered up. A panel of lights sprang to life, blinking sequences danced on the board.

"I want to fly it," whined Riccardo.

"Get him away from me, Surge," she hissed through clenched teeth, "before I waste precious time smashing his face."

"Hey—I'm the one who saved the day—"

Sergio dragged his brother away from the command array. Shoving him into a seat, he strapped him in. Then he dragged the Doc over and got her secured in a seat. He was heading for the Major when a lurch shook the ship and tossed him to the floor. G-forces pinned him there.

The ship engaged in no vertical ascent. The thrusters sent the Lynx200 thundering forward. Clouds of moondust billowed in every direction.

As this sudden propulsion kicked in, Sergio was thrown back and pinned against the row of seat. Nearby, Major Dummheit slid across the floor and thumped against the rear wall. Sergio clutched at the struts that mounted the seats to the deck. With anxious eyes, he stared across the chamber.

Marshall stood fast at the controls, her knees bent and leg servos locked against the forces of momentum that swept through the ship. On the wall screen, the lunar landscape came zooming toward them. The two nearest craters loomed large. Struggling with the controls, Marshall acti-vated auxiliary jets that would introduce some altitude to their hell-bent trajectory. For a terrifying instant it looked as if the yacht was going to collide with the craters, then their stark embankments veered from sight and a starscape replaced them on-screen. A panorama of desolate gray raced along at the bottom of the view-screen. Traveling at supersonic velocity, the yacht careened across the lunar terrain, barely thirty meters above the surface. Only Marshall's deft maneuvers avoided flying the ship directly into mountain ranges or other obstacles.

As Sergio watched, a secondary screen lighted up above the pilot, showing a rear view. A flash blossomed low on the receding horizon and that flare swiftly ballooned into a radiance of enormous proportion. The lunar landscape came apart and huge chunks of rock retreated from the edge of the eruption. For a perilous moment these pieces were silhouetted against the incandescent blast, then the glow expanded and swallowed this debris.

The Eiger reactor had finally reached critical mass and exploded. The unleashed cataclysm vaporized the installation and everything in it: dormant corridors, bloodstained labs, the torn remains of the Eiger staff and the terrorist invaders, Corporal Hibbs and his dreaded witch. Not even the unearthed alien spacecraft could withstand the hellish nuclear blast; in fact there was every chance that its own foreign drive system contributed to the holocaust. When the glow faded, only a jagged pit would remain to mark the location of the underground research base.

The yacht's hell-bent acceleration prevented Sergio from lifting an arm to give his friend a farewell salute. He silently bid Hibbs adios.

Achieving escape velocity, the appropriated racing yacht left behind the Moon and relegated the survivors' ordeal to unpleasant memories that would haunt their dreams for years to come.

41

With the exception of Dr. Holmes, it came as no surprise that the Authorities viewed the squad's debriefing with a momentous degree of skepticism. Outright disbelief was more like it.

References to an alien spacecraft were summarily dismissed by investigators. Nor was any credence given to accounts of reanimated corpses or a panther that could walk through solid walls.

Each fantastic aspect of the squad's misadventure was attributed to delusions brought about by some chemical contaminant, although no traces of any foreign substance could be found in the participants' blood.

The vessel used by the survivors to escape the holocaust was traced back to individuals with connections to Green Vengeance, a group of ecological extremists who had been linked to several terrorist strikes to Brazilian and North American wildlife preserves. This led the Authorities to presume that the Eiger staff had been secretly conducting illegal experiments in hallucinogenic weaponry. Apparently the base's personnel had fallen prey to an outbreak of their own diabolical concoction. Residue of that same chemical had clearly distorted the perceptions of the Marine squad sent in to rescue everyone. This contagion had claimed the lives of Corporal Green, Corporal Hibbs, Private Scarpetti and Private Danford, just as the unknown chemical had caused the widespread suicidal activities of the Eiger weapons makers and their Green Vengeance coconspirators.

None of this could be formally proven. With the complete destruction of the lunar installation, all potential evidence had been atomized. But the conjectured scenario satisfied the Big Brass.

To mollify public curiosity, a story was released to the press that a private research installation located on the dark side of the Moon had suffered an accidental reactor core breach. It was futile to deny that a nuclear explosion had occurred, the blast had been witnessed by a variety of satellites and ships in transit, but at least this "official" account offered a feeble explanation for the catastrophe.

No one paid much attention to Dr. Holmes' allegations that an alien contagion had been the cause of all the mayhem. Everyone laughed at her assertion that the Eiger base had discovered an alien spacecraft buried beneath the lunar surface. Her reputation as a UFO fanatic discredited her outrageous claims. Her descriptions of a flying saucer and bodies of Gray aliens were too cliché to be taken seriously. The video logs contained in the soldiers' gear were spotty; corrupted by radiation, presumably from the cataclysmic meltdown, they offered no validation of Holmes' incredible account. Once Global had concluded their investigation and released her, Dr. Holmes found that even her SETI employers had little sympathy for her zealous indictment of a cover-up. She was advised to resign and spare the Cause any further embarrassment.

An infuriated Major Dummheit accused the members of his Marine squad of mutiny. Much to the Major's outrage, fragments of video records provided by the survivors' gear vindicated the actions of his soldiers. All charges were dropped; in fact, the two remaining squad members were awarded citations of bravery for their valor in connection with the attempted rescue of the Eiger personnel. Dummheit was decommissioned and warned to accept the quiet life of a civilian lest evidence of his unsavory protocol garnered him a stretch in a military prison. His wife promptly filed for divorce and did not join him in his Earthside exile.

Only Riccardo Denk mentioned the witch in the course of Global's investigation into the Eiger base disaster. His flamboyant history marked him as an unreliable witness. When the Authorities refused to believe his wild story, Riccardo turned violent. Only the intervention of his influential father spared him from facing charges of sedition. The Denk family had him committed to a groundside psychiatric institution.

Anticipating official cynicism, Corporals Sergio Denk and Anne Marshall had kept their stories simple. Both soldiers had acknowledged that *something* had impaired their perceptions while they were at Eiger base, for the things they'd thought they'd seen and experienced were patently impossible. They were commended for shaking off this delusional bias and reverting to conduct becoming members of the Global military force.

Their testimony earned posthumous citations of valor for Corporal Hibbs, Corporal Green, Private Scarpetti, and Private Danford.

Although he continued his amorous relationship with Marsh for several years, Sergio never confided certain facts to her concerning their final hours at the Eiger installation. No one ever learned of the witch's existence, nor the sacrifice Hibbs had made to keep the unholy bitch dead.

Perhaps best known as the writer/artist of the Those Annoying Post Bros. *comic book series, Matt Howarth has many outlets for his twisted creativity. And all of them are notoriously "strange".*

During his career of four decades, Matt has authored and drawn a variety of unconventional comic books and graphic novels, and contributed graphic fiction to numerous publications in the field of comics and science fiction…and music. For, among all of Matt's creative outlets, there runs the insidious influence of alternative and electronic music. He has found several ways to achieve this crossover of diverse genres.